PENGUIN CLASSICS

TRISTAN

WITH THE 'TRISTRAN' OF THOMAS

Nothing is known about THOMAS except what emerges from his story. There is a passing reference to him by a poet, and Gottfried terms him 'Thomas of Britain'. However, this is ambiguous as the word 'Britain' could mean either Great Britain or Brittany.

•

GOTTFRIED VON STRASSBURG (*fl.* 1210) was probably a member of the urban patriciate in Strassburg. Judging from his writing he appears to have been a cultured man, well read in Latin, French, and German; a lover of music and of the hunt; and a skilled linguistic stylist. He chose Thomas as his source for *Tristan* and completed five-sixths of it.

•

ARTHUR THOMAS HATTO was Head of the Department of German, Queen Mary College, University of London, from 1938 until his retirement in 1977, and was Professor of German Language and Literature at the same university from 1953 to 1977. He is now Professor Emeritus in German in the University of London. He was assistant for English at the University of Berne (1932–4), and during the Second World War worked in the Foreign Office (1939–45). Since 1960 he has been a Governor of the School of Oriental and African Studies, University of London, where in 1970 he gave the Foundation Lecture, with the title 'Shamanism and Epic Poetry in Northern Asia'.

His other publications include *The Memorial Feast for Kökötöy-khan* – a Kirghiz epic, edited, translated and with a commentary. His translations for the Penguin Classics are Gottfried's *Tristan* and the fragments of Thomas's *Tristan* (together in one volume) and the *Nibelungenlied*, and with Wolfram von Eschenbach's *Parzival*, his third volume for the series, he has made available to the English-reading public a substantial portion of the finest narrative poetry of the medieval German Golden Age.

Professor Hatto is now living in retirement in the enjoyment of a Leverhulme Emeritus Fellowship in support of his studies of epic poetry in Central Asia and Siberia. He is married and has one daughter.

GOTTFRIED VON STRASSBURG

TRISTAN

TRANSLATED ENTIRE FOR THE FIRST TIME

With the surviving fragments of the

TRISTRAN

of

THOMAS

With an Introduction by A. T. Hatto

PENGUIN BOOKS

Penguin Books Ltd, Harmondsworth, Middlesex, England
Viking Penguin Inc., 40 West 23rd Street, New York, New York 10010, U.S.A.
Penguin Books Australia Ltd, Ringwood, Victoria, Australia
Penguin Books Canada Limited, 2801 John Street, Markham, Ontario, Canada L3R 1B4
Penguin Books (N.Z.) Ltd, 182–190 Wairau Road, Auckland 10, New Zealand

—

This translation first published 1960
Reprinted 1965
Reprinted with revisions 1967
Reprinted 1969, 1970, 1972, 1974, 1975, 1976, 1978,
1980, 1982 (twice), 1984, 1985, 1987

—

Copyright © A. T. Hatto, 1960
All rights reserved

—

Made and printed in Great Britain by
Hazell Watson & Viney Limited,
Member of the BPCC Group,
Aylesbury, Bucks
Set in Monotype Poliphilus

CONTENTS

INTRODUCTION 7

ACKNOWLEDGEMENTS 37

Tristan

BY GOTTFRIED VON STRASSBURG

PROLOGUE 40

1. Rivalin and Blancheflor 45
2. Rual li Foitenant 65
3. The Abduction 70
4. The Hunt 78
5. The Young Musician 87
6. Recognition and Reunion 93
7. Tristan's Investiture and Gottfried's Literary Excursus 104
8. Return and Revenge 111
9. Morold 121
10. Tantris 138
11. The Wooing Expedition 150
12. The Dragon 159
13. The Splinter 173
14. The Proof 184
15. The Love-Potion 191
16. The Avowal 198
17. Brangane 205
18. Gandin 214
19. Marjodoc 219
20. Plot and Counterplot 222
21. Melot 229
22. The Assignation by the Brook 234
23. The Ordeal 240
24. Petitcreiu 249

25. *Banishment*   257
26. *The Cave of Lovers*   261
27. *Discovery*   269
28. *The Parting*   274
29. *Isolde of the White Hands*   284

Tristran

BY THOMAS

30. *The Wedding*   301
31. *Cariado*   311
32. *The Hall of Statues*   315
33. *The Bold Water*   319
34. *Tristran's Return*   321
35. *Brengvein's Revenge*   324
36. *Reconciliation*   332
37. *Tristran Returns Again*   336
38. *The Poisoned Spear*   338
39. *Caerdin's Mission*   342
40. *The Death of Tristran and Ysolt*   349

APPENDICES

1. *A Note on Thomas's Tristran*   355
2. *The Scene in the Orchard*   364
3. *Tristran's Angevin Escutcheon*   365
4. *Notes on the Poets referred to by Gottfried in the Literary Excursus*   367
5. *Gottfried's Geography*   369
6. *A Glossary of Geographical Names*   371
7. *A Glossary of Characters' Names*   372

INTRODUCTION

THE story of Tristram and Yseult,* which began in these islands, affords an outstanding example of how to have the best of both worlds. Conceived in an age when morals were watched over by priests altogether more powerful than the clergy of today, it told a desperate tale of forbidden love in which much that is dubious was excused. This was accomplished by means of a brilliant device. In the belief that it is wine, Tristram and Yseult drink a magic potion which unites them in everlasting love. So far as we can recover his thoughts, the author of the earliest discernible version of the story seems to be saying: 'Well, if the Lord *will* permit such things as love-philtres to ensnare innocent mortals, be it on his own head!' And so, in this poet's version, the lovers, driven from hazard to hazard though they are, come to no real harm till their end. And however passionately we side with them, our consciences are salved.

In this early version of the story, however, Queen Yseult's love-potion had more to it than its mere convenience as a sop to the conscience, since it had positive symbolic qualities which are not easily exhausted. It stands for something that threatens to overwhelm the senses and ultimately the will of the best-intentioned people, something that assails them from without, often suddenly, as a fate, something that infects their whole being to the point of frenzy – like a poison. 'Poison', it must be said, is the form in which our Latin-derived word 'potion' appears in Old French, and it means any draught that is drunk, whether for good or ill. In its baleful sense 'poison' plays an important part in our story, since Tristram and Yseult not only drink the poison together, and with it their death, but Tristram is also twice wounded by poisoned weapons near the loins. On the first occasion he is healed by Yseult's mother, the

---

* 'Tristram' and 'Yseult' have come to be regarded as the English forms of the names. I use them here when speaking of the romance in general. I use 'Tristran' and 'Ysolt' for Thomas's pair, and 'Tristan' and 'Isolde' for Gottfried's, as a ready means of distinguishing them. Gottfried also uses the form 'Isôt'. Gottfried's story is essentially the life of Tristan, courtier, warrior, and lover, into which Isolde enters only at a later stage. Poets who followed Gottfried refer to his work as the *Tristan*, correctly, beyond all question, and I have followed them in turn, resisting the temptation to name it 'Tristan and Isolde', as readers might have expected. For typographical reasons I use 'Brangane' (dissyllabic) instead of Gottfried's 'Brangæne'.

Queen Yseult, who must have derived this function from her daughter, together with her name. On the second occasion Tristram dies because young Yseult cannot come in time to heal him. This is all linked with the potion, though medieval poets may not always have been aware of it.

The earliest discernible literary version of the *Tristram* referred to above was composed *c.* A.D. 1150 quite possibly in Anglo-Norman. Although there were earlier versions extending back into Celtic antiquity, nothing positive can be said of them. It is therefore with pardonable inaccuracy that scholars call the version of *c.* 1150 'the archetype', since they do so as a charm against idle speculation. They understand by this term the archetype of the literary versions, the first literary source of which we have any certain knowledge. Even this archetype is no longer extant. But it can be reconstructed, often in great detail, so far as its narrative data are concerned, by comparing its derivatives, the versions of Eilhart von Oberge (between 1170 and 1175), Béroul (about 1200), and Thomas (about 1160), the last of whom radically revised it. The style of the continental Norman Béroul recalls the style of oral narration and may even intentionally revive it. In spirit this version surely comes nearest to the archetype. In the version of Eilhart, a North German knight of all too wooden temperament, the spirit of the original is largely lost. He was not the man to deal adequately with ill-fated passion, adultery-cum-lese-majesty, and perjured oaths. We find him always playing for safety. Only fragments of his own authentic version survive; but a metrically smoother recension of it by a later hand has come down to us entire in several manuscripts. Comparison shows that the second writer did not tamper with the narrative.

The versions of Eilhart and Béroul constitute what might be called the older version of the *Tristram*. They have it in common that the powers of the love-drink abate after three or four years sufficiently for Tristram to go into exile, marry Yseult of the White Hands, scorn her embraces, and embark on a series of dangerous visits to his first love in Cornwall; for all of which, no doubt, the absurdity of the two-phase love-potion was originally conceived, allowing as it did for the inseparable love of the first half of the story and the love-in-separation of the second. But as early as about 1160 the archetypal version of the story was radically revised and extended by the poet Thomas, in all probability to suit the taste of the Angevin court. In North-French-speaking territories, courtly society had now achieved its autonomy in literature as it had in Queen Eleanor's Provençal land of Aquitaine at least a generation before, and the passion of love had come to be regarded rather less as a random stroke of fate and more as a positive, even educative and purifying, force. It had come to be seen as the mark of a generous and well-bred nature in those who would receive it. It certainly needed no excuse, and Thomas required no abatement of the love-potion. It is significant of Thomas's outlook that he caused Mark, too, to partake of the philtre, a trait which the Middle English *Sir Tristrem* with prophetic insight into the English temperament extends to the dog Hudain, who, as a result, is attached to the lovers in canine affection for life.

> þai loued wiþ al her miȝt,
> And Hodain dede al so.

Thomas's recension will be discussed in a separate introduction below. What is important here is that Thomas's already very courtly version of the romance was adapted into the German tongue by one of the world's great poets.

The *Tristan* of Gottfried von Strassburg (*fl.* 1210) has every right to be considered the classic form of the romance. Few European poems of comparable length from Virgil to the present day can have so much formal artistry to show, alternating with purest narrative. Much of the verbal beauty of the original is inevitably lost in translation, but it is with some satisfaction that I offer readers of English the first unabridged rendering of Gottfried's *Tristan* and indeed of any masterpiece of this great generation of German poets, in a form which (whatever its defects) is not intrinsically absurd – plain prose.

By a curious fate the names of Thomas and Gottfried have, many years after their deaths, come to be as inseparable as the rose-bush and the vine (or, as some say, the hazel and the honeysuckle), which by virtue of the love-potion grew above the lovers' graves; not only because Gottfried chose Thomas's *Tristran* as his source, making a far more marvellous thing of it than it had ever been before, but because the surviving text of the one begins where the other's leaves off. Gottfried died when he had covered no more than five-sixths of the story; and now only the last sixth of Thomas's completed poem remains, and even then with some gaps. But by adding one part to the other, we are able to tell the tale to an end in the only way of which Gottfried would have approved – through Thomas, his chosen source, to whose narrative data he remains loyal to an astonishing degree, considering his own genius, and whom he admired as surely as he surpassed him.

Except that later writers tell us Gottfried's name, we know nothing about him but what we can learn from his poem and from two philosophical strophes of no great distinction. In the opening acrostic, Gottfried appears to dedicate his poem to one Dieterich, but this person has not been identified. Later poets and collectors of poetry give Gottfried the title not of 'hêr', which would in the first place indicate a knight, but of 'meister', that is, one who has concluded a prolonged course of study at an ecclesiastical centre of learning. We do not know it for a fact: but Gottfried is most readily imagined as a member of the urban patriciate of Strassburg, a class of men who, by the beginning of the thirteenth century, were growing in wealth and self-assurance and were soon to play a part in literature. Gottfried does not share the knights' condescension towards the merchant class, but on the contrary uses such expressions as 'courtly' or even 'noble merchant', which to a petty knight like Wolfram von Eschenbach,* great poet though he was, would have been a contradiction in terms. Gottfried seems to be looking back to his own exacting education when he writes of Tristan's: 'This was his first departure from his freedom. ... In the blossoming years, when the ecstasy of his springtime was about to unfold and he was just entering with joy into his prime, his best life was over ... the frost of care (which ravages many young people) descended on him and withered the blossoms of his gladness!' Gottfried was assuredly highly trained in theology, law, and rhetoric, but we cannot guess how he was employed after finishing his education. One suggestion which is as plausible as any is that he was in the local urban or episcopal secretariat. Whether or not he was ever engaged on

* See page 367.

confidential missions, his treatment of certain incidents in his story shows him to have been the shrewdest of diplomats, though some scholars have dubbed him 'non-political'. His understanding of French can safely be said to be perfect. It may have come from study in France.

Gottfried was a very cultured man. He was well read in Latin, French, and German literature. He is one of the greatest stylists, if not the greatest, in German literature of any period. His rare gift for language enabled him to transpose every formal artifice from the medieval Latin *ars poetica* into German and to invent others of his own. His virtuosity in such matters is astonishing. His classical allusions are more accurate than those of most who wrote in the vernacular at this time, and, what is more important, they are far more suggestive in tone. Classical poetry and mythology appealed to his fancy mightily. It is as if he had a premonition of the Renaissance. For inspiration he invokes not God, the Supreme Poet of more pious authors, but Apollo and the Nine Muses, at a time when most laymen thought of Apollo as a member of the Moslem 'Trinity'. He was utterly devoted to music, which echoes through his story. In his literary excursus he appears not only as a critic and aesthete but also as a judge of *Minnesang,* the double art of words and melodies. He was deeply versed in hunting-lore and no doubt a keen hunter, so that his distinction between 'those who were skilled in the chase' and 'those who wished to pass the time hunting' contains a sly dig. Altogether, we may rely on it that he was adept in all those graces which make for good breeding in society. It is remarkable that, at a time when the petty nobility of the Hohenstauffen era were acquiring social refinement with an *élan* of which only upstarts are capable, this townsman of Strassburg presents us with an ideal of courtly life more brilliant and accomplished than any. Gottfried beat the knights at their own game. He will scarcely have succeeded in doing so without drawing on the culture of their tutors, the priests.

Gottfried's attitude towards that other aspect of knightly endeavour, the art of chivalry, suits what we already know of him. He affects not to wish to compete with knightly poets in descriptions of arms and battles. 'If you wish to know the details of the tournament you must ask the squires – it was they who arranged it.' But in fact, in his own manner, he can be as vivid as Wolfram and shows some slight trace of his influence. In the scene in which Tristan is knighted, Gottfried of course presents chivalry as a splendid ideal; but in action it is shorn of its glory. Instead, he gives us shrewd calculation. With knights, the stress is on tactics; and he is always careful to show how a mere man might slay a giant or a monster by a combination of luck, opportunism, and piecemeal disposal. In his story the archangels do not invisibly lay low thousands for the hero at a flourish of his sword, as in crusading narratives. As to Arthurian romance, we may assume that Gott-fried had seen through its follies, for he steers clear of them all. Thomas places Tristran a generation later than King Arthur and Gottfried does nothing to change this.

Unlike his great counterpart Wolfram, Gottfried never laughs from the heart, but he smiles now and again. He had a subtle, scathing wit, and we shall never plumb the depths of his irony. The way in which the two Isoldes dispose of the Steward's pretensions to the younger is masterly: the older woman is cool and assured and plays him like a fish on a line; the girl shelters behind her mother and is rude and waspish; the Steward blunders from trap to trap. We see Gottfried in a lighter vein, too, in the scene in which Melot the Dwarf tries unsuccessfully to ensnare Tristan with a forged mes-sage from Isolde. Here the humour is delicate and restrained – till Melot runs on to the barb. Nevertheless, there are other passages in which Gottfried goes too far with his mockery, notably at the end of the Morold episode, where the big man is returned to his king in pieces. Gottfried's taunts on the carved-up state of a warrior who has fought bravely, if arrogantly, would be unthinkable in a poet like Wolfram, who often risked his life in the field (as Gottfried probably did not), and they confirm our suspicion that Gottfried's was not a magnanimous nature. In keeping with this, there is another revealing passage in which Gottfried sophistically cuts Tristan in half to share between his two 'fathers', Mark and Rual. He argues that a man is compounded of his wealth and his person: take the former away, and you will have but half a man. There is much wisdom here; but it has a distinctly worldly flavour.

Apart from his doctrine of love, which must soon engage our attention, Gottfried tells us little of himself, and even then he keeps his mask. Although he brings God and the Church into his story more frequently perhaps than any of his contemporaries, he strikes the reader as correct in such matters but no more. He is as cool on this subject as he is ardent on that of love, and, indeed, the language in which he conveys his thoughts on love often draws on the language of religion in its intensest form. Thus it follows that his views on love and religion must be treated together.

Since Gottfried is so reticent it is not surprising that some of those most concerned to elicit his *personalia* should have put him on the rack of their scholarship and obtained the confessions they required. Some found that he was an atheistical mocker and blasphemer, others an art-loving hedonist of strangely recent type, others a Catharist heretic leading a double life, others an anti-Christian demonist, and yet others a mystical amorist. It cannot be said too emphatically that there is not a shred of evidence in favour of any of these labels, and that there is some evidence against them. But whatever we learn of him, it is never to be forgotten that we learn it by his grace, not by violation of his poem.

The way to an understanding of Gottfried's story lies through his Prologue, and, with less assurance, through the discourses which accompany his story at critical points, since these are often opportunist in character.

In the first forty lines of his Prologue, Gottfried makes a modest beginning. They deal with the relation of criticism to art, and are formed into succinct quatrains in the gnomic manner which use the subtlest play on forms and meanings, above all in the rhymes, and whose opening letters make an acrostic. One discerning critic has had the courage to say that Gottfried, who is so very brilliant elsewhere, has attempted too much here, so that the matter has suffered from the form. Certainly these forty lines are hazardous to interpret and, divested of their verbal brilliance in translation, make a dull beginning to such a poem. I have, therefore, quoted them in the original, which has the virtue of saving the acrostic, and have set a tentative rendering confronting them. They need not detain us further. It is the true Prologue that matters now.

Gottfried informs his listeners that he has decided to busy himself with something that will bring pleasure and contentment not to courtly society at large, since it was bent on having a good time, but to a select circle of 'noble hearts' who accepted and even welcomed love in the totality of its antitheses – the sweet and the bitter, joy and sorrow, life and death. To such a mode of life he is so fervently devoted that he will be damned or saved with it. To those of like mind he proposes to tell a tale that will half-assuage their pain, such being the function of a love-story: he will tell of Tristan and Isolde. After gracefully acknowledging the existence of other versions of the story and the good intentions of their authors, he names his source, the *Tristran* of Thomas, as the authentic version, and he clearly means to adhere to it. And now, in lines of classic beauty with a rhythmic flow that rises to incantation, he reveals his amatory doctrine. A tale of true love ennobles the spirit, reinforces constancy, and enhances life's good qualities; and this is because love is so blessed a thing that, unless love instruct him, no one has worth or honour. How tragic, then, that all but a few are doomed to lose love's benefits because they will not bear its sorrows! For ...

> *swem nie von liebe leit geschach,*
> *dem geschach ouch liep von liebe nie.*

'He that never had sorrow of love never had joy of it either!' Joy and sorrow were ever inseparable in love. We must win honour and glory with the two or go to perdition without them. Had not the lovers of whom this story tells endured sorrow for the sake of love, they would never have comforted so many. Although they are now dead, their sweet name lives on, ever-renewed for the living.

> *Their death, their life are our bread.*
> *Thus lives their life, thus lives their death.*
> *Thus they live still and yet are dead,*
> *And their death is the bread of the living.*

The liturgical nature of this language is startlingly obvious. The difficulty is to say just which sacred context Gottfried had in mind, though we must remember that poetic language may embrace several contexts at once. Is the allusion direct to such canonical sayings as 'I am the living bread ... If any man eat of this bread he shall live for ever; and the bread that I give is my flesh, which I shall give for the life of the world'? Does it come from the liturgy? Or does it come from sources derived from these?

Careful study in recent years has revealed that, while it would be foolish to discount powerful echoes from the Scriptures and the liturgy, our passage and others like it are derived from only one source with any consistency, namely, from the language of the mystics and, above all, from that of St Bernard in his Sermons on the Song of Songs, mystically interpreted.

Just as St Bernard in his Prologue offers 'bread', that is, solid nourishment for the spirit, to the experienced initiates who can digest it, so Gottfried offers the 'bread' of his story to the band of noble hearts who alone are fit to receive it. Another parallel which, no doubt, gave life to our passage was this, that just as the priest preached a sermon before the Eucharist in order to awaken an intense desire for the Body of Christ in the communicants, so Gottfried in his Prologue excites the longing of his listeners for the 'bread' of the tale of Tristan, the tale of martyred love.

The architectural features of the Lovers' Cave, to which Tristan and Isolde withdraw on being banished by King Mark, show similar treatment by Gottfried. They are given allegorical interpretations recalling the traditional allegorization of the Christian Church as a building. The roundness of the Cave betokens Simplicity; its breadth the Power of Love; its height Aspiration; and so on. But, again, closer and more convincing analogies have been found to link them with a mystical interpretation of the 'Cubicle' in which the Soul suffers Union with God; and, most strikingly, with a mystical interpretation of the Tabernacle, which accounts, among other things, for the Bed.

Within the precincts of their Cave the lovers take no food: they nourish themselves merely by gazing at one another. To recur to the language of the mystics, they are consumed by one another like Christ and the Soul, and, consuming, are sustained. Like the Blessed in Paradise, they are rapt in the beatific vision and, in the words of the Book of Revelation, 'They shall hunger no more, neither thirst any more.' They may also, though less compellingly, be regarded as Love's anchorites, who are nourished by invisible manna.

Gottfried's 'noble hearts' (an expression he is the first to use in German) have a close parallel in the 'noble soul' of the mystics, as has their capacity to suffer for love. 'Noble' in mystical contexts means raised to the divine plane – for how else could the Soul unite with God? The novelty of Gottfried's secular usage lies in the fact that the word for 'noble' normally took its meaning from rank in feudal society, not from qualities of the heart. Half a century before the Bolognese Guido Guinizelli conceived his humane and thus anti-feudal philosophy of the *cuore gentile*, the Strassburger Gott-fried formulated his doctrine of the *edelez herze*, which similarly opened the doors to those of the highest culture, whatever their social origins. But behind both Gottfried and Guinizelli we may suspect medieval Latin authors.*

A crowning analogy with the language of the mystics is found in the words in which Gottfried formulates the bond that unites the lovers, words that seek to bridge the antitheses which dominate the lives of ordinary men and women. Though these and other pairs of words ring in our ears throughout his poem, it is not they but their fusion that is of supreme importance to Gottfried. 'What I have to say does not concern that world and such a way of life; their way and mine diverge sharply. I have another world in mind which together in one heart bears its bitter-sweet, its dear sorrow, its heart's joy, its love's pain, its dear life, its sorrowful death, its dear death, its sorrowful life. To this life let my life be given, of this world let me be part, to be damned or saved with it.' When one comes to such passages one wonders why one ever thought of trans-lating, so poor is the return. For the rhythm of Gottfried's verse, the music of his rhymes binds opposites together triumphantly, strange though it all is in logic. I quote the passage here, so that the reader may form some idea of what is lost:

> *Der werlde und diseme lebene*
> *enkumt min rede niht ebene:*
> *ir leben und minez zweient sich.*
> *ein ander werlt die meine ich,*
> *diu samet in eime herzen treit*
> *ir süeze sur, ir liebez leit,*
> *ir liebez leben, ir leiden tot,*
> *ir lieben tot, ir leidez leben:*
> *dem lebene si min leben ergeben,*
> *der werlt wil ich gewerldet wesen,*
> *mit ir verderben oder genesen.*

Such passages convince us that Gottfried is in deadly earnest and that this is not an example of the clever dialectic of love to which

* Only in the Prologue does 'noble hearts' bear this esoteric meaning.

one is accustomed in other medieval poems, much though a prose rendering might suggest it.

It is clear from these examples that whatever other religious matter Gottfried has drawn on, the one consistent theme is that of twelfth-century mysticism.* The question now arises as to how to use this insight. In the form of the crassest alternatives: was Gottfried merely utilizing the ready-made language of the mystics, those pioneers in the discovery of the inner self, in order to say things about love that had never been said before? Or was he preaching a new religion of love while at the same time rejecting Christianity, or at least Christian teaching on love? Much depends on the answer.

Lest the reader should imagine that the conception of love which Gottfried recommends as lofty and difficult of attainment is a form of 'platonic' love, it must be said at once that it is grounded in willing and full surrender on both sides. Gottfried has some curt words for prudish lovers who deny themselves to each other. On the other hand, the love which he conceives is far from being the mere worship of the instincts as with certain modern authors. Between lovers, at least, constancy and other good qualities are demanded to their highest degree, and, if need be, the suffering entailed by true love must be borne with fortitude. Thus Gottfried's ideal of love presents a fusion of the sensual and the spiritual; how successfully I leave others to judge.

Was Gottfried utilizing religious language or preaching a new religion? To begin with, one may concede that his attitude and language imply a new *cult* of love. This in itself would amply account for his appropriation of religious and, above all, mystical language, since such language was a highly developed vehicle of ecstasy, anything short of whose intensity clearly would not have suited Gottfried. But was he preaching a religion? Surely not. His pronouncements concern relations between lovers, while those of religion concern communities. Gottfried uses scathing words on current amorous behaviour. He says that deceived husbands have only themselves to blame, for they are blinded by lust; that the close-keeping of women is abominable, since it incites them to evil

---

* It is not without interest that when Wagner was exploiting Gottfried's story for his music drama he had recourse to the quasi-mystical philosophy of Schopenhauer for its elaboration.

courses – rather should they be trusted; that love is hounded to the far corners of the earth, or goes begging from door to door. But when we examine such statements, we find that they do not amount to a coherent and positive system, and sometimes contradict each other. They are based on ready-made home-truths, however cleverly Gottfried elaborates them. Trenchant though such observations are in themselves, they offer no prospect of reform in any social sense. If Gottfried thought that his cult of love contained the seeds of universal regeneration between the sexes he does not say so; rather does he place his hopes in a minority. One doubts whether his heroic conception of love, so securely founded on suffering, could survive in conditions where all could wed as they pleased. Lovers as Gottfried conceived them can no more do without the Jealous One's doorkeepers, spies, and 'slanderers' (who seem always to tell the truth) than revolutionaries without the police. In an ideal world free of *mésalliance* such as Gottfried implies but never describes, his lovers would go to pieces for sheer lack of opposition: they are heroes of the Resistance, of the underground army of love. It is well observed that they should leave their paradise of their own free will in the episode of the Cave of Lovers in order to resume their hunted life, which must inevitably end in separation.

In the absence of any positive statements on Gottfried's part, we must imagine him to have been resigned to the existing social order and to have accepted it as a fact of life that an absolute attachment of lovers must often or always run counter to society and find its own way of survival in desperate opposition to it. He does not say so explicitly, but there is small risk in believing him to have thought that the social order and the mighty passion of love were facts of the creation for whose conflict he was not responsible, and, moreover, that the solution offered by the clergy (of whose whole apparatus he was master) was far from satisfactory. It would be unsafe to go any further. This does not necessarily make him a heretic, though his outlook might well have gained in freedom from the mutual attrition of Christianity and Catharism in his native Strassburg in his own lifetime. Schooled in medieval and in some classical learning, Gottfried may have been a lover who could think for himself on what mattered most to him – no unusual thing in a great poet, though not very common then.

It would be hard to assert that Gottfried is anything more than correct in religious matters. He can draw a majestic picture of the power of God as it reveals itself in a tempest. He most affectionately sets heavenly crowns on the heads of that happy pair, Rual and Floraete, when they are dead. But in other contexts he cannot escape the suspicion of using the name of God lightly, or on occasion of making a mere narrative device of it, even to the point of slickness. After burying Rivalin he commends his soul to God and smartly transfers our interest to the sad death of Blancheflor on giving birth to Tristan, only to repeat the process with her and conclude with the pointed phrase: 'And now let us tell what God did with the babe that had neither father nor mother'. He executes such manoeuvres almost too adroitly and leaves us wondering. His characters sometimes voice sentiments which we may fairly claim as his. A case in point is Tristan's fluent assumption of the rôle of David to Morold's Goliath, prior to their duel. For Tristan tries to assuage the Cornishmen's fears by the argument that if a warrior who stakes his life in a good cause falls in battle, then a swift death and a people's long-drawn agony are rated differently in Heaven and on earth.* In the sequel we learn that God did succour Tristan against Morold; but he came to Tristan's aid only at the last moment after a sharp reminder from Gottfried, and even then was but one ally among three.

Gottfried's alarming comment on the outcome of Isolde's trial by ordeal for adultery, in which Heaven seems to uphold her innocence, has often been adduced in discussions of his theological position. Indeed it is even now regarded, quite mistakenly, as the key passage for this purpose. When the red-hot irons leave Isolde's hands unscathed, Gottfried observes: 'Thus it was made manifest and confirmed to all the world that Christ in His great virtue is pliant as a windblown sleeve. He falls into place and clings whichever way you try Him, closely and smoothly, as He is bound to do!' Surviving rituals of such trials show that what was expected to be 'manifested' was not the nature of any member of the Trinity but the divine judgement of the case. *Tristan* was written in about 1210. Five years later the Lateran Council forbade the clergy to con-

---

* Such sentiments have their bearing, for example, on the débâcle of the Second Crusade, for which the priesthood promised victory.

secrate trials by ordeal. The Church has never liked to be less than five years behind well-informed public opinion, and it suits our situation excellently to suppose that this brilliant poet of an enlightened and somewhat rationalistic circle in the Bishop's town of Strassburg should be indulging in irony (as so often elsewhere) at the expense of those who still believed in ordeals.

There is no compelling reason to regard this passage in its context as blasphemous, or heretical or demoniac, or indeed as anything more sensational than the utterance of an intelligent and alert man who was indifferent enough in religious matters to be critical of pious excess among the ignorant. It is as if he suspected that the clergy were not on such intimate terms with their Maker as their words and behaviour implied and – despite the one occasion when the Deity thwarted the plans of young Tristan's abductors with a storm at sea – believed that God does not intervene in human affairs by fits and starts, but holds aloof till the appointed day. It has further been well observed that, in contrast to almost any comparable poem of Gottfried's day, there is no passage in *Tristan* in which its author shows a positive relationship towards any member of the Trinity but the first. Various explanations are possible, but we have no means of choosing between them.

To conclude this discussion, which, in the absence of a common opinion, it was not possible to spare the reader, it can be said that although Gottfried is propagating an esoteric cult of worldly love by means of a story as if predestined for it, and with an intensity which others devoted to the joy or the salvation of their souls, he is not preaching a new religion, nor challenging the Church head-on. Instead, he seems to emerge as a scholar, lover, sceptic, and poet with a rare power of taking words from other spheres, both emotional and rational, and suiting them to the ever-changing needs of his story, a story of passion beyond the law.

The rack and the police filing-system are not the best means of getting truth out of dead poets. There is far more to be learnt about reticent authors by trying to visualize their situation as they take their work in hand. We know that Gottfried used as his source the poem of a lesser artist, but that, for reasons of literary integrity as he understood them, he meant to keep to the story. He might smile to himself over some of the matter to be recounted, but as a question of principle he made the best case he could for it. In other words, his attitude towards his story was that of an advocate. His heart was most assuredly in all that had to do with love, and here his pleading is inspired. But where the tale goes against him, laying some strain on his advocacy, we find him cool and calculating and at times even specious. He makes damaging admissions against his clients only when he must. When Isolde asks Brangane, who is still a virgin, to do duty for her at the nuptials, Gottfried's brief comment, 'Thus Love instructs honest minds to practise perfidy, though they ought not to know what goes to make a fraud of this sort', lays the blame on Lady Love's shoulders which (we see) are broad as well as handsome. Having disposed of the matter, he never hints at guilt again, except to say that it was Mark's fault that he was deceived, because he closed his eyes – the lovers concealed nothing! Isolde's success with her doctored oath at her ordeal must also have left Gottfried exposed; but, as we have seen, he extricates himself brilliantly by means of scathing irony. This advocacy of Gottfried's makes it very difficult to penetrate to the man, and it is more profitable to study him where he reveals himself all the time – in his work, as an artist.

Gottfried's *Tristan* lies half-way between romance and novel. Its archaic narrative matter, often frankly pure fairy-tale, is set in motion by Gottfried with as much realistic psychology as it will bear. For whole stretches one feels that one is reading a novel – and then the old tale reasserts itself. At times we find him shaking his head over the story's love of the irrational, either obliquely through irony, as when dealing with monsters, or directly, as when he ridicules a widespread variant to the effect that a swallow chanced to bring a golden hair from Ireland to Cornwall, leading to the marriage of Isolde. We often have the feeling that Gottfried was more mature in outlook than he was permitted to show by the literary media of his time. Having made his choice, he adhered faithfully to the convention that a writer does not foist tales of his own imagining on a credulous public, as he accused Wolfram von Eschenbach of doing. He names his source and keeps to it, deepening here, broadening there, adding circumstantial detail and always embellishing and embroidering.

If Gottfried's *Tristan* does not arrive at being a novel, of which literary form Gottfried was no doubt capable but at which he was not aiming, it has nevertheless passed beyond romance. Nor are we losers by it. Of the two, novel and versified romance, the latter was better suited to Gottfried's unique gift of lyrical narrative. The one structural weakness which a modern critic might be tempted to ascribe to his work, were he to apply our standards to it, would be that the discrepancy between the traditional plot and Gottfried's deep understanding of human motives at times leads us to question the consistency of some characters.

A case in point is Isolde's attempt to have Brangane murdered soon after the latter has saved Isolde's reputation and perhaps her life by the sacrifice of her own virginity in Mark's bed. But for the unforeseeable compassion of Isolde's agents, the deed would have been done beyond recall. However sincerely Isolde may have repented her action, she was morally a murderess. The motive for her attempt is her fear that Brangane, once having tasted the pleasures of the bed, might conceive a liking for them and seek to oust her by exposing her. This reveals Isolde as inhumanly ruthless and utterly unworthy of a story whose confessed purpose was to show us an exemplary pair of lovers, unless we admit that love takes absolute precedence over moral considerations even to the point of murder. Gottfried does not say as much, but instead eludes the problem, which was none of his seeking. It was his source which demanded of him that he recount Isolde's attempt on Brangane's life as best he might, and this he does brilliantly within the confines of the episode. But we cannot always rhyme it with other episodes, at least with those prior to the drinking of the potion.

Yet Gottfried is not beyond all hope of rescue. For, although as a young princess Isolde had been nurtured most tenderly under the eyes of a discerning mother at a court of great refinement, Gottfried has nevertheless prepared us for her pitiless attempt on Brangane. Two hundred and fifty lines back he has made it not Tristan's or Brangane's but Isolde's idea that her cousin should replace her at the nuptials. It is but a short step from the violation of a friend's integrity to the destruction of her life. In turn, the substitution of Brangane for Isolde was dictated by fear for her life, a fear made resourceful by love; and this was all because love had forced Isolde to surrender to Tristan. For its part (as Gottfried tells the tale) love had come because Tristan and Isolde had chanced to drink a magic draught together. Thus the chain of human motivation holds as far back as this, till we are suddenly face to face with magic; which suggests that, if the consistency of Isolde's character has been impaired by anything at all, it was by the direct action of the philtre as much as by the apparently incongruous events of the tale. But, in fact, far from being no more than an uncouth survival from a cruder age (as it was historically), the Brangane episode is an integral part of the events which arise from the drinking of the potion, and is wholly congruent with that fateful act, showing as it does how swiftly love can drive Isolde to the depths. In the Brangane episode the malign aspects of love as it was released by the philtre are shown to the full in action. And how sudden was that release!

> Nu daz diu maget unde der man,
> Isot unde Tristan,
> den tranc getrunken beide, sa
> was ouch der werlde unmuoze da,
> Minne, aller herzen lagærin. ...

Now when the maid and the man, Isolde and Tristan, had drunk the draught, in an instant that arch-disturber of tranquillity was there, Love, waylayer of all hearts. ...

The brief but menacing syllable 'sa' ('at once') on which the two halves of the poem hinge, the carefree and the enamoured, marks the opening of a box that can be compared to Pandora's: the passion of love flies out, and with each of its heroic virtues comes a vice – arrogance, deceit, treachery, ingratitude, and finally the will to murder.

If we compare the scene in which Tristan lies helpless in his bath and Isolde ponders whether she shall avenge her uncle Morold's death on Tristan then and there, we observe that she finds it impossible to carry out the deed. Sentimental critics, wise in the wisdom of latter-day psychology, attribute Isolde's inability to kill Tristan to her being more or less unconsciously in love with him, even before drinking the love-potion, a conception which was foreign to Gottfried. Gottfried's own explanation, which one may be excused for preferring, despite its not being entirely free from prevarication, is that Isolde's womanly instincts forbade her to kill. Between this passage and her attempt on cousin Brangane's life something must have happened to Isolde. That the potion was indeed the true cause of the lovers' passion and of all that followed from it and no mere outward symbol will be shown by other means below. But we have learned enough to understand that, for some time, the potion changed Isolde's character much for the worse.

We may not leave Isolde without dwelling on one further trait. Like Eve in the popular medieval interpretation of the scene in Genesis, Isolde is the one who first overcomes the lovers' sense of shame by leaning her elbow against Tristan; it is she who entices her Adam to her orchard at great risk in the noonday heat and so brings about their discovery, separation, and fall from happiness; it is she again who, at the moment of parting, restrains Tristan from too hasty a leave-taking and solemnly pronounces the doctrine of their identity, as priestess of their amorous cult. Gottfried rates woman lower than man as a being of spirit and intelligence, but concedes her the priority in love.

Tristan's character shows no such apparent break as Isolde's. Conceived when his father seemed mortally wounded, born to sorrow by a mother who died in childbirth at the news of his father's death, Tristan was destined to be a tragic lover. In German law (but not in English law, which Thomas may have followed) Tristan was a bastard, since he was conceived out of wedlock, a state which no subsequent marriage of his parents could legitimize. On being set ashore in Cornwall the boy lied his way to safety with the utmost assurance. He soon proved himself as an infant prodigy at court in all imaginable accomplishments and ousted the Chief Huntsman and the Master Musician from their positions of pre-eminence without any sign of compunction. During his struggle with Morold as an initiate to knighthood, Tristan showed great political foresight, as well as courage, as in all his subsequent dealings with the anti-Tristan party at court. When he went to Duke Morgan to claim a fief which his father had held and was reminded of his illegitimacy, he forced the argument round to where Morgan cast aspersions on his mother, thus offering Tristan the one chance of 'righting' his bad case in law, which he promptly seized; for without warning he dispatched Morgan with ruthless efficiency, and later defeated his army, so that his *de facto* position was unassailable. Next, in pursuit of higher honours at the court of his maternal uncle, Tristan virtually abandoned his own loyal Parmenians – and commended them piously to God. Gottfried himself is so sensitive to the impression this might make that he washes his hands of Tristan's action by means of a literary device. – His audience is represented as insisting that Tristan should pursue his ambitions, regardless of his obligations to Parmenie, and the poet acquiesces.

Thus after Tristan has drunk the love-potion it does not strike us as unthinkable that he should succumb to its effects after a sharp struggle with Loyalty and Honour. And we must in any case regard this pair as a rhetorical convenience, because, when Gottfried has to unite Tristan and Isolde for the first time, Loyalty and Honour lose to Love; whereas, when Gottfried has to land the lovers in Cornwall at a time when they were free to go to Tristan's country, Loyalty and Honour (for what they are worth) are momentarily in the ascendant – probably the poorest piece of work in the story. Now come a series of intrigues which make it clear that no one less adroit and unconcerned for moral issues than Tristan has been since childhood (despite his upbringing by honest Rual) could ever have stayed near his mistress so long. And when at last he is caught in flagrant delict and goes into exile, he singes his wings in a new flame under the fatal fascination – so we are told – of the lady's name, Isolde of the White Hands. Gottfried's description of the passing disintegration of Tristan's love for Isolde the Fair to the point where he can marry, but not love, the other Isolde, is masterly; but we are aware that Tristan's loyalty even within the sacred bond of love has received a permanent scar.

The characters of Tristan and Isolde thus oscillate between the ideal, if judged by amatory standards, and the criminal, if judged by others. Gottfried barely hints whether he regards this as inevitable; but in his Prologue to *Parzival*, Wolfram von Eschenbach shows that he has noticed the discrepancy. In Wolfram's eyes there is but one standard of loyalty, which reveals Gottfried's lovers to be false.

The account of the loves of Tristan's parents, Rivalin and Blancheflor, makes one of the finest short stories in German of any period. Clearly Tristan has inherited some of his parents' qualities. They fall madly in love with each other without the aid of a love-potion and give themselves up to their passion with the same disregard for the consequences as Tristan and Isolde, and with an even more reckless disregard for their lives. But the father is far less circumspect than his son. He is mettlesome, ambitious, and revengeful, to his own undoing. He has been excellently described as 'constitutionally incapable of doing anything but loving and fighting. He is improvident in the extreme.' Blancheflor's reason is flooded to drowning by warm emotions. Having abandoned her whole future to the dashing Rivalin's whim, she reminds him apologetically of the plight in which she would find herself, were he to go away and leave her, and finds a swift and at last adequate response in her lover's impetuous heart.

The shadows in Gottfried's ideal pair are deepened by contrast with the happily married couple Rual and Floraete, who move with ease in courtly society and yet remain uncorrupted and touchingly devoted to Tristan, their fosterling and overlord, who belongs to quite another world. Brangane and Curvenal, too, are patterns of loyal love towards their respective principals, the former especially in that, having failed to guard the potion well, she pays the price in full on demand, and even pardons her would-be murderess. (Thomas, however, in a later scene which Gottfried did not reach, shows Brangane turning against her mistress when the load becomes too heavy for her.) In the minor character Marjodo there is a well-conceived change of behaviour. A friend of Tristan's and a secret admirer of Isolde, he becomes their implacable enemy on discovering that the Queen is not so unattainable as he had thought, so that, withered by jealousy, he descends from being Tristan's bosom-friend to the level of Melot, the insidious dwarf, to make a pair who henceforth hunt together as the Serpent and the Cur.

The most problematic figure is that of Mark. He sets the tone of a court famed for its gaiety and high breeding, qualities which are not always borne out in later episodes, in which his barons intrigue against Tristan. We find Mark magnanimous and then ever more devoted to the child of his sister's elopement, both before and after discovering his identity, often against his own political interest, about which he does not seem to care. His love of pleasure shows its first signs of weakness, as Gottfried tells the tale, when he fails to detect the deception at his nuptials – 'one woman was like another to him'. At first he will not credit the rumours linking the names of the two he loves best in the world. But when suspicion grows and it is time for him to act, he is blinded by lust for his beautiful Queen and will not see the truth. At length, in language of great nobility and tinged with a tragic quality that we meet with only here, yet somewhat undermined by its belatedness, Mark stands aside from their company of three and banishes the lovers, not finding it in himself to harm them. Soon, at the flimsiest sign of Isolde's innocence, Mark falls victim once again to his desire for the wife who does not love him. He wavers for a long time in suspicion and doubt, unable to make up his mind, till at last crass certainty tears illusion from his eyes. The last we hear of him in Gottfried's unfinished poem is that instead of killing the lovers in the act as the law (both written and unwritten) would have allowed or even required, he returns to the Palace to fetch witnesses; but finding Tristan gone and with him all proof of the deed, he is lectured by his councillors, after an ineffective show of annoyance, into taking Isolde back as a woman who has been much wronged.

Thomas had raised the figure of Mark from that of a royal cuckold given to black fits of rage to one who was for ever in doubt because he could find no proof by which to convict his dear ones. Gottfried no doubt perceived that such a figure harboured tragic possibilities. This may well be one of the reasons why he fixes the guilt on Mark so squarely – only the lovers must have his listeners' sympathy, he has none to spare for a rival. Altogether, the men and women of the Middle Ages had little sentiment to spare for husbands. For these and other reasons Mark can at best be a pathetic, but not a tragic, figure. It is our gentler, or should one say less robust, modern outlook alone which suspects that he might be otherwise.

Some further light is thrown on the situation by an inquiry into the nature of the love-potion. Was it a cause of love, or a mere symbol of the passage from unconscious to conscious love? Tristan and Isolde are certainly occupied with each other in some way prior to drinking the potion, and it would be very modern and therefore very profound of Gottfried to have them unconsciously in love. But unfortunately, if one combs this part of the story, one finds no explicit statement to this effect, so that any who assume it are without question placing psychological constructions on the narrative of a poet who was well able to do this for himself. They do so at their own risk. It was seen above that Gottfried's motive for Isolde's failure to kill Tristan in his bath was her womanly nature. The woman who kills is a she-devil, like Kriemhild in the *Nibelungenlied*. After Isolde's admiration of Tristan's handsome looks and physique as he sits naked in his tub before she has discovered his identity, this somewhat ambiguous motive of her womanhood is disappointing, but it must be borne. Other comparable scenes occur, in which a reader of *Peg's Paper* might detect unconscious love, as, for example, on board ship shortly before the mishap with the philtre, when Isolde rejects Tristan's respectful and strictly permissible familiarities (compare how Hermione gives her hand to Polixenes in *The Winter's Tale* in all innocence and propriety according to the fashion of the times). In such scenes Gottfried plays with his listeners. He executes a double finesse. For he knows as well as they that the two must fall in love. He has told us twice over that they are fated to do so, when on two occasions Isolde was the first to discover her future lover. He, too, knows of unconscious love, and half tempts us to jump to conclusions. But, in fact, with the conventions at his disposal, he adheres closely to the tradition of his story, namely that it was a philtre which made his lovers fall in love.

At first sight it would seem that no philtre is needed to involve two high-spirited young people in a fatal passion, since Tristan's parents Rivalin and Blancheflor fall in love in much the same way without one. But their tragedy is brought about by Rivalin's arrogance, which is external to their love; and although they ran away from one court, they might easily have lived at another had Rivalin not fallen in battle. The loves of Rivalin and Blancheflor nevertheless do offer a clue to the problem. Rivalin's falling in love is compared to the ensnarement of a free bird on the limed twig, an image which Chaucer uses later in his *Troilus*:

> For love bigan his fetheres so to lyme ... [I, 353]

Like Claudius's 'limèd soul' in *Hamlet*, Rivalin struggles to be free, but is more engaged. And when Gottfried comes to tell of the fruitless efforts of Tristan and Isolde, especially of the latter, to free themselves from the insidious clinging of love, he renews this image. There were no hints of unconscious love in Rivalin before Blancheflor sighed at him; so that this parallel alone is enough to suggest that there was no unconscious love between Tristan and Isolde. But Gottfried was more explicit. Before Tristan has finally won Isolde for his uncle at the court of Dublin, she is compared to the free falcon on its bough that turns its gaze where it pleases, an image rich in associations with medieval German love-poetry. In this same scene Isolde is also referred to as Love's bird of the chase. Later, this image too is revived; but now Isolde has drunk the draught, she has been caught in the lime (as falcons were sometimes caught in practice), and has succumbed; so that her predatory eyes, now in company with her heart, go out to one man alone, her fated lover Tristan. Thus it would seem that any change in Isolde's character must be attributed to the potion.

The inference is clear. At the Irish court, Isolde, the falcon on her bough, was fancy-free. But now, thanks to the fateful error with the potion, she is Love's captive. There is proof that Gottfried uses symbols in this way. For in Marjodo's dream a mighty boar ranges from the forest, plunges up to Mark's bedchamber and fouls the royal linen with his foam at the very moment when Tristan is lying in the Queen's arms. Looking back over the story we recall that the device on Tristan's shield at his knighting ceremony is precisely that of the Boar, just as the boar of Troilus' dream tallies with the heraldic Boar of his rival Diomede in Chaucer. These magnificent images of the Boar and the Falcon are used sparingly but consistently by Gottfried in his *Tristan*.

It would be fair to say that although Gottfried employs the love-philtre symbolically (how could it fail to symbolize fatal passion?), this does not preclude it from being the cause of Tristan and Isolde's love. In Thomas's version Mark also drinks of the potion. But Gottfried will have none of that. He causes Brangane to throw the cursed fatal flask into the sea so that Mark should be unable to drink of it. For what part could sensual Mark have in the unique and heroic passion of which Tristan and Isolde are the martyrs? And be it noted: when the ships put to land, the sea is such that they can make good headway, but, as the love-drink falls into its lap, we are told that it is wild and raging! Evidently the sea has claimed something very potent and out of the ordinary. This innovation of Gottfried's, slight in itself yet highly significant in effect, must serve for many other instances of his discreet yet far-reaching changes.

One final word remains to be said on Gottfried's attitude towards love. Although, while the tale is on, Chaucer sympathizes warmly with his pair of lovers in *Troilus*, he takes it all back at the end and again in his last will and testament. It is possible, though very unlikely, that Gottfried might have done so, had he finished his story. He seems to have committed himself too deeply. But because of the mask that he wears we shall never know for sure. One feels in the end that he was an idealist and also a pessimist in love. He tells us that he has known the passion since his twelfth year, has found his way to the Cave (though he never went to Cornwall), and blundered up to the Bed, without ever resting on it. Even his lovers, who do repose there, do not stay there long, but resume their place of 'honour' in society, after which Tristan's love is to suffer cruel attrition. Gottfried has prepared us for this. For when Love brings the pair together for the first time, he discreetly engages our attention in a discourse on love as love had come to be – cheapened, prostituted, and hounded to the corners of the earth. Gottfried despairs from the outset of the ability of the common herd to attain it. But even the hopes which he places in his chosen band of noble hearts appear slender.

Comparison with his source shows that Gottfried was tactful in his handling of the lovers' amours beyond what we might expect in a man of his generation. To the modern mind the relationship of the three, and then four, main characters is unpalatable. As soon as a situation of this sort threatens to arise in the *Forsyte Saga* on Soames's reassertion of his rights, Galsworthy stages Bosinney's exit – scarcely credibly for us – by having him run over by a hansom-cab. From a natural delicacy of feeling and in the interests of the beauty of the tale as he wished to tell it, Gottfried passes over disturbing elements as lightly as he can; whereas Thomas, always the analytical psychologist, tends to wallow in outraged feelings.

To place Gottfried's *Tristan* in its true perspective it must be stressed that it is but one of four great narrative poems in medieval German, the others being the *Parzival* and the *Willehalm* of Wolfram von Eschenbach, and the epic *Nibelungenlied*, all written within twenty years of one another at the beginning of the thirteenth century. Together with the songs of leading Minnesinger like Heinrich von Morungen, Walther von der Vogelweide, and Neidhart von

Reuental, these longer poems make an age of great literature as yet unsuspected by readers of English at large. German genius has sometimes been over-cried in its native land, so that where there is a hindrance to its appreciation as here – only a discipline as exacting as that of classical studies will unlock the door to it – others have taken the line of least resistance and ignored the just claims to their attention of this fascinating poetry. Even that great master of medieval literatures, W. P. Ker, shows few signs of having savoured the poetry of the Hohenstauffen age of Germany. Here, then, is a lost world of the imagination awaiting discovery by the curious, and here, as a beginning, is Gottfried's *Tristan*, which, unless I have sadly betrayed it, should bring a shock of delight to those who were expecting an Arthurian romance, a Tennysonian idyll, or a Wagnerian melodrama; or who imagined that in the year A.D. 1210 Germany was still altogether in the Dark Ages.

*

To translate fine literature is to invite defeat in battle to gain a higher end. The enlightened translator is fey: he knows that the best that he can do is to make a good showing in a cause that is doomed from the start. After enjoying Gottfried's poem for thirty years I would never have dared translate it but for the unending pleasure, despite the incalculable loss, which translations of otherwise inaccessible masterpieces have given me, even renderings that were manifestly poor or misconceived. I know from this experience that it is possible to succeed whilst failing, and how grateful a reader can be for a translator's courage, or maybe rashness.

In justice to his author a translator must account to his readers in general terms for the loss suffered by the original.

First of all, Gottfried's *Tristan* is in verse. It is in short rhyming couplets, no great metre to sustain a poem of nearly twenty thousand lines, but a metre, nevertheless, which is more than adequate for recitations of one or two longer episodes each evening after supper. Gottfried handles this rather light verse with such tact that the reader rarely perceives anything but its beauties. All – barring a poet of comparable gifts – who ventured to render this long poem in kind, would run the constant risk of lapsing into doggerel, as examples in several languages have shown. Indeed, the difficulties that would beset a modern poet would be far greater than those confronting Gottfried, since short couplets were an accepted convention at court and well suited to the language. Anything less than the most distinguished verse would be a gross disservice to such an author. To announce that one had reproduced a poem of this sort in verse would raise the highest expectations, which anyone but a born poet must inevitably disappoint. May this prose version be found useful by a good English poet one day!

In this medium, in passages of lyrical or philosophical concentration, Gottfried reveals himself as a formal artist of astonishing virtuosity. His verbal subtleties and intricacies are unmatched in any period of German literature. Gottfried learned his art directly and indirectly from the medieval Latin *Ars Poetica*; yet for comparable passages of highly formal poetry in narrative one might have to go as far as Persia or India. It is only because Gottfried is a great storyteller, too, with an impeccable plain style, which he uses in the greater part of his poem, that translation offers chances of success. His verbal *tours de force*, serving to underline his interpretation of the story, are based on structures of sound and of grammar often peculiar to medieval German, as for example in these beautiful lines, already quoted above:

> *swem nie von liebe leit geschach,*
> *dem geschach ouch liep von liebe nie.*

It seemed pointless to try to copy such things in English. (They cannot be copied in modern German either, though some attempt it.) Another related field in which effort would have been wasted is where Gottfried plays, as he often does, on nuances of meaning within one and the same word. Here it must be understood that in all this verbal brilliance there is no trace of the facetious exuberance of Shakespeare's courtiers; it is managed gravely and with the decorum of a man who was at the same time poet, critic, and aesthete. In my rendering all this is lost. There is some small comfort in the thought that the modern world has even less time for such things than the majority of Gottfried's contemporaries had.

At the beginning of the Prologue the reader will find in the original Middle High German ten (out of eleven) quatrains of sententious utterance, with the plain prose sense opposite them. Their repeated rhymes sometimes play on nuances of meaning or on etymological relationships. The first letters, together with the first letter of the first long paragraph, give the acrostic

G[otfrid] DIETERICH T[ristan] I[sot]

The acrostic continues through pairs of large initials to where the poem breaks off, and, since it is incomplete, remains insoluble. In each case the first initial of a pair introduces a gnomic or otherwise emphatic quatrain, which I have always printed in italics. The verbal intricacies of these quatrains are naturally lost in translation. The following example (ll. 1751 ff.) will show to what extent:

> *Owe der ougenweide*
> *da man nach leidem leide*
> *mit leiderem leide*
> *siht leider ougenweide!*

(Alas for the sight where, after dire grief, one sees a sadder sight with grief more dire!)

The formal loss is only too evident. Any attempt to render this in verse and in kind must inevitably offend. But in refraining from giving such offence thus negatively in prose, I hope to make it possible for the other virtues of my author to be enjoyed without distraction.

Since Gottfried had received a thorough schooling in rhetoric, theology, and law, I considered it possible that he might have attempted to convey his knowledge of the emotions in terms of a systematic psychology. The first thousand lines were sufficient to banish the idea. Despite his highly developed dialectic of life and death, joy and sorrow, Gottfried's psychology was unlearned and intuitive. With him, such words as those for 'heart', 'mood', 'sense', and even 'body' and 'soul' often overlap or are synonymous. Thus he was in the happy position of being nearer to those who locate the emotions in the kidneys or in the feet than to the precise authors of today. I therefore soon gave up referring to my glossary to see how I had last dealt with such terms, and confined myself entirely to the context. Thus in instances where Gottfried had made a pattern with such words and their derivatives, and where it was important to render the play of the emotions in a sense acceptable to modern readers, the pattern has been effaced.

No doubt as a result of his learned upbringing as much as his great fluency, Gottfried's style favours a profusion of double expressions, an inclination which is strongly encouraged by the tendency of the metre to divide the line at its middle, as in the case of the antithetical formulations referred to above. I have often deliberately copied such expressions as an intrinsic element of Gottfried's style; but where I felt that a double expression was an obstacle to smooth reading – Gottfried's own acknowledged aim – I replaced it by a simple one. Another liberty which I permitted myself was the straightforward translation into English of numerous phrases in medieval French with which Gottfried spices his German, a thing he does with excellent good taste. To have left these phrases embedded in modern English would have been incongruous; to have given them in modern French would have created an effect very different from what Gottfried intended. I have, of course, changed pronouns into names where convenient, and vice versa.

In my version I have avoided the pseudo-medieval jargon in which it was customary to render medieval stories as recently as a generation or two ago, and which lingers on curiously into our own times. One asks oneself, what have Tennyson, Sir Walter Scott, or Malory to do with Gottfried von Strassburg? Why then bring them to the feast? Arthur Waley and E. V. Rieu have shown us what can be achieved in a straight argument with their authors, with all third parties excluded. Only in the two hunting scenes have I consciously employed some archaic terms, and even then sparingly. (Turberville's *Boke of Huntinge* could have furnished many more.) For a host of reasons I could not run the risk of having the ancient and poetic Grand Chase of the Hart read in terms of a modern stag-hunt.

Gottfried makes a highly personal use of an already subtle idiom, the well-bred colloquial language of the Hohenstauffen courts further refined by literary usage. But medieval German lexicography is in a parlous state, not having been systematized since 1878, though much new material has been made available. Furthermore, there is only one commentary on Gottfried's *Tristan*, that of R. Bechstein (1889), which, though excellent for its day, has never been brought up to date, and in any case applies to Bechstein's edition of the text below which it runs, and not to the more modern edition of F. Ranke (1930), on which the present translation, but for a word or two, is based. Ranke in turn published few comments involving close textual interpretation, and one sometimes has the feeling that he may not always have been in a position to know the precise meanings of passages which he could nevertheless edit with confidence. Thus for a full understanding of *Tristan* at the purely linguistic level there is still some way to go.

It was accordingly something of an adventure to set about translating Gottfried's masterpiece. Yet I dare to send out my rendering in the hope that it may not only entertain the general reader, but also serve those who have some acquaintance with medieval German as a running commentary on the text, a commentary which, in the nature of things, can permit itself none of those disquieting silences of which textual commentators at times avail themselves. Scholars might kindly note that I intend to account for my readings elsewhere and that for them to point out my errors convincingly now would both contribute to the subject and improve any later edition of this translation.

Apart from the losses and difficulties which I have recorded, I have felt sustained by Gottfried's supreme ability to tell a story. If I have succeeded in conveying this feeling to my readers the pleasure I have had from my labours will be all the sweeter for not being confined to myself.

A. T. H.

Queen Mary College, London
August 1959

The story of Gottfried's *Tristan* has been made known to readers of English before by Jessie L. Weston in *The Story of Tristan and Iseult, rendered into English from the German of Gottfried von Strassburg* (1899), 2 vols., and by E. H. Zeydel in *The Tristan and Isolde of Gottfried von Strassburg, translated with Introduction and Notes and Connecting Summaries* (Princeton, 1948). The former is a much abbreviated paraphrase, the latter a rendering into couplets of longer portions, with connecting summaries in prose. I have consulted neither.

ACKNOWLEDGEMENTS

The interpretation of Gottfried's and Thomas's poems of Tristan is far from concluded, and I have therefore sought more light on my problems from friends and colleagues in my own and in other fields. Their response was overwhelmingly generous.

First of all I must thank Professor F. P. Pickering for answering textual questions concerning Gottfried's Tristan promptly, as often as he was asked, especially during the early stages of my translation, when I was finding my feet. He and three others, Professor Hugo Kuhn, Mr Hugh Sacker, and Dr Roy Wisbey, replied to two pages of questions for which I required others' opinions. My colleague Dr Herbert H. K. Thoma very kindly cleared up some knotty points of grammar. I have to thank Professor Jean Fourquet, Dr H. Furstner, Dr Rainer Gruenter, Professor W. Schwartz, and Professor Jost Trier for the gift of valuable offprints. My warm thanks are due to my colleague Dr Rosemary Combridge, who, as good fortune would have it, was engaged in writing a thesis on legal problems in Gottfried's Tristan while I was translating the poem. Dr Combridge not only allowed me to read her illuminating thesis as she was writing it, but she also discussed with me during many months fine points of character and of story-telling involved in Gottfried's oblique references to the law. For some information on medieval nautical matters I have to thank Captain S. W. Roskill, R.N. (Retd), and Dr David Ross. I owe my tutor, Professor F. Norman, O.B.E., an incalculable debt for having grounded me in Medieval German studies, and I must also record that I read passages from Tristan for the first time under the late Professor Robert Priebsch.

I owe a deep debt of gratitude to Professor Arthur L. Basham, who undertook the tiresome task of reading and criticizing my first typed draft of Gottfried's Tristan, and to my wife Margot for so patiently listening to my readings from it; and again to Professor Leonard W. Forster and Professor Bernard Lewis for reading and criticizing the second draft, together with the Introduction. These good friends did their best to help me find a way, hitherto untrodden, of rendering Medieval German verse into some kind of contemporary English prose. I must also thank the editor of the Penguin Classics, Dr E. V. Rieu, C.B.E., for his penetrating advice, besides the practical example afforded by his own translations.

I am grateful to Professor Count Roberto Weiss for advice concerning Guido Guinizelli and on Italian terms of heraldry, to Professor Gunnar Tilander, Dr D. H. Evans, and Mr Terry Dalby for advice on hunting terms, and to Mr R. J. Taylor for advice on medieval musical matters. My grateful thanks are due to Dr Combridge for reading the first proofs, and to Professor Norman for reading the second.

With regard to the Tristran *of Thomas, Professor Jean-Pierre Collas and Dr Frederick Whitehead not only answered separately a hundred-and-fifty questions on the corrupt and elusive fragments, but also compared my translation with the original, an act of kindness for which it would be hard to find a name. Without their invaluable assistance I could never have dared publish my rendering. But – it goes without saying – for errors or wrong-headed notions in conflict with their advice I myself am entirely to blame.*

For the provision of books and articles and for failing to recall them, in the unshakable belief that I was actively engaged with them, I have to thank Mr Adrian Whitworth, M.A., my College Librarian.

It gives me lively pleasure to record that I have learned more about the enchanting early ramifications of the story of Tristan (the later ones tend to be as boring as they are spurious) from the unpublished work of Dr F. Whitehead and from long correspondence with him, than from any other single source. He read and improved my draft introductions to the poems of both Gottfried and Thomas.

The names of the late Professor F. Ranke, Professor J. Schwietering, and Professor F. Ohly also demand mention wherever there is question of interpreting Gottfried's Tristan. *My debt to Professor R. S. Loomis, an earlier translator of Thomas, is recorded in its appropriate place below, as is my debt to A. Colin Cole, Esq., Portcullis Pursuivant of Arms, for bringing his science to bear on heraldic problems in* Thomas.

There are incorporated in this reprint many improvements which I owe to the accurate and sensitive scholarship of Dr L. Okken of Harmelen, Holland. Dr Okken compared my translation in its entirety with the original text of Gottfried.

A. T. H.

Incorporated in this further reprint are improvements for which I am indebted to the published work of Professor Werner Betz of the University of Munich and Professor C. Stephen Jaeger of Evanston, Illinois. It goes without saying that many of the scholars whom I thanked in the acknowledgements to the first impression now enjoy higher titles.

A. T. H.

GOTTFRIED VON STRASSBURG

Tristan

*G*edæhte man ir ze guote niht,
von den der werlde guot geschiht,
so wærez allez alse niht,
swaz guotes in der werlde geschiht.

*D*er guote man swaz der in guot
und niwan der werlt ze guote tuot,
swer daz iht anders wan in guot
vernemen wil, der missetuot.

*I*ch hœre es velschen harte vil,
daz man doch gerne haben wil:
da ist des lützelen ze vil,
da wil man, des man niene wil.

*E*z zimet dem man ze lobene wol,
des er iedoch bedürfen sol,
und laze ez ime gevallen wol,
die wile ez ime gevallen sol.

*T*iur unde wert ist mir der man,
der guot und übel betrahten kan,
der mich und iegelichen man
nach sinem werde erkennen kan.

*E*re unde lop diu schepfent list,
da list ze lobe geschaffen ist:
swa er mit lobe geblüemet ist,
da blüejet aller slahte list.

*R*eht als daz dinc zunruoche gat,
daz lobes noch ere niene hat,
als liebet daz, daz ere hat
und sines lobes niht irre gat.

*I*r ist so vil, die des nu pflegent,
daz si daz guote zübele wegent,
daz übel wider ze guote wegent:
die pflegent niht, si widerpflegent.

*C*unst unde nahe sehender sin
swie wol diu schinen under in,
geherberget nit zuo zin,
er leschet kunst unde sin.

*H*ei tugent, wie smal sint dine stege,
wie kumberlich sint dine wege!
die dine stege, die dine wege,
wol ime, der si wege unde stege!

PROLOGUE

If we failed in our esteem of those who confer benefits on us, the good that is done among us would be as nothing.

We do wrong to receive otherwise than well what a good man does well-meaningly and solely for our good.

I hear much disparagement of what people nevertheless ask for. This is niggling to excess, this is wanting what you do not want at all.

A man does well to praise what he cannot do without. Let it please him so long as it may.

That man is dear and precious to me who can judge of good and bad and know me and all men at our true worth.

Praise and esteem bring art on where art deserves commendation. When art is adorned with praise it blossoms in profusion.

Just as what fails to win praise and esteem falls into neglect, so that finds favour which meets with esteem and is not denied its praise.

There are so many today who are given to judging the good bad and the bad good. They act not to right but to cross purpose.

However well art and criticism seem to live together, if envy comes to lodge with them it stifles both art and criticism.

O Excellence! how narrow are thy paths, how arduous thy ways! Happy the man who can climb thy paths and tread thy ways!

If I spend my time in vain, ripe for living as I am, my part in society will continue to fall short of what my experience requires of me. Thus I have undertaken a labour to please the polite world and solace noble hearts – those hearts which I hold in affection, that world which lies open to my heart. I do not mean the world of the many who (as I hear) are unable to endure sorrow and wish only to revel in bliss. (Please God to let them live in their bliss!) What I have to say does not concern that world and such a way of life; their way and mine diverge sharply. I have another world in mind which together in one heart bears its bitter-sweet, its dear sorrow, its heart's joy, its love's pain, its dear life, its sorrowful death, its dear death, its sorrowful life. To this life let my life be given, of this world let me be part, to be damned or saved with it. I have kept with it so far and with it have spent the days that were to bring me counsel and guidance through a life which has moved me profoundly. I have offered the fruits of my labour to this world as a pastime, so that with my story its denizens can bring their keen sorrow half-way to alleviation and thus abate their anguish. For if we have something before us to occupy our thoughts it frees our unquiet soul and eases our heart of its cares. All are agreed that when a man of leisure is overwhelmed by love's torment, leisure redoubles that torment and if leisure be added to languor, languor will mount and mount. And so it is a good thing that one who harbours love's pain and sorrow in his heart should seek distraction with all his mind – then his spirit will find solace and release. Yet I would never advise a man in search of pleasure to follow any pursuit that would ill become pure love. Let a lover ply a love-tale with his heart and lips and so while away the hour.

Now we hear too much of one opinion, with which I all but agree, that the more a love-sick soul has to do with love-tales the more it will despond. I would hold with this opinion but for one objection: when we are deeply in love, however great the pain, our heart does not flinch. The more a lover's passion burns in its furnace of desire, the more ardently will he love. This sorrow is so full of joy, this ill is so inspiriting that, having once been heartened by it, no noble heart will forgo it! I know as sure as death and have learned it from this same anguish: the noble lover loves love-tales. Therefore, whoever wants a story need go no further than here. – I will story him well with noble lovers who gave proof of perfect love:

A man, a woman; a woman, a man:
Tristan, Isolde; Isolde, Tristan.

I am well aware that there have been many who have told the tale of Tristan; yet there have not been many who have read his tale aright.

But were I now to act and pass judgment as though I were dis-pleased by what each has said of this story, I would act otherwise than I should. This I shall not do; for they wrote well and with the noblest of intentions for my good and the good of us all. They assur-edly did so well-meaningly, and whatever is done well-meaningly is indeed good and well done. But when I said that they did not tell the tale aright, this was, I aver, the case. They did not write according to the authentic version as told by Thomas of Britain, who was a master-romancer and had read the lives of all those princes in books of the Britons and made them known to us.

I began to search assiduously both in Romance and Latin books for the true and authentic version of Tristan such as Thomas nar-rates, and I was at pains to direct the poem along the right path which he had shown. Thus I made many researches till I had read in a book all that he says happened in this story. And now I freely offer the fruits of my reading of this love-tale to all noble hearts to distract them. They will find it very good reading. Good? Yes, profoundly good. It will make love lovable, ennoble the mind, fortify constancy, and enrich their lives. This it can well do. For wherever one hears or reads of such perfect loyalty, loyalty and other virtues commend themselves to loyal people accordingly. Affection, loyalty, constancy, honour, and many good things besides, never endear themselves anywhere so much as when someone tells a love-tale or mourns love's tender grief. Love is so blissful a thing, so blessed an endeavour, that apart from its teaching none attains worth or reputation. In view of the many noble lives that love in-spires and the many virtues that come from it, oh! that every living thing does not strive for sweet love, that I see so few who, for their lover's sake, will suffer pure longing in their hearts – and all for the wretched sorrow that now and then lies hidden there!

Why should not a noble mind gladly suffer one ill for a thousand boons, one woe for many joys? He that never had sorrow of love never had joy of it either! In love, joy and sorrow ever went hand in hand! With them we must win praise and honour or come to nothing without them! If the two of whom this love-story tells had not endured sorrow for the sake of joy, love's pain for its ecstasy within one heart, their name and history would never have brought such rapture to so many noble spirits! Today we still love to hear of their tender devotion, sweet and ever fresh, their joy, their sorrow, their anguish, and their ecstasy. And although they are long dead, their sweet name lives on and their death will endure for ever to the profit of well-bred people, giving loyalty to those who seek loyalty, honour to those who seek honour. For us who are alive their death must live on and be for ever new. For wherever still today one hears the recital of their devotion, their perfect loyalty, their hearts' joy, their hearts' sorrow –

This is bread to all noble hearts. With this their death lives on. We read their life, we read their death, and to us it is sweet as bread.

Their life, their death are our bread. Thus lives their life, thus lives their death. Thus they live still and yet are dead, and their death is the bread of the living.

And whoever now desires to be told of their life, their death, their joy, their sorrow, let him lend me his heart and ears – he shall find all that he desires!

1

RIVALIN AND BLANCHEFLOR

THERE was a lord in Parmenie of tender years, as I read. In birth (so his story truly tells us) he was the peer of kings, in lands the equal of princes, in person fair and charming, loyal, brave, generous, noble: and to those whom it was his duty to make happy this lord all his days was a joy-giving sun. He was a delight to all, a paragon of chivalry, the glory of his kinsmen, the firm hope of his land. Of all the qualities which a lord should have he lacked not one, except that he over-indulged himself in pleasures dear to his heart and did entirely as he pleased. For this he had to suffer in the end, since, alas, it is the way of the world, and ever was, that oncoming youth and ample fortune bear fruit in arrogance. It never occurred to him to overlook a wrong, as many do who wield great power; but returning evil for evil, matching force with force: to this he gave much thought.

Now it cannot last for ever when a man pays back each wrong that he suffers in coin of the realm. Heaven knows that in the give-and-take of life a man must shut his eyes to a great deal, else he will often come to grief. If one cannot overlook a hurt, many hurts will grow from it. It is a fatal style of living – one catches bears with it. For a bear gives blow for blow till he is overwhelmed with blows.* That is what happened to him, in my opinion, since he went on revenging himself till he reaped disaster from it. But his downfall was due not to malice, which is the ruin of many, but to the tender years that accompanied him. His warring against his own happiness, as he flowered into early manhood with a young lord's temper and breeding, was caused by his wanton youth, which blossomed

* A 'bear-hammer' or beam was suspended before a hive in a tree. A bear coming for the honey found himself thwarted by the beam and fought it till he was dazed and fell on the pointed stakes which had been prepared for him below.

in his heart with arrogance. He did as all young people do who never think ahead, he shut his eyes to care and lived for the sake of living. When his life began in earnest to rise up like the day-star and look out smiling on the world, he thought – but it did not happen so – that he would always live like this and revel in the sweets of living. But no, his life that had scarce begun was soon spent. Just when the early sun of his wordly joy was about to shine out dazzlingly, his evening, hidden from him till then, fell suddenly and blotted out his morn.

As to his name, this tale makes it known to us, his story reveals it. His true name was Rivalin, his byname Canelengres. Many affirm and believe that this same lord was a Lohnoisan and King of the land of Lohnois: but having read it in the sources, Thomas assures us he was of Parmenie* and held a separate land from a Breton called Duke Morgan, and owed him allegiance for it.

Now after lord Rivalin had been a knight for some three years as befitted his high rank and had acquired the whole art of chivalry and all the resources of war (he had land, men, and means), whether he was provoked or whether it was from arrogance I do not know but (so his story tells) he attacked Morgan as if Morgan had done him some wrong. He came riding into his land in such strength as to raze not a few of his fortresses. Towns were forced to yield and, dear as they held them, ransom their lives and goods till he had amassed the means so to increase his troops that he could impose his will, be it on town or fortress, wherever he marched his army.

Rivalin, too, often took an injury; he paid with many a worthy man, for Morgan was on his guard. Rivalin met Morgan in open battle time and again and often did him mischief; for loss and gain attend war and chivalry – that is how wars advance, feuds proceed by losses and gains. Morgan no doubt served him likewise: he razed castles and towns in return, despoiled him of subjects and possessions now and then, and harmed him as much as he could. But this was of little avail, for Rivalin penned him in again, inflicting heavy losses, and continued with him thus till he had so far reduced him that he was quite unable to defend or see any chance of saving himself, unless in his most formidable strongholds. These Rivalin invested. He launched attacks and skirmishes against them in plenty

* See p. 371, below.

and thrust him at all times clean back into the gates. He often held tournaments before the walls, too, and fine displays of chivalry. Thus Rivalin brought great force to bear on Morgan and ravaged his land with fire and pillage, till he offered to parley and with great difficulty achieved it that they should put their quarrel by and agree on a year's truce. And with oaths and sureties this was duly confirmed.

Thereupon Rivalin returned with his men in gay and happy mood. He rewarded them handsomely and made them all happy too. He sent them home in good spirits and with much credit to himself.

It was not very long after these achievements that Rivalin decided to travel again, this time for pleasure, and he equipped himself once more with great magnificence like all who aspire to honour. All the baggage and stores that he would need for a year were taken on board ship. He had often heard people say how noble and distinguished the young King Mark of Cornwall was, whose fame was in the ascendant and who then ruled Cornwall and England.

Now Cornwall was Mark's heritage; but as to England matters stood thus. He had held it since the time when the Saxons of Gales had driven out the Britons and made themselves masters there, thanks to whom the land that had been known as 'Britain' lost its name and was at once renamed 'England' after the men of Gales.*
When they had seized the land and shared it amongst themselves, all wished to be kinglets and lords in their own right, but all were the losers by it; for they took to killing and butchering one another and ended by placing themselves and their lands under Mark's protection. From this time on, England served him so well and reverently in every way that no kingdom ever served king to better purpose. Moreover, this history tells of him that in all the neighbouring lands where his name was known, no king was so esteemed. Here was where Rivalin longed to be. Here he planned to spend a year with Mark in order to acquire merit from him, devote himself to chivalry, and add polish to his manners. His noble heart informed him that were he to acquaint himself with the manners of foreign lands he would thereby improve his own, and himself be for them.

* Gottfried sees a connexion here between 'Gales' (which normally means 'Wales') and 'Engelant' as England was named in Medieval German.

With this in mind he set out. He entrusted his land and people
to his marshal, Rual li Foitenant, a lord of that country and one he
knew to be loyal. Then Rivalin crossed the sea, together with twelve
companions. He had no need of more: with these he had an ample
following.

Now when after due lapse of time he arrived off Cornwall and
learned while still afloat that noble Mark was at Tintagel, he set his
course for that city. He landed there, he found him there, and was
heartily glad to do so. He then attired himself and his followers
magnificently and in a way befitting his rank. When he came to
court, Mark, noble man, received him with much distinction, and,
with him, all his followers.

The honours and reception accorded there to Rivalin surpassed
in splendour any shown him before in other places. The thought of
it delighted him, it made life at this court agreeable for him. 'In-
deed,' he thought repeatedly, 'God Himself has brought me to these
people. Fortune has been kind to me. All I ever heard on the sub-
ject of Mark's excellence is here borne out in full. His is a good and
courtly way of life.' And so he told Mark what had brought him,
and having learned his business Mark answered, 'Welcome, in
God's name! I and my possessions and all that I have shall be at
your command!'

Rivalin was pleased with the court: and the court was full of his
praises. He was liked and esteemed by rich and poor. No stranger
was ever loved more. For his part he could well deserve it, for
Rivalin, excellent man, was ready to serve them all in friendship,
both personally and materially, as he well knew how. Thus he
lived in high esteem and in the true goodness which his mind de-
rived from the daily pursuit of excellence, till Mark's festival came
round.

By behest and by request Mark had so established this festivity
that when he summoned his knights they promptly made the
journey from the kingdom of England to Cornwall once in every
year. They brought bevies of charming ladies with them and many
other lovely things.

Now the festivities were fixed, agreed, and appointed for the four
weeks of blossom-time from the entry of sweet May until its exit,
and as near to Tintagel as allowed all to see each other, in the

fairest meadow that eyes ever shone on, before or since. Charming, gentle spring had busied himself about it with a sweet assiduousness. Of little wood-birds (fit delight for the ear), flowers, grasses, leaves, and blossoms and all that soothes the eye and gladdens noble hearts, that summer-meadow was full. Of all that May should bring, one found whatever one wished there: shade together with sunshine, lime-trees by the fountain, tender, gentle breezes regaling Mark's company each according to its nature. The bright flowers smiled up from the dewy grass. May's friend the greensward had donned a summer smock of flowers so lovely that they shone again from the dear guests' eyes. The delightful blossom on the trees smiled out at one so pleasantly that one's heart and all one's soul went out to it through eyes that shone, and gave back all its smiles. The soft, sweet, lovely singing of the birds, that often assuages ears and soul, filled hills and valleys. The heavenly nightingale, that enchanting little bird – may its sweetness abide with it for ever! – was trilling among the blossoms so wantonly that many a noble heart took joy and zest from it.

There in great joy and merriment this company were lodged on the greensward, each according to his whim. As his hope of pleasure prompted him, so was each encamped. The princely camped in princely, the courtly in courtly, fashion: some were encamped under silk here, others elsewhere beneath blossoms. Lime-trees sheltered many: many were lodged in arbours made of boughs of leafy green. Neither household nor guests had ever been lodged so delightfully. There were endless stocks of viands and fine clothes, of which all had laid in a fabulous store, as is the way at feasts. Moreover, Mark entertained them so lavishly that they enjoyed themselves greatly and were happy.

Such was the beginning of that festival. And if a man who loved a spectacle took a fancy to seeing anything, opportunity was there to indulge him. One saw what one wanted to see: some went to note the ladies, others to see dancing; some watched the bohort,* others jousting. Whatever one fancied was found in abundance; for all who were of pleasurable years vied in seeking pleasure at that feast. And Mark the good, the courteous and magnanimous, had a rare marvel of his own apart from the beauty of other ladies, whose

* An equestrian game with shields and blunt lances, but usually no armour.

pavilions he had placed in his ring – his sister Blancheflor, a girl so lovely that you never saw a lovelier, there or anywhere. It is said of her beauty that no man of flesh and blood had ever gazed at her with enamoured eyes and not loved woman and noble qualities better ever after.

This heavenly vision made many a man on the heath gay and mettlesome, and exalted many a noble heart. But there were many other lovely women in that meadow, too, of whom each might well have been a great queen for beauty. They too afforded zest and joy to all present, and gladdened many hearts.

Meanwhile retainers and guests set the bohort going. The best and noblest rode up from all directions. Noble Mark was there and Rivalin, his friend, not to mention others of his retinue who had also gone to much trouble as to how to cut a figure that would be talked of to their credit. Many chargers could be seen, most carefully draped with rare silk and cendale; many housings of snowy white, of yellow, violet, red, green, blue. Elsewhere you could see others woven of fine silk and these were variously cut, chequered or parti-coloured, and adorned in diverse ways. The knights paraded garments cut and slashed with marvellous splendour. Summer, too, showed clearly that he wished to keep Mark company, for among that assembly you could see many lovely garlands which he had brought him as a May-gift.

In the sweet fulness of this springtide they began a charming knightly sport. The company merged again and again in a tangled mass, meandering in and out, and long continued so till the bohort had moved to where noble Blancheflor – a miracle on earth – and many other lovely women sat watching the display; for these knights rode so superbly, so truly magnificently, that many loved to watch them. But whatever feats were performed there, it was courtly Rivalin, and no denying it, who excelled all others utterly that day. The ladies were quick to note him, declaring that no man among them rode with such expert horsemanship, and they praised him in every detail. 'Look!' they said, 'what a heavenly young man that is! Everything he does, how divinely it becomes him! What a perfect body he has! How evenly those magnificent legs of his move together! How tightly his shield stays glued in its place! How well the spear-shaft graces his hand! How elegant all his robes! How noble his head and hair! How charming his whole bearing! What a divine figure he makes! O happy, lucky woman, she that will enjoy him!'

Now good Blancheflor was taking in what the ladies were saying, for whatever any of them did, she prized him greatly in her thoughts. Into her thoughts she had received him, he had come into her heart, and in the kingdom of her heart wore crown and sceptre with despotic sway. But this she hid so profoundly that she kept it from them all.

Now that the bohort was over and the knights were dispersing and each making his way to where his thoughts inclined him, it chanced that Rivalin was heading for where lovely Blancheflor was sitting. Seeing this, he galloped up to her and looking her in the eyes saluted her most pleasantly.

'God save you, lovely woman!'

'Thank you,' said the girl, and continued very bashfully, 'may God Almighty, who makes all hearts glad, gladden your heart and mind! And my grateful thanks to you! – yet not forgetting a bone I have to pick with you.'

'Ah, sweet woman, what have I done?' was courteous Rivalin's reply.

'You have annoyed me through a friend of mine, the best I ever had.'

'Good heavens,' thought he, 'what does this mean? What have I done to displease her? What does she say I've done?' and he imagined that unwittingly he must have injured a kinsman of hers some time at their knightly sports and that was why she was vexed with him. But no, the friend she referred to was her heart, in which he made her suffer: that was the friend she spoke of. But he knew nothing of that.

'Lovely woman,' he said with all his accustomed charm, 'I do not want you to be angry with me or bear me any ill will. So, if what you tell me is true, pronounce sentence on me yourself: I will do whatever you command.'

'I do not hate you overmuch for what has happened,' was the sweet girl's answer, 'nor do I love you for it. But to see what amends you will make for the wrong that you have done me, I shall test you another time.'

And so he bowed as if to go, and she, lovely girl, sighed at him most secretly and said with tender feeling:

'Ah, dear friend, God bless you!' From this time on the thoughts of each ran on the other.

Rivalin turned away, pondering many things. He pondered from many sides why Blancheflor should be vexed, and what lay behind it all. He considered her greeting, her words; he examined her sigh minutely, her farewell, her whole behaviour, and so doing began to construe both her sigh and her sweet benediction as manifestations of love, and indeed arrived at the belief that both had been uttered with love alone in mind. This fired his spirit too, so that it returned and took Blancheflor and led her straightway into the land of his heart and crowned her there as his Queen. Blancheflor and Rivalin, the King and the sweet Queen, made equal division of the kingdoms of their hearts: hers fell to Rivalin, his became hers in return. Yet neither knew how it fared with the other. They had claimed each other in their hearts with one harmonious accord. Justice had come into its own, for she, too, oppressed his heart, causing the same pangs as she endured for him. But since he was uncertain of her motive – whether she had acted from enmity or love – he wavered in perplexity. He wavered in his thoughts now here, now there. At one moment he was off in one direction, then suddenly off in another, till he had so ensnared himself in the toils of his own desire that he was powerless to escape.

Rivalin proved by his own example that a lover's fancy acts like a free bird which, in the freedom it enjoys, perches on the lime-twig; and when it perceives the lime and lifts itself for flight stays clinging by the feet. And so it spreads its wings and makes to get away, but, as it does so, cannot brush against the twig at any part, however lightly, without the twig's fettering it and making it a prisoner. So now it strikes with all its might, here, there, and everywhere, till at last, fighting itself, it overcomes itself and lies limed along the twig. This is just how untamed fancy behaves. When it falls into sad love-longing and love works its miracle of love-lorn sadness on him, a lover strives to regain his freedom: but love's clinging sweetness draws him down and he ensnares himself in it so deeply that, try as he may, he cannot get free of it.

So it went with Rivalin, whom his longing ensnared in love for his heart's Queen. His entanglement had placed him in a quandary, for he did not know whether she wished him well or ill; he could not make out whether she loved or hated him. No hope or despair did he consider which did not forbid him either to advance or retreat – hope and despair led him to and fro in unresolved dissension. Hope spoke to him of love, despair of hatred. Because of this discord he could yield his firm belief neither to hatred nor yet to love. Thus his feelings drifted in an unsure haven – hope bore him on, despair away. He found no constancy in either; they agreed neither one way nor another. When despair came and told him that his Blancheflor was his enemy he faltered and sought to escape: but at once came hope, bringing him her love, and a fond aspiration, and so perforce he remained. In the face of such discord he did not know where to turn: nowhere could he go forward. The more he strove to flee, the more firmly love forced him back. The harder he struggled to escape, love drew him back more firmly. Thus love persevered with him till hope won the victory and put despair to flight, and Rivalin was certain that his Blancheflor loved him. Now that there was no opposition, his heart and all his mind were centred on her in concord.

Though sweet Love had now brought his heart and mind to where it was her pleasure, he still had no idea that love was so keen a sadness. When he considered the marvel that had befallen him in his Blancheflor and went through it all in detail from beginning to end, her hair, her brow, her temples, her cheeks, her mouth, her chin, the joyous Easter Day that lurked smiling in her eyes, Love, the one and true incendiary, came and kindled her flames of desire, the flames that set his heart on fire and revealed to him in a flash what keen sadness and lovers' pining are! For now he laid hold of a new life, a new life was given him; so that he changed his whole cast of mind and became quite a different man, since all that he did was chequered with strangeness and blindness. His native disposition had grown as wild and capricious from love as he had asked for. His life took a turn for the worse. No longer did he laugh from the heart, as was his way. The only life he knew was silent moping, since all his gaiety had given way to love-sickness.

Nor did love-lorn Blancheflor escape his amorous plight. She, too, was weighed down by the same hurt through him as he through her; for Love, the tyrant, had entered her soul somewhat too tempestuously, and robbed her of her composure for the greater part. Contrary to her custom, she was, in her demeanour, out of step both with herself and with the world. Whatever pleasures she had turned to, whatever pastimes she was partial to before, they all came amiss to her now. Her life took shape only on sufferance of the torment that oppressed her.

And with all the pangs and ardours she endured, she had no idea what was troubling her, for she had never before felt such heaviness and heartache. 'Alas, Lord God, what a life I lead!' she said to herself over and over again. 'Whatever has happened to me? After all, I have seen many men, and none ever made me suffer. Yet ever since I saw this man my heart has not been free and happy as once it used to be. This constant looking at him has brought me the keenest sorrow. My heart, which had never suffered torment, has been deeply wounded by it. Body and soul, it has altogether changed me. If what has happened to me is to happen to all women who hear and see him, and if this is his nature, then much beauty will be wasted on him and the man is a pest! But if he has learnt some witchcraft of which this strange marvel and miraculous torment are the outcome, he were far better dead, and women should never set eyes on him. What unhappiness and sorrow I suffer because of him! Truly, I never looked at him or any man with hostile eyes nor bore ill will to any. Through what fault of mine can it be that a man whom I regard with a friendly eye should make me suffer?

'But why do I reproach the good man? He may well be innocent of this. The heartache that I have from and because of him, is, God knows, mostly the doing of my own heart. I saw many men there – and him! How can he help it that my feelings have settled on him alone among all those others? When I heard so many noble ladies bandying his magnificent body about like a ball, and his fame as a knight, too, with their praises, and saying so much to his credit, and saw with my own eyes the fine qualities they gave him, and dwelt on all his virtues, I became infatuated, and that is why my heart was fixed on him! Yes, it dazzled me, this was the witchery that has made me so forget myself. He has done me no harm, the dear man who makes me suffer and whom I name and accuse. My foolish, unbridled fancy – that is what harms me so, that is what is out to ruin me! It wants too much that it should not want, if it but cared for what is right and proper. But now it consults only its own wishes concerning this heavenly man, on whom it has settled so swiftly. And, Heaven help me, I shrewdly suspect (if I may with honour suspect it and need not blush at the word because I am a maiden) I think the pangs that I suffer in my heart for him are caused by love, and love alone. This I know from my longing to be with him. And whatever this all may mean, there is something shaping for me here that points to love and a man! For what I have heard all my life about tender feelings and women truly in love has entered my own heart. Sweet pain-at-heart, which racks so many noble spirits with its dear torment, lies within my heart!'

Now that the noble young lady perceived within her heart with her whole being (as lovers do) that her companion Rivalin was destined to be her heart's joy, her high hope, her best life, she gave him look on look and saw him whenever she could. When it could be done with propriety she greeted him covertly with tender glances. Her love-sick gaze rested upon him time and again, lingeringly and amorously. When the enamoured man, her friend, grew aware of this, Love and the hope he placed in her began to nerve him in earnest, now indeed his desire took fire, and from now on he returned the sweet girl's looks more boldly and tenderly than he had ever done before. When opportunity offered, he, too, greeted her with looks. And now that the lovely girl discerned that his thoughts ran on her as her thoughts on him, her greatest care was past – for she had imagined all along that he had no desire for her. But now she was sure that his feelings towards her were tender and kind, as a lover's feelings for his love should be. And he was as sure of her. This set the thoughts of them both on fire, so that with all their hearts they fell to loving and doting on each other. They experienced the truth of the saying that where lovers gaze into each other's eyes they feed love's fire apace.

Now when Mark's festival was over and the nobles had dispersed, news came to him that a king, an enemy of his, had invaded Cornwall in such force that unless he were soon repelled he would destroy all he overran. There and then Mark summoned a mighty army and met him in great strength. He fought with him and defeated him, killing and taking so many of his men that those who got away or survived on the field did so by great good fortune. There noble Rivalin was run through the side with a spear and so severely wounded that his friends bore him home to Tintagel in great grief as one half dead. They set him down, a dying man. At once it was rumoured that Rivalin of Canoel had been struck in battle and mortally wounded. This gave rise to doleful laments, at court and in the country. Those who knew of his good qualities deeply mourned his undoing. They regretted that his prowess, his handsome person, his tender youth, his admired high temper and breeding, should pass away so soon with him and have so untimely an end. His dear friend Mark lamented him with a heart-rending vehemence he had never felt before for any man. Many a noble-woman wept for Rivalin, many a lady lamented him; and all who had ever seen him were moved to pity by his plight.

But whatever the sorrow they all felt for his disaster, it was his Blancheflor alone, that faultless, noble lady, who in utter steadfast-ness, with eyes and heart, bewept and bewailed her dear love's pain. And indeed, when she was alone and able to vent her sorrow, she laid violent hands on herself. A thousand times she beat with them *there* and only *there*, *there* where she was troubled, above her heart – *there* the lovely girl struck many a blow. Thus did this charming lady torment her sweet young lovely body in such an access of grief that she would have bartered away her life for any death that did not come of love. In any event, she would have perished and died of her sorrow, had not hope refreshed her and expectancy buoyed her up, set as she was on seeing him, however that might be: and once having seen him she would gladly suffer whatever might be in store for her. With such thoughts she held on to life, till she re-gained her composure and considered means of seeing him, as her sufferings required. In this way her thoughts turned to a certain nurse of hers who had sole charge of her upbringing and never let her out of her keeping. She drew this woman aside and went to a private place and there made her sad complaint to her, as those in her position have always done and still do today. Her eyes brimmed over, the hot tears fell thick and fast down her gleaming cheeks.

'Ah, woe is me,' she said, clasping her hands and holding them out imploringly. 'Ah,' she said, 'woe, woe is me! Oh dearest nurse, prove your devotion now, of which you have such a fund. And since you are so good that my whole happiness and deliverance rest on your aid alone, relying on your goodness I will tell you what troubles my heart. I shall die if you do not help me!'

'Tell me, my lady, what distresses you so and makes you complain so bitterly?'

'Darling, dare I tell you?'

'Yes, dear mistress, come tell it now.'

'This dead man Rivalin of Parmenie is killing me. I would very much like to see him, if that were possible and if I knew how to go about it before he is quite dead – for alas! he is past recovery. If you can help me to this I will deny you nothing as long as I live.'

'If I allow this thing,' her nurse reflected, 'what harm can come of it? Half dead already, this man will die tomorrow or even today, and I shall have saved my lady's life and honour and she will always love me more than other women. Sweet mistress,' she said, 'my pet, your misery saddens my heart, and if I can avert your sufferings by any act of mine, never doubt that I shall do so. I will go down myself and see him, and then return at once. I will spy out the whole situation, how and where he is bedded, and also take stock of his suite.'

And so, pretending to go and mourn his sufferings, Blancheflor's nurse gained admittance and secretly informed him that her mistress would much like to see him, if he would allow it in accordance with honour and decorum. This done, she returned with the news. She took the girl and dressed her as a beggar-woman. Masking her lovely face in the folds of heavy veils, she took her mistress by the hand and went to Rivalin. He, for his part, had packed his people off one after another and was alone, after impressing it on them all that solitude brought him relief. For her part Blancheflor's nurse declared that she had brought a physician-woman, and she succeeded in getting her admitted to him. She then thrust the bolt across the door.

'Now, madam,' she said, 'go and see him!' And Blancheflor, lovely girl, went up to him, and when she looked into his eyes, 'Alas,' she said, 'alas for this day and evermore! Oh that I was ever born! How all my hopes are dashed!'

Rivalin with great difficulty inclined his head in thanks as much as a dying man might. But Blancheflor scarcely noticed it and paid no attention, but merely sat there unseeing, and laid her cheek on Rivalin's, till for joy but also for sorrow her strength deserted her body. Her rosy lips grew wan, the hue of her flesh quite lost the glow that dwelt in it before. In her clear eyes the day turned dark and sombre as night. Thus she lay senseless in a swoon for a long time, her cheek on his cheek, as though she were dead. And when she had rallied a little from this extremity she took her darling in her arms and laying her mouth to his kissed him a hundred thousand times in a short space till her lips had fired his sense and roused his mettle for love, since love resided in them. Her kisses made him gay, they brought him such vigour that he strained the splendid woman to his half-dead body, very tenderly and close. Nor was it long before they had their way and the sweet woman received a child from him. As to Rivalin he was all but dead, both of the woman and love. But for God's helping him from this dire pass he could never have lived; yet live he did, for so it was to be.

Thus it came about that Rivalin recovered, and Blancheflor's heart was burdened and unburdened of two different kinds of pain. She left great sorrow alongside the man and bore greater sorrow away. She left the anguish of a love-lorn heart, but what she bore away was death. She left her anguish when love came; death she received with the child. Yet, however it was she recovered, in which-ever way she had been burdened and unburdened by him (on the one hand to her loss, on the other to her gain), she regarded nothing else but dear love and the man who was dear to her. Of the child or tragic death within her she knew nothing: but love and the man she did know, and behaved as a living person should and as a lover does. Her heart, her mind, her desire, were centred entirely on Rivalin, and his in return on her and on the passion she inspired in him. Between them they had in their minds but one delight and one desire. Thus he was she, and she was he. He was hers and she was his. There Blancheflor, there Rivalin! There Rivalin, there Blancheflor! There both, and there true love!

Their life was now intimately shared. They were happy with each other and heartened one another with much kindness shared in common. And when they could decently arrange a rendezvous, their worldly joy was so entire, they felt so appeased and contented, that they would not have given this life of theirs for any heavenly kingdom. But this did not last for long. For in their prime, when they were at the summit of their joys and revelling in bliss, messengers came to Rivalin. His enemy Morgan had summoned a great muster against his country. At this news a ship was at once made ready for Rivalin, and all his gear was stowed aboard. Victuals and chargers, it was all got ready for the voyage without delay.

When charming Blancheflor heard the fateful news about her beloved man her troubles began in earnest. For the second time the sorrow in her heart robbed her of sight and hearing. The hue of her flesh became like that of a dead woman. From her mouth came the one wretched word 'Alas!' This alone and nothing more did she say. 'Alas!' she said for a long while, 'Alas! Alas for love, and alas for the man! What a legacy of toil I have with you! Love, affliction of all the world, brief as is the joy in you, fickle as you are, what is it that all love in you? You reward us as an arch-deceiver, this I do clearly see. Your end is less good than what you promise us when, with short-lived joy, you lure us to lasting sorrow! Your fairy enticement floating amid such feigned sweetness cheats all living things, as my example shows. From all the happiness that should have been mine I have only mortal pain; for the man I have set my hopes on is going away and leaving me!'

In the middle of this tale of woe her true love Rivalin entered with weeping heart to take his leave of her. 'Madam,' he said, 'your servant! I shall and must sail home! God protect you, lovely woman. Stay happy and well always!' At this she fainted yet again, again she swooned before him in her governess's lap, like one dead, from the anguish in her heart. When her loyal fellow-sufferer in love saw how great was the distress of his beloved, he gave her good companionship, since what she suffered for love he shared in tender sympathy. His colour and all his strength began to ebb away from him. He sat down dejectedly, as one does on such sad occasions, and could scarce wait for her to gain strength for him to take the unhappy woman in his arms and clasp her to himself most tenderly, and kiss her cheeks, her eyes, her mouth some few times, and caress her thus and thus; till at last by degrees she came to herself and sat up of her own accord.

When Blancheflor returned to her senses and had her friend in her sight again, she looked at him sorrowfully. 'Ah,' said she, 'good

man, how I have suffered through you! Why, sir, did I ever set
eyes on you, if it was for so much anguish that I have in my heart –
from you and all because of you! If by your leave I dare mention it,
treat me with greater kindness and friendship. My lord and friend,
I have endured much for your sake and three things in particular
that are deadly and unalterable. The first is that I carry a child
whose birth I fear I shall never survive, unless God be my help-
mate. The second is even more serious. When my royal brother
sees this remissness in me, not to mention his own dishonour, he
will bid me be destroyed and put to a shameful death. But the third
is the greatest hardship and worse than death by far. I know that if
matters go well to the extent that my brother lets me live and does
not make an end of me, he would nevertheless disinherit me and
deprive me of my honour and property; so that for the rest of my
life I would lose my standing and be of no account. I would then
have to rear my child without the support of a father, though it had
a father living. Nor would I ever complain of this if I could bear
the shame alone, and my most noble family and royal brother live
in honour, and free of the scandal and me! But when the whole
world gossips it round that I have got a bastard child, this and the
other kingdom, Cornwall and England, will suffer open disgrace.
Ah me, when the day comes for them to accuse me with their eyes
for having caused two lands to be humiliated, I, lonely woman,
were better dead! Oh my lord,' she said, 'this is the plight, this
is the abiding anguish in which all my days I must die a living
death. Sir, unless it come about by your help and God himself
bring it to pass, I shall never be happy again!'

'Dearest lady,' he answered, 'if you are in any distress on my ac-
count I will mend it, if I can, and from this day on see to it that no
further shame or suffering befall you through any fault of mine.
Whatever the future holds in store, you have made me so very happy
that it would be an outrage if I let you suffer any hardship. Madam,
I will tell you candidly what is in my heart. From sorrow and
joy, bad and good, and all that the future holds for you, I will
not divorce myself! I shall always be there to share, however irk-
some it be. And I offer you a choice between two things, let your
heart be judge: shall I stay – or go? Consider this yourself when
choosing – if you wish me to stay and see what comes of your

affairs, so be it. But if it is your pleasure to sail away home with me, I myself and all that I have shall always be at your service. You treat me here so well that I must repay it with all imaginable kindness. Now tell me, madam, what you have in mind, for whatever you wish, I wish it too!'

'Thank you, sir!' she said, 'may God reward you for your kind words and treatment, for which I must ever thank you on bended knee! My friend and lord, as you well know, there can be no question of our staying here; for, alas, I cannot hide my fears for my child. If only I could steal away in secret! That would be the best way out for me in my position. My lord friend, advise me.'

'Then listen to me, my lady,' he said. 'Tonight, when I go aboard, see that you get there first very secretly (by then I shall have taken my leave) and that I find you with my retinue. Do this, for so it has to be!'

After this talk, Rivalin went to Mark and told him the news that had been brought to him about his land and people. He took leave of Mark at once, and then of all his court. The regret they showed for Rivalin then and later was such as he had never experienced. Many pious farewells were sent after him, with a prayer that it please God to have his life and his honour in His keeping.

And now that night was falling and Rivalin had come to his ship and taken all his gear on board, he found lovely Blancheflor his lady there. At once they put to sea: and so they sailed away.

When Rivalin had landed and learned of the great peril that Morgan had brought upon him with over-mastering force, he summoned his marshal, in whom (knowing him to be loyal) he placed his greatest trust, and who administered his country for him. He was called Rual li Foitenant, a very mainstay of honour and loyalty, who had never swerved from his fealty. Rual told him various things well known to himself about the fearful trouble that had arisen for their land. 'Nevertheless,' he said, 'now that you have come in time, and God has brought you back again to the great relief of us all, things will come straight in the end and we shall pull through safely! So let us be of good cheer and put our fears aside.'

Then Rivalin took occasion to tell him about the dear romance of his Blancheflor. Rual was heartily glad of it. 'I can well see, my lord,' he said, 'that your honour increases in every way! Your esteem and reputation, your happiness and joy mount like the sun! You could advance your name through no other woman in the world so much as her! Therefore, my lord, take my advice. If she has been kind to you, let her reap the benefit. When we have settled this affair and thrust the peril from us that now weighs on our backs, appoint a great festivity, a splendid and magnificent one, and in the presence of kinsmen and vassals take her publicly to wife. Moreover, I advise you that first of all, in church, in sight of priests and laymen, you please to avow your marriage with her according to the Christian rite.* To do so will bring down blessings on yourself. And believe me truly when I say it: you will prosper for it all the more in honour and possessions.'

Indeed so it came to pass, it was duly done, and he achieved his purpose. And when he had taken her in marriage he delivered her with due form into the hands of the loyal Foitenant, who conveyed her to Canoel, to that same castle after which his lord (as I read) was called Canelengres: Canel from Canoel. In this castle Rual kept his own wife, who had moulded her body and mind to life in courtly society with all a woman's steadfastness. He conveyed his lady to her and arranged for her comfort in keeping with her station.

When Rual returned to his lord the two of them reached agreement concerning the perils that confronted them. They sent messengers over all their territories and gathered their knights together. They applied their strength and resources to warlike ends alone. And so they rode out with their army against Morgan; and Morgan and his men for their part awaited them in exemplary fashion – they received Rivalin with sharp fighting. Oh what a host of stout warriors were laid low and done to death there! How few of them were spared! How many men got into desperate straits, how very many from either army lay dead or wounded there! In this deadly defence of his country that most pitiable man was slain, whom all the world might well lament – if doleful lamentation were of any avail when a man is dead! Good Rivalin of Canoel, who had never anywhere swerved so much as a foot's breadth – nor even

* In the eyes of the law, Rivalin and Blancheflor had consummated a clandestine, runaway love-match which needed only to be declared in church to obtain full validity.

half! – from the sentiments of a true knight or from the high breed-
ing of a great lord, lay there pitifully slain. Yet in the midst of all
this strife his men rode up and gave him cover, and managed to get
him away. With many a woeful cry they bore him off and laid him
to rest as a man who took with him to his grave no more nor less
than the glory of them all! If I were now to speak at length of wild
lamentation and of their grief and what each said in his sorrow,
what would be the good of it? It would be vain. They had all died
with him in honour and possessions and in all the zest which, by
rights, should give good people bliss and a happy life.

It has come to pass, it has to be: good Rivalin is dead. No more
is required of them than to pay him the dues of a dead man, for
there is nothing else to be done. They shall and must let him go!
And may God in Heaven, who has never forgotten noble hearts,
have him in His keeping! And let us continue with the story and
how it fared with Blancheflor.

When the lovely woman heard the grievous news, Lord God
preserve us from ever knowing what she felt in her heart! I do not
doubt that if any woman suffered mortal pain on account of a man
who was dear to her, such pain was present in her heart. Her heart
was full of mortal anguish. The signs were there in her for all to
see that his death had pierced her to the heart. Yet in all this grief
her eyes never once grew moist. But God Almighty, how came it
that there was no weeping there?

Her heart had turned to stone. There was no life in it but for the
living love and very lively anguish that, living, warred against her
life. Did she lament her lord at all with words of lamentation? Not
she. She fell mute in that same hour, her plaint died in her mouth.
Her tongue, her mouth, her heart, her mind were all spent. The fair
lady had done with lamenting. She cried neither woe! nor alas! She
sank to the ground and lay in agony till the fourth day, more pite-
ously than ever any woman. She twisted and turned and writhed,
this way, that way, to and fro, and continued so until, with much
labour, she bore a little son. But see, it lived, and she lay dead.

*Alas for the sight where, after dire grief, one sees a sadder sight with grief
more dire!**

---

* First Rivalin's death, then Blancheflor's.

The grief of those whose honour was vested in Rivalin and whom he cherished in accordance with his station so long as it pleased God that he should do so, was, alas, too great, surpassing all other grief; for their high hope, their strength, their whole activity, and all their chivalry, their honour and esteem, were laid low. His death nevertheless was glorious; but hers was more than pitiable. However ruinous for land and people the hardship was which their sovereign's death entailed, it was not so distressful as the agony and piteous death of that sweet lady. Let every good man lament her grief and distress. And whoever had joy of woman or ever aspires to it, let him ponder in his mind how easily disaster may befall good people in matters of this sort, how easily their happiness and their lives may end in grief, and pray that the blameless woman be well received of God, and that it please Him to help and console her in His power and goodness. And now let us tell what God did with the babe that had neither father nor mother.

2

RUAL LI FOITENANT

Grief and steadfast loyalty ever renewed after the death of a friend renew one's friend. This is supreme loyalty.

When a man grieves for his friend and acts loyally towards him when he has died, this ranks above all reward, this is the very crown of loyalty. With this same crown (so I read) the Marshal and his good wife were crowned, who before God and the world were one flesh and one fidelity, of which they showed the signs both to the world and God; for they practised perfect loyalty according to God's command and maintained it without fail till their end. If any two on earth were to become king and queen for the sake of their loyal devotion it would most certainly be they, as I can prove from how each behaved.

After their lady Blancheflor had died and Rivalin had been buried, the affairs of the orphan who survived went as well as could be expected in his adverse situation, as though he were meant to prosper. The Marshal and his wife took the little orphan and hid him away from all eyes. They said, and they had it proclaimed, that their lady had been with child and that it had died with her in her womb. From this threefold affliction the laments of the people rose higher, their laments rose higher than ever before – laments that Rivalin was dead, laments that Blancheflor had perished, laments that the little child, too, had perished, who held all their hopes for the future.

In addition to all these troubles the mighty fear which Morgan inspired in them affected them as keenly as the death of their lord. For the greatest distress in which any man can be is to see his deadly enemy before his eyes, day and night. Such peril grips at one's heart; it is a living death. Amid all this anguish of the living, Blancheflor was carried to her grave over which much observance was done with weeping and wailing. You must know that there was wild lamentation, much and overmuch. But I must and will not afflict your ears with matters which are too distressing, since too much talk of grief offends them and there is nothing so good that it does not pall from being said too often. Therefore let us leave long-drawn laments and apply ourselves to what we shall tell of the orphan from whom this tale takes its rise.

Men's affairs often turn to ill fortune, then back from ill fortune to good.

At the height of his peril and whatever the outcome, a valiant man should think how to save himself. As long as he is alive he should live with the living and nourish his own hopes of life. This is what the Marshal Foitenant did. Since his situation was an anxious one, he thought in the midst of his peril of the ruin of his land and of his own death; but since his defence was unavailing and he could not save himself from his enemy by force, he saved himself by policy. He at once conferred with the barons from all over his lord's country and got them to make peace, since there was nothing they could do but surrender and ask for mercy. They surrendered their lives and property to Morgan's pleasure. They settled the aggressions between Morgan and themselves by diplomacy, and so saved their land and people.

Loyal Foitenant the Marshal went home and consulted with his good wife, and then commanded her most strictly on pain of death to lie in like a woman in childbed and after the appropriate time to say that she had borne the child (who was really her young lord), and to keep to her story. The good wife of the Marshal, worthy, constant, chaste Floraete, mirror of womanly honour and gem of true virtue that she was, was easily urged to what, after all, tended much to her honour. She assumed the pose of one in pain, like a woman about to give birth. She ordered her rooms and amenities to be got ready for a confinement: and since she had full knowledge of how to act the part she drew on it for her simulated labour. She feigned great distraction of body and mind, like a woman about to enter her pangs and like one fully ready for labour of this kind. And so in the greatest secrecy the babe was laid beside her and in such a way that apart from her midwife none knew of it.

At once the rumour went round that the good wife of the Marshal had been brought to bed of a son. And indeed this was true, she had been in fact. She lay in with a son who held her in filial affection until they both were dead. That same sweet child had the same sweet childish craving for her that a child should have for its mother; and this was as it should be. She devoted all her thought to him in motherly affection and was as constant in her attentions as if she had carried him under her own heart. As the story tells us, it never happened before or since that a man and a woman reared their lord with such love, as we can see as this tale proceeds – what paternal cares and how many toils the faithful Marshal endured for him.

Now that the good wife of the Marshal was deemed to have recovered from her labour and after her six weeks (as is laid down for women) was due to be churched of the son I have been speaking of, she took him in her arms and carried him, as well became her, thus tenderly to the House of God. And when she had been churched in godly fashion and had returned from making her offering with her splendid retinue, Holy Baptism awaited the little child, so that it could receive its Christianity in God's name and, however it should fare in days to come, nevertheless be a Christian.

Now when the priest who was to baptize him had everything ready in the way that is customary at a christening, he asked what the child's name was to be. The gracious lady then went and spoke with her husband the Marshal in private and asked him what he wished to have him called. For a long while the Marshal was silent, pondering narrowly in his mind what name was suited to his circumstances, and at the same time reviewing the child's affairs from the beginning and how they had come to be as they were, just as he had learned them.

'Listen, madam,' he said, 'in view of what I heard from his father – his experience with his Blancheflor, the great sorrow in which her desire for him was assuaged, in what sorrow she conceived this child, and the sorrow with which she bore him – let us call him "Tristan"!'

Now 'triste' stands for sorrow, and because of all these happenings the child was named 'Tristan' and christened 'Tristan' at once.

His name came from 'triste'. The name was well suited to him and in every way appropriate. Let us test it by the story, let us see

how full of sorrow it was when his mother was delivered of him,
see how soon trouble and pain were loaded upon him, see what a
sorrowful life he was given to live, see the sorrowful death that
brought his anguish to a close with an end beyond comparison of
all deaths, more bitter than all sorrow. All who have read this tale
know that the name accorded with the life: he was the man that his
name said he was, and his name of Tristan said what he was. And
if anyone would have liked to know what subtle calculation
prompted Foitenant to spread the rumour that the infant Tristan
had died in the throes of childbirth in his dead mother's womb, we
will tell him: he did it out of loyalty. The trusty man did this
because he feared Morgan's enmity – that, knowing the child was
there, Morgan would either by force or cunning make an end of
him and deprive the land of its heir. And so the faithful man
adopted the orphan as his child and reared him so well that all
should wish him the grace of God for payment – he well deserved
it of that orphan.

When the child had been blessed and baptized according to the
Christian rite, the Marshal's excellent lady took her darling child
into her closest care again. She wished to see for herself all the time
if he were comfortable or no. His dear mother applied her thought
to him with such tender solicitude that, if she had had her way, he
would always have walked on velvet. And when she had thus
continued with him till his seventh year and he could understand
what people said and did (and in fact did understand), his father
the Marshal took him and placed him in the care of a man of ex-
perience and promptly sent him abroad with him to learn foreign
languages and begin at once to study books, and ply them more
than any other branch of study. This was his first departure from
his freedom; with it he joined company with enforced cares which
had been hidden and withheld from him till then. In the blossom-
ing years, when the ecstasy of his springtime was about to unfold
and he was just entering with joy into his prime, his best life
was over: just when he was beginning to burgeon with delight the
frost of care (which ravages many young people) descended on him
and withered the blossoms of his gladness. With his first experience
of freedom his whole freedom was cut short. The study of books
and all its stern discipline were the beginning of his cares. Yet once

having started on it he applied his mind and industry to it with such vigour that he had mastered more books in that short space than any child before or after him.

During the time that he was engaged on these two studies of books and languages, he also spent many hours playing stringed instruments of all kinds, persevering from morning to night till he became marvellously adept at them. He was learning the whole time, today one thing, tomorrow another, this year well, next year better. In addition to all this he learned to ride nimbly with shield and lance, to spur his mount skilfully on either flank, put it to the gallop with dash, wheel and give it free rein and urge it on with his knees, in strict accordance with the chivalric art. He often sought recreation in fencing, wrestling, running, jumping, and throwing the javelin, and he did it to the utmost of his strength and skill. And we hear from this narrative that none (whoever he might be) ever learned to track or hunt as well as he. He excelled at all manner of courtly pastimes and had many at his command. To crown all, his person was such that no young man more fortunate in his gifts was ever born of woman. Everything about him was of the rarest, both in qualities of mind and of manners. But (as I read) his fair fortune was chequered with lasting adversity, for, alas, he was blessed with trouble.

Now when Tristan's fourteenth year came round the Marshal fetched him home and told him to ride and travel all the time and take note of the land and its people so that their ways should be well known to him. This the admirable young man did in exemplary fashion and so successfully that at this time no youth in the whole kingdom led so noble a life as he. Everyone met him with good will and a friendly eye, as one rightly treats a man whose thoughts tend only to excellence and who is averse to all unworthiness.

3

THE ABDUCTION

❧

AT this time it chanced that a lone merchantman arrived off Parmenie over the sea from Norway and made its landfall there and put to shore at Canoel, at the foot of that same castle where the Marshal and his young lord Tristan resided. And when the foreign merchants had displayed their wares it was quickly reported at court what merchandise was for sale. At the same time news arrived which brought ill luck for Tristan – there were falcons to buy and other fine birds of the chase. This was so much talked of that at last two of the Marshal's sons (for boys are much given to such things) decided to take Tristan, their supposed brother, with them as a third and begged and entreated their father then and there to have some falcons bought for him. Noble Rual would have been loth to leave anything undone that his friend Tristan had asked, for he cherished him more and treated him better than any at court or in the country. He was not so devoted to his own sons as he was to Tristan. In this he plainly showed what perfect loyalty was his, and how virtuous and honourable he was. He rose and at once took Tristan by the hand as a loving father would. His other sons went with them, and many retainers too, who either seriously or for amusement followed them down to the ship. And whatever gave pleasure and took one's fancy was for sale in full supply. Jewels, silk, rich clothes – there was a fabulous store of it, and also of fine hunting birds. There were peregrines in plenty, merlins, sparrowhawks, hawks that had mewed, and red-feathered eyasses – of all there were ample stocks. Word was given to buy Tristan some falcons and merlins, and, to please him, some were purchased for the boys who were deemed to be his brothers. Whatever each wished for was obtained for them, all three.

When they had been given all they wanted and were about to turn back, it so happened that Tristan caught sight of a chess-board

hanging in the ship, with its field and its fence very marvellously
decorated. Beside it hung a set of men superbly carved in noble
ivory. Tristan, accomplished boy, regarded it attentively. 'Oh,' he
said, 'noble merchants, in Heaven's name, don't tell me you play
chess?' and said it in their language. Hearing him use their speech,
which next to none in those parts knew, they looked at the boy
with mounting interest and took stock of him minutely. And to
their minds no youth was so blessed with looks or had such beauti-
ful manners. 'Yes,' answered one of them, 'quite a few of us here
are versed in the game. You can easily put it to the test if you like.
Come, I will take you on!' 'Done!' answered Tristan. And so
they two sat down over the board.

'I shall go back home, Tristan,' said the Marshal. 'You can stay
here if you like. My other sons will go up with me. Your tutor must
keep you company here and see that you come to no harm.'

And so the Marshal and all who were with him went back in
again, with the exception of Tristan and his tutor, of whom I
can truthfully tell you by the testimony of this story that no squire
was ever reared more gently for courtesy and noble instincts. His
name was Curvenal. He had learned many accomplishments, as
well fitted him to instruct a boy who in turn, under his tuition, ac-
quired many noble attainments.

Tristan, gifted well-bred youth, sat and played on so elegantly
and politely that the strangers kept looking at him as one man and
confessed in their hearts that they had never set eyes on any young
person adorned with so many excellences. But whatever address he
showed in his deportment or at the game, it was in their eyes noth-
ing to what follows. They were amazed that a child could speak so
many languages, which flowed to his lips in a way they had never
heard in any port they had called at. Every now and then this
polished young courtier interposed with fashionable small-talk and
exotic terms of chess. These he pronounced well – he knew a great
many of them – and with them he adorned his game. Then he
also sang most excellently subtle airs, 'chansons', 'refloits', and
'estampies'. He persevered with these and other polite acquire-
ments to such a point that the traders resolved that if, by some ruse,
they could get him away they would reap great profit and honour
from him. So they promptly bade their rowers stand by while they

themselves weighed anchor as if they attached no importance to it.
They put to sea and got under way so gently that neither Tristan
nor Curvenal was aware of it till they had carried them well on a
league from the landing-place. For the two players were so absorbed
in their game that they had thought for nothing else. But when they
had finished it with Tristan as the winner, and the latter began to
look about him, he saw only too well what course events had taken.
You never saw mortal man so thoroughly woe-begone as he. He
leapt to his feet and standing among them, cried: 'Oh noble
merchants, in God's name, what are you going to do with me? Tell
me, where are you taking me?'

'Listen, my friend,' said one of them, 'nobody can save you from
sailing away with us, so cheer up and put a good face on it.'

At this, poor Tristan raised such a pitiful dirge that his friend
Curvenal began to weep with him from the bottom of his heart and
evince such misery that the crew to a man grew wretched and sullen
because of him and the boy. So they set Curvenal in a tiny skiff and
placed an oar beside him to scull with and a small loaf against his
hunger, and told him to head for wherever he pleased – but Tristan
must go with them. Having said this they sailed on and left him to
drift, a prey to many cares.

Curvenal was adrift on the sea. He suffered distress of many
kinds: distress at the plight he saw Tristan in, distress at his own
peril, since he feared that he would die (for he could not sail a boat
nor, till that moment, had he ever tried). And he cried out in his
heart, 'Lord God, what shall I do? I have never known such fear!
I am here without a crew and I do not know how to sail. Lord God
preserve me and be my shipmate out of here! Trusting in Thy
Grace I will attempt what I have never put my hand to. Guide me
out of this peril!'

With this he laid hold of his sweep and departed in God's name
and (as God of His grace vouchsafed him) arrived back home in a
short space and reported what had happened. In their grief the
Marshal and his good lady used themselves so hard that had Tristan
died before their eyes, they could not have been more deeply affected.
Thus in their common sorrow they went with all their household to
weep for their lost child, down beside the sea. Many a tongue im-
plored God to succour him. Many were their laments, now one

way, now another. And when evening came and they had to separate, their mourning, which till then had been so varied, changed to perfect unison. They said one thing only; they chanted it here, they chanted it there, this solitary refrain:

> *Beas Tristant, curtois Tristant,*
> *tun cors, ta vie a de commant!* *
>
> May thy dear life, thy body fair
> This day be in our Father's care!

Meanwhile the Norwegians sailed on with him and had so contrived it that they would have realized all their wishes concerning him. But He that orders all things and ordering sets them to rights, whom winds, sea, and all the elements subserve in fear and trembling, frustrated it. By His will and command a tempest arose on the sea so perilous that they could no longer send for themselves, but just left their ship to drift where the wild wind drove it, while they despaired of their lives. They had abandoned themselves utterly to that poor prop called 'Chance'. They left it to fate whether they should survive or not, for they had no choice but to mount as if to the heaven and plunge again to the depths, at the sea's will. The raging billows tossed them now up, now down, now hither, now thither. Of all these men not one could keep his feet for a moment. Such was their life for well on eight days and nights, as a result of which they were near to exhaustion.

'By God, masters,' one of them now said, 'to my mind this terrible life we are leading is at the command of the Almighty. Our tossing here on the raging seas more dead than alive has no other cause than our sinful treachery in kidnapping Tristan from his friends.' 'Yes,' they all answered together, 'you are right there, that is just what it is!' They accordingly resolved that, if winds and water were to give them a lull which would let them put to shore, they would gladly set him free to go wherever he pleased. And at once, as soon as they were all agreed, the rigours of their voyage were assuaged. In that same instant the winds began to slacken, the waves abate, the sea subside, the sun shine brightly as be-

* Handsome Tristan, courteous Tristan, I commend your life and body to God. (The couplet which follows is a rendering of Gottfried's free translation of the French.)

T.—4

fore. And now they were swift to act; for during those eight days the wind had beaten them to Cornwall and they were then so near to land that it was hard before their eyes, so they put to land at once. They took Tristan with them and set him ashore, handing him some bread and other food of theirs. 'God give you good luck, friend,' they said, 'and have your life in His keeping!' Then they all bade him farewell and immediately turned back.

Now what did Tristan – homeless Tristan – do? Well, he just sat down and cried. For when anything crosses them children can do nothing but cry. The forlorn and homeless boy joined his hands and raised them in earnest prayer to God. 'Oh, almighty God, abounding in mercy as Thou art, great as is Thy goodness, sweet Lord, I beg Thee extend Thy mercy and goodness to me this day, seeing that Thou hast suffered me to be abducted in this fashion! Lead me, I pray, to where I can soon be with fellow men! I now look all about me and see no living thing. How I dread this great wilderness! Wherever I bend my eyes I see the end of the world, wherever I turn I see nothing but desert, wasteland, wilderness, wild cliffs, and sea as wild. How the terror of it afflicts me! But more than this I fear that, whichever way I turn, wolves and other beasts will devour me. The day, too, is fast sinking towards evening. It will be bad for me if I delay any longer and do not leave this spot. If I do not soon go, I shall spend the night in this forest and then it will be all over with me. Now I see there are many high cliffs and hills hard by. I think I will climb one, if I can, while I still have light, and see if there is any habitation, either near at hand or further off, where I shall find people I can join, and in whose company I can somehow or other keep body and soul together.'

With such thoughts, he rose and turned away. He was wearing a cloak and robe of magnificent brocade, marvellous in its texture; for it had been finely embroidered and interwoven with slender cords of silk to rare effect by Saracens in the infidel style, and was so well cut to his handsome figure that fine clothes were never cut better by man or woman. Moreover, the story tells us that this brocade was of a green greener than May grass and its lining of ermine so very white that it could not possibly be whiter.

Now since there was no staying there, Tristan prepared himself for his toilsome march, downcast and weeping. He tucked his robe up somewhat higher under his girdle, rolled his cloak, laid it over his shoulder, and made his way at speed through forest and open country up towards the wilds. He had no other track or path but what he trod for himself – working forward on legs and arms he made a track with his feet and opened a path with his hands. He went climbing on uphill over stick and stone till he came to an up- land where he chanced on a forest-path, winding and narrow and overgrown with grass. This he followed down on the further side, hoping it would lead to a straight one.

In a short while it led him to a fine road, ample in breadth and well beaten to and fro. Weeping, he sat down to rest at its verge. And now his heart took him back to his dear ones and to the land where the people were known to him, and this made him very de- jected. And again he lamented his woes to God, most pitifully. 'Oh, God,' he said, gazing fervently up to heaven, 'good Lord, how utterly lost I am to my father and mother! Ah, how well I would have done to refrain from my cursed chess-playing, which I shall loathe eternally! God damn sparrow-hawks, falcons, merlins! – they have torn me from my father; it is all their fault that I have left my friends and acquaintances. Those who wish me well are all very sad and dejected on my account. Dearest mother, I know how you are tormenting yourself for grief. Father, your heart is full of sorrow. I know you are both bowed down with it. Oh, if only I knew you knew that I am alive and well, great would be God's mercy to you and to me! For I know you will never be happy unless by the will of God you learn that I am alive. Comforter of all that are troubled, Lord God, will it so!'

Meanwhile, as he sat there and lamented, as I have said, he caught sight of two old pilgrims approaching in the distance. They were of godly aspect, advanced in days and years, hairy and bearded, as God's true children and pilgrims often are. Those wayfarers wore cloaks of linen and such other clothing as is appropriate to pilgrims, and on the outside of their clothes there were sewn-on sea-shells and many other tokens from distant lands. Each bore a staff in his hand. Their head and leg-covering was well suited to their kind. These servants of God wore round their thighs linen hose trussed close to the leg and reaching down within a hand's breadth of their ankles. Feet and ankles were bare to the obstacles under foot. They also bore saintly palms on their backs which showed that they were penitents. At this moment they were intoning their psalms and prayers and all the good things they knew. On seeing them, Tristan held anxious soliloquy. 'Merciful Lord, what will become of me now? If those two coming along there have seen me, once again they may well lay hands on me!' But as they drew nearer and he recognized the nature of their staves and of their clothing, he soon knew what they were and began to pluck up courage and feel a little happier. 'Praise to Thee, O Lord!' he said fervently. 'These are surely good people, I need not be afraid of them.'

Very soon now they saw the boy sitting ahead of them. As they approached he politely leapt up to meet them, his fine hands crossed on his breast. The two men scanned him intently and noted his courteous ways. They went up to him kindly and saluted him most charmingly with this pleasant greeting: 'God keep you, dear friend, whoever you are!' Tristan bowed his thanks to the old men. 'Oh,' he said, 'God in His power bless such saintly company!' 'Dear child,' they replied, 'where are you from – or who brought you here?'

Now Tristan was very shrewd and cautious for his years and started to tell them a pretty tale. 'Good sirs,' he told them, 'I was born in this country and with some others was to have ridden out hunting in this forest here today, but (myself I do not know how) I rode out of touch with both huntsmen and hounds. Those who knew the forest-paths all fared better than I, because, having no track, I rode astray and got lost. I then hit on a cursed trail which brought me to the edge of a gully where, try as I would, I could not curb my horse from plunging headlong down. We ended up, my horse and I, lying in a heap together. Then I failed to get to my stirrup in time to prevent its snatching the reins and careering off into the forest. And so I came to this path, which has brought me as far as this. But I cannot say where I am, nor in which direction I must go. Now, good people, please tell me where you are going?' 'If Our Lord grant it, friend,' they answered, 'we intend to be in Tintagel tonight.' Tristan then asked them politely whether they would let him go with them. 'By all means, dear child,' said the palmers. 'If that is where you are making for, come along!'

Tristan set out together with them. And, as they went, they

talked of many things. Courtier as he was, Tristan was so wary of his speech that whichever way they questioned him he answered them no more than need and circumstance required. He had his speech and bearing under such fine restraint that these grey and venerable sages ascribed it to heavenly favour, and studied his ways and demeanour and his handsome person, too, with ever keener interest. His clothes held their attention, for they were very splendid and of marvellous texture. 'Good God,' they mused, 'who is this boy and where is he from, that has such beautiful manners?' And so, making it their pastime to watch and consider his every peculiarity, they marched for well on a mile.

4

THE HUNT

Now events were swift to follow. His uncle Mark of Cornwall's hounds (as this true tale informs us) had at that very moment chased a hart of ten to a spot not far from the road. It let them overtake it, and there it stood at bay. Hard running to escape had robbed it of all its strength. And now the huntsmen, too, were there with a great clamour, blowing for the kill.

When Tristan saw the bay, he addressed the pilgrims with his usual discretion. 'Gentlemen, these hounds, this hart, these people are those I lost today. But now I have found them again – these are my friends and acquaintances. I will join them, if you will excuse me.'

'God bless you, child,' they answered, 'good fortune attend you!'

'Thank you, and God keep you!' was good Tristan's answer. He bowed and turned away in the direction of the hart.

Now when the hart had been killed, the one who was Huntsman-in-Chief laid it out on the grass on all fours like a boar.

'How now, master, what is that meant to be?' interposed Tristan, bred as he was to courtly ways. 'Stop, in God's name! What are you at? Whoever saw a hart broken up in this fashion?'

The huntsman fell back a pace or two. He looked at him and said: 'What do you want me to do with it, boy? When we flay a hart we know of no better way in these parts than to split it clean down from the head and then into four, so that none of the quarters is much bigger than another. That is the custom of this country. Are you versed in the art, boy?'

'Yes, master,' he replied. 'The usage is different in the land where I was reared.'

'How so?' asked the huntsman.

'There they excoriate a hart.'

'On my word, friend, unless you show me, I shall not know the meaning of "excoriate"! Nobody in this kingdom knows the trick of it. I have never heard it named, either by us or by strangers. Dear boy, what is "excoriate"? Good as you are, do show it me. Come along – "excoriate" this hart!'

'Dear master,' answered Tristan, 'since you ask about excoriation, by your kind permission (and if it will give you pleasure) I will gladly show you my country's usage, so far as I have retained it.'

The Master-Huntsman looked at the young stranger with a kindly smile, for he was well-bred himself and was versed in all the graces that a good man should know. 'Indeed, dear friend,' said he, 'please do! Come along, and if it is beyond your strength, my dear young fellow, I myself and my companions will lend a hand and lay it out and turn it over for you, as you shall prescribe by pointing with your finger.'

Tristan, the boy so far from home, removed his cloak, placed it on a tree-stump, tucked up his robe, and rolled up his sleeves. Then he smoothed down his hair and laid it above his ears. Those present at the break-up of the hart eyed him with ever-growing interest. They inwardly considered his bearing and behaviour, and it pleased them so much that they delighted to watch it. They confessed to themselves that everything about him was noble, his clothes rare and magnificent and his figure of perfect build. They all flocked round to watch what he would do.

And now the homeless boy, young master-huntsman Tristan, went up to the hart and, taking hold of it, tried to lay it on its back, but failed to shift it on to it because it was too heavy. Then he asked them politely to place it to his liking and prepare it for breaking up. This was quickly done. He took his stand at the hart's head and then began to strip it. After making an incision he slit it from the muzzle down under the belly. Then he returned to the forequarters. These he stripped in due order, first right then left. Next he took the two hind-quarters and flayed them likewise. He then started to peel away the hide from the flanks and everywhere from the holds, working down from the head. Then he spread his hide on the ground. He again went back to his fore-quarters and detached them from the breast, leaving the latter entire. The quarters he laid on one side. He addressed himself next to severing the breast from the chine and from the flanks, including three ribs on either side. (That is the way to break up a hart. Those who know how to take out the breast are sure to leave these ribs on it.) Then he quickly turned and removed the hind-quarters most expertly, both together, not one by one. To the two steaks where the back sweeps over the loins towards the scut for a palm and a half, and which those who know how to break up a beast call 'the haunch', he left what duly belongs to them. He severed the ribs on both sides, cut them away from the chine and then the paunch as far as the great gut. And since this ill became his beautiful hands he said: 'Two serving-men, here, quick! Move this further off and get this ready for us!'

Thus the hart was dismembered and the hide removed according to the rules of the chase. He laid the breast, sides, and quarters, both fore and hind, in a neat pile on one side. With that the Break-up was over.

'There, master,' said our homeless stranger, Tristan, 'this is Excoriation; this is how the art is plied! Now, please, you and your attendants, step up and do the fourchie.'

'"Fourchie", dear boy, what is that? What on earth can you have named? You have shown us this piece of hunting lore – and rare and excellent it is – like a master. Now, do go on with it and display your skill to the full. We shall assist you as before.'

Without more ado, Tristan ran off and cut a fork to his hand which those who are versed in the fourchie call the 'fourche' (though 'fourche' and 'fork' are identical; there is nothing to choose between them). Having returned with his stick, he cut out the liver entire, and then severed the net and the numbles. He removed the pizzle from its limb. Seating himself on the grass, he took all three pieces, bound them firmly with his net to the 'fourche', and then tied it round about with green bast.

'Observe, gentlemen,' he said, 'they call this "fourchie" in our hunting usage, and the art is so called from its being on the "fourche", and this is most appropriate, since the "fourche" is the proper place for it. Some groom come and hold it! The day must not pass without your remembering your quarry.'

'"Quarry"? Bless us!' they all said. 'What is that? We should understand Arabic sooner! What is "quarry", dear man? Don't say a word of explanation – do the thing itself so that we can see it with our eyes, as you are a courteous man.'

Tristan was ready to oblige as before. He took the pluck (I mean that on which the heart is strung) and cleaned it of all its appendages. He cut off half of the heart towards its pointed end and, taking it in his hands, cut it crosswise into four and threw this down on the hide. He then returned to his pluck. He removed the milt and lungs, and the pluck was bare of its contents. When this had been placed on the hide, he quickly cut both pluck-string and gorge, above, at the curve of the breast. Then swiftly he removed the head and horns from the neck, and told them to place these with the breast. 'Here, quick!' he said to the men. 'Take this chine away! If any poor person should have a mind to it, make him a present of it or deal with it according to your own custom. This is how I do the quarry.' The company closed in and inspected his woodmanship.

Tristan called for the pieces which he had asked to be made ready for him. And, indeed, it was all in its place, ready and prepared, just as he had told them. The four quarters of the heart had been laid on the four parts of the hide following the usage of the chase, and lay thus arranged. He chopped the milt and the lungs, and then the paunch and the great gut (and what other dogs' fare there was) into suitably small pieces, and spread it all out on the hide. This done, he summoned the hounds with a loud 'Ça, ça, ça!' They were all there in a trice, standing over their reward.

'There you are,' said the eloquent youth, 'this is what they call the quarry at home in Parmenie, and I will tell you the reason why. The food one gives the hounds from the hide they call "quarry" because it lies on the hide or "cuire". So hunters have taken the term and coined "quarry" from "cuire". Thus "quarry" comes from "cuire". And believe me, it was devised for the good of the hounds. It is a beneficial practice, since the bits one lays on the hide serve to flesh the hounds, being sweet to their taste from the blood. Now consider this style of quartering – this is all there is to it. Judge to what extent you like it.'

'Lord!' they all said, 'what do you mean, dear child? We clearly see that these arts were devised to the great good of bloodhounds and pack!'

'Now take your hide away,' good Tristan continued, 'since I have done all I can. And believe me truly, could I have served you further, I gladly would have done so. Now each of you cut your own withies and truss your portions separately. Convey the head in your hands, and take your present to court with all appropriate ceremony: this will enhance you as courtiers. You know yourselves how a hart must be presented. Present it in the approved manner!'

The huntsman and his men were once again amazed that the boy should propound so many hunting usages one after another and with such discernment, and be so well versed in such lore.

'Listen, good child,' they said, 'these marvellous distinctions which you draw and have drawn for us are so bewildering that, unless we see them to a finish, we shall consider what you have done so far as of small account.' They therefore quickly fetched a horse and begged him of his goodness to ride with them to court in the style which his craft prescribed and show them his country's usage to an end.

'Very well,' said Tristan, 'take up the hart, and off we go!' and mounted and rode away with them.

The others had scarce been able to await the opportune moment when they should be riding in company, and now they all began to speculate on his affairs – where he was from and how he had come there. They longed to know all his circumstances. And this is just what Tristan was shrewdly considering. He proceeded very subtly to fabricate his story; and whichever way one looked at it, his tale was not that of a child.

'To the far side of Britain,' he began very artfully, 'lies a land called Parmenie. My father is a merchant there and leads a graceful, sociable life in keeping with his station – I mean such as is given to a merchant. And, that you may know all, he is not so rich in chattels as in qualities of mind. It was he who had me learn what I know. Now merchants often came from other countries, and I studied their speech, manners, and peculiarities so intently that, finally, I was seized with an urge that ceaselessly nagged me to go into foreign lands. And since I longed to acquaint myself with strange lands and peoples, I so had my thoughts on it, day and night, that at last I eluded my father and sailed away with some merchants. That is how I came to this country. And now you have heard all about me. I don't know how you like it.'

'Ah, dear child,' they all answered, 'it was a noble urge in you. It does many people good to live abroad, and teaches one many good things. My dear young man, may God bless the land where so excellent a child was ever reared by a merchant! Of all the kings in the world not one would rear a child better. But now, dear boy, tell us this: what name did your courtly father give you?'

'Tristan,' he answered, 'Tristan is my name.'

'Heaven help us!' cried one of them. 'Why in Heaven did he call you that? *Juvente bele et la riant* – "Fair youth and smiling" – would have been a better name for you, believe me.'

And so they rode conversing each in his own way, with this boy for their sole entertainment. The attendants put questions such as were fitting for each to ask.

It was not long before Tristan saw the citadel. He broke two leafy garlands from a lime-tree. One he set on his head, the other he made of larger size and gave it to the huntsman.

'Oh,' he said, 'what stronghold is this, dear master? It is a castle fit for a king!'

'Tintagel,' answered the huntsman.

'Tintagel? What a splendid castle! God save you, Tintagel, and all who dwell inside you!'

'Bless you, dear child,' answered his companions. 'May you be ever happy, and prosper as we would wish it!' And so they arrived at the gate.

Tristan halted before it. 'Gentlemen,' he said to them, 'since I have not met you before, I do not know any of your names. But ride two and two together and keep close beside one another, preserving the shape of a hart. Let the horns go ahead, the breast follow in their track, the ribs come after the fore-quarters. Then arrange for the hind-parts to follow on the ribs. After that, you should see to it that the quarry and fourchie bring up the rear – such is true huntsman-ship. And do not be in too great a hurry – ride in due order, one behind another. My master, here, and myself as his groom will ride together, if it meets with your approval.'

'Indeed, dear boy,' they all replied, 'as you wish it, so do we!'

'Very well,' he said. 'Now lend me a horn that I can manage, and bear in mind that, when I begin, you must listen to me, and whatever I blow, you blow the same.'

'Blow up, dear friend, and play whatever you like – we shall all follow you in it, I and my companions.'

'Excellent!' said the boy. 'Very well – agreed!' They handed him a little horn, high-pitched and clear. 'Off you go,' he said.

So they rode in, troop-wise, two and two, as was right and proper. And when the troop were right inside, Tristan took his little horn and blew so splendidly and so entrancingly that all who rode with him could scarcely wait to join him for sheer joy and all took their horns and blew with him rarely, to his measure. He led them excellently, and they followed well and skilfully in his tune. That castle was filled with music!

When the King and his household heard this strange hunting-measure they were shocked to the very marrow, since it had never before been heard there at court. But now the troop was at the Palace door, to which a crowd of retainers had run up, attracted by the fanfares. They were all most curious to know what the din was about. Illustrious Mark himself had also come to find out, attended by many courtiers. Now when Tristan first saw the King, he took a liking to him more than to all the rest. His heart singled him out, for Mark was of his own blood – instinct drew him towards him. Looking him in the eyes he made ready to salute him and embarked on a new fanfare in a foreign measure, winding his horn so lustily that none could follow now.

But this was soon over, and the noble waif had done with his horn-blowing and was silent. He made the king a fine bow and, smiling with all his great charm, said in French: 'God save the King and his household!'

Mark the Debonair and all his retainers thanked the boy courteously as a man of worth deserves. 'Ah,' they all answered together in the same language, both great and small, 'may God give kind fortune to such a charming creature!'

The King took stock of the boy and summoning his huntsman said: 'Tell me, who is this child whose speech is so well-trimmed?'

'He comes from Parmenie, my lord, and he is so marvellously well-bred and accomplished that I never knew the like in a child. He says his name is "Tristan" and that his father is a merchant; but

I do not believe it. For how could a merchant, with all his affairs to see to, ever have devoted so much leisure to him? Could a man whose occupation is business have the leisure to spend on him? God in heaven, he is so versatile! Look at this new art we displayed on coming to court! We learned it all from him. And hear this cunning arrangement: as a hart is shaped, so was it brought to court. Did you ever see anything so ingenious? Observe: the head precedes, the breast follows in its track. The quarters fore and hind, one thing and the next, these were never presented at court with greater elegance. Look there, did you ever see a fourchie made in such style? Never did I hear of such refinements of the chase! Before this, moreover, he showed us the way to "excoriate" a hart. I like this craft so well that if I ever hunt again, I shall never hack deer into four, be it hart or hind.' And he proceeded to tell his lord all about Tristan from beginning to end, how perfect he was in the noble art of venery, and how he had set the quarry before the hounds.

The King paid close attention to all that the huntsman said. He had the boy called and sent the hunt to their lodgings to attend to their duties. They turned back and rode away.

Master-Huntsman Tristan returned his little horn and alighted on the ground. The young pages ran up to the boy and, putting their arms round him, conducted him ceremoniously into the royal presence. As to Tristan, he could proceed with elegance, too. His form, moreover, was shaped as Love would have it. His mouth was as red as a rose, his colour radiant, his eyes clear; his hair fell in brown locks, crimped at the ends; his arms and hands were shapely and dazzling white; his figure was tall to the right degree; his feet and legs (in which his beauty most appeared) deserved such praise as a man may give a man. His clothes, as I told you, were most elegantly cut to his figure. He was so well favoured in presence and manners that it was a joy to watch him.

'My friend,' asked Mark, looking Tristan in the eye, 'are you called Tristan?'

'Yes, sire – "Tristan". God save you!'

'And you too, my dear young gentleman.'

'Thank you, noble King of Cornwall,' he replied. 'May the Son of God bless you and your household eternally!'

5

THE YOUNG MUSICIAN

Now, as you have heard, Tristan has unwittingly come home, though he imagined he was homeless. Noble Mark, his unsuspected father,* acted with magnanimity, and there was truly great need that he should. He asked or commanded the household one and all to be kind and gracious to the young stranger and to honour him with their company and conversation, and they were all very glad to comply. Thus good Tristan was now a royal retainer. The King liked to see him and was glad to have him, since he was drawn to him in his heart. He loved to observe him and often did so, for Tristan was at all times discreetly at his side, ministering to his needs whenever he found occasion. Wherever Mark was or wherever he went, Tristan always made a second. This Mark took in very good part. He held Tristan in high favour, and it cheered him when he saw him.

Meanwhile, before the week was out, it happened that Mark himself rode out hunting with Tristan, together with many of the court, to study his skill in the art of woodmanship. Mark sent for his own hunter and gave it him. Tristan was never better mounted, for it was strong, swift, and handsome.

Mark asked them to give the boy a little horn of clear and melodious tone.

'Tristan,' he said, 'remember you are my Huntsman. You must show us your hunting-lore. Take your hounds, ride off and post your relays wherever you judge they should be.'

'No, Sire,' answered Tristan courteously, 'it cannot be done like this. Tell the huntsmen to go, let them man the relays, let them cast off the hounds. They know their way about country here, and are better informed than I where the hart withdraws and flees before the

* Legally, had the truth been known, Mark stood in the position of a father towards Tristan.

hounds. They know the lie of the land. As for me, I have never ridden this country, I am an utter stranger.'

'In God's name, Tristan, you are right! You cannot show your worth there. The huntsmen must go themselves and make their arrangements between them.'

And so the huntsmen left, coupled their hounds, and quickly set up their relays in places they well knew. They roused a hart at once and all hunted it par force till towards evening, when the hounds caught up with it. At that same moment Mark and Tristan (and with this pair many courtiers) raced up for the kill. There was a great clamour of horns in many different measures – the men blew so splendidly that it did Mark and many others with him good to hear it.

When they had killed the hart they placed their Chief, Tristan, this stranger grown so familiar, beside the beast and begged him to show them the Excoriation from first to last. 'Certainly,' said Tristan, and he thereupon made himself ready.

Now I am much of the opinion that there is no need for me to serve you with the same account twice running. Just as I described it for you with the first hart, so did Tristan break up this. As they watched the break-up, the fourchie, and the art of the quarry, they declared with one voice that no one could improve on these practices or ever devise better.

The King told them to truss up the hart, and then he turned away. He and his huntsman, Tristan, together with all his train, then rode home again with horns and fourchie.

From this time on Tristan was a courtier much beloved among them. The King and his household kept good company with him, and he, too, was so obliging to rich and poor alike that, had it been possible to pamper them all, he gladly would have done so. God had bestowed on him the grace of being willing and able to live for his fellows. Laughing, dancing, singing, riding, running, leaping, being on his best behaviour and letting himself go, this he could do with everyone. He lived as people wished him to live, and as young people should. If any of them started anything he fell in with him at once.

Now it happened one day a little after supper, when people seek entertainment, that Mark had sat down somewhere and was listening intently to a lay which a harper was playing. (The man was a master of his art, the best they knew, and a Welshman.) And now Tristan of Parmenie came and sat at his feet and was soon so engrossed in the lay and its sweet music that, had he been forbidden on pain of death, he could not have kept silent about it. For his spirits began to soar and his heart was overflowing.

'Master,' he said, 'you play well. You produce your notes correctly and with the sad passion they were meant to have. The lay was composed by Bretons about Sir Gurun and his Paramour.'*

The harper took this all in, but gave ear to his playing till he had finished his lay, as if he had not heard what was said. He then turned to the boy.

'How do you know where this music comes from, dear child?' he asked. 'Are you perhaps versed in the art?'

'Yes, dear minstrel, there was a time when I, too, had mastered it. But my skill is now so feeble that I dare not play in your hearing.'

'Don't say that, my friend. Take this harp – let us hear the sort of music they play in your country.'

'If you command me, and if it is by your leave that I play to you?' said Tristan.

'It is, dear fellow. Here, harp up!'

When Tristan took the harp it was as if made for his hands, which (as I have said) were of surpassing beauty; for they were soft and smooth, fine and slender and dazzling white as ermine. Passing them over the strings he struck up some preludes and phrases, fine, sweet, and haunting, recapturing his lays of Arthur.† Then, taking his key, he adjusted pegs and strings, some up, some down, until they were to his liking. This was soon done, and Tristan, the new minstrel, began his new office with his mind full upon it. He drew his snatches and preludes, his haunting initial flourishes so sweetly from his harp and made them so melodious with lovely string music, that all came running up, one calling another. The household arrived for the most part at a run. Nor did they think that they had come too soon.

---

* For the contents of a Lay of Guirun as sung by Ysolt, see Episode 31, p. 313.

† The text says 'of Briton' or 'of Breton'. The adjective may be used here as a proper name to indicate King Arthur, the Briton *par excellence*.

Now Mark was absorbed by the scene and sat turning it over in his mind and watching his friend Tristan; and he greatly wondered how Tristan had been able to conceal so polite an accomplishment and such virtuosity as he saw at his command. But now Tristan was playing the opening strains of a lay on 'Graland the Fair's Proud Mistress'. He made such excellent sweet music on his harp in the Breton style that many a man sitting or standing there forgot his very name. Hearts and ears began to play the fool and desert their rightful paths. Thoughts found varied expression there: 'Ah,' they mused, 'blessed be the merchant that ever sired such a noble son!' But nimbly his white fingers went dipping among the strings, scattering sweet sound till the palace was full of it. Nor was there sparing of eyes: a host of them were bent on him, following his hands.

And now this lay was ended, and the good King sent to ask him to play another. 'With pleasure,' said Tristan. In fine style he struck up a second lay, full of yearning like the first, about Noble Thisbe of Old Babylon. He played it so beautifully and went with his music in so masterly a fashion that the harper was amazed. And at the appropriate places, sweetly and rapturously, the accomplished youth would wing his song to meet it. He sang the notes of his lay so beautifully in Breton, Welsh, Latin, and French that you could not tell which was sweeter or deserving of more praise, his harping or his singing. Much talk and discussion arose on the subject of himself and his acquirements. All were agreed that in their country they had never known such talent in one man. 'Oh, what kind of child is this?' asked one here, another there. 'What companion have we here? All the pages in the world are nothing compared with our Tristan.'

When Tristan had ended his lay to his liking, Mark said: 'Tristan, come here. May your tutor be honoured in the eyes of God, and you together with him! This is very good. I would like to hear your lays of an evening, sometimes, when you cannot fall asleep. You will do this for me, won't you, and on your own account as well?'

'Yes, indeed I will, Sire.'

'Now tell me, can you play any other stringed instruments?'

'No, Sire,' he said.

'Oh, but surely you can? I ask you this, Tristan, by the love you bear me.'

'My lord,' answered Tristan swiftly, 'you need not have pressed me so far to tell you, despite myself, since, if you wish to know it, I am bound to tell. I have applied myself to stringed instruments of every description and yet play none so well but that I would gladly play it better. I have not studied this art for long, and to tell the truth I have been at it on and off for seven years, or little more, believe me. Parmenians taught me the fiddle and organistrum,* Welshmen the harp and rote – they were two masters from Wales; Bretons from the town of Lut grounded me in the lyre and also in the sambuca.'†

'Sambuca? What is that, dear man?'

'The best stringed instrument I play.'

'You see,' said the retainers, 'God has heaped his bounty on this child for a life of sheer delight!'

Mark questioned him further. 'Tristan, I heard you singing in Breton just now, and in Welsh, good Latin, and French. Do you know these languages?'

'Yes, tolerably well, Sire.'

At once the crowd pressed in on him, and those who had any acquaintance with the tongues of neighbouring countries lost no time in testing him, one in one language, the next in another. While this was going on he courteously replied to what they had to say – to Norwegians, Irishmen, Germans, Scots, and Danes. Then many a heart began to yearn for Tristan's talents. Many would have loved to be like him. Desire in countless hearts invoked him with tender fervour. 'Ah, Tristan, how I wish I were like you!' 'Tristan, life is worth living for you!' 'Tristan, you have been given the pick of all the talents that a man can possess in this life!' And with all this they made a great hubbub. 'Just listen!' said one, 'just listen!' said another. 'Do listen everybody! A fourteen-year-old child has learned all the arts there are!'

'Tristan, listen to me,' said the King, 'you can do everything I want – hunting, languages, music. To crown it let us be com-

---

* An instrument with three or four strings manipulated mechanically, and a keyboard.

† Here probably a member of the lute family.

panions. You be mine and I will be yours. By day we shall ride out
hunting, at night here at home we shall sustain ourselves with
courtly pursuits, such as harping, fiddling, and singing. You are
good at these things; do them for me. For you, in return, I will play
a thing *I* know, which perhaps your heart desires – of fine clothes
and horses I will give you all you want! With these I shall have
played well for you. Look, my companion, I entrust my sword,
spurs, cross-bow, and golden horn to you. Take charge of them,
look after them for me – be a merry courtier!'

And so the homeless boy became a favourite at court. You never
saw such felicity in a child as could be seen in him. Whatever he
did, whatever he said seemed (and was) so good, that all cherished
friendly feelings and tender affection for him.

And with that enough of this matter. We must lay this theme
aside and take up the other again to narrate what steps his father,
the Marshal loyal Don Rual li Foitenant, having lost him, took to
find him.

6

RECOGNITION AND REUNION

DON Rual li Foitenant took ship without delay and crossed the sea with ample baggage, for he had resolved never to return before hearing definite news of some kind as to his young lord's whereabouts. He put to shore in Norway and inquired after his friend Tristan up and down the land from morn till night. But what was the good of it? Tristan was not there: all his searching was in vain. And so, not finding him, Rual set his course for Ireland. But here again he failed to discover any more about him than before. But now his resources began to dwindle to such an extent that he dismounted, had his horses sold, and sent his people home with the baggage. He was left quite destitute and went begging for his bread, and continued to do so from kingdom to kingdom, land to land, searching for Tristan for some three years or more, till he had so lost his handsome appearance, and his colour had so deteriorated, that anyone who had seen him then would never have admitted he was of noble birth. Worthy Don Rual endured his load of shame like a vagabond born and bred without allowing his poverty to rob him of his good humour at all, as Heaven knows happens to many.

Now when his search was advancing into its fourth year Rual was in Denmark making urgent inquiries to and fro from place to place, when, by the grace of God, he chanced upon the two pilgrims whom his young lord Tristan had met on the road through the forest. He questioned them at once, and they told him how long it was since they had seen just such a boy as Rual had described to them, and how they had let him go along with them; all his peculiarities of face, hair, speech, behaviour, body, and clothes; and the various languages and accomplishments he was versed in. Rual saw at once that the description tallied. He then begged the palmers for the sake of our Lord to name the place where they had left him, if they knew it. They answered him that it was near Tintagel in

Cornwall, and he asked them to name him the town over and over again.

'Now in which direction does Cornwall lie?' he asked them.

'It marches with the land of Britain on the far side,' they promptly answered.

'Ah,' thought Rual, 'Lord God, this is surely Thy mercy. If, as I have learned, Tristan has gone to Cornwall in this way, truly he has gone home, for Mark is his uncle. Lead me there, dear Lord! Lord God, by Thy command, vouchsafe me the sight of Tristan! May this news I have heard bring me joy! It seems good and indeed it is so. It has rallied my drooping spirits and heartened me.'

'Good people,' said he, 'may the Son of the Maid preserve you! I will start on my road and see if I can find him.'

'May He that hath power over all the world guide you to the boy!'

'Thank you,' said Rual. 'By your leave I shall delay no longer.'

'Adieu, friend, adieu!' they answered.

Then Rual went his way, never resting his body so much as half a day, till he came to the sea. There he did rest, much to his annoyance, for no ships were ready to sail. But when at length he found a passage, he sailed to Britain. Through Britain he tramped so manfully that no day was so long that he failed to trudge on into the night. What gave him the strength and the courage was the hope he took from his news. It made his efforts light and easy.

On arriving in Cornwall Rual at once asked to be told where Tintagel was, and was very soon informed. He then resumed his journey and came to Tintagel early one Saturday morning, as people were going to mass. He accordingly took up his stand before the minster where people were passing to and fro and looked in all directions and probed with his eyes here, there, and everywhere to see if he could find anyone whom it would be right and proper for him to question. For he kept on thinking to himself: 'These people are all more respectable than I. I fear that whomever I engage in conversation will think it beneath him to answer any questions about the boy, seeing me so down-at-heel. Counsel me, O Lord, what to do!' But now King Mark was approaching with a delightful entourage. The loyal man looked again, but he did not see what he wanted.

When the King left mass to return to court, Rual moved out of their path, drawing aside with him an aged courtier.

'My lord,' said Rual, 'kindly tell me. Do you know if there is a page here at court called "Tristan"? They say he attends on the King?'

'A page?' rejoined the other. 'I will tell you nothing of a page. There is a young squire who is a retainer here. He is soon to be made a knight. The King values him highly, for he is versed in many arts and has acquired many accomplishments and courtly ways. He is a strong young man of fine carriage with brown hair falling in locks, and an exile. We call him "Tristan".'

'Oh, my lord,' said Rual eagerly, 'are you a retainer at court here?'

'Yes.'

'By your honour, my lord, do one trifle more – for you are very kind. Tell him there is a poor man here who wishes to see and speak with him. And please assure him I am from his country.'

The other accordingly told Tristan that a fellow countryman of his was there, and Tristan went along to him at once. And the moment Tristan saw him he said, his words chiming with his feelings: 'Now may our Lord be sanctified for ever, father, that it is given to me to see you!' This was his very first greeting. After this he ran to him, laughing, and kissed the loyal man as a child should kiss its father. This was as it should be: Rual was his father, he was Rual's child. None of the fathers now alive, or who were ever born before us, treated their children in a more fatherly way than Rual treated Tristan. Yes, Tristan held father, mother, kinsmen, vassals – all the friends he ever had – together in his arms there.

'Oh, my good and trusty father,' he said affectionately, 'tell me, are my dearest mother and my brothers still alive?'

'I do not know, dear son,' answered Rual, 'but they were alive when I last saw them, though they were much distressed because of you. I cannot tell you how they have fared since, because I have seen nobody I knew for a long time, nor have I been home since that cursed hour when I suffered such disaster in you.'

'Dear father,' asked Tristan, 'what is the matter? Where have your good looks gone?'

'You took them from me, my son.'

'Then I shall give you them back again.'

'My son, we may yet live to see it.'

'Now, father, come to court with me.'

'No, son, I will not go there with you – surely you can see that I would not pass muster at court like this?'

'But, father,' said Tristan, 'you must. My lord the King must see you.'

Good, courteous Rual reflected: 'My nakedness doesn't matter. In whatever state the King sees me now, he will be glad to see me, if I tell him about his nephew here. When I tell him all that I have done from the outset, what I am now wearing will seem to him very fine.'

Tristan took him by the hand. Rual's outfit and clothes were as one might expect – a miserable little robe, worn right through and threadbare, and tattered in many places. Nor did he have a cloak. The garments the good man wore beneath his robe were thoroughly wretched, utterly worn out and soiled. The hair of his head and beard was as thickly matted from neglect as if he were from the wilds. Moreover, the praiseworthy knight went barefoot and bare-legged and was weather-beaten too, as all are bound to be whom hunger and cold, sun and wind, have robbed of their fresh complexion. In this state he appeared before Mark, near enough to look him in the face.

'Tell me, Tristan,' said Mark addressing him, 'who is this man?'

'My father, Sire,' answered Tristan.

'Do you mean it?'

'Yes, my lord.'

'We bid him welcome!' replied the noble King.

Rual thanked him with a courtly bow. This was a sign for the knights to come running up in crowds and, with them, the royal household, and 'God save you, sir!' they cried one and all.

Now you must know that however unpresentable Rual was so far as clothes were concerned, he was truly magnificent and faultless in both physique and bearing. His form was princely. His limbs and stature were huge, like those of a hero of old, his arms and legs were of generous length, his gait was fine and stately, his whole frame well-proportioned. He was neither too young nor old but in his prime, when youth and years give life its best vitality. For true majesty he was the peer of any emperor. His voice rang out like a clarion, his speech was well-trimmed. He stood there in sight of all their lordships with magnificent allure. Nor was it the first time that he had done so.

And now there was great whispering among knights and barons discussing it up and down. 'Oh,' they all said, 'is that he? Is that the well-bred merchant about whom his son Tristan has told us so many fine things? We have heard tale upon tale of his excellence. Why has he come to court like this?' and they gossiped on in this fashion.

The mighty King then ordered that Rual should be shown to a chamber and there provided with some fine clothes. Tristan soon had him bathed and well attired. A cap was ready to hand. Tristan put it on Rual's head and it suited him perfectly, for he had a handsome countenance. He cut a splendid figure. Tristan took him by the hand affectionately, as he felt, and led him back to Mark.

Now Rual pleased them greatly. 'Look how soon fine clothes have transformed the man! Those clothes suit the merchant splendidly, and in himself he is superb! Who knows if he is not a most distinguished man? To tell the truth, he behaves as if he were. Now look at the stately way he walks, and how elegantly he bears himself in his noble robes, and judge of his qualities above all through Tristan. For how could a man of trade have reared his child so beautifully, unless from a noble heart?'

They had washed, and the King had come to table. He seated his guest Rual at his own board and had him served well and courteously as befits a well-bred man. 'Tristan,' he said, 'go and wait on your father yourself.' And believe me this was done. Tristan showed him all the honour and attention in his power, in the measure of his affection. Rual ate readily for his part, since Tristan was the best comfort he could have.

When they left the table, the King engaged his guest in conversation, asking him various questions about his country and his travels. And while he questioned him the knights all listened, and attended to Rual's story.

'Sire,' said Rual, 'I declare it is just on three and a half years since I set out. But wherever I have chanced to go since then, I have asked no news but of what I was obsessed with and what has led me here.'

'And what was that?'

'Tristan, here. And believe me, Sire, I have other children that God has blessed me with, and I wish them as well as any man his children: three such sons that, had I been with them, one or other would surely now be a knight. – But if I had undergone half the trouble for all three that I have endured for Tristan, stranger though he is to me, very much indeed would have been done.'

'Stranger?' asked the King. 'Tell us, how can that be? Surely he is your son, as he says?'

'No, Sire, he is no concern of mine except inasmuch as I am his vassal.' Tristan started and looked at Rual fixedly.

'But tell us why you have suffered this hardship,' the King rejoined, 'and stayed away from your wife and children so long (as you say), seeing that he is not your son.'

'Only God and I know that, my lord.'

'But enlighten me, too,' said Mark kindly. 'I am very curious.'

'If I knew that I should not regret it, and if it were seemly for me to say it in this place,' said the faithful man, 'I could tell you a whole history as to how this affair came about and how things have shaped for Tristan, here.' The whole household, Mark and his barons, shot the question at him as with a single voice: 'Tell us, good and trusty man – *who is Tristan?*'

'Sire,' began good Rual, 'it happened in time past, as you and those who were here in those days well know, that my lord Rivalin, whose liege I was and would be now, had it pleased God that he should live, was told so much and much again about your excellence that he entrusted his whole land and people to my keeping, and came to this country; for he wished very much to know you, and joined your suite. And you know the story of what happened to Blancheflor – how he won her as his lover, and she ran away with him. When they had arrived home and received each other in marriage (this happened under my roof with myself and many others to witness) he entrusted her to my charge, after which I always cared for her to the best of my ability. But he promptly assembled an expedition in his country, together with his kinsmen and vassals, set out at once, and was killed in battle, as you no doubt have heard. And when the news got abroad, and the lovely woman learned of the turn that things had taken, mortal grief struck so hard into her heart, that with Tristan here in her womb she fell into her pangs, from which she wrested him, and herself lay down and died.'

At this the faithful man was assailed by such heartfelt grief that he could not conceal it, for he sat and wept like a child. The eyes of all the others, too, began to brim over at his story. The heart of good King Mark was so strongly pierced with grief that tears of pain flowed from his eyes and streamed down his cheeks and robes. This news was a cause of deep distress to Tristan for no other reason than that he had lost a father in the person of this faithful man, and the belief that he had a father.

Meanwhile good Rual sat dejectedly and told the court about the pitiful child: how strictly he had told them to nurse it after its mother had borne it; how he had had it hidden away in a secret place; how he had spread the rumour and had it proclaimed to his countrymen that it had died in its mother's womb; how (as I told you earlier) he had commanded his wife to lie in as a woman lies in childbed, and, after the appropriate time, to keep on telling every-one that she had borne the child; how she had gone to church with Tristan, and how he had been baptized there; why he had been named 'Tristan'; how he himself had sent the boy abroad and had him taught all the skills which he had mastered, both of tongue and hand; how he had left Tristan on board ship, how Tristan had been stolen away from there and he himself had come in search of him under great hardship. And so he sat telling his tale from begin-ning to end. One passage brought the tears from Mark, with an-other Rual caused himself to weep, with a third he reduced all to tears, with the sole exception of Tristan, who had no laments for anything he had heard, so sharply did the words assail him. But whatever heart-rending things good Rual told the court about the lovers Rivalin and Blancheflor, those moving events were as noth-ing beside the devotion which Rual had shown for Rivalin through the deeds that he had done after Rivalin had died, as you have heard in detail. In the eyes of the court this was the most steadfast love a vassal ever bore his lord and lady.

When this account was finished, Mark asked his guest: 'Is what you say a fact, my lord?'

Good Rual handed him a ring. 'Now, Sire,' he said, 'bear in mind what I have told you!'

Good, upright, Mark took it and examined it. His old grief re-
turned with new force. 'Alas,' he said, 'sweet sister, it was I who
gave you this ring, which my father gave me on his deathbed. I can
well believe this account. Tristan, come here and kiss me! I swear
that, if you and I live, I will be your father by right of succession.
May God have mercy on the souls of Blancheflor your mother and
of your father Rivalin, and may it please Him to give them life ever-
lasting together! Since it has come about that, after all, my sweet
sister has left me you, I shall, if God grant, be happy for the rest of
my life! Now, dear friend,' he went on to his guest, 'tell me, who
are you and what is your name?'

'Rual, Sire.'

'Rual?'

'Yes.'

Mark now recollected in a flash – for in the past he had heard
much about him – how wise and honourable and loyal he was.
'Rual li Foitenant?' he asked.

'Yes, Sire, that is my name.'

And good Mark got up and kissed Rual, and received him
with the noble honours that were due to him. Their lordships fol-
lowed hard and kissed him one by one, they put their arms round
him in embrace upon embrace, and courteously saluted him. 'Wel-
come, noble Rual, you marvel among men!'

Rual was welcome there. And indeed the king took him by the
hand, led him away, and seated him beside him most affectionately
while they resumed their conversation and talked about various
matters touching both Tristan and Blancheflor, and the whole
history of what Rivalin and Morgan had inflicted on one another
and how it had all ended. Very soon the conversation turned to
where the King described to Rual by what subterfuge Tristan had
come there and how he had told a tale of his father being a
merchant.

Rual looked at Tristan. 'My friend,' he said, 'for love of you I
have long, intently, and unremittingly followed my merchant's
trade in poverty this far. But it has all ended well, for which I shall
always render thanks to God!'

'It is clear to me,' said Tristan, 'that what has been said here is
not of a sort to make me happy in a hurry. I have arrived, so I learn,

at a strange state of affairs. I hear my father say that my father was killed long ago. With this he renounces me, and I must go minus a father – I who had come to have two! O father, and belief that I had a father, how you have both been taken from me! Through that same man of whom I averred "my father has come!" I lose two fathers – himself and the one I never saw!'

'How now, friend Tristan,' said the Marshal, 'do not say that, it is all without foundation. As a result of my coming you are in fact of more consequence than you thought you were, and have received lasting honour from it. And, despite what you say, you have two fathers as before, my lord here, and myself. He is your father, as I am. So take my advice and henceforth be the peer of kings! Say no more, and do just this. Ask my lord your uncle to knight you here and help you to get back home, since you can see to your own affairs yourself now. Your lordships, I call on you all to declare that his Majesty should be pleased to do so!'

'It is very fitting,' they all replied together. 'Tristan has the strength and is a well-grown man.'

'Nephew Tristan,' asked the King, 'tell me, how do you feel about it? Would you like me to do so?'

'My dear lord and sovereign, I will tell you how I feel. If I were wealthy enough to be a knight as I should wish to be, and in such style that I need not blush at the name, nor it at me, and the glory of chivalry would not be debased in me, then I would love to be a knight, to train my idle youth and wean it to worldly honours. For chivalry, they say, must make its start in childhood or else it will never grow hardy. That I have so seldom exercised my untried youth in pursuit of renown and distinction was very wrong, and I reproach myself for it bitterly. But I have long been aware that ease and knightly renown go ill with one another in every way. I myself have read that honour desires the body's pain, and comfort is death to honour, if, in one's youth, one indulges it too long. Indeed let me tell you this: had I known a year or more ago that my fortunes were as high as I have been informed here, I would not have gone unknighted till now. However, since it remained undone, it is right that I should now make up for it; for I stand fairly well so far as strength and aspirations go. May God help me to property, so that I achieve my aspirations!'

'Nephew,' said Mark, 'consider for yourself how you would act if you were a king, and lord over all Cornwall. Here sits your father Rual, who loves you with all his heart: let him help and advise you so that your fortunes prosper to your liking. My dear nephew Tristan, have no truck with poverty: Parmenie is yours and will remain your free possession while your father Rual and I remain alive. Furthermore, I will give you this revenue: my land, my people, and all that I have shall be at your disposal! If you aspire to high distinction and your ambitions are such as I have heard you say, do not spare what is mine merely because it is so. Let Cornwall be your domain, my crown your tributary! If you wish to be honoured in the world, see that you have lordly aspirations – I will give you the wherewithal. Now you have the wealth of an emperor – do not fall below your own level! If you have any regard for yourself and if you have the spirit that you ought to have and such as you have avowed to me, you will not need long to convince me. Look, if I find you have a lordly temper, you will now and ever after find me a horn of plenty: Tintagel shall always be your abundant treasure-house. If you outstrip me in munificence and I fail to follow with the means, may all that I own in Cornwall fall to ruin!'

This was greeted with a profusion of bows. Those who were present at this declaration acknowledged it one and all. They paid him a tribute of honour and praise with joyful acclamation. 'King Mark,' they all said, 'you speak as a man of breeding should. Your words well grace the Crown. May your tongue, your heart, and your hand rule over this realm for ever!'

The trusty Marshal Sir Rual and Tristan his young lord went to work on the sumptuous scale which the King had laid down for them. But now I shall wrangle about their two generations, the father's and the son's; for, since age and youth never agree in one particular quality – youth rating wealth lightly, and age pursuing it – someone will ask us how they could arrange between them for each to have his way and assert his peculiar rights; so that Rual should observe measure in wealth, and Tristan sate ambition with abundance? I will sift this without prevarication: the affection which Rual and Tristan bore each other was so evenly matched that neither suggested good or bad other than as his fellow wished it, or could have done with propriety. Rual was a judge of character and made allowance for Tristan in consideration of his youth; while Tristan deferred to Rual's proven worth. This carried them on with one accord to a single goal; the one wished the same as the other. In this way they two were one in mind and purpose, and thus, in this one quality, age and youth agreed. Here pride stooped to good sense. And so they preserved between them, Tristan his right to high spirits, Rual moderation in wealth; with the result that neither denied his own nature.

7

TRISTAN'S INVESTITURE AND
GOTTFRIED'S LITERARY
EXCURSUS

🦋

AND so Rual and Tristan set about their arrangements, judiciously
and according to their means. During the next month they acquired
clothes and equipment for thirty knights whom noble Tristan
wished to sponsor as comrades.

Now if anyone asks me about their clothes, how splendid they
were and they were got together, I am quickly resolved to tell
him just as my source affirms it. If I tell him otherwise let him refute
me and give a better account himself.

Their clothes were made by four different Splendours of which
each was happy in its duty: the first was Mettle, the second Affluence,
the third Discretion who cut these two to match, the fourth was
Courtesy who stitched for them all. All four worked skilfully in
their several ways: Mettle desired, Affluence granted, Discretion
set to work and cut, Courtesy stitched all their clothes and other of
their adornments – pennants and housings and other chivalric gear
pertaining to a knight. In whatever confers the hall-mark of chivalry
on man and beast, their caparisons were all very splendid, so much
so that each would have graced a king had he been knighted in it.

Now that the companions have been equipped with splendour
as described, how shall I begin my account and prepare their noble
captain, Tristan, for his knighting so that people will gladly listen
and the account be in keeping with my story? I do not know what
to say on the subject that would please and content you and also
adorn my tale. For during my lifetime and earlier, poets have spoken
with such eloquence of worldly pomp and magnificent trappings
that had I at my command twelve times my inspiration, and were
it possible for me to carry twelve tongues in my one mouth, of which

each could speak as I can, I should not know how to begin to describe magnificence so well that it had not been done better before. Knightly pomp, I declare, has been so variously portrayed and has been so overdone that I can say nothing about it that would give pleasure to anyone.

Ah, how Hartmann of Aue* dyes and adorns his tales through and through with words and sense, both outside and within! How eloquently he establishes his story's meaning! How clear and transparent his crystal words both are and ever must remain! Gently they approach and fawn on a man, and captivate right minds. Those who esteem fine language with due sympathy and judgement will allow the man of Aue his garland and his laurels.

But if some friend of the hare, high-skipping and far-browsing, seeks out Poetry's heath with dicing terms, and, lacking our general assent, aspires to the laurel wreath, let him leave us to adhere to our opinion that we too must have a hand in the choosing. For we who help to gather the flowers with which that twig of honour is entwined to make a floral wreath, we wish to know *why* he asks. Since if anyone lays claim to it, let him leap up and add his flowers! We shall judge from them if they grace it so well that we should take it from the poet of Aue and confer the laurel on him. But since none has yet come who has a better claim, then in God's name let us leave it as it is! We shall not allow anyone to wear it whose words are not well-laved, and his diction smooth and even; so that if someone approaches at the trot, well-poised and with an upright seat, he will not stumble there. Inventors of wild tales, hired hunters after stories, who cheat with chains and dupe dull minds, who turn rubbish into gold for children and from magic boxes pour pearls of dust! – these give us shade with a bare staff, not with the green leaves and twigs and boughs of May. Their shade never soothes a stranger's eyes. To speak the truth, no pleasurable emotion comes from it, there is nothing in it to delight the heart. Their poetry is not such that a noble heart can laugh with it. Those same story-hunters have to send commentaries with their tales: one cannot understand them as

* For the poets to whom Gottfried refers in this literary excursus see Appendix 4. The 'friend of the hare', whom he declines to name, is Wolfram von Eschenbach.

one hears and sees them. But we for our part have not the leisure to seek the gloss in books of the black art.

But there are other 'dyers'.* Bligger of Steinach's words are delightful. Ladies worked them with silk and gold on their embroidery-frames – one could trim them with fringes from Byzantium! He has a magic gift of words. And I fancy his limpid invention was wondrously spun by the fairies and cleansed and refined in their well – for he is surely inspired by the fairies! Thus his tongue, which bears a harp,† has two utter felicities: words and inspiration. These two between them harp out their tales with rare excellence. See what marvels of verbal ingenuity this master of words traces meanwhile on his tapestry, how deftly he throws couplets like knives, or glues them together as if they had grown there. I even believe he has books and letters tied on for wings, for – if only you will look – his words ride the air like eagles!

Whom else can I single out? There are and have been many, inspired and eloquent. Heinrich of Veldeke had every poetic gift. How well he sang of love! How finely he trimmed his invention! I imagine he had his insight from Pegasus' spring, from which all wisdom comes. I have never seen Heinrich myself; but I hear the best (those who were masters in his day and since) voice their opinion and accord him the glory of having grafted the first slip on the tree of German poetry. From this have sprouted branches whence the blossoms came from which they drew the cunning of their masterly inventions. And now this skill has spread its boughs so far and has been so diversely trained that all who are now writing break blossoms and sprays to their hearts' content, in words and melodies.

'Nightingales'‡ there are many, but I shall not speak of them, since they do not belong to this company. Thus I shall say no more of them than what I must always say – they are adepts at their task and sing their sweet summer songs most excellently. Their voices are clear and pleasing, they raise our spirits and gladden our hearts within us. The world would be full of apathy and live as if on

---

* Narrative poets.

† The escutcheon of the Steinachs displayed the Harp.

‡ Lyric poets or *Minnesinger*, who composed both the words and airs of their songs.

sufferance but for this sweet bird-song, which time and again brings back to any who has loved, things both pleasant and good, and varied emotions that soothe a noble heart. When this sweet bird-song begins to tell us of its joy it awakens intimate feelings that give rise to tender thoughts.

'Oh, do tell us about the Nightingales!'

They all know their calling and can all express their pining so well in words and song. So who is to bear the banner, now that their lady marshal, the Nightingale of Hagenau, who bore the master-secret of all music sealed in her tongue, has fallen thus silent to the world? I often think of her – I mean her sweet and lovely music – and wonder where she acquired such a store and whence she received her wondrously flexible airs. I should think that Orpheus' tongue, which had power over all music, sounded through her mouth.

But since she is no longer with us, give us some advice! Let some kind man offer an opinion here. Who is to lead the charming bevy, who is to marshal this retinue? I think I shall find the one who must bear the banner! Their mistress is well able to do so, the Nightingale of Vogelweide! How she carols over the heath in her high clear voice! What marvels she performs! How deftly she sings in organum! How she varies her singing from one compass to another (in that mode, I mean, which has come down to us from Cithae-ron,* on whose slopes and in whose caves the Goddess of Love holds sway)! She is Mistress of the Chamber there at court – let her be their leader! She will marshal them admirably, she knows where to seek Love's melody. May she and her company sing with such success that they bring their sad love-plaints to a joyful consumma-tion, and may I live to see it!

Now I have discoursed long enough to an indulgent audience on the poetic achievement of these good people. Tristan is still un-equipped for his knighting, and I do not know how to equip him. My imagination shies away from it, so that alone and unhelped by inspiration, from which it has its office, my tongue does not know what to do. Yet I will tell you what is clogging my tongue and in-spiration. What has confused the pair of them is a thing that

* A confusion of the mountain with Aphrodite's island of Cythera.

troubles thousands. If one who is no great speaker is joined by an eloquent man, the things he was able to say die on his lips. I think this has happened to me. I see and have always seen so many eloquent men that there is nothing I can write that does not seem trivial against the present style of writing. People nowadays are so well spoken that I am bound to watch my words and see to it that they are such as I would have in other men's tales and would approve in another author.

Now I do not know how to begin. My tongue and native gifts are powerless to help me, the words I could have uttered have been snatched clean out of my mouth. I do not know what to do about it, unless it is just this – a thing, I swear, that I have never done before. Only now, with heart and hands, will I send my prayers and entreaties up to Helicon, to the ninefold throne whence the fountains pour from which flow the gifts of words and meaning. Its lord and the nine ladies, Apollo and the Camenae – nine sirens of the ears who, at their court, preside over those gifts and dispense their favours to people as they choose – they give their springs of inspiration to many so completely that they cannot with honour deny me just one tiny drop! And if I can obtain that drop, I shall maintain my position where it is fitting to do so with poetry. And however minute this single drop, it will restore to their old path my tongue and imagination, in respect of which I have strayed so far. It must pass my words through the glowing crucible of Camenian inspiration, and refine them for me there most wondrously and prepare them to perfection like Arabian gold! These same divine graces of true Helicon, the highest throne from which the words well out that echo through one's ear, that laugh into one's heart and make poetry as limpid as a gem most rare, may they deign to hear my voice and prayer, up there in their heavenly choirs, and just as I have implored them.

Now suppose that this has been done: that I have been granted all that I asked concerning words, and possess a full abundance; that I make my words agreeable to all ears, give shade to every heart with the green, green leaf of the lime, go with my verse so smoothly that at every step I sweep the way for it and do not leave in its path the slightest speck of dust that has not been removed, and my poetry walks altogether on gay flowers and clover: even then I shall scarcely turn my invention (slight as it is) to where so many have gone astray in pursuit of their quarry. Truly, I must avoid this. For if I applied my whole resource to the equipment of a knight as, Heaven knows, many a man has done, and were to tell you how Vulcan, the wise, the famous, the good artificer, set his own hands to the making of Tristan's sword, jambs, hauberk, and other pieces pertaining to a knight, in superb and masterly fashion; how he drew and cut out the image of him whose courage is boundless – the Boar – on his escutcheon; how he devised his helmet and in token of Love's torment raised the Fiery Dart upon it; how one by one he fashioned this and that to marvellous perfection and how my lady Cassandra, the wise Trojan woman, had used all her wit and art on arranging Tristan's clothes and preparing them for him with her best insight (her spirit, as I read, had been endowed by the gods in heaven with supernatural powers): what effect could all this have, other than when, further back, I was equipping Tristan's company for his investiture? Saving your disagreement, it is my opinion (and I am convinced of it) that if to these two aids – Mettle and Means – you add Discretion and Courtesy, the Four between them will serve as well as any others. Certainly Vulcan and Cassandra never equipped knights more splendidly than they.

Now, since these four Splendours are thus able to arrange a brilliant belting ceremony, let us entrust our friend Tristan to the four of them! Let them take him in hand and (since nothing better can be done) array the noble man for us in the same style and trappings as those in which his companions-in-arms have been accoutred so elegantly. And so let them lead Tristan to court and to the jousting-ring, in all his gear the replica of his companions, equally trim and fine – in the clothes, I mean, that were sewn by the hand of man; not in those that we are born with, which come from the wardrobe of the heart, which go by the name of 'Noblesse', which make a man light-hearted and dignify life and living: such clothes were not given to the companions in the same measure as the lord. For God knows, gay, aspiring Tristan wore clothes altogether his own, graced to a rare degree by ease and distinction of bearing. In fine manners and good qualities his cut was quite superior. Yet in the clothes that were sewn by human hands there was no difference, the noble captain wore the same as his comrades.

8

RETURN AND REVENGE

If any living man suffered constant woe with lasting good fortune, Tristan always did so, as I shall explain to you.

An ultimate limit had been set for Tristan in the twin spheres of success and misfortune; for in everything that he set his hand to he succeeded for the most part; yet his success was dogged by misfortune, little though the latter has in common with it. Thus these two opposites, constant success and abiding misfortune, were paired together in one man.

'Now in God's name, tell on! Tristan has just been knighted and achieved a brilliant success in matters of knightly honour – come tell us, what misfortune does he suffer with it?'

Heaven knows, there is one thing that has always harassed every heart, as it did his: that his father had been killed. This tormented his soul. Thus good and bad, success and disaster, pleasure and pain, were constant allies within one heart.

All are agreed that anger besets a young man more relentlessly than a mature one.

Over all Tristan's honours there brooded always the sorrow and hidden grief (of which none ever saw a sign in him) that arose because Rivalin was dead and Morgan alive. This sorrow beset him with care. Thus care-laden Tristan and his trusty counsellor the good Foitenant (whose name still speaks of loyalty)* at once got ready a fine barque with rich furnishings, of which the best imaginable were to hand there, and then appeared before Mark.

'My dear lord,' said Tristan, 'please give me leave to sail to Parmenie and, in accordance with your advice, see how our affairs

* 'Foitenant' – 'he who keeps faith'.

stand there regarding the land and the people, which (as you say) are mine.'

'Nephew,' answered the King, 'it shall be done, I will grant this request, sorely though I shall miss you. Sail home to Parmenie, you and your company. If you need more knights, take them at your pleasure, take horses, silver, gold, and whatever you will need, as you choose to need it! And whomever you receive as companions, treat them so bounteously and with such good comradeship that they will be glad to serve you and wait on you loyally. Dearest nephew, act and live by the advice of your father, trusty Rual here, who all this time has behaved so faithfully and honourably towards you. And if God grant that you set your affairs to rights with honour and advantage, then you must return – return again to me! I promise you one thing, and I shall do it – here is my hand on it – that I shall always share my land and my wealth with you equally. And if it is your fortune to survive me, then receive them all as your possession, since I intend for your sake to stay unmarried all my life. Nephew, you have clearly heard what I ask and what I have in mind. If you love me as I love you, if you bear me equal affection, let Heaven be witness, we shall spend our days happily together. With this I give you leave to go. May the Son of the Maid watch over you! Your affairs and your honour are now in your own hands – guard them well!'

Without further delay, Tristan and his friend Rual, together with their retinue, took ship from Cornwall back home to Parmenie.

If you would care to hear about the welcome of these lords, I will tell you, as I learned it, how well they were received.

The leader of them all, honest, trusty Rual, stepped ashore ahead of them. He laid his cap and mantle courteously aside and running up to Tristan all laughing, kissed him and said: 'My lord, welcome in God's name and in your country's name and mine! Look, sir, do you see this fair land beside the sea? – fortified cities, strong defences, and many a fine castle? I tell you your father Canel left it to you. If you are manly and watchful, nothing of what you see here will ever be lost to you – I shall be your surety for that!' With these words he turned with a happy and joyful heart and gladly received the knights, one after another, saluting and greeting them most de-

lightfully with his gracious words. Thereupon he led them up to
Canoel. He faithfully surrendered to Tristan those cities and castles
in the whole land which had been in his keeping since Canel's
time, together with his own, which had come down to him from
his forebears. Why continue? He had the rank and means, and
he supported his lord accordingly, like a man of rank and means,
and, with Tristan, all his followers. You never saw such kind-
hearted effort and pains as he went to, to please them all in every
way.

But what *have* I done? Oh where are my senses? I have made a
blunder! To have passed over the Marshal's good wife, the faultless
and constant lady Floraete – how unmannerly! But I will make
amends to the sweet woman. I know for sure that the courteous,
virtuous, good-tempered, most noble, and excellent lady will not
have received her guests with words alone. For whenever a word
passed her lips, good will had gone before it. Her heart rose up to
meet her guests as if it were borne on wings. Her words and her
feelings were in perfect harmony, and I know they overflowed most
amicably when she was receiving guests. Believe me, the joy which
the heart of good Floraete felt towards her lord and child – the boy
who is the hero of this story (her son Tristan, I mean) – I divine it
from the many virtues and accomplishments which, as I read, the
good lady possessed. And that there were not a few of them she
showed in the way best open to a woman, for she bestowed on her
child and his following all the honour and comfort that ever came
the way of knights.

After this, all the lords and magnates who ruled the cities and
castles were summoned from the whole land of Parmenie. When
they had assembled in Canoel, had seen and heard the truth about
Tristan as the tale tells us concerning him and as you yourselves
have heard, a thousand welcomes flew from the mouths of all. The
country began to awake from its long sorrow and entertain happy
thoughts to an astonishing degree. One by one they received their
fiefs from the hand of their lord Tristan, with their vassals and their
lands. They took the oath of fealty and became liege men. All this
while Tristan suffered the secret pain that was hidden in his heart,
of which Morgan was the cause. Day and night, it never left him.
Thus he took counsel with his kinsmen and vassals and declared

that he would hasten away to Brittany to receive his fief from his enemy's hands so that he could hold his father's territories with better title. He not only said but did so. He and his company left Parmenie well-equipped and prepared as men must be who are bent on a desperate venture.

When Tristan arrived in Brittany he chanced to hear a reliable report that Duke Morgan was out riding from forest to forest at the hunt. He accordingly told his knights quickly to make ready and wear their hauberks and other gear beneath their robes in such a way as would allow no link of mail to show outside their garments. Now this was given effect, it was done. And over his gear each man donned his travelling cloak, and mounted his horse thus accoutred. They told their train to ride back quietly and stop for nobody, then divided their knights into two contingents. The larger force was detailed to retire and cover the train as it went on its way. When this had been done, those who turned off with Tristan had among them some thirty knights, those of the return-party sixty or more.

It very soon happened that Tristan caught sight of some huntsmen and hounds, and he inquired of the former where the Duke might be. They told him promptly, and off he went at once in that direction. True enough, he soon found a crowd of Breton knights beside a woodland stream, for whom lodges and pavilions had been erected on the grass with a wealth of greenery and gay flowers set both around and within them. They had their hawks and hounds close at hand. They returned Tristan's greeting together with that of his party civilly and according to courtly custom, and in their turn told him straightway that their lord Morgan was riding in the forest but a short way off. Those from Parmenie quickly made for the spot and duly found Morgan and many Breton knights, waiting on their Castilians. As they trotted up to him Morgan received the foreigners, whose purpose was unknown to him, with the courtesy due to strangers. His countrymen did likewise – each hastened up with his greeting. When this bustle of greetings was over, Tristan addressed Morgan.

'Sir, I have come for my fief and ask you to invest me with it here and not deny me what I have a title to! That would be just and courteous.'

'Sir,' said Morgan, 'where do you come from and who are you?'

'I am of the House of Parmenie,' answered Tristan, 'and my father's name was Rivalin. I should be his heir, sir. My own name is Tristan.'

'You accost me with such idle tales, sir, they were as well unsaid as uttered! My mind is quickly made up. Were you entitled to have anything of me, your claim would soon be met: for nothing would disqualify you as a man fit for any distinction, wherever you sought it. But we all know – the country is full of the tale – how Blanche-flor ran away with your father, the honours that befell her, and how their love-affair ended.'

'Love-affair? What do you mean?'

'I will tell you no more now, for that is how the matter stands.'

'Sir,' rejoined Tristan, 'you have said enough to leave me in no doubt. You mean that I am a bastard, and so will have forfeited my fief and my claim?'

'Indeed, my dear young knight, that is how it strikes me and many others.'

'You speak slanderously,' said Tristan. 'I thought that when one man wronged another it was seemly and proper for him to observe sense and decency towards him, at least in his choice of language. Had you any sense or decency, in view of the wrong that you have done me, you would have spared me your remarks, which rouse fresh grief and resurrect old scores. After all, you killed my father! Yet you do not think me wronged enough but you must say that my mother who bore me, bore me out of wedlock! Almighty God! I know that so many nobles – I cannot name them here – have placed their hands in mine in token of their homage! Had they re-cognized the fault in me that you allege, not one of them would have done so! They know it for a fact that not long before his death my father Rivalin made my mother his lawful wife. If I must prove and attest this on your person, I swear I shall attest it to the full!'

'Away!' said Morgan. 'Devil take you! What good is your attestation? You may not draw sword on anyone who was ever made free of a court!'

'That we shall see!' said Tristan. He whipped out his sword and ran at him. With a downward sweep he struck through skull and brain, ending only at the tongue, then at once plunged the sword into his heart. Thus the truth of the proverb was evident which says that debts lie, yet do not rot.

Morgan's companions the gallant Bretons were unable to be of any use to him or come to his aid so quickly as to save him from destruction; yet they stood to their arms as best they might. Very soon there were a great number of them. Taken by surprise though they were, all attacked their enemies courageously. They paid no attention to tactics or defence, but pressed forward in a mass and forced them out into the open at the outskirts of the forest. Here there arose much shouting, weeping, and mourning, so that Morgan's death, amid varied lamentation, flew as if on wings. Up in the castles and over the country it told its tale of grief. Through that land there flew this one lament: 'Alas for our lord – he is dead! What will become of our country now? Now, you fine warriors, come this way from towns and fortresses and pay these strangers back for the wrong that they have done us!' And so they harried their enemies' rear with ceaseless attacks, and themselves met with a hot reception from the intruders at all times; for these returned to the attack repeatedly, at full squadron strength, and threw many to the ground and yet maintained their flight, withdrawing all the time to where they knew their main body to be. At last the intruders came up with their knights and made their quarters there on a well-defended hill, and here they passed the night.

During the night the home force grew so strong and compact that as soon as day was dawning they were pursuing their hated guests irresistibly for the second time, thrusting many down and breaking into their mass repeatedly with spear and sword. (Such did not last long, believe me! Swords and spears were very short-lived there. Many were used up when they charged into that squadron.) In return the little army defended itself so valiantly that heavy losses were inflicted when their ranks were broken into. The formations on both sides time and again suffered heavy losses, they received and inflicted cruel injury, involving many men. And so they continued with each other till the resistance of the inner force began to weaken, for their strength was declining, the others' gaining – they were improving day and night both in dispositions and in numbers, so that some time before nightfall they once more encompassed the intruders, this time in a watery fastness from which the latter fought back and so saved themselves overnight. Thus the one army was penned in and completely encircled by the other as if enclosed by a fence.

Now how did those anxious strangers, Tristan and his men, tackle the matter in hand? I will tell you how they fared, how their anxiety abated, how they got away and won a victory over their enemies.

Ever since Tristan, following his counsellor Rual's advice, had gone abroad to receive his fief and hasten back at once, Rual had been haunted by a suspicion of just how Tristan had fared, though he had not advised Morgan's downfall. He mustered a hundred knights and took the same path as Tristan had taken. In a very short time he arrived in Brittany and learned at once how things had gone. In accordance with local rumours he aimed his march at the Bretons' siege position and, as he and his men came in sight of the enemy, not one of them disgraced himself by being out of line, either at the rear or on the flanks. They sped on all together with flying pennants. There was a great shouting of war-cries in their ranks: 'Chevelier Parmenie! Parmenie chevelier!'* Pennant after pennant raced through the guy-ropes of the Bretons' tents chasing ruin and disaster, they thrust the Bretons through their own pavilions with deadly wounds. And now that the beseiged descried their country's pennants and heard their slogans called, they gave themselves more room and rode out into the open. Tristan launched a strong attack, and much harm was done to the Bretons. Grappling and felling, hacking and thrusting – this began to disrupt their formation on both flanks of the army. And what also broke their resistance was the great shouting the two parties sustained, of 'Chevelier Parmenie!' And so the resistance of the Bretons was at an end, they had no heart to return to the attack nor any fight left in them other than to sneak off unobserved and hurry and scurry towards castle and forest. The fighting grew very confused. Flight was their best defence and their surest salvation from death.

After this rout the knights of Parmenie dismounted and quickly set up camp. They ordered those of their countrymen who lay dead on the field to be buried. They had the wounded laid on litters and then turned for home. With this, Tristan's fief and separate territory had been conferred on him by his own hand. He was now both

* 'Knights of Parmenie!'

lord and vassal of one from whom his father had never acquired a thing.* Thus he set himself to rights and smoothed out his affairs: 'set to rights' regarding his property, 'smoothed out' in respect of his feelings. His wrong was now a right, his sad heart buoyant and even. He was now in uncontested possession of his father's entire legacy so that no one at that time laid claim to any of his property.

This achieved, Tristan turned his thoughts back to Cornwall again, as his uncle had bidden him when he left him. Yet, on the other hand, he could not detach his feelings from Rual, who in fatherly devotion had shown him so much kindness. His affections were firmly fixed both on Rual and on Mark. His whole mind was bound up with these two, and drawn in opposite directions.

Now some kind man might say: 'How will good Tristan go about it now, if he is to give each his due and recompense each as he ought?' Every one of you knows full well that Tristan must inevitably renounce one to be with the other. You tell us how it should go! If he returns to Cornwall he will lower the pride of Parmenie, and Rual, too, will be dashed in spirits and in all the good things that should gladden him. But if Tristan chooses to stay there, he refuses to seek higher honours and ignores Mark's advice into the bargain, on whom his whole honour depends. How can he act without harming himself? – 'In God's name he must return, he must have our sanction for that! – If he is to have a good and happy fate he must enrich himself in honours and mount in aspiration! He has every right to aspire to and seek out any honour. And if Fortune for her part grants them to him, she has the right to do so, since his whole mind runs that way.'

Tristan, clever youth, decided most ingeniously to share himself as equally between his two fathers as if he had been cut in half. He divided himself as neatly and equally as one divides an egg and gave to either man what he knew would go best with his circumstances. If none of you has ever heard of the division you can make of a whole man, I will tell you how it is done. Nobody doubts that two things go to make a man – his wealth and his person. These two breed noble sentiment and much honour in the world. But if any-one tries to part them, wealth turns to poverty, and the person of a

* Rivalin had despoiled Morgan in war but apparently not acquired a sovereign title to the fief for which he owed allegiance.

man, now denied its due, falls into disrepute, and he becomes but half a man, though physically entire; and the same goes for a woman. Man or woman, it is the way of the world that their persons and possessions, making common cause, should create their whole personality; and that, if these two things are divorced, nothing will come of either.

Tristan embarked on this course with a will and concluded the matter skilfully. He ordered handsome mounts to be procured, fine clothes, viands, and other stores, such as one has on festive occasions, and then he gave a great feast. To it he summoned and invited the great nobles in whom the power of that country was vested, and they did as friends do and came as they were bidden. Tristan was no less ready with his arrangements. Having asked for two of his father Rual's sons to be his heirs in further succession to Rual, he knighted the young men, and whatever he could contribute from his treasure towards their dignity and honour, he was as devotedly ready to give it as if they had been his own children. Now, when these two were knighted, twelve companions were knighted with them, of whom one was courtly Curvenal. Well-bred and courteously inclined as he was, Tristan took his brothers by the hand and led them away. His kinsmen and vassals and all who were of ripe judgement, whether from mother-wit or experience or both together, were invited and summoned to the court forthwith. Now, sir, all are assembled.

Tristan rose at once and addressed them. 'My lords one and all, whom I shall always be glad to serve in every way loyally and sincerely to the utmost of my power – my kinsmen and dear vassals, by whose grace I have what honour God has given me: with your help I have put straight all that I wished in my heart. Although God vouchsafed it to me, I know that it was accomplished through your skill and courage. What more can I say? In these few days you have shown me honour and kindness in so many ways that I do not doubt that the world must pass away before you would deny me a wish! Friends, vassals, and all who have come for love of me or out of the goodness of their hearts, do not be deeply offended by what I have to say: I proclaim to you all, as my father Rual here has witnessed it, that my uncle has made me co-regent and intends to stay unmarried in my favour so that I shall succeed him, and he desires me to attend him wherever he is or goes. Now I am resolved (and all my heart is set on it) to do as he wishes and return to him. My revenues and my Honour, which I derive from these lands, I will grant in fee to my father Rual. And if my fortunes in Cornwall should be other than fair, and whether I die or survive there, this shall be his hereditary fief. Now his sons are standing here, too, and with him other of his children; any subsequent heirs of his shall all have a title to the land. My vassals and household officers and my fiefs throughout the country I will keep in my possession all my years and days.'*

At this there was great distress and outcry among the assembled knighthood. They all lost heart. Their spirit, their faith were all gone. 'Ah, my lord,' they said among themselves, 'it would have been far better for us had we never seen you – then we should have been spared this grief with which you now afflict us! My lord, our hope and faith were so firmly pinned on you that, in you, we had something to live for. But alas, no! If you go away, the happy life we all might have had will be dead and buried. You have made our sorrows greater, not less, my lord. Our happiness had risen some-what, but now it has sunk again.'

I know this as sure as death, that however deep the grief of all the others and however great their sorrow at this news, although it was to Rual's advantage and he received great profit from it and much material honour, it wrung his heart more cruelly than theirs. Heaven knows, he never received a fief in such misery as the fief he accepted here.

Now that Rual and his sons had been enfeoffed and installed as heirs by the hand of their lord Tristan, he commended the land and its people to God, and left the country. With him went Curvenal, his tutor. Was Rual's grief and that of his other vassals, indeed of the whole population – was their sadness of heart for their dear lord a trifle, do you think? Believe me, I know. Parmenie was full of woe, and for good reason. The Marshal's wife, Floraete, who was possessed both of honour and loyalty, subjected herself to such tor-ments as a woman may fairly inflict on herself to whom God has vouchsafed a life well-suited to her honour as a woman.

* Tristan retains his sovereign title, but all else goes to Rual and his heirs in perpetuity.

9

MOROLD

WHAT fresh matters shall I now set in train? When landless Tristan arrived in Cornwall he heard a rumour which greatly displeased him; that mighty Morold had come from Ireland and was demanding tribute from both Cornwall and England under threat of armed combat. In the matter of the tribute things stood thus. As I read the history and as the authentic story says, the man who was king of Ireland was called Gurmun the Gay and he was a scion of the house of Africa, where his father was king. When the latter died, his country passed into the possession of Gurmun and Gurmun's brother, who was co-heir with him. But Gurmun was so ambitious and high-tempered that he disdained to share anything with anybody – his heart insisted that he should rule as monarch. And so he began to choose strong and steadfast men, the best that were known for desperate encounters, both knights and sergeants, whom he was able to attach to himself by his wealth or his charm; and he left all his land to his brother there and then.

Quickly forsaking those parts, Gurmun obtained leave and authority in writing of the mighty, illustrious Romans that he should have possession of all he could subdue, yet concede them some right and title to it. Nor did he delay any longer, but ranged over land and sea till he came to Ireland and conquered that country and compelled its people, despite themselves, to take him as lord and king; after which they came round to helping him to harry their neighbours at all times with battles and assaults. In the course of these events he subdued Cornwall and England, too. But Mark was a boy at the time and irresolute in war, as children are, and so lost his power and became tributary to Gurmun. It further helped Gurmun greatly and added to his power and prestige that he married Morold's sister. This led to his being much feared. Morold was a duke and would have liked to rule a country of his own, for he was very bold and possessed lands, much wealth, a good person, and a resolute spirit. He was Gurmun's champion.

Now I will tell you truly and precisely what tribute it was that was sent from Cornwall and England to Ireland. In the first year they sent them three hundred marks of bronze and no more; in the second silver; in the third gold. In the fourth year Morold the Strong arrived from Ireland armed both for battle and single combat. Barons and their peers were summoned before him from all over Cornwall and England, and in his presence they drew lots as to which should surrender to him such of their children as were capable of service and as handsome and acceptable in their appearance as courtly usage required. There were no girls, only boys. Of the latter there were to be thirty from either land, and there would be no way of opposing such degradation other than by single combat or by a battle between peoples. Now the Cornish and English were unable to obtain justice by means of open warfare since their lands had declined in strength. On the other hand Morold was so strong, pitiless, and harsh that scarcely anyone he looked in the face dared risk his life against him more than would a woman. And when the tribute had been sent back to Ireland and the fifth year had come round again, at the solstice they had always to send to Rome such envoys as were acceptable to her to learn what instructions her mighty Senate would dispatch to each subject land. For each year there was proclaimed to them how they were to dispense the laws and statutes of the land in the manner of the Romans, and how conduct their courts of justice. And indeed, they had to live in strict accordance with the directions they received in Rome. Thus every fifth year these two lands submitted their Presentation and statutory tribute to Rome, their noble mistress. Yet they did her this honour less as a due, either in law or religion, than by command of Gurmun.

Let us now return to the story. Tristan had heard all about this infamy in Cornwall; and the pact by which this tribute was levied was well known to him before. Yet, from the talk of the people, he heard every day of the country's shame and suffering wherever he rode past castles or towns. And when he returned once more to court at Tintagel, I tell you he witnessed such woeful scenes on the roads and in the streets that he was deeply angered. The news of Tristan's arrival quickly reached Mark and his court, and they were all glad of it – I mean as glad as their sorrowful state would allow; for the greatest lords of all Cornwall were, as you have heard, now assembled at court for their dishonour. The noble peers of the realm were resorting to drawing lots for the ruin of their sons! And it was thus that Tristan found them all, kneeling and at prayer, each man on his own, but openly and without shame, with streaming eyes, and in an agony of body and soul, as he begged the good God to shield his race and offspring.

Tristan went up to them while they were all at their prayers. How was he received? You are easily answered. To tell the truth, Tristan was not welcomed by a single soul of all the household, not even by Mark, as affectionately as he would have been had this annoyance left them free. But Tristan overlooked it and boldly went to where the lots were being apportioned and where Mark and Morold were seated. 'You lords, one and all,' he said, 'to name you all by one name, who hasten to draw lots and sell your noble blood, are you not ashamed of the disgrace you are bringing on this land? Brave as you always are in all things, every one of you, you ought by rights to make yourselves and your country honoured and respected, and advance its glory! But you have laid your freedom at the hands and feet of your enemy by means of this shameful tribute, and, as in the past, you give your noble sons into serfdom and bondage, who ought to be your joy, your delight, your very life! And yet you cannot show who is forcing you to do so, or what necessity compels it, but for a duel and one man! No other necessity is involved. Nevertheless, you cannot hit on one among you all who is willing to pit his life against a single man to try whether he shall fall or prevail. Now assuming that he falls, well then, a quick death and this long-lived tribulation are valued differently in Heaven and on earth. But if he wins and the unjust cause is overthrown, he will have honour in this world and God's regard in the next for ever. After all, fathers should give their lives for their children, since their lives are one and indivisible: this is to go with God. But it is utterly against God's commandments when a man yields the liberty of his sons up to serfdom, when he hands them over as bondsmen and himself lives on in freedom! If I may advise you on a course that would be fitting both in piety and in honour, my counsel is that you choose a man, wherever you can find him among the people of this country, who is fit for single combat and willing to leave it to fortune whether he survives or no. And all of you pray for him in God's name, above all, that the Holy Ghost grant him honour and a happy outcome, and that he fear not Morold's strength and stature overmuch. Let him place his trust in God, who has never yet deserted any man that had right on his side. Take counsel quickly, deliberate with speed how to avert this disgrace and save yourselves from but a single man! Dishonour your birth and good names no more!'

'Oh, sir!' they all replied, 'it is not like that with Morold – none can face him and live!'

'Enough of that!' said Tristan. 'For God's sake, consider who you are! By birth you are peers of all kings, and equals of all emperors, and you mean to barter away and disown your noble sons, who are just as noble as you, and turn them into bondsmen? If it is a fact that you cannot inspirit anyone so far that he dares to fight in God's name and in a just cause against that one man for the wrong suffered by you all and the plight of this land, and if you would be good enough to leave it to God and to me, then indeed, my lords, in God's name I will give my young life as a hostage to fortune and undertake the combat for you! God grant it turn out well for you and restore you to your rights. Moreover, if somehow I should fare otherwise than well in this battle, your case will not be harmed. If I fall in this duel it will neither avert nor bring on, reduce nor increase the distress of a single one of you. Matters will stand as before. But if it turns out happily, then indeed God willed it so and God alone will be thanked for it. For the man I shall face single-handed (as I am well aware) is one whose strength and spirit have long stood the test of warfare, whereas my powers are just developing and I am not so eligible for deeds of arms as our present need requires, except that I have two victory-bringing aids in battle – God and our just cause! They shall go into battle with me. I have a willing heart, too, and that is also good for duelling. So that, if these three help me, I feel sure that I shall not succumb to one man, however untried I may be in other respects.'

'My lord,' said all those knights, 'may the holy power of God that created all the world requite you for your help and inspiration, and for the dear hope which you have held out to us all. Let us tell you what it amounts to, sir. Our deliberations are of little avail. Had Fortune meant to favour us we need not have waited till now, such efforts have we made each time this question arose. We men of Cornwall have not debated our affliction on merely one occasion: many a discussion have we had, but never yet found one of us who would not sooner have made serfs of his sons than lose his own life fighting this devilish man.'

'How can you say so?' asked Tristan. 'All sorts of things do happen. Time out of number one has seen lawless arrogance humbled by puny strength, and it might easily happen again, if someone dared the deed.'

Now Morold was listening all this time and, seeing Tristan's boyish appearance, was annoyed that he had claimed the duel so insistently, and was secretly very angry with him.

But Tristan continued: 'My lords all, state your opinion! What in effect do you wish me to do?'

'Sir,' they all replied, 'if the hope that you have raised in us could ever be fulfilled, we would all wish the matter to go forward.'

'Is that your pleasure?' asked Tristan. 'Since it has been reserved all along for me, God willing, I will put it to the test whether he intends to favour you through me, and whether I myself am blessed with any luck.'

At this, Mark tried to wean Tristan from his purpose with all his skill, fancying that he need only ask him to renounce it for his sake, and he would do so. Not he! Tristan did nothing of the sort. He could be brought neither by commands nor by entreaties to do as Mark wished and abandon his purpose. On the contrary, he went to where Morold was sitting and continued with what he was saying.

'Tell me, sir, in God's name, what brings you here?'

'Why do you ask, my friend?' retorted Morold. 'You know very well what brings me here, and what it is that I have come for!'

'Listen to me, all you nobles – my lord the King and his vassals!' answered subtle Tristan. 'Lord Morold, you are right. I know it and admit it. Shameful though it is, it is a matter which none can ignore. Tribute has been sent to Ireland from here and from England now for many a day without sanction of law. This was achieved only after a long time, and under great duress and many acts of violence. These countries saw many of their towns and fortresses levelled; and their inhabitants, too, suffered such heavy and frequent losses that in the end they were overwhelmed by injustice, and the stout warriors who had managed to survive were forced to submit to dictation, since they feared for their lives and were unable to act otherwise than as circumstance allowed. Thus, as you can see today, great wrong has been done them ever since, and the time is long past when they should have repudiated their servitude by resort to war. For they have made great progress – the two lands have grown in population, both native and foreign, in the number of towns and fortresses and in material wealth and prestige. We must now be given back what has hitherto been lost to us. From now on our common salvation must depend on force! If we are ever to have better times we must clinch it by war and campaigning. So far as manpower goes, we are in good shape: both lands are stocked with people. The Irish must now give us back what all our lives they have robbed us of. We shall pay them a visit ourselves as soon as Heaven permits. Whatever they have of ours, big or small, if only you will do as I say and follow my advice, they will have to make it good again, down to the last trinket. Our humble bronze may even yet turn to ruddy gold! Many strange things have happened on earth that one was little prepared for. These barons' noble sons who have become serfs over there in Ireland may yet regain their freedom, however little they dream it. Please God to grant me that favour! For I desire in His name that it be given to me to plant my standard in Ireland with my own hand, together with these noblemen, and humble that nation and the very soil they tread!'

'Lord Tristan,' rejoined Morold, 'I think it would profit you if you were to concern yourself less with such matters, for whatever is said meanwhile will not make us yield what is ours by right.' Having said this he went and stood before Mark. 'King Mark,' he said, 'speak! You and all who are present here to discuss the matter of their sons with me, let me hear your opinions, tell me more of this matter. Is it your common will, and are your intentions such as your advocate Tristan has stated?'

'Yes, my lord. Whatever he says or does, that is our common policy, our will and our intention!'

'Then you are breaking your oath of allegiance, both to my lord and me, and all the terms that we agreed on!'

'By no means, my lord!' answered Tristan courteously. 'Your tongue is running away with you. It does not sound well to impugn a man's loyalty. Not one of them is breaking his oath of allegiance. A treaty was sworn between you some little time ago, and it will be upheld today: namely, that of their good will they were to send to Ireland every year from Cornwall and England the tribute that was there determined for them; or alternatively, that they were to defend themselves by single combat or with the forces of the land. If they are willing to meet you thus far and redeem their oath of allegiance by means of tribute or by battle, they will be dealing justly by you. My lord, consider this, take counsel with yourself and tell me which you prefer. Whichever of the two you consent to – single combat or war – you can count on us to give it you any time from now. For spear and sword must decide between you and us. Now make your choice and tell us. – We no longer like this tribute!'

'Lord Tristan,' Morold replied, 'my choice is easily made. I know precisely which of the two I want. There are not enough of my men here for me to ride to war in a proper state of defence. I sailed over here with a private force and arrived in this dual king-dom most peaceably, as I have done before. Little did I dream that matters would turn out thus! I did not foresee this happening with these noblemen. I imagined I would sail away with my just dues and with good will. But now you have offered me war, and I am unprepared.'

'My lord,' said Tristan, 'if it is war you want, return at once, sail home to your own country, summon your knights, assemble all your forces, and return, and then let us see what becomes of us. And if in fact you have not done so within these six months, watch out for us at home – we shall not fail to come! We have been told before now, you know, that violence must be met by violence, force by force. Since the land and its rights are to be humbled by war and noblemen made serfs, and this is to be deemed equitable, we put our trust in God that our humiliation will yet be visited on you!'

'By God, Lord Tristan,' said Morold, 'I well understand that your words would fill a man with dread who had never met such bragging and never heard such threats! But I trust I shall emerge unscathed. It is not the first time that I have met such bluster and impudence! But it is my belief that your power and ensign are no threat to make Gurmun fear for his realm. Furthermore, unless you mean to break your loyal oath to us, this arrogance will not go unchecked so far as Ireland. We shall decide now between the two of us on the duelling-ground with our own hands whether you or I am in the right!'

'With God's help I myself will prove it, and may He doom to death whichever of us two is in the wrong!' Tristan drew off his glove and offered it to Morold. 'Gentlemen,' he said, 'take note. My lord the King and all present, hear the terms in which I appoint this duel, lest I spoil my case: That neither my lord Morold here, nor he who sent him, nor any other man rightfully obtained tribute from Cornwall or from England! This much I will prove and verify with my own hand and confirm before God and the world on the person of his lordship here, who all along has been the author of the trouble and degradation that have come upon our two countries.'

At this many a noble tongue cried out to God with fervour, imploring Him to remember their sorrow and shame in his verdict, and free them from their bondage. But however dejected they all were on account of this combat, it failed to pierce Morold to the marrow – in fact he was quite unmoved by it. The seasoned warrior did not turn the challenge down; he proffered Tristan the gage of combat in return with a harsh mien and a disdainful countenance. This hazard was much to his liking and he counted on emerging from it in excellent shape.

Now that this had been confirmed in these terms, their lordships were excused combat till the third day. When this duly arrived the whole baronage assembled and such a crowd of commoners that the shore was covered with people. Morold went to arm himself.

I will not blunt or encumber my inner perception or the sharp vision of my poetic faculty with close scrutiny either of Morold's strength or of his armour, though he has often been reckoned one of the best for valour. The qualities which have been attributed to him are manifold – that he was renowned in every land for such courage, strength, and stature as make a perfect knight. Let this praise of him suffice. I know he was well able, then as ever, to do justice to his strength of body as the knightly code required, both in battle and single combat – he had achieved so much in the past.

Good King Mark was so deeply distressed by this duel that the timidest woman could not have suffered so much for a man. He was sure that Tristan would die and would gladly have gone on suffering the other hardship of the tribute, if only the duel could be waived. But things took their course: first, because of the tribute; second, because of the man.

Tristan, as yet untried in desperate encounters, armed himself in chain-mail without delay to the best of his ability. He encased his body and limbs neatly in one piece. Over this he laid a dazzling pair of jambs and a hauberk, noble pieces wrought with all the armourer's skill and industry. His friend and loyal servitor Mark buckled on two fine, strong spurs, with weeping heart. He fastened all the straps on his armour for him with his own hand. They then brought him a coat-of-arms whose seams and gatherings everywhere (so I heard) had been designed by fair hands with needles in embroidery frames most rarely, and had been even more marvellously executed! Oh what a story it would make to tell how charming and admirable he looked in it, when he had put it on! Only I do not wish to draw things out – this would grow too wordy if I were to exhaust each topic as it deserved. And you must accept this fact: the man graced his tabard and conferred more lustre on it than the tabard conferred on the man. However fine, however splendid that coat-of-arms, it was nothing like equal in worth to the man who had put it on.

Mark girded on a sword above it that proved the very life of him, thanks to which above all he escaped alive from Morold, and many times since then. It swept down so cleanly and lay on its path so pliantly that it whipped neither up nor down but sped straight down its track to its quarry. A helmet was sent for, which had the appearance of crystal: it was hard and gleaming, the finest and best that a knight ever took in his hands. Nor do I imagine that as good a one ever came to Cornwall. On it stood the Dart, foreteller of Love, which Love's effects in him proved a true prophet in days to come, however long the respite.

Mark placed the helmet on his head. 'Alas,' he cried, 'I will complain most bitterly to God that I ever set eyes on you, nephew! I will renounce all that makes a man happy, if I must suffer calamity in you!'

A shield was sent for, too, on which an accomplished hand had lavished all its industry. It had a silver sheen all over, to match it with the helmet and the chain-mail. It had been burnished again and again and embellished with a lustre like that of a new mirror! A Boar had been cut out over it most skilfully from coal-black sable. This weapon, too, his uncle hung round him, and it suited the splendid man and fitted his side as if it had been glued there, then and on all occasions.

And now that Tristan (excellent, agreeable young man!) had assumed the shield, these four pieces – helmet, hauberk, shield, and jambs – illumined each other so beautifully that if the armourer had designed all four to enhance each other with their beauty and be beautified in return, their splendour could never have been matched more evenly.

But what of the new marvel that was hidden within and beneath it, to the peril of his enemies? – was that of no account beside the rare masterpiece fashioned on the surface? I know it as true as daylight that however it was with the exterior, the subject within was designed and executed with greater artistry to make the pattern of a knight than all the outward embellishment. The work of art inside was most excellently contrived in form and conception. How the craftsman's art appeared in it! Tristan's breast, his arms and legs were lordly, splendid, well-formed, and noble. His casing of iron became him marvellously well.

Tristan's horse was held there by a squire – no finer mount was bred in Spain or anywhere. It was not sunken in any part, but deep and broad in the chest and quarters, strong in the flank, perfect in all its points. Its feet and legs met every formal canon: the hooves were rounded, the legs were straight, all four tall as a wild deer's. And it was of excellent line in that its build forward of the saddle and round the chest was just as it should be in the best type of war-horse. Over it lay a dazzling barding, bright and gleaming as sunlight, which matched the rest of the mail and was sufficiently long and ample to fall at even length just short of the horse's knees.

Now that Tristan was well and splendidly equipped for battle in accordance with the code of chivalry and the rules of judicial com-

bat, those who were judges of men and iron alike all agreed that iron
and man together had never made a fairer picture. But however fine
it was now, it was incomparably finer when he had mounted his
charger and taken up his lance – then it made a delightful picture,
then the knight was splendid both above and below the saddle! His
arms and shoulders had free play. He was adept at slipping into
a tight seat when saddles had to be climbed. His handsome legs
dangled at his horse's shoulders straight and clean as a wand. Man
and beast were so in keeping with one another, you might think they
had been born and had grown in one piece. Tristan's seat on horse-
back was firm, even, and distinguished. Moreover, however agree-
able Tristan was in outward appearance, his mind within was
so good and of such fine quality that a nobler soul and finer nature
were never encased in helmet.

Meanwhile a battle-ground had been appointed for the cham-
pions, an islet in the sea, yet near enough to the shore for the crowd
to see with ease what happened there. It was further agreed that apart
from these two men none should set foot on it till the battle was over.
And indeed this was well honoured. Accordingly, two pontoons
were sculled along for them, of which each could ship a man and a
horse in armour. The boats were waiting. Morold boarded one and,
taking the sweep, ferried himself across. Arriving at the island he
quickly beached the boat and made it fast. He mounted at once,
took hold of his spear, and wheeled and galloped his horse at full
tilt in grand style over the length and breadth of the island. The
charges he delivered with lowered lance within that battle-ground
were as light and sportive as if it were a game.

When Tristan had embarked in his craft and taken his gear –
that is, his horse and his lance – on board with him, he stationed
himself in the bows. 'Your Majesty,' he said, 'my lord Mark, do
not be over-anxious for me or for my safety. Let us leave it in God's
hands. Our fears are of no avail. What if we fared better than we are
led to believe? Our victory and good fortune would be due not to
skill in arms but to the power of God alone. Leave all your dreads
and fears, for I may yet emerge unscathed. As to me, this affair
weighs lightly on me. So let it be with you. Take heart! It will fall
out only as it must. But whatever turn my affairs should take, what-
ever the end in store for me, commend your land this day to Him on

whom I rely. May God himself go with me to the duelling-ground and restore justice to its own. God must either win or suffer defeat with me! May He watch over the issue!'

With these words he gave them the sign of the cross and, pushing off in his pontoon, left in God's name. Many lips now commended his life to God, many hands sent tender farewells after him.

When he had landed on the farther shore he set his craft adrift and quickly mounted his charger. Morold was there in an instant.

'Tell me,' asked Morold, 'what does this mean, what had you in mind when you set your boat adrift?'

'I did it for this reason. Here are two men and a boat. It is certain that unless both fall one of them will be killed, so that the victor's needs will be met by this one boat which brought you to the island.'

'Clearly there can be no turning back from this duel,' answered Morold. 'If you were to stop it even at this late hour and we parted company amicably on the understanding that my dues from these lands were confirmed to me, I would think you fortunate, for indeed I should be very sorry if it fell to me to kill you. No knight that I ever set eyes on has pleased me as much as you.'

'If peace is to be made between us the tribute must be abolished,' was Tristan's spirited answer.

'Take my word for it,' said the other, 'peace will not be made on those terms! We shall not make friends that way. The tribute must go with me!'

'Then we are wasting our time parleying. Since you say you are so sure to kill me, Morold, defend yourself, if you wish to live – there is no other way about it!'

Tristan threw his horse round, flattened the curve into a dead straight line, and galloped right ahead with lowered spear with all the zest of which his heart was capable. With thighs that beat like wings, with spurs and ankles, he took his horse by the flanks. Why should the other man dally, whose life was now at stake? He did as all men do whose minds are resolved on prowess. At his heart's bidding he, too, wheeled rapidly away and more rapidly back again, raising and lowering his lance. And now he came spurring along like one drawn by the Devil. Horse and rider, they came flying at Tristan swifter than a merlin, and Tristan was as eager for Morold. They flew along with equal dash and keenness so that they broke their spears, which shivered in their shields into a thousand pieces. Then swords were snatched from sides and they went at it hand to hand from the saddle. God himself would have joyed to see it!

Now I have heard everyone declare (and indeed it stands in the story) that this was single combat, and all are agreed that no more than two were involved. But now I shall show that it was a general engagement between two whole detachments, and though I never read this in the tale of Tristan, I shall nevertheless make it credible. As the true version has always said and says today, Morold had the strength of four, making a force of four men. Such was the one side. On the other it comprised: first God; second Right; the third was their vassal and servitor, loyal Tristan; the fourth was Willing Heart, who works wonders in extremities. From the first four and the second, though I am no marshal, I quickly form two detach, ments, otherwise eight men.

At first you thought this tale grotesque for saying that two com, panies on as many mounts should ever come to blows. But now you have learnt how in fact on either side four knights under one helmet – or a fighting strength of four – were met together here. These now proceeded to ride hard at each other to the attack. Thus one group – Morold, four men strong – fell upon Tristan like a thunderclap. This cursed limb of Satan struck at him so powerfully that his blows all but robbed him of strength and reason. Had his shield not stood him in good stead, under which he had learned to guard and pre, serve himself with skill, neither his helmet nor his hauberk nor any other piece would have served him, but Morold would have killed him through his chain,mail. Morold gave him no chance to look up, such a rain of blows did he deal him. And so Morold went on hacking at him till he mastered him with blows, and Tristan, hard put to it to meet them, thrust out his shield too far and held his guard too high, so that finally Morold struck him such an ugly blow through the thigh, plunging almost to the very life of him, that his flesh and bone were laid bare through hauberk and jambs, and the blood spurted out and fell in a cloud on that island.

'What now?' asked Morold. 'Will you own yourself beaten? You can see for yourself by this that you should never plead an un, just cause. The wrongness of your case is now clearly revealed. If you wish to live, think how it can be done, while you still have the time. For believe me, Tristan, your plight must irrevocably end in your death! Unless I alone avert it you will never be cured by man or woman – the sword that has wounded you is bated with deadly poison! No physician or medical skill can save you from this pass, save only my sister Isolde, Queen of Ireland. She is versed in herbs of many kinds, in the virtues of all plants, and in the art of medicine. She alone knows the secret, and no other in the world. If she does not heal you, you will be past all healing. If you will listen to me and admit your liability for tribute, I will get my sister the Queen herself to cure you. I will share all I have with you in friendship and deny you nothing you fancy.'

'I shall not abandon my oath and my honour either for you or your sister. I have brought here in my free hand the freedom of two countries, and back it shall go with me, else I must suffer greater harm for them, even death itself! Know that I am not driven to such straits by a single wound, so that all must stand or fall by it. We are still very far from having decided this duel. The tribute will end in your death or mine, there is no help for it!' With this, Tristan attacked him again.

Now some may well ask (and I myself ask it too): 'Where are God and Right now, Tristan's comrades-in-arms? Are they going to help him, I wonder? Their company has taken heavy punishment, yet they are slow to put in an appearance. If they do not come soon they will be too late: so let them come quickly! Here are two men riding against four, they are fighting for their lives, which are in jeopardy. If they can ever be saved, this must happen very soon!'

God and Right rode in with a just verdict to the salvation of their company and the destruction of their enemies. Only now were they ranged in equal numbers, four to four, so that troop rode against troop. When Tristan sensed the presence of his comrades his courage and mettle rose: his friends brought him strength and encouragement. He set spurs to his horse and came galloping along at such a pace that in his joyous onrush he thrust his horse's chest against his enemy with a mighty clash and so bowled him over, charger and all.

And when Morold had collected himself somewhat from his fall and was making for his horse, Tristan was already upon him and in a flash had struck his helmet a blow that sent it flying. At this, Morold took a run at him and struck off a foreleg of his horse above the knee clean through the barding, so that the beast sank on its haunches beneath him, while Morold was content to leap aside. Then, moving his shield on to his back as his seasoned instincts prompted him, the wily man groped down and retrieved his helmet. In the light of his experience he calculated that when he was back in the saddle he would don his helmet and attack Tristan again. And now that he had collected it, had run to his mount and come near enough to seize the bridle, thrust his left foot home into the stirrup and grasp the saddle with his hand – Tristan had overtaken him. He struck Morold across the pommel so that his sword and his right hand, mail and all, fell upon the sand. And as it fell, Tristan struck him another blow, high upon the coif, and the blow went home so deeply that, when Tristan jerked back his sword, the wrench left a fragment embedded in Morold's skull. (This, as it turned out later, drove Tristan to fear and desperation. It all but proved the death of him.)

When that doomed company, Morold, shorn of his strength and defences, went reeling, tottered, and collapsed, 'How now?' asked Tristan, 'as God help you, Morold, tell me, have you any idea what this means? It strikes me you are seriously wounded. You are in a bad way, I fancy. Whatever comes of my wound, you could do with some good medicaments! You will need all the physic Isolde your sister ever read of, if you intend to recover! By his infallible decree God, the just and true, has judged of your wrong and, through me as His instrument, restored justice to its own again. May He long continue to watch over me! This arrogance has been humbled!' He then strode up to Morold and taking his sword and laying it in both hands, struck off his enemy's head, together with the coif.

And so Tristan returned to the haven, where Morold's boat was waiting. He sat himself down in it and quickly made for the crowded beach. There beside the sea he heard great joy and lamentation: joy and lamentation as I shall explain to you. For those whose happiness depended on his victory, great joy and a blissful day had dawned. They clapped their hands, they praised God with their lips and, there and then, sang many hymns of triumph to Heaven. Yet for the foreign people, those cursed strangers who had been sent there from Ireland, the day had dawned with tragedy. There was as much of their keening as singing by the others. They wrung their hands in torment of their grief.

As these wretched foreigners, these keening Irishmen, were about to hasten aboard their ships in their sorrow, Tristan drew near and met them on the beach.

'Gentlemen,' said Tristan, 'go and collect the tribute which you see there on the island, take it home to your lord and tell him that my uncle, King Mark, and his two peoples send him this Present. And proclaim to him further that whenever it is his royal will and desire to send his messengers here for tribute of this kind, we shall not let them go empty-handed. We shall send them back to him with such honours as these, whatever it costs us to do so.'

During this whole parley Tristan hid his bloody wound from the foreigners beneath his shield, a ruse that saved his life in days to come; for they went back home without any of them observing it. They now quickly left him, crossed over to the island and, in lieu of their lord, found a man hewn to pieces. With him they sailed away.

When the Irish reached land they took up the wretched Present which had been sent by them – all three pieces, I mean. They laid them together so that nobody should lose any. They carried them before their master and faithfully repeated their message in the terms I have narrated. I assume and expect what I have a right to expect – that King Gurmun the Gay was far from gay and deeply vexed and had every reason to be so; for in this one man he had lost his heart, his courage, his hope, and his vigour, and a fighting-strength equal to that of many knights. The hoop of Fortune which held his fame aloft and which Morold had trundled unchallenged through all the adjacent lands, had now toppled over. But the grief of his sister the Queen, and her sorrow and lamentation, were much more vehement. She and her daughter Isolde tormented themselves in one way and another – you know in what a heart-rending fashion women behave when they are deeply afflicted. They looked on this dead man for the sole purpose of grief so that the sorrow in their hearts should swell the more. They kissed the head and the hands which had subjected countries and peoples, as I have related before.

They eyed his head-wound, closely and ruefully, from above and from below. And now the wise, discerning Queen espied the splinter that was embedded in it. She sent for a forceps, inserted it, and so removed the fragment. She and her daughter viewed it mournfully, and they took it together and laid it in a casket, where, in days to come, it brought Tristan into jeopardy.

So now Lord Morold is dead. If I were to make a long story of all their grief and lamentation what would be the use? Who could bewail all their sorrow? Morold was borne to his grave and buried like other men. Gurmun took it to heart and at once sent an edict through the Kingdom of Ireland that his men were to keep sharp watch for any living thing, male or female, coming there from Cornwall, and kill it! This decree was given such stern effect that no member of the Cornish race could repair there at any time without its costing him his life, whatever the ransom he offered, till many a mother's child, though guiltless, paid the penalty. And this was without cause, for Morold was justly slain. He had placed his trust not in God but in his own strength, and had always come to battle with violence and pride, in which he was laid low.

10

TANTRIS

Now I shall return to the story where I left it. When Tristan had landed without his horse and spear, groups of people on horseback and on foot pressed forward in their thousands to salute him. They received him joyfully. Never had the King and his country experienced so happy a day – so they said, and one may well believe them, for great honour had come to them from him. Single-handed, he had brought to an end the shame and suffering of them all. As to the wound which he bore, they expressed much sorrow over it and were deeply grieved by it. But imagining he would soon recover from this annoyance, they made light of it and escorted him straight to the palace. They unarmed him at once and saw to his comfort as he or some bystander directed. They summoned the best doctors to be had from town and country.

What, then? The doctors were summoned, they applied their whole command of the art of medicine to him. Where did it get them and what was the use of it? He was not a whit the better for it. Their whole assembled knowledge of medicine was of no advantage to him. The poison was such that they quite failed to draw it from the wound, till it suffused his whole body, which then assumed a hue so wretched that one scarcely recognized him. Moreover, the place where the blow had fallen took on a stench so fearsome that life became a burden to him and his body an offence. Further, his greatest grief the whole time was the realization that he was beginning to weigh upon those who, till now, had been his friends; and he understood more and more the meaning of Morold's words.

Tristan had often heard in days past how beautiful and accomplished Morold's sister Isolde was, for there was a saying about her that flew from mouth to mouth in all the adjacent lands where she was known:

> Wise Isolde, fair Isolde,
> She shines out like the Dawn!

Care-laden man that he was, Tristan was always pondering on this, and was convinced that, if he was ever to recover, it could only be by the skill of the woman who knew the secret – the subtle Queen! Yet how this was to come about he could not fathom. Nevertheless he began to reflect, since it was a matter of life or death, that there was little to choose between risking his life or dying, and this death-like extremity. He accordingly fixed his resolve on going to Ireland of all places (whatever fate God might hold in store for him) in order to be cured, if such were to be his lot. He sent for his uncle and told him his secret intention in detail, as friend to friend, and what he meant to do in the light of Morold's information. Mark liked it well and ill. Yet one should suffer loss as best one may when forced to do so; a man must choose the lesser of two evils – this is a useful maxim. Thus they agreed on everything together: how he was to effect his voyage; how they were to hush it up that he was bound for Ireland; how they should spread the rumour that he was in Salerno to be cured – and all went according to plan.

When this was resolved, Curvenal was summoned and they told him at once of their common will and purpose. Curvenal gave his approval and declared that he would accompany him, to live or die with him.

When evening came, a barque and a skiff were made ready for their voyage and a full stock of victuals and other ship's stores was laid in. Then, with many expressions of grief, poor Tristan was carried aboard in such great secrecy that, apart from those who had been sent to attend to it, few knew of this embarkation. He commended his retinue and his effects most earnestly to Mark, with the request that not a farthing of his property should be allowed to go astray till they had certain news of his fate. He sent for his harp – this he took aboard with him alone of his possessions. After these preparations Tristan and Curvenal put to sea and sailed away with only eight men, who had pledged their lives and sworn in the name of God to swerve not an inch from their commands.

When they had embarked and Mark was gazing after Tristan, I know for sure that he had little pleasure or ease – this parting pierced him to the heart and to the very marrow of his bones. (Only it turned out happily and pleasantly for them in the end.) And when the nobility heard under what hardship Tristan had sailed for

Salerno in order to be cured, his suffering could not have touched them more deeply had he been their own child. And since he had sustained this misfortune in their service, it moved them all the more.

Now, taxed to the utmost of his strength and resources, Tristan sailed on in the direction of Ireland, steered by the experienced hand of his master-mariner. When the ship drew near enough to Ireland for them to make out the land, Tristan told the helmsman to change his course for the capital city of Dublin, since he knew that the wise Queen had her residence there. He made good speed towards it, and when he had come near enough to recognize it clearly, 'Look, sir!' he cried to Tristan, 'I can see the city! What are your orders?'

'Let us ride at anchor,' answered Tristan, 'and spend the evening and part of the night here.'

They dropped anchor and remained there for the evening. In the course of the night Tristan gave orders to put towards the city, and when this had been done and they were near enough to have taken up their station half a mile from the town, he asked them for the very worst clothes in the barque. When they had dressed him in them, he ordered them to remove him from the barque without delay and place him in the skiff. He also told them to place his harp inside it and food enough to sustain him for three or four days. This was all soon done to his satisfaction. He then summoned Curvenal into his presence, together with the crew.

'Friend Curvenal,' said Tristan, 'take charge of this ship and these men, and always care for them well, for my sake. When you get back, reward them richly so that they will keep our secret faithfully and never tell anyone about it. Return home with speed. Greet my uncle for me and tell him that I am still alive and by the bounty of God may yet live on and be cured. He is not to be downcast because of me. And tell him truly that if I am destined to recover I shall return within a year. If my affairs should prosper, he will soon get to hear of it. Put it out at court and in the country that I succumbed to my malady and died on the way. Take very good care that the retainers whom I still have there do not disband. See that they wait for me till the time which I have named for you. But if luck has not come my way within one year from now, you may give me up for lost. Let God take care of my soul, and look to your own welfare. Take my attendants, sail back home to Parmenie, and settle down with my dear father Rual. Tell him from me that, as he loves me, he shall repay my love for him through you, and treat you well and handsomely, as is his wont. And further instruct him in this: let him grant me this one wish regarding those who have served me till now – that he thank and reward each man in proportion to his services. And now, dear people,' he concluded, 'with this I commend you to God. Sail on your course and leave me to drift. Now is the time for me to wait upon God's mercy. It is high time for you, too, to put to sea and save your lives – dawn is fast approaching.'

And so they drew away with much grief and lamenting and, shedding many a tear, left him adrift on the stormy sea. No parting ever pained them so. Every loyal man who has ever had a friend and knows how one must love him, will understand Curvenal's distress, believe me. But however sorry he was in his heart he nevertheless kept to his course. Tristan remained there alone, drifting to and fro, in misery and anguish, till the bright morning came.

When the Dubliners saw the pilotless skiff amid the waves they gave orders to hurry and inspect it. Messengers repaired there at once. And now that they were approaching and nevertheless failed to see anyone they heard the sweet strains of a harp float out to them, softly and to their hearts' delight, and, accompanying it, a man sing so enchantingly that they took it for a greeting most marvellous and rare, and were rooted to the spot as long as he harped and sang. But the pleasure they had from him was short-lived, since the sounds that he made for them with hands or lips did not come from the depths – his heart was not in his music. For it is of the nature of music that one cannot play for any length of time unless one is in the mood. Although it is a very common thing, what one plays superficially in a heartless and soulless way cannot really claim to be music. Except that Youth made Tristan entertain her with lips and hands by playing and singing for her, it was torment and hardship for the sufferer.

When he left off playing, the other boat hove to. They laid hold of his skiff and vied to be first to look inside.

When they set eyes on him and saw how wretched he looked and the condition he was in, it offended them that he could perform such marvels with his hands and lips, yet they greeted him as one well able to earn a welcome by singing and playing, and asked him to tell them what fate he had undergone.

'I will tell you,' answered Tristan. 'I was a court minstrel and was master of many accomplishments and courtly ways, such as talking and letting others talk, playing the lyre, fiddle, harp, and crowd, and jesting and joking. I was well versed in it all as such folk have to be. With this I acquired enough, till my wealth turned my head and I wanted more than my due. And so I took up trade, and this has proved my undoing. I found a rich merchant as partner, and, back at home in Spain, the two of us loaded a ship with whatever cargo we pleased and set our course for Britain. But out at sea a band of pirates attacked us in their ship and robbed us of everything, big and small, and murdered my partner and every living soul. That I alone survive with the wound which I have was thanks to my harp, from which all could see that I was a minstrel born and bred, as I myself assured them. And so with great difficulty I obtained this skiff from them and provisions enough to live on till now. In this way I have been drifting alone in great pain ever since, for well on forty days and nights, wherever the winds buffeted me and the wild waves bore me, now one way, now another. I have no idea where I am, and know even less where to go. Now, gentlemen, kindly help me to where there are people, that our Lord may reward you!'

'You shall reap the benefit of your sweet voice and playing at once, my friend,' answered the messengers. 'You shall not float helpless or hopeless any longer. Whatever it was brought you here, whether God or wind or water, we shall take you to where there are people!'

And they kept their word. They towed him, skiff and all, right into the city as he had asked them to do. They made his skiff fast to the shore and said: 'Look, Minstrel, open your eyes! Look at this castle and the fine city here at hand! Have you any idea now what place it is?'

'No, sir, I do not know what it is.'

'Then we shall tell you. You are in Dublin, in Ireland!'

'The lord be praised that I am with people again! For there must be someone among them who will be kind to me and give me some assistance.'

The messengers then made for the town and busily discussed his circumstances with every mark of astonishment. They reported that they had experienced an amazing thing in one you would never have suspected of it. They told the tale as it had happened – that while they were still at some distance they had heard the strains of a harp float over to them so sweet, and accompanied by a song so ravishing, that God himself would love to hear it in His heavenly choirs. They declared that it was a poor sufferer, a minstrel wounded to death. 'Go and look, you will see that he will die tomorrow or even today. Yet, through all his sufferings, he has so lively an air, you would not find a soul in any land so little concerned for such misfortune.'

The citizens made their way to the spot and gossiped with Tristan on various topics and asked him sundry questions. He repeated to each the same story as he had told the messengers. They then asked him to play for them on his harp, and he gave all his mind to meeting their request, for he did it very willingly. Whatever he could do by singing or playing to win their favour, this was his desire, to this did he put his mind and this did he accomplish. And when the poor minstrel performed so sweetly, harping and singing beyond his bodily strength, it moved them all to pity, and so they had the poor man carried from his skiff and asked a physician to take him into his house and in return for their money diligently attend to whatever might be good for him and afford him help and easement.

This was duly performed. And when the doctor had taken Tristan home and done all he could to the best of his skill to make him comfortable, it did him little good. The tale was on every tongue throughout the city of Dublin. One crowd came in as another went out, voicing their regret at his sufferings.

It happened meanwhile that a priest entered and saw how accomplished he was with his hands and voice, for he was himself a skilful and dextrous performer on every variety of stringed instrument, and master of many languages. He had devoted his life and talents to the cultured pursuits of the court. He was tutor to the Queen and a member of her suite, and had sharpened her mind since childhood with many a good precept and many a rare maxim which she had learnt under his tuition. He sedulously tutored her daughter, too, Isolde, the exquisite girl, of whom the whole world speaks and who is the heroine of this story. Isolde was her only child, and since the day when her daughter was able to learn any art with hand or voice, the Queen had devoted all her attention to her. The priest had her, too, in his charge, and was always teaching the girl her books, and how to play stringed instruments.

Seeing so many arts and acquirements at Tristan's command this priest was moved to deepest pity for his sufferings and, delaying there no longer, went to the Queen and told her that there was a minstrel in the town, a man racked with pain suffering a living death, and that no man born of woman was ever so rare in his art or of a more cheerful disposition. 'Ah, noble Queen,' he said, 'if only we could give thought to taking him somewhere, where you might decently come and hear the miracle of a dying man who can harp and sing so ravishingly, yet whose condition is past all help! For he will never be cured – the doctor of physic who has attended him till now has discontinued his treatment, having failed to serve him with his science.'

'Look,' said the Queen, 'I will tell the chamberlains that, if he can at all stand being handled and moved about, they are to bring him up to us, to see if anything can be done for him in his condition, or if anything will cure him.' This was duly done.

When the Queen had seen his terrible state to the full, and the colour of the wound, she diagnosed it as poison. 'Oh you poor minstrel,' she said at once, 'you have a poisoned wound!'

'Have I?' Tristan was quick to ask. 'I cannot tell what it is, since no treatment will help me or do me any good. I do not know what to do next, other than place myself in God's hands and live as long as I can. But if anyone takes pity on me, seeing my wretched state, may God reward him! I am in dire need of help, I suffer a living death!'

'Tell me, minstrel, what is your name?' asked that knowledgeable lady, addressing him again.

'My name is Tantris, ma'am.'

'Now, Tantris, believe me when I say that I am going to cure you for certain. Take heart and be of good cheer! I myself will be your doctor!'

'Thank you, gracious Queen! May your tongue flourish eternally, your heart never die, your wisdom live for ever to give succour to the helpless! May your name be praised on earth!'

'Tantris,' answered the Queen, 'if it is within your capacity (for no wonder you are so weak) I would like to hear you play your harp – they tell me you are an excellent performer.'

'No, do not say so, ma'am! No misfortune of mine shall prevent me from doing (and doing very well) anything you require.'

And so they sent for his harp, and the young Princess, too, was summoned. Lovely Isolde, Love's true signet, with which in days to come his heart was sealed and locked from all the world save her alone, Isolde also repaired there and attended closely to Tristan as he sat and played his harp. And indeed, now that he had hopes that his misfortunes were over, he was playing better than he had ever played before, for he played to them not as a lifeless man, he went to work with animation, like one in the best of spirits. He regaled them so well with his singing and playing that in that brief space he won the favour of them all, with the result that his fortunes prospered.

During the whole time that he was playing, there and elsewhere, his vile wound exhaled such an odour that none could remain with him for as much as an hour.

'Tantris,' said the Queen, 'if you should ever happen to reach a point where this stench has left you and people can abide your company, let me commend this girl, Isolde, to your care. She studies hard at her books and music and, allowing for the time she has been at it, is tolerably well versed in them. And if you have any knowledge or accomplishments beyond her tutor's or mine, pray instruct her in them. In return, as a reward, I will restore your life and body to you in perfect health and looks. I can give or refuse: both are in my power!'

'If matters stand thus that I can recover in this way,' said the sick minstrel, 'and be cured through my music, God willing, I shall be cured! Good Queen, since your thoughts for your young daughter are as you say, I am sure that I shall be healed. The extent of my reading encourages me to believe that I shall deserve your good will through her. Moreover, I know it to be true of me that no man of my years plays such a variety of noble stringed instruments. Whatever you please to ask me shall be done, so far as lies in my power!'

Thereupon they appointed a small room for him and furnished him daily with all the attentions and comforts that he himself prescribed. Only now did he reap the benefit of his prudence in the pontoon, when he had slung his shield over his side and hidden his wound from the foreign Irish folk, as they were leaving Cornwall. It accordingly remained unknown to them, and they had no idea that he was wounded. For, had they heard of his being wounded in any way, knowing as they did what wounds Morold dealt with the sword which he always took to battle with him, Tristan would not have fared as he did. But the foresight he had shown helped him to save his skin. From this one may see and know how it may often happen that a man who is prudent and circumspect can reap the profit of his foresight. The well-versed Queen bent all her thought and intelligence to the task of healing a man to lay hold of whose life she would dearly have given her own, and her good name into the bargain. She hated him more than she loved her own self. Yet whatever she could devise for his well-being, ease, and advantage, she set her mind to it and busied herself about it day and night! But there was nothing strange in this, for she failed to recognize her enemy. Had she known on whom she was lavishing her care and whom she was helping from death's door, if there is anything worse than death, I assure you she would have given it him far more gladly than life. As it was, she knew nothing but good, and good will was all that she bore him.

Now if I were to speak at length and deliver you a long discourse on my lady's skill as a physician, on the marvellous efficacy of her medicines and how she treated her patient, what good would it do and what would be the point of it? A seemly word sounds better in noble ears than one from the druggist's box. To the best of my contrivance I shall refrain from uttering any word in your hearing that could displease your ears or offend your hearts. I will say less on all topics rather than make the tale harsh and unpleasant for you with language not of the court. With regard to my lady's medical skill and the recovery of her patient, I will tell you briefly that within twenty days she helped him so far that people suffered him everywhere, and none who desired his company held aloof because of his wound.

From this time on the young Princess was constantly under his tuition, and he devoted much time and energy to her. One by one he laid before her for her consideration the best things that he knew, both in book-learning and the playing of instruments, which I shall not name in detail, so that she could make her own choice for study as it suited her.

Here is what fair Isolde did. She quickly mastered the pick of his attainments and diligently pursued whatever she took up. The tuition she had already received stood her in very good stead. She had previously acquired a number of refinements and polite accomplishments that called for hands or voice – the lovely girl spoke the language of Dublin, and French and Latin, and she played the fiddle excellently in the Welsh style. Whenever they played, her fingers touched the lyre most deftly and struck notes from the harp with power. She managed her ascents and cadences with dexterity. Moreover, this girl so blessed with gifts sang well and sweetly. She profited from the accomplishments which she had already acquired, and her tutor, the minstrel, much improved her.

Together with all this instruction Tantris engaged her in a pursuit to which we give the name of Bienséance, the art that teaches good manners, with which all young ladies should busy themselves. The delightful study of Bienséance is a good and wholesome thing. Its teaching is in harmony with God and the world. In its precepts it bids us please both, and it is given to all noble hearts as a nurse, for them to seek in her doctrine their life and their sustenance. For unless Bienséance teach them, they will neither prosper nor win esteem. This was the chief pursuit of the young Princess, she often refreshed her mind with it and so grew to be courteous, serene, and charming in her ways. Thus the enchanting girl was brought on so much both in her studies and deportment in these six months that the whole land talked of her felicity. Her father the king, too, took great pleasure in it, and her mother was delighted.

Now it often happened when Gurmun was in pleasurable mood or knights from other parts were at court before the throne, that Isolde was summoned to her father in the Palace to while away the time for him and many others with all the polite attainments and pretty ways she knew. Any pleasure she gave her father was pleasure to them all. Were they rich or poor, she was a rapturous feast for their eyes and delight to their ears and hearts – without and within their breasts their pleasure was one and undivided! Sweet and exquisite Isolde, she sang, she wrote, and she read for them, and what was joy to all was recreation for her. She fiddled her 'estampie',* her

* A dance played on instruments, often without vocal accompaniment.

lays, and her strange tunes in the French style, about Sanze* and St Denis (than which nothing could be rarer), and knew an extraordinary number. She struck her lyre or her harp on either side most excellently with hands as white as ermine. Ladies' hands never struck strings more sweetly in Lud or Thamise than hers did here – sweet, lovely Isolde! She sang her 'pastourelle', her 'rotruenge' and 'rondeau', 'chanson', 'refloit', and 'folate'† well, and well, and all too well. For thanks to her, many hearts grew full of longing; because of her, all manner of thoughts and ideas presented themselves. No end of things came to mind, which, as you know, happens when you see such a marvel of beauty and grace as was given to Isolde.

To whom can I compare the lovely girl, so blessed by fortune, if not to the Sirens, who with their lodestone draw the ships towards them? Thus, I imagine, did Isolde attract many thoughts and hearts that deemed themselves safe from love's disquietude. And indeed these two – anchorless ships and stray thoughts – provide a good comparison. They are both so seldom on a straight course, lie so often in unsure havens, pitching and tossing and heaving to and fro. Just so, in the very same way, do aimless desire and random love-longing drift like an anchorless ship. This charming young princess, discreet and courteous Isolde, drew thoughts from the hearts that enshrined them as the lodestone draws in ships to the sound of the Sirens' song. She sang openly and secretly, in through ears and eyes to where many a heart was stirred. The song which she sang openly in this and other places was her own sweet singing and soft sounding of strings that echoed for all to hear through the kingdom of the ears deep down into the heart. But her secret song was her wondrous beauty that stole with its rapturous music hidden and unseen through the windows of the eyes into many noble hearts and smoothed on the magic which took thoughts prisoner suddenly, and, taking them, fettered them with desire!

Thus, with Tristan for tutor, lovely Isolde had much improved herself. Her disposition was charming, her manners and bearing good. She had mastered some fine instruments and many skilled accomplishments. Of love-songs she could make both the words and

* Possibly Sandde, the saintly father of St David of Wales.

† The *rotruenge* was a rollicking popular dance-form, with refrain; *folate* remains unexplained.

the airs and polish them beautifully. She was able to read and write.

Meanwhile Tristan was well and fully healed so that his skin and his colour began to clear again. He was in continual fear lest he should be recognized by some courtier or other native, and he was always turning over in his mind some polite way of obtaining his dismissal and so escaping from his cares: for it was clear to him that the Queen and the Princess would be most loth to let him go. He reflected nevertheless that his life was exposed all the time to great uncertainty. He went to the Queen and turned an elegant speech, as was his custom everywhere.

'May God make good to you in the Everlasting Kingdom,' he said, kneeling before her, 'the favour, comfort, and help which you have extended to me. You have treated me so perfectly that I pray God will always repay you. I myself shall seek to deserve it until my dying day wherever I can advance your good name, poor man though I am. Good Queen, by your kind leave I will sail home. My affairs have reached a point where I can stay no longer.'

The lady laughed at him. 'Your wheedling will not help you,' she said. 'I shall not give you leave to go. I tell you, you will not get away within a year!'

'Oh, no, noble Queen, consider the nature of holy wedlock and of the love that joins two hearts! I have a wife at home who is as dear to me as life, and I am sure she assumes beyond all doubt that I am dead and gone. And this do I fear and dread: if she were given to another, my life and solace would be gone, and with it all the joy on which I pin my hopes, and I should never be happy again.'

'Upon my word, Tantris,' said the discerning woman, 'the necessity you plead is binding. No well-intentioned person should ever divide such partnership. May God be gracious to you, man and wife. Reluctant though I am to do without you, I shall do so in God's name. I will assuredly let you go and shall remain your well-wisher and friend. My daughter Isolde and I will give you two marks of red gold for your journey and upkeep – accept them from Isolde!'

The poor exile joined his hands both in body and in spirit in token of thanks to each of the royal ladies, the mother and the girl. 'May you both be thanked and honoured in God's name,' he said. And delaying no longer he sailed away to England, and from England straight back home again to Cornwall.

11

THE WOOING EXPEDITION

When his uncle Mark and the people heard that Tristan had returned in full health, they rejoiced with all their hearts throughout the kingdom. His friend the King asked him how he had fared, and Tristan told him his story in all detail as precisely as he could. They were all amazed, and in the course of his narrative joked and laughed a good deal about his voyage to Ireland and how well he had been healed by her who was his enemy, and about all his doings among the Irish. They declared that they had never heard of any exploit like it.

Now when all the hearty laughter about his voyage and cure had subsided, they pressed him with questions about the maid Isolde.

'Isolde,' said Tristan, 'is a girl so lovely that all that the world has ever said of beauty is nothing beside hers. Radiant Isolde is a girl of such charm, both in person and in manner, that none was born, nor ever will be, so enchanting and exquisite. Dazzling, radiant Isolde, she shines like gold of Araby! I have abandoned the idea I had gained from reading books, which praise Aurora's daughter and her glorious offspring Helen, namely, that the beauty of all women was laid up in her one flower. Isolde has rid me of this notion! Never again shall I believe that the sun comes from Mycene. Perfect beauty never shone forth over Greece – here is where it dawns! Let all men in their thoughts gaze only at Ireland, let their eyes take pleasure there and see how the new Sun following on its Dawn, Isolde after Isolde, shines across from Dublin into every heart! This dazzling, enchanting maiden sheds a lustre on every land! All that people say and discuss in praise of woman is nothing compared with this. Whoever looks Isolde in the eyes feels his heart and soul refined like gold in the white-hot flame; his life becomes a joy to live. Other women are neither eclipsed nor diminished by Isolde in the way many claim for their ladies. Her beauty makes others beautiful, she adorns and sets a crown upon woman and womankind. None needs to be abashed because of her.'

When Tristan had finished telling what he knew of his lady, the enchanting maid of Ireland, the hearts of those who were listening and taking it all in were refreshed by his words as blossoms by the May-dew – it gave them all a fillip.

Tristan resumed his old life, with a joyful heart. A second life had been given him, he was a man newborn. Only now did he begin to live. He was merry and gay again, and the King and his court were willing to do his pleasure – till cursed meddlesomeness, damned envy, that seldom if ever sleeps, began to stir among them and cloud the minds and behaviour of many lords, with the result that they begrudged him the honour and distinction which the court and people accorded him. They began to run him down and hint that he was a sorcerer. His past deeds – how he had slain their enemy Morold, how his affair had passed off in Ireland – had been done by recourse to witchcraft, so they began to declare to one another. 'Look,' they all said, 'consider this, and tell us how he could ever live in face of mighty Morold? How did he manage to deceive his mortal enemy, the clever Queen, into caring for him so well that in the end she healed him with her own hands? Listen, is it not a mystery how this trickster manages to pull the wool over people's eyes and succeeds in all his enterprises?'

Thereafter Mark's councillors adopted a policy of importuning him morning and evening with urgent advice to take a wife from whom he could get an heir, either a son or a daughter.

'Heaven has given us a good heir,' answered Mark, 'God help us by keeping him alive! While Tristan lives, know it once for all: there will never be a Queen and lady here at court!'

At this their malice only mounted, the envy they bore Tristan increased more than ever and began to break out in many of them with such virulence that they could not hide it from him any longer, and adopted such an attitude towards him and such language, time and again, that he went in fear of his life and was in constant anxiety that sometime, somehow, they would conspire to murder him. He begged his uncle Mark in God's name to give thought to his fears and the danger he was in, and fulfil the barons' wishes; he did not know when his end might come.

'Say no more, nephew Tristan,' said his faithful uncle, 'I wish for no heir but you. Nor shall you go in fear of your life. I will give you sure protection. Now in Heaven's name, how can the malice and envy of that faction harm you? A worthy man is bound to suffer malice and envy: a man grows in worth so long as he is envied. The pair of them, worth and envy, are like mother and child; worth bears fruit in envy all the time. Who earns more malice than your lucky man? That fortune is poor and feeble which never knows any malice. Live in the constant endeavour to be free of people's spite for but a single day – you will never succeed in escaping it! But if you wish to be spared the malice of villains, sing their tune and be a villain with them – they will not hate you then. Whatever other people do, Tristan, aim always at loftiness of spirit. Weigh what is to your honour and advantage from all angles in advance, and urge on me no more what may well turn out to your detriment. Whatever is said on this subject, I shall follow neither them nor you!'

'Sire, with your permission I will leave the court, I am no match for them. I have not a hope, living in the midst of such enmity. I would rather always be landless than rule the whole earth in such fear!'

When Mark saw how serious he was, he stopped him and said: 'Nephew, however much I should like to prove my steadfast love towards you, you will not let me do so. Whatever comes of this, I shall not be to blame. But I am ready to do whatever meets your wishes. Tell me, what do you wish me to do?'

'Summon your court councillors who have put you up to this, and sound the mind of each. Ask what course they would think it well for you to take and spy out their intentions, so that the affair can be settled satisfactorily.'

No time was lost in summoning them all. And with Tristan's death as their sole aim they resolved at once that if a marriage could be brought about, lovely Isolde would be a fitting wife for Mark in birth, breeding, and person; and they confirmed this as their counsel. They then had audience of the King. One who was apt in such matters voiced through his one mouth the joint will and purpose of them all. 'Sire,' he said, 'this is our considered opinion. As is well known to our neighbours and those of the Irish, fair

Isolde of Ireland is a maiden on whom the spirit of womanly perfection has showered all possible blessings, as indeed you yourself have often heard concerning her that she is Fortune's darling and perfect in life and limb. If you can get her for your wife and we for our lady, no greater good on earth could ever come our way so far as a woman is concerned!'

'Explain, my lord,' answered the King. 'Granted that I wished to have her, how could it ever come about? For you must bear in mind how matters have stood between us and the Irish for a long time now. That whole nation hates us! Gurmun is deeply incensed with me, and with good reason – I feel the same towards him. Who could effect such great amity between us?'

'Sire,' they all replied, 'it often happens that there is mischief between two countries; but then let the two sides seek and find a remedy and make peace, together with their children. Hostilities often give way to friendship. If you bear this in mind you may yet live to see the day when Ireland is yours. The King and Queen have Isolde as their sole heir, she is their only child: Ireland goes with these three.'

'Tristan has made me think of her a great deal,' answered Mark. 'She has been much in my thoughts since he praised her to me. As a result of such reveries, I, too, forgetful of all others, have become so obsessed with her that, if I cannot have her, I will marry no other, I swear by God and my life!' He swore this oath not because his feelings were inclined that way more than any other, but as a subterfuge, never dreaming it would ever come to pass.

But the royal councillors replied: 'If you arrange for my lord Tristan here, who is acquainted with that court, to conduct your embassy, it will all be concluded and settled. He is prudent and discerning, and lucky in all his works: he will accomplish it successfully. He has an excellent knowledge of their language. He completes every task he is set.'

'This is wicked advice that you give,' answered Mark. 'You are far too intent on harming Tristan and getting him into difficulties. Has he not died for you and your heirs once already? – and you wish to make an end of him for the second time! No, you lords of Cornwall, you must go there yourselves. Do not come plotting against Tristan any more!'

'But, Sire,' interposed Tristan, 'there is nothing wrong in what they have said. It would be very fitting for me to undertake more boldly and readily than another man anything that you fancied, and indeed it is right that I should do so. I am the very man for it, Sire. I assure you none will do it better. Only, command them all to come with me themselves, there and back again, to maintain your honour and interests.'

'No, you shall not fall into the hands of the Irish a second time, now that God has brought you back to us!'

'I insist, Sire. Whether the barons live or die, I shall have to share their fate. I shall make them see for themselves whether it will be my fault, if this land should remain without an heir. Tell them to make ready. I will steer and pilot the ship with my own hands to the blessed land of Ireland, back to Dublin and the sunshine that gladdens many hearts! Who knows if we shall not win the beauty? Your Majesty, if lovely Isolde were yours and we all dead as a result, little harm would be done!'

When Mark's councillors saw which way the wind was blowing, they were more downcast than ever in their lives. But it was fixed and irremediable. Tristan told the King's secretary to pick from the household twenty dependable knights, those most fit for battle; he himself recruited sixty mercenaries, both native and foreign; and from among the councillors he took twenty barons without pay, making exactly a hundred companions. These were Tristan's complement, and with them he crossed the sea. He took such store of clothes, provisions, and other cargo that no ship with as many people was ever so well furnished for its voyage.

One reads in the old Tale of Tristan* that a swallow flew from Cornwall to Ireland and there took a lady's hair with which to build its nest – I have no idea how the bird knew that the hair was there – and brought it back over the sea. Did ever a swallow nest at such inconvenience that, despite the abundance in its own country, it went ranging overseas into strange lands in search of nesting materials? I swear the tale grows fantastic, the story is talking nonsense here! It is absurd, too, for anyone to say that Tristan, with a company, sailed the seas at random and failed to attend to how long

* The Archetype or one of its descendants, such as Eilhart's version, which, however, has two swallows.

he was sailing or where he was bound for, nor even knew whom he was seeking! –What old score was he settling with the book, who had this written and recited? The whole lot of them, the King, who dispatched his parliament, and his envoys (had they gone on a mission in this style) would have been dolts and fools.

Tristan and his company were under way and sailing on their course. But some – I mean the barons, those twenty comrades and councillors of Cornwall – were very uneasy. During this time they were in great trepidation, for they all feared in their hearts – and said as much aloud – that they would die. They cursed the hour in which this expedition over the sea to Ireland was ever thought of. They could suggest no plan how to save themselves. They considered one thing and another, yet failed to find any course of action worthy of the name. Nor was this surprising. For, whichever way one looked at it, their choice lay between two things: they had to save their lives either by a ruse or a gamble. But resource was in short supply there, and none of them dreamt of adventure – those barons were lacking in both subtlety and courage. Yet some few of them said: 'This man is very clever and versatile. If God is kind to us, and if Tristan will only curb his blind foolhardiness, of which he has more than his share, we shall come out of this alive with him. Heedless of what the next day brings, he does not care what he does. He would not give a crust either for us or for his own life. Yet our best hopes are tied to his fortunes. His resourcefulness must teach us how to save ourselves.'

When they had reached Ireland and made their landfall at Wexford (where, as they had heard, the King was sojourning), Tristan gave orders to anchor just out of bowshot from the harbour. His barons begged him in God's name to tell them his plans for winning the lady – their very lives depended on it! They thought it would be wise if he told them his intentions.

'Enough of this,' answered Tristan. 'Take care that none of you shows himself to these people. You all lie low inside. Crew and servants only are to ask for news on the gangplank from the loading-port. None of you is to appear. Keep quiet, and go along in with you! Knowing the language, I shall stand outside myself. People will soon be coming to confront us with hostile messages from the townsmen. I must lie to them for all I am worth today. Keep hidden below deck; for, if they get wind of you, we shall have a fight on our hands and the whole country on top of us. While I am away tomorrow – since I mean to ride out very early to try my fortunes, success or no success – let Curvenal stand out on the gangway near the port with others who know the language. And bear this one thing in mind: if I stay away for three or four days do not wait any longer, but escape back over the sea and save your lives! Then I alone shall have paid with my life to win the woman, and you can choose a wife for your lord wherever you please! This is what I think you should do.'

The Royal Marshal of Ireland, who had power and authority over the whole town and harbour, came spurring down towards them, armed and ready for battle with a great troop, both of citizens and their emissaries, as they had been commanded from court and as this tale narrates above (as you will see if you turn back). Their orders were to seize whoever put to shore till it was clearly established whether he was a native of Mark's country. These torturers, these cursed murderers, who had done many an innocent man to death to please their master, came marching down to the harbour with bows and cross-bows and other arms, like a regular band of brigands. Shipmaster Tristan donned a travelling-cloak, the better to disguise himself, and had a goblet fetched for him of beaten gold marvellously wrought in the English style. He then stepped into a skiff, with Curvenal following after, made for the harbour and saluted and bowed across to the citizens with all the charm he could muster. But, ignoring his greeting, a crowd of them ran up to his skiff, while many others shouted from the foreshore 'Put to land! Put to land!'

Tristan promptly put her into port. 'Gentlemen,' he said, 'tell me, why do you come like this? What do you mean by such behaviour? You all look very grim. I do not know what to expect. Do me this honour, in God's name. If there is any one among you in this harbour in a position of authority, let him give me a hearing!'

'There is!' said the Marshal. 'Here I am! You will find my looks and treatment grim in as much as I shall stop at nothing to find out what you have come for, down to the last detail!'

'I assure you, sir,' answered Tristan, 'that I am entirely at your disposal. If someone would call for silence and let me have my say, I would ask him to see to it that I am heard in a seemly fashion and as the honour of this country requires.' At this he was granted a hearing.

'Sir,' said Tristan, 'our station, birth, and country are such as I shall tell you. We are people who live by gain, and we need not be ashamed of it. In fact, I and my company are merchants, and we hail from Normandy, where out wives and children are. We travel from country to country chaffering in various goods, here, there, and everywhere, and earn enough to keep ourselves. We put to sea, I and two other merchants, less than a month ago. The three of us were in convoy, bound for Ireland, and it is now just on a week that, early one morning, a wind drove us far away from here, as winds often do, and broke up our company of three by parting me from the others. Nor do I know what has become of them, only God keep them, dead or alive! During these eight days I have been buffeted about most cruelly on many a foul course. And yesterday, at noon, when the gale had spent itself, I recognized the hills and the landscape. I turned and anchored at once and lay there till today. This morning, as soon as it was growing light, I followed on my course all along here to Wexford. But here things are worse than there! My life still seems to be in danger, though I hoped to have found safety, for I know the town and have been here with merch⁄ants from time to time and so hoped all the more to find good treat⁄ment and security. But I have sailed into a gale with a vengeance! – though God may yet preserve me. Since I find no safe anchorage here among these people I will put to sea again where I shall be a match for anyone and give battle enough in flight! But if you care to treat me with honour and courtesy, I shall be happy to make you a gift such as my present means allow in return for a brief stay, on the understanding that you protect me and my property in this har⁄bour, till I have tried whether I shall be lucky enough to discover my compatriots. If you mean to let me stay, then see to it that I receive protection – God knows who these people are, closing in so fast in their little boats! If you do not, I shall row back to my men and snap my fingers at the lot of you!'

The Marshal hereupon ordered them all to put back to land, and promptly asked the stranger: 'What will you give the King, if I guarantee your life and goods in this country?'

'I will give him a mark of red gold a day, my lord, however I scrape it together,' answered the foreigner. 'And if I can depend upon you, your reward shall be this goblet.'

'Indeed you can!' they all cried at once. 'He is the Marshal of the Realm!'

The Marshal accepted his gift, which he thought princely and handsome, and then bade him put into port. He ordered good treatment and security for Tristan and his effects. Princely and red they were – I mean their dues and emoluments! The King's gold, princely and red. The reward of his envoy, red and princely! They were both of them magnificent. This indeed played its part in gaining shelter and protection for Tristan.

12

THE DRAGON

TRISTAN has gained protection; but nobody yet knows what he intends to do. You shall be told, then you will not weary of the story.

The tale speaks of a serpent that was then living in that country. The cursed fiendish monster had burdened the land and the people with such an excess of harm that the King swore by his royal oath that he would give his daughter to whoever would make an end of it, provided he were a knight and of noble birth. This wide-spread report and the enchanting young woman between them caused the death of thousands who came to do battle and met their end there. The country was full of the tale, and Tristan knew all about it; for it was the one thing that had encouraged him to em-bark on his expedition, the thing he placed most reliance in, other than which he had no hope.

It is time, get going! Early next morning Tristan armed himself as a man must arm for a desperate encounter. He mounted a sturdy war-horse and told his followers to hand him a long stout spear, the strongest and best in the ship. He immediately rode on his path through fields and open country. He made many a twist and turn through the wilds, and, as the sun began to climb, he galloped to-wards the vale of Anferginan, where (as one reads in the French source) the dragon had his lair. There, far away in the distance, he saw four armed men galloping across country in full flight at a pace rather swifter than an amble! One of the four was Steward to the Queen and aspired to be the Princess's lover, entirely against her wishes. And whenever knights rode out to try their valour and fortune, the Steward also appeared, somewhere, sometime, for no other reason than that it should be said that he, too, had been seen where men rode out on adventure. But otherwise he did not partici-pate, for he never set eyes on the dragon without valorously turning tail.

Tristan saw very clearly from the fleeing band that the dragon must be near by, so he paced off in that direction and had not ridden long before he saw a thing that pained his eyes, the grisly dragon! Belching smoke, flames, and wind from its jaws like the Devil's brat it was, it turned and came straight at him. Tristan lowered his spear, set spur to his horse and, charging along at speed, thrust the spear through its gullet so that it tore through the jaw and barely stopped at the heart, while he and his charger met the serpent with such a shock that his horse died under him and he all but failed to get away. But the dragon attacked his horse again, scorching it and devouring it, till it had consumed everything as far as the saddle, monster that it was. But now the spear that had wounded it was galling it so much that it turned away from the horse and made for a rock-strewn region with Tristan its antagonist hot on its tracks. The doomed beast ranged on ahead so vehemently that it filled the forest with its dreadful voice and burned and uprooted many thickets in its rage. This it continued to do till it was overcome with pain and wedged itself in under a beetling cliff.

Tristan now drew his sword and thought to have found the beast defenceless – but no, the danger was now greater than before. Yet, however arduous it was, Tristan attacked the dragon for the second time and the dragon the man in return, reducing him to such straits that he thought his end had come. But for the fact that he never let it get to grips with him, it would soon have robbed him of the power either to strike or parry. And indeed, it was an army in itself. It took smoke and steam into battle with it and other equipment in the shape of fire and teeth, and also claws with which to strike, so sharp and finely set that they were keener than a razor. With these it chased him round and round from tree to bush, through many a dreadful twist and turn. He had to take cover and hang on as best he could, since to fight was not to his advantage. Yet he had ventured such resolute counter-attacks that the shield which he held was all but charred to cinders, for the dragon attacked him with fire, so that he barely eluded its onslaught.

This, however, did not last very long. The murderous reptile soon reached a point where it began to lose heart, and the spear so told on it that the beast sank to the ground and lay writhing there in agony. Tristan lost no time. He raced up at speed and plunged his sword into its heart beside the spear, all the way up to his hand. At this the dying monster let out a roar from its vile throat as grim and grisly as though heaven and earth were falling, and this death-cry echoed far over the countryside, and greatly startled Tristan.

When the dragon pitched over and Tristan saw that it was dead, with much effort he wrenched its jaws apart, cut off from the tongue in the cavity as much as he wanted with his sword, thrust the piece into his bosom, and let the jaws snap to. He then made for the wilds, meaning to lie up and rest somewhere during the day in order to recover his strength, and return at night to his compatriots. But the heat which he suffered, both from his own exertions and from the serpent, dragged at him and wearied him so much that from now on he was hard put to it to keep alive. But he espied the shimmer of a fair-sized pool into which a cool rill tumbled from a rock. Into this he dropped, all in armour as he was, and let himself sink to the bottom, leaving only his mouth above water. He lay there that day and night, for the cursed tongue which he had on him robbed him of his senses. The fumes alone that assailed him from it ravaged his strength and colour, so that he did not leave that place until the Princess delivered him.

The thoughts of the Steward, who, as I have said, aspired to be the knight and lover of the charming girl, were vastly inflated at the sound of the dragon's roar, which had echoed so grim and grisly over field and forest. In his heart he read it all as it had happened. 'It is dead for certain,' he thought, 'or, if not, so far gone that I can get the better of it with a little ingenuity.' He stole away from the other three, paced down a slope and then urged his mount at speed to where the cry had come from. When he came to Tristan's horse he paused and lingered by it for a long while, weighing things narrowly in his mind – this short advance already filled him with dread. Nevertheless after some time he plucked up some courage and rode in a mechanical, scared, half-hearted sort of way, following the traces of scorched grass and leaves. And soon, before he was aware of it, he suddenly came upon the dragon as it lay there, and he, the Steward, had such a mighty shock from having been so close and having ridden so near to it that he almost tumbled off! But he was quickly in command again. He threw his horse round so rapidly that he collapsed in a heap together with it!

F

When he had picked himself up (from the ground, I mean) he had no chance so much as to mount his charger, so terrified was he. This villainous Steward just left it and fled! But, since no one pursued him, he halted and crept back, reached down for his lance, took his horse by the reins, marched up to a fallen tree, mounted, and breathed again. He galloped a good way off and looked back at the dragon again to see what sort of an aspect it bore, and whether it was dead or alive. Seeing that it was dead, 'God willing, I am in luck!' he exclaimed. 'Here is treasure trove! It was a good and lucky hour that brought me here!' With this he lowered his spear, gave rein to his horse, hacked it with his spurs, put it to the gallop, and charged full tilt ahead, shouting as he did so:

> 'Schevalier damoysele,
> ma blunde Isot, ma bele!'*

He thrust at the dragon with such power that the strong ashen shaft slithered through his hand. That he battled no more was due entirely to this calculation: 'If the man who killed the dragon is alive,' he thought, 'what I have just been scheming will not help me at all.'

The Steward turned away and rode searching here and there in hope of finding the man somewhere so exhausted or badly wounded that there would be some sense in fighting him. Then he would do battle with him with the intention of killing him, and, having killed him, of burying him. But, finding no trace of him anywhere, he soon thought 'Enough of this! Whether he is dead or alive, if I am first on the scene, no one will turn me away. I have kinsmen and vassals so estimable and reputable that, were anyone to take up the case, he would be bound to lose it.' He now spurred back to his adversary, dismounted, and, resuming his battle just where he had stopped, fell to stabbing and hacking at his foe with his sword here, there, and everywhere till he had cut him to shreds in sundry places. He made many attempts on the neck and would dearly have liked to sever it, but it was so huge and hard that he wearied of his exertions. He broke his spear over a stump and rammed the front half into the dragon's gullet as if it were the outcome of a jousting blow. Then he mounted his Spaniard and cantered gaily into Wexford, where he ordered a waggon and four

---

* 'Knight of a young lady, my fair and lovely Isolde!'

to be driven from the town at speed to fetch the head, and told the news of his success to everyone and the danger and hardship he had suffered for it.

'There, you see, everybody!' he said. 'Just listen, contemplate the miracle of what a brave man and steadfast courage can do to win a charming woman! I shall never cease to marvel that I ever emerged alive from the peril I was in, and I am positive I would never have survived, had I been soft like the other – I do not know who he was, but some gentleman of fortune who had also ridden out for adventure, doomed man that he was, had come upon the dragon ahead of me and there met his end. God had forsaken him. They were gobbled up, the two of them, man and beast are dead and done for! Half of the horse still lies there chewed and scorched. But what do you gain if I make a long story of it? I have suffered greater trials over this than a man ever suffered for a woman.'

He assembled all his friends, returned to the serpent, and showed them his marvel. He asked them all to bear witness to the truth as they had seen it there, then carted off the head. He invited his kinsmen, summoned his vassals, and ran to the King to remind him of his promise. A day was appointed for this business at Wexford in the presence of the realm, and the realm was summoned at once – by which I mean the barons, who all made ready as the royal summons required of them.

The ladies at court were promptly told the news, and you never saw ladies suffer such torment and vexation as it occasioned in them all. As for lovely Isolde, the enchanting girl, her heart died within her. Never had she known so hateful a day.

'Oh, no, my pretty daughter. Gently,' her mother Isolde said to her, 'do not take it so to heart! For whether it was done by fair means or foul, we shall see that nothing comes of it! And indeed the Lord will protect us. Do not cry, my darling daughter, those bright eyes of yours must never grow red for such a petty vexation!'

'Oh, mother,' said the lovely girl, 'my lady, do not dishonour your most noble person! Before I comply, I will stab a knife through my heart! I shall take my own life before he has his pleasure of me! He shall never win a wife or lady in Isolde – unless he has me dead!'

'No, sweet daughter, have no fear of that. Whatever he or anybody says, it is of no importance at all. He shall never be your husband, not if all the world had sworn it!'

When night began to fall, the wise woman consulted her secret arts (in which she was marvellously skilled) on her daughter's distressful situation, with the result that she saw in a dream that these things had not happened as rumoured.

As soon as daylight came, the Queen called Isolde and said: 'Daughter, are you awake, darling?'

'Yes, my lady mother,' Isolde answered.

'Well, do not be afraid any more, I have some good news to tell you! He did not kill the dragon! It was killed by a stranger, whatever the adventure that brought him here. Up we get, we must hurry to the scene and investigate for ourselves! Brangane, get up quietly, tell Paranis to saddle for us quickly, and say that all four of us, I and my daughter, you and he, will have to ride out together. He is to bring our palfreys to our secret postern where the orchard overlooks the fields, as soon as ever he can!'

When this was all ready the company mounted and rode in the direction where the dragon was said to have been slain. Finding the horse, they closely examined its harness. They reflected that they had never seen such gear in Ireland, and they all came to the conclusion that whoever he was whom the horse had carried there, that man had slain the dragon. They at once rode on and came upon the serpent. Now this fellow fiend of Satan was so huge and monstrous that the radiant bevy turned pale as death in dread at the sight of him.

'Oh, how certain I am that the Steward never dared face him!' the mother told her daughter. 'We can say good-bye to our fears. And indeed, daughter Isolde, whether this man is dead or alive, something tells me that he is hidden hereabouts – I feel it in my bones! If you agree, let us leave this spot and go and search, in the hope that by the grace of God we may find the man somewhere and, with his aid, make an end of this fathomless suffering which weighs on us like death!'

They quickly made their plan. All four companions rode off in different directions; one woman looked here, another there. And now it happened, as it was meant to happen and as an equitable fate would have it, that Isolde, the young Princess, was the first to set eyes on her life and her death, her joy, her sorrow. A gleam coming from his helmet betrayed the presence of the stranger to her. Catching sight of the helmet she turned and called to her mother.

'Quick, madam, ride over this way! I can see something shining, Heaven knows what! It looks just like a helmet! I think I have made it out correctly.'

'Yes,' her mother answered. 'I think so, too. God means to favour us. I think we have found the man that we are looking for.' They at once called the other two to join them, and all four rode that way.

When they drew near to him and saw him lying thus, they all thought that he was dead.

'He is dead!' said both Isoldes. 'This dashes all our hopes! The Steward has foully murdered him and carried him into this bog.'

They all dismounted and in a moment they had dragged him out on to dry land. They quickly unlaced his helmet and then unbound his coif. Experienced Isolde examined him and saw that he was alive but that his life was hanging by a thread.

'He is alive!' she said. 'That is certain. Now quickly take off his armour! If I am lucky enough to find that he has no death-wound, the situation can be remedied!'

When these three beauties, this radiant company, began to unarm the poor stranger with their snow-white hands, they found the dragon's tongue.

'Oh look,' said the Queen, 'what is this, what can it be? Brangane, my noble niece, what do you think?'

'It looks to me like a tongue.'

'You are right, Brangane, I have an idea that it was the dragon's! Our luck has not gone to sleep. My darling daughter, my pretty Isolde, I know we are on the right track as sure as I shall die! The tongue, don't you see, has robbed him of strength and consciousness!' At this they finished unarming him and, failing to find either wounds or bruises, were all of them very glad.

The skilled woman then took some theriac and dosed him with it till he broke out into a sweat. 'This man is going to live,' she said. 'The fumes which attacked him from the tongue are yielding quickly. He will soon be talking and opening his eyes.' And this in fact soon happened.

Tristan did not lie there long before he opened his eyes and looked about him. Seeing this heavenly company beside and around him, he thought to himself: 'Ah, merciful Lord, Thou hast not forgotten me! Three lights encompass me, the rarest in all the world, joy and succour to many hearts, delight of many eyes – Isolde, the bright Sun; her mother Isolde, the glad Dawn; and noble Brangane, the fair Full Moon!' With such thoughts he rallied, and with difficulty managed to say 'Oh, who are you, and where am I?'

'Knight, can you speak? Then do!' answered Isolde. 'We shall help you in your need.'

'Yes, dear lady, heavenly woman. I have no idea how my body has grown so weak and my strength ebbed away so swiftly.'

Young Isolde looked at him closely: 'If I ever set eyes on him, this is Tantris the Minstrel!' she said.

'Upon my word, I think so too,' said the two others.

'Are you Tantris?' asked the wise woman.

'Madam, I am.'

'Tell us where you have come from,' the Queen continued, 'and by what means, and the business that brings you here?'

'Alas, most angelic lady, I have not the strength in my body to account for my doings in detail. In God's name, have me conveyed or carried somewhere where I can receive attention this coming day and night. Then, if I recover my strength, it will be only right that I should do and speak your pleasure.'

Accordingly, all four took hold of Tristan, lifted him on to a palfrey and conveyed him away between them. Then, returning by their postern, they smuggled him in so that none got wind of their expedition. Inside, they gave him attention and made arrangements for his comfort. Of the tongue, which I mentioned before, of his armour and other belongings not a bit was left behind, they had taken it all along with them, both the man and his equipment.

When the second day dawned, the wise Queen took him in hand. 'Now, Tantris,' she said. 'Tell me by the favours I have done you, now and once before (since I have twice saved your life and wish you well), and with the trust you place in your own wife – when did you come to Ireland? How did you kill the serpent?'

'Madam, I will tell you. Some few days past – three days ago today – I and some other merchants entered this harbour in our ship, whereupon a band of brigands came down from the town, why I do not know; and, had I not prevented it by making them a gift, they would have robbed us of our goods and of our lives into the bargain. Now, our condition is such that we have to make a home and dwell in foreign lands without knowing whom to trust, for we are subject to much molestation. Thus I am convinced that if I could somehow achieve it, it would be in my interest to receive official recognition in foreign lands. Recognition abroad will make a merchant wealthy. You see, my lady, that was what I had in mind. For I have long known the report of the serpent, and I killed it for no other reason than that I imagine I shall find protection more easily among the people here.'

'May peace, security, and protection attend you with lasting honour till your dying day!' said Isolde. 'Your coming here is most auspicious for both you and us. Now think of your dearest wish. It shall be granted, I shall see that you obtain it, from my lord and me.'

'Thank you, my lady. This being so, I will commend my ship and myself utterly to your honour. See to it that I never regret having confided my life and goods to you!'

'No, Tantris, it shall not happen. Have no further fear for your life or for your goods. Here is my hand to assure you on my honour that so long as I live no ill shall befall you in Ireland! Do not deny me a request, but give me some help in an affair that touches my honour and indeed my whole happiness!' And she told him (as I have narrated) of the arrogant pretensions of the Steward on the subject of this exploit – with what persistence he laid claim to Isolde and how he would drag a trumped-up case to the duelling-ground, were anyone to cross him and take the matter up.

'Dear lady,' said Tristan, 'do not let this distress you. With God's help you have twice restored my life to me and it is only right that it should be at your service in this combat, as in all other perils, as long as I have it unimpaired!'

'Heaven reward you, dear Tantris! I readily believe you. More-over, I assure you that if this scandal should ever materialize, both Isolde and I will suffer a living death!'

'No, no, ma'am, do not say another word! Now that I have your protection, have staked my life and goods on your honour and shall find security in it, dear lady, you must take heart! Help me back to my strength and I shall settle it all single-handed. And tell me, ma'am, do you know if the tongue which I had on me was left behind, or where someone may have put it?'

'No, indeed it was not left behind, for I have it here, together with all your belongings. We brought it all along with us, Isolde, my pretty daughter, and I.'

'This is just what we shall need,' said Tristan. 'Now, good Queen, say good-bye to your cares. Help me back to my vigour and it shall all be finally settled.'

The Queen and the Princess, the one like the other, then took him in hand, and whatever they knew would benefit and heal him, they made their chief concern.

Meanwhile his ship's company were in a wretched state. Many were so alarmed as to think that they were lost. Not one had hopes of surviving, since for two days they had had no news of Tristan. They had also heard the rumour which had spread concerning the dragon. There was a great deal of gossip of a knight having lost his life, only half of whose horse remained there. Thus Tristan's men were quick to think: 'Who could this be but Tristan? There is no doubt about it at all – if death had not hindered him, he would have been back by now.'

They thereupon took counsel and sent Curvenal out to view the horse. This he duly did. Curvenal rode out there, he found the horse and recognized it. But then he rode on farther, and at once came upon the dragon. Finding no trace of Tristan's things, either of his clothes or of his chain-mail, he was assailed by great perplexity. 'Oh,' he thought, 'are you dead or alive? Alas, alas, Isolde,' he said, 'alas that your fame and glory ever came to Cornwall! Was your noble beauty framed for such ruin of one of the finest natures ever confirmed by lance and whom you pleased too well?'

With these words Curvenal returned weeping and lamenting to the ship, and reported things as he had found them. His intelligence was displeasing to many, though not to all – this doleful news did not depress them all, for many bore it well. On the other hand, you could see that it brought great sorrow to many others, and these were in the majority. Thus their feelings and intentions were variously good and ill. At such cross purposes the divided ship fell to

gossiping and whispering. Far from regretting the doubts and un-
certainties that had been voiced to them, the twenty barons thought
that they might employ them to make good their escape, and they
all demanded with one voice that they should wait no longer for
him – the twenty only, I mean. They proposed sailing away in the
night. But others were for staying and for learning more of his fate.
Thus they were at odds among themselves. Some wished to be off,
others to remain. Finally it was left at this, that since it was not plain
or certain that he was dead, they would stay to make their inquiries
for at least two days – much to the barons' regret.

Meanwhile the day had come which Gurmun had fixed for the
assembly at Wexford to hear the case of his young daughter and the
Steward. Gurmun's noble neighbours, his kinsmen, and his vassals,
whom he had summoned to his diet to ask them for their counsel,
were all assembled there. He took them aside and sought their advice
in this affair most urgently, like a man nothing less than whose whole
honour was at stake. He also summoned his dear spouse, the Queen,
to counsel; and well might she be dear to him, since in her he had
two distinct blessings, the rarest a man can find in a beloved wife.
She was endowed so richly with both beauty and wisdom that she
might well be dear to him! And so the most favoured of Queens,
that wise and lovely woman, was present there as well. Her royal
friend and lover led her apart from the Council.

'Tell me,' asked Gurmun, 'what do you advise? This all weighs
on me like death!'

'Take heart,' answered Isolde, 'we shall come out of it well – I
have foiled the whole plot!'

'How, dearest lady? Tell me, too. Then I shall share your
pleasure!'

'Well, our Steward did not kill the dragon as he claims, and I
know the man who did! I shall prove it at the right moment. Put
aside your fears. Go back quickly to your Council. Declare to
them all that, as soon as you have heard and seen the Steward's
proof, you will gladly redeem the oath which you swore to the
realm. Tell them all to go with you, and take your seats in judge-
ment. Have no fear at all, but order the Steward to plead and say
whatever he wishes to say. When the right moment comes, Isolde
and I shall be there. If you command me, I will speak for you,

Isolde, and myself. Let that suffice for now – I will go and fetch my daughter. We shall come back at once.'

The Queen went to fetch her daughter, and the King returned to the Palace. He took his seat at the assize together with many barons, the peers of the realm. There was a splendid array of knights, a great throng, who were there not so much in honour of the King as because they were curious to know what would come of the great rumour. This is what they were all wondering.

When the two heavenly Isoldes entered the Palace together they greeted and welcomed their lordships each in turn, during which time a great deal was being thought, said, and uttered on the subject of their perfections, though more was said about the Steward's good luck than on the subject of the ladies. 'Now, look, all of you!' they said (and thought as much). 'Just consider. If this wretched Steward who has not a grace to his name is to have this angelic girl, the greatest good fortune will have smiled on him that he or any man could enjoy in a young woman!' Thus the two ladies went in to the King, who rose to receive them and then seated them affectionately beside him.

'Well, Steward,' said Gurmun, 'you speak. What is your request?'

'Most willingly, my lord King. What I request, Sire, is that you do not violate royal custom and wrong the realm in me. You said, and indeed promised on oath, if you will admit it, that you would give your daughter Isolde as a reward to whichever knight would slay the serpent unaided. This oath has ruined many men, but I took no notice of that because I loved the young woman and kept on risking my life more desperately than any man, till, at last, I succeeded in slaying the beast. If this is sufficient – here lies the head, look at it! I brought this evidence back with me. Now redeem your promise! A King's word should stand. A royal oath should be honoured!'

'Steward,' said the Queen, 'I tell you it is intolerable when a man who has done nothing to deserve it aspires to so rich a reward as my daughter Isolde!'

'How now, madam?' answered the Steward. 'You do wrong, why do you speak in this way? My lord, who will settle the case, is well able to speak for himself. Let him speak and answer me!'

'Madam,' rejoined the King, 'speak for yourself, for Isolde, and for me!'

'Thank you, Sire, I shall,' replied the Queen. 'Lord Steward, your love is honest and good, and you have such a valiant heart. You deserve a good wife, most assuredly. But I vow it is a scandal for a man to lay claim to so exalted a reward without deserving it. You have adorned yourself with an exploit of which you are totally innocent, so someone has whispered in my ear!'

'You are talking nonsense, madam. I have this visible proof!'

'You took a head away with you, as another might easily do – that is, if he thought he could win Isolde with it! But she is not to be won with such trifles.'

'I should think not!' said young Isolde. 'Such paltry hardships will never buy me!'

'Come, come, my young lady Princess!' rejoined the Steward, 'how can you speak so maliciously of my concerns, and of the many hardships I have borne for love of you?'

'A lot of good your loving me will do you!' said Isolde. 'I swear I was never your sweetheart, nor shall I ever be!'

'I understand,' retorted the other. 'I can see that you behave just like other women. You are all so constituted in body, nature, and feelings that you must think the bad good and the good bad. This vein is very strong in you. You are altogether contrary. To your mind, fools are all wise, wise men fools. The straight you make crooked, the crooked straight again. You have hitched all possible contradictions to your rope – you love that which hates you, you hate that which loves you! This bent is very strong in you. How enamoured you are of contradictions, of which one sees so many in you! The man who wants you, you do not want at all; but you do want the man who loathes you! Of all the games one can play on the board you are the most bewildering. The man who risks his life for a woman without security is out of his senses. But take my word for it, despite anything you or my lady says, this will be settled very differently, or some one will break his oath to me!'

'Steward!' countered the Queen, 'to those who can judge of discernment, your views are strong and discerning – they seem to have been formed in the intimacy of the boudoir. Moreover, you have expressed them as befits a ladies' man. You are too deeply versed in femininity, you are far too much advanced in it. It has robbed you of your manhood! You, too, are over-fond of contradictions, and in my opinion this suits you. You have hitched these same feminine traits very tightly to your rope – you love that which hates you, and that which you want does not want you! But this is our woman's game – why do you have any truck with it? In Heaven's name, you are a man – leave us our womanish ways! They won't do you any good. Keep to your manly disposition and love that which loves you, want that which wants you – this game offers excellent chances. You keep on telling us that you desire Isolde and that she will have none of you? Such is her nature: who can change it? She lets many things pass her by which she might easily have. Some men she detests who would like her very much – of whom you are the prime example! Here she takes after me: I never loved you either. Nor does Isolde, I know – in this she takes after me. You are wasting a lot of passion on her. Lovely, exquisite girl, how cheap she would be if she wanted every man that wanted her. Steward, my lord must be ready to honour his oath towards you, as you have said. Take care you keep up with your pretensions and lose nothing on the way! Follow up your case! I hear that the dragon was killed by another man – think, how will you answer that?'

'Who could he be?'

'I know him well and will produce him when required.'

'Madam, the man does not exist who could take up this case and presume by a deception to part me from my honour and – if he gave me an opportunity for legal redress – against whom I would not pit my life, hand to hand, on such terms as this court laid down, before I would retract!'

'I swear it,' replied the Queen, 'and will myself be surety for it that I accept this declaration and will bring the man that slew the dragon to do judicial combat with you on the third day from now, since at present I cannot do so.'

'That will suffice,' said the King, and all the barons assented: 'In such terms it will suffice, Steward. This is but a short delay. Step forward and ratify the duel, and let my lady do the same.'

The King thereupon took a pledge from them both with firm security, to the effect that this duel would be decided on the third day without fail. With this, these events were concluded.

13

THE SPLINTER

THE ladies thereupon withdrew and resumed their nursing of the
minstrel. With tender solicitude they devoted their care exclusively
to matters that would benefit him. And indeed he was soon well
again; his flesh shone with healthy colour. Isolde kept on looking
at him; she scanned his body and his whole appearance with un-
common interest. She stole glance after glance at his hands and face,
she studied his arms and legs, which so openly proclaimed what he
tried to keep so secret. She looked him up and down; and whatever
a maid may survey in a man all pleased her very well, and she
praised it in her thoughts. And now that her scrutiny had shown
his figure to be so magnificent and his manner so princely, her heart
spoke within her.

'O Lord, Worker of Miracles, if anything that Thou dost or hast
done, and anything Thou hast created falls short in any way, there
is a failure here, in that this splendid man, whom Thou hast en-
dowed with such physical perfections, should seek his livelihood
wandering from land to land so precariously. By rights he should
rule a kingdom or some land of suitable standing. It is an odd world,
where so very many thrones are filled by men of inferior race and not
one has fallen to his lot. So proper and well-nurtured a person
should have honour and possessions. He has been greatly wronged:
Lord, Thou hast given him a station in life out of keeping with his
person!'

The girl repeated this often. Her mother, too, had told her father
about the merchant in all those details which you yourselves have
heard, how the whole affair had come about and how he had no
other wish than to be granted protection on any future occasion
when he repaired to the kingdom of Ireland. All these things she
had told him privately from beginning to end.

Meanwhile, the girl had told her page Paranis to scour and

polish his armour and carefully attend to other of his belongings. Well, this had been duly done, his arms had been made presentable again and lay neatly piled in a heap. The girl then stole in and examined each piece in turn.

Now it again happened to Isolde as an equitable fate intended it that for the second time, before all the others, she discovered her heart's torment! Her heart was turned, her eye impelled to where his equipment lay. I have no idea how she could do such a thing, but she took up the sword in her hands. (Young ladies and children are given to whims and hankerings and, God knows, so are many men.) She drew it, looked at it, and studied it closely in one place and another. Then she saw where the piece was missing and examined the gap, long and minutely, and thought: 'Heaven help me! I think I have the missing piece, and what is more, I shall try it!'

Isolde fetched the piece and inserted it – and the gap and the cursed splinter fitted each other and made as perfect a whole as if they were one thing, as indeed they had been, not two years past. But now her heart froze within her on account of the old wrong that she had suffered. Her colour came and went from red to deathly pale and fiery red again, for grief and anger. 'Oh,' she said, 'luckless Isolde, alas, who brought this vile weapon here from Cornwall? With it my uncle was slain, and his slayer was called Tristan! Who gave it to this minstrel? – After all, his name is Tantris.' At once she began to turn the two names over in her mind and consider their sound. 'Oh,' she said, 'these names trouble me. I cannot think what there is about them. They sound so very similar. "Tantris",' she said, 'and "Tristan". They surely somehow go together?' Trying the names over on her tongue she seized on the letters of which each is formed and soon found that they were the same. She divided their syllables and, reversing them, found the key to the name. She found what she had been looking for. Forwards she read 'Tris-tan', backwards she read 'Tan-tris'. With this she was certain of the name.

'I knew it!' said the lovely girl. 'If this is how things stand, my heart informed me truly of this deception. How well I have known all the time, since I began to take note of him and study him in every detail of his appearance and behaviour and all that has to do with him, that he was a nobleman born. And who would have done this but he? – sailing from Cornwall to his deadly enemies, while we have twice saved his life. Saved? Nothing will save him now! This sword shall make an end of him! Now, quick, avenge your wrongs, Isolde! If the sword with which he slew your uncle lays him low in turn, ample vengeance will have been done!' She seized the sword and stood over Tristan where he was sitting in a bath.

'So you are Tristan?' she said.

'No, my lady, I am Tantris.'

'I know you are Tantris *and* Tristan, and the two are a dead man! Tantris will have to answer for the wrong that Tristan has done me! You will have to pay for my uncle!'

'No, dear young lady, no! In God's name, what are you doing? Consider your sex and spare me! You are a woman, well born and of tender years. If you earn the name of murderess, enchanting Isolde will be dead to honour for ever. The sun that rises from Ireland and has gladdened many hearts, alas, will be extinguished. Shame on those dazzling white hands – how ill a sword becomes them!'

At this point her mother the Queen entered at the door. 'How now?' she asked. 'What is this, daughter, what do you mean by this? Is this ladylike behaviour? Are you out of your senses? Is this some joke, or are you really angry? What is that sword doing in your hands?'

'Oh, my lady mother, remember the great wrong that has been done to us. This is the murderer Tristan, the man who killed your brother! Now is our opportunity to revenge ourselves by plunging this sword through him – we shall never have a better chance!'

'Is this Tristan? How do you know it?'

'I am certain it is Tristan! This is his sword, look at it and note the fragment beside it, and then judge if the man be he! But a moment ago I inserted the piece into this cursed gap, and, oh, misery, I saw it made a perfect whole!'

'Ah, Isolde, what memories have you revived in me?' was her mother's swift reply. 'That I was ever born! If this is Tristan, how deceived I am!'

But now Isolde went and stood over him with poised sword.

'Stop, Isolde!' said her mother, turning towards her. 'Stop! Do you not know what I have pledged?'

'I do not care. I swear he is going to die!'

'Mercy, lovely Isolde!' cried Tristan.

'Oh, you villain?' answered Isolde. 'Are you asking for mercy? Mercy is not for you. I shall have the life out of you!'

'No, daughter,' interposed her mother, 'we are not in a position to take vengeance, except by breaking our oath and dishonouring ourselves. Do not be so hasty. His life and goods are under my protection. However it came about, I have granted him full immunity.'

'Thank you, my lady,' said Tristan. 'Bear well in mind, ma'am, that relying on your honour I entrusted my goods and my life to you, and that you received me on those terms.'

'You liar,' said the girl. 'I know very well what was said. She did not promise Tristan her protection, either for life or property!' – and with these words she ran at him for the second time, and Tristan again cried 'Lovely Isolde, mercy, mercy!'

But her mother, the most trusty Queen, was there and he had no need to be anxious. And even if he had been tied to the bath at this time, and Isolde had been there alone with him, he would not have died at her hands. How could the good, sweet girl, who had never known bitterness or rancour in her womanly heart, ever kill a man? Only, because of her grief and anger, she outwardly behaved as if she wished to do so, and indeed might easily have done so, had she had the heart – but it failed her utterly for so bitter a deed! Yet her heart was not so good that she knew no hate or animosity, since she saw and heard the cause of her grief. She heard her foe and saw him, and yet was unable to slay him. Her tender womanliness was not to be denied, and it snatched her from her purpose.

Those two conflicting qualities, those warring contradictions, womanhood and anger, which accord so ill together, fought a hard battle in her breast. When anger in Isolde's breast was about to slay her enemy, sweet womanhood intervened. 'No, don't!' it softly whispered. Thus her heart was divided in purpose – a single heart was at one and the same time both good and evil. The lovely girl threw down the sword and immediately picked it up again. Faced with good and evil she did not know which to choose. She wanted and yet did not want, she wished both to do and refrain. Thus uncertainty raged within her, till at last sweet womanhood triumphed over anger, with the result that her enemy lived, and Morold was not avenged.

Isolde then flung the sword away, burst into tears, and cried: 'Alas, that I ever lived to see this day!'

'My dearest daughter,' that wise woman her mother replied, 'the sorrows that weigh on your heart are the ones I share, only mine are worse and much more cruel, I say it to my grief. Mercifully this grief does not touch you so deeply as me. My brother, alas, is dead. This was my greatest affliction. But now I fear further grief through you, which, I tell you, daughter, affects me far more deeply than the other, for I have loved nothing so much as you. Rather than that anything should happen to you which I should hate to see, I would renounce this feud. I can abide one sorrow more easily than two. Because of that vile man who is proceeding against us by threat of judicial combat, I find myself so placed that unless we see to it urgently, your father the King, and you and I, will suffer lasting disgrace and never be happy again.'

'My dear ladies,' said the man in the bath, 'it is true that I have made you suffer, though under great duress. If you care to recollect (as you ought), you will know that my hand was forced by nothing less than death, to which no man willingly submits so long as he can save himself. But however events turned out then, and however matters stand now in respect of the Steward, set it all aside. I shall bring it to a happy conclusion – that is, if you let me live and death does not prevent me. Lady Isolde and again – Isolde, I know that you are always thoughtful, good, sincere, and understanding. If I may broach a certain matter to you in confidence, and if you will refrain from unfriendly behaviour towards me, and from the animosity, too, which you have long borne towards Tristan, I have some good news to tell you.'

Isolde's mother Isolde looked at him for some time, and her face grew redder and redder. 'Oh,' she said, her bright eyes filling with tears, 'now I hear it clearly and know for a fact that you are he! I was in doubt until this moment. Now you have told me the truth, unasked. Alas, alas, lord Tristan, that I should ever have you in my power as well as I have now, yet not so as to be able to use it or so that it could serve me! But power is so very varied: I think I may use this power on my enemy and pervert justice thus far against a wicked man. God, shall I, then? I think most assuredly – yes!'

At this point noble, discerning Brangane came softly gliding in, smiling, and beautifully attired. She saw the naked sword lying there and the two ladies looking very woe-begone.

'What is the matter?' asked Brangane discreetly. 'What is the reason for this behaviour? What are you three up to? Why are these ladies' eyes so dimmed with tears? This sword lying here – what does it mean?'

'Look,' said the Queen, 'Brangane, dearest cousin, see how deceived we are! Too blindly have we reared a viper for a nightingale, and ground corn for the raven that was meant for the dove. Almighty God, how we have saved our foe, thinking him a friend, and twice with our own hands shielded Tristan, our enemy, from grim death! Look at him sitting there – that man is Tristan! Now I am in two minds as to whether to avenge myself. Cousin, what do you advise?'

'Do not do it, my lady, put it from your mind. Your happy, sensible nature is too good for you ever to think of such a crime or abandon yourself so far as to contemplate murder, and against a man, at that, to whom you have given your protection! You never meant to do so, I trust to God. You should be thinking of the business you have with him which wholly concerns your honour. Should you barter your honour for the life of an enemy?'

'What would you have me do, then?'

'Think it over for yourself, my lady. Withdraw, and let him leave his bath. You can discuss what will suit you best in the meantime.' And so all three retired to their private chamber to talk the matter over.

'Listen, you two,' said the elder Isolde, discerning woman that she was. 'Tell me, what can this man mean? He informed us that if we would renounce the enmity which we have long borne him, he would have some good news to tell us. I cannot imagine what it could be.'

'Then my advice is that nobody should show him any untowardness till we have discovered his intentions,' said Brangane. 'They may well be good and tend to the honour of you both. One should turn one's coat according to the wind. Who knows if he has not come to Ireland to enhance your reputation? Take care of him now and never cease to praise the Lord for one thing – that through him this monstrous, scandalous fraud of the Steward's is going to be exposed. God was looking after us while we were searching; for, had Tristan not been quickly found, I vow he would soon have died. In that event, my young lady Isolde, things would be worse than they are. Do not show him any unfriendliness, for if he were to grow suspicious and succeed in escaping, nobody could blame him. Therefore think this over, both of you. Treat him kindly as he deserves. This is my advice – do as I say. Tristan is as well born as you are, and he is well bred and intelligent, and lacking in no fine quality. Whatever your feelings towards him, entertain him courteously. You can rely on it that, whatever his motives were, some serious purpose has brought him. The object of his endeavours will be some matter of weight.'

The ladies rose and left their chamber, and went to the secret place where Tristan was sitting on his couch. Tristan did not forget himself – he leapt up to meet them, threw himself before them, and lay in supplication at the feet of those gracious and charming women, saying as he prostrated himself: 'Mercy! Dear ladies all, have mercy on me! Let me profit from having come to your country for the sake of your honour and advantage!' The dazzling trio looked away, and exchanged glances. And so they stood, and so he lay.

'My lady,' said Brangane, 'the knight has lain there too long.'

'What do you wish me to do with him?' the Queen asked swiftly. 'My feelings do not let me be his friend. I cannot think of anything that I could suitably do.'

'Now, dear lady,' replied Brangane, 'do as I say, you and mistress Isolde. I am utterly certain you can scarcely love him in your thoughts because of your old grief; but at least promise him his life, the two of you, then perhaps he will say something to his advantage.'

'Very well,' said the ladies. And with that they told him to get up. When the promise had been duly given, all four sat down together.

Tristan returned to the matter in hand. 'Now, your Majesty,' he said, 'if you will be my good friend, I will arrange within these two days – but, believe me, without guile – for your dear daughter to wed a noble king well-suited to be her lord – handsome and magnanimous, a rare, illustrious knight in the use of lance and shield, born of a lineage of kings and, to crown all, far wealthier than her father!'

'On my word,' said the Queen, 'if I could be sure of this I should willingly do whatever I was asked.'

'I will soon provide you with guarantees, ma'am,' answered Tristan. 'If I do not confirm it at once, following our reconciliation, then withdraw your protection and leave me to my ruin.'

'Speak, Brangane,' said the prudent woman, 'what do you advise, what is your opinion?'

'I approve of what he has said, and I advise you to act accordingly. Put your doubts aside, stand up, both of you, and kiss him! Though I am no queen, I mean to share in this peacemaking – I too was related to Morold, however humble my station.' And so they all three kissed him: but it was long before the younger Isolde could bring herself to do so.

When they had made their peace, Tristan again addressed the ladies. 'Now the good Lord knows that I have never felt so happy as now! I have anticipated and weighed all the dangers that could befall me, in the hope that I might win your favour – only now I do not hope, I am sure of it! Lay your cares aside. I have come from Cornwall to Ireland for your honour and advantage. After my first voyage here, when I was cured, I sang your praises continually to my lord Mark, till my prompting turned his thoughts so strongly towards you that he summoned the resolution for the deed, but only just, and I will tell you why. He feared your enmity, and in any case wished to stay single for my sake, so that I could succeed him when he died. But I urged him against it till he began to give way to me. In the end we two agreed on this expedition. That is why I came to Ireland, and why I killed the dragon. And now in return for your having tended me so kindly and assiduously, my young lady shall be Queen and Mistress both of Cornwall and England! So now you know the reason for my coming. My dear, good ladies, all three, let this be a secret!'

'Tell me,' asked the Queen, 'would it be remiss of me if I were to inform his Majesty and effect a reconciliation?'

'By no means, ma'am,' answered Tristan. 'He has every right to know it. But take good care that I come to no harm from it.'

'Have no fear, my lord. That danger is past.'

This concluded, the ladies withdrew to their cabinet and considered his good fortune and success in every detail of this enterprise. They all spoke of his cleverness, the mother from one angle, Brangane from another.

'Mother,' said the daughter, 'listen to the astonishing way in which I discovered that his name was Tristan! When I had solved the mystery of the sword, I turned my attention to the names, "Tantris" and "Tristan". As I passed them over my tongue it struck me that they had something in common. I then examined them closely and found that the letters needed for either were exactly the same. For, whichever way I read it, it contained only "Tantris" or "Tristan", and both were comprised in either. Now, mother, divide this name Tantris into a "tan" and a "tris", and say the "tris" before the "tan", and you will say "Tristan". Say the "tan" before the "tris", and you will say "Tantris" again!'

'Bless me!' said her mother, crossing herself. 'However did you come to think of that?'

When these three between them had discussed a great number of things that had to do with Tristan, the Queen sent for the King.

'Listen, my lord,' said the Queen. 'You must grant us a request which the three of us earnestly desire. If you comply, we shall all reap the benefit of it.'

'I will deny you no reasonable request. Whatever you wish shall be done.'

'Is the matter entirely in my hands?' asked the good Queen.

'Yes, whatever you wish shall be done.'

'Thank you, Sire, I am satisfied. My lord, I have the man who killed my brother – Tristan – here in the Castle! I want you to receive him into your grace and favour! His errand is such that a reconciliation is justified.'

'Upon my word, I leave it to you to decide, without any hesitation. As a nearer relation your brother Morold concerns you more than me. As you have renounced his quarrel, I shall do so, too, if you wish.'

Isolde now told the King of Tristan's mission just as the latter had told her himself, and the King was well pleased by it. 'Now see that he keeps his word,' he answered her.

The Queen then sent Brangane to fetch Tristan, who, on entering, threw himself down at the King's feet.

'Mercy, your Majesty!' he cried.

'Rise, lord Tristan,' answered Gurmun, 'come here and kiss me. Loth as I am to do so, I nevertheless renounce this feud, seeing that the ladies have done so.'

'Are my Sovereign and his two lands included in this peace, Sire?' asked Tristan.

'Yes, my lord,' answered Gurmun immediately.

When peace had been made, the Queen took Tristan, sat him down beside her daughter, and asked him to repeat to her lord from the beginning the whole story of how these events had taken shape, both concerning the dragon and the suit of King Mark. This Tristan told all over again.

'Now how shall I assure myself of this matter, lord Tristan?'

'Very easily, Sire. I have my master's great barons near at hand. Name whatever guarantees you please: so long as I have a single one your wishes shall be met.'

The King then left them, and the ladies and Tristan were alone again. Tristan turned swiftly to Paranis: 'My friend,' he said, 'go down, and you will find a ship in the harbour. Approach it unseen and ask which of its company bears the name of Curvenal. Then quickly whisper to him that he is to come to his master. Tell no one else, but bring him quietly, as you are a courteous page.' Well, then, Paranis did so. He fetched him so quietly that nobody noticed him.

When Paranis and Curvenal appeared before the ladies in their chamber, of those present only the Queen inclined her head in greeting. The reason why the others ignored him was that he did not come as a knight. Seeing Tristan safe and happy in the care of the ladies, Curvenal said in French: 'My dear lord, in God's name what are you doing, lying under cover in this delightful paradise and abandoning us to our fears? We all thought we were lost. Up to this moment I would have sworn you were not alive. How wretched you have made us! Your ship's company were declaring only this morning that you are dead and are convinced that it is true. They were persuaded with great difficulty to remain here last night, and have resolved to sail this evening!'

'They were wrong,' said the good Queen, 'he is alive and safe and happy.'

Tristan then addressed him in Breton. 'Curvenal,' he said, 'quickly go and tell them down below that all is well with me and that I shall accomplish the mission on which we were sent.' He then proceeded to tell him of his success in all detail as precisely as he could. And when he had told him of his exertions and the good fortune that had crowned them, he said: 'Now go down quickly, tell my barons and knights that every man of them is to be ready with his things tomorrow morning, well-groomed and dressed in the finest clothes that each has with him, to await my messenger. When I send him to them at the ship, they are to ride to me here at court. I shall also dispatch someone to you early tomorrow by whom you are to send me my jewel-casket and my clothes, those of the best cut. You must also dress yourself as becomes a courteous knight.' Curvenal bowed and left.

'Who is that man?' asked Brangane. 'He really thought it paradise here! Is he a knight or a servant?'

'Madam, whatever you take him for, he is a knight and a man. Have no doubt about it: the sun in the sky above never shone on one of finer character!'

'God bless him!' said the Queen and the Princess, and my lady Brangane, too, the courteous, well-bred maiden.

When Curvenal arrived at the ship and delivered himself of his speech in the terms which had been laid down for him, he repeated what he had been told and how he had found Tristan. And now, suddenly, they behaved like men who have died and come back to life – so happy were they! But many were glad more because of the peace-treaty than for the honour that Tristan had reaped. The envious barons returned as before to their whispering and their gossiping. Citing his splendid success they accused him more than ever of dealings in sorcery. Not one of them but said 'Here is a mystery, all of you – the miracles this fellow performs! God, the things this man can do, accomplishing every task to which he sets his hands!'

14

THE PROOF

AND now the day had come which had been appointed for the duel, and many lords and a great press of the nobility were assembled in the hall before the King. There was a good deal of talk among the young stalwarts as to who would fight the Steward on behalf of the maiden Isolde. The question was bandied to and fro, but no one knew anything about it.

Meanwhile, Tristan's chest and clothes had arrived. From it he selected a girdle for each of the three ladies, so fine that no queen or empress ever had a better. The chest was full to the lid of chaplets, brooches, purses, and rings, all of such quality that in your fondest fancy you could think of nothing finer. None of this left the chest, save what Tristan took for himself: a girdle that suited him, and a small clasp and a chaplet that did not ill become him. 'Lovely women all three,' he said, 'dispose of this chest and everything in it as you please.' Having said this he left. He put on his fine clothes and went to great pains to adorn himself as a proud, gay knight should do. And, indeed, they suited him perfectly.

When he rejoined the ladies they turned their critical gaze on him and secretly took stock of him. It was the verdict of all three that he was *divinely* handsome! These three heavenly women were all thinking at once 'Gracious, what a manly creature he is! His clothes and figure make a splendid man between them, they go so well together. He is altogether fortunate!'

Now Tristan had sent for his company, and they had come and taken their seats in the hall, one after the other. The whole assembly then went over and gazed with minute attention at the marvellous clothes they saw on them. Some few declared that clothes of such uniform quality had never been worn by so many men at one time. The barons all kept silent and refrained from speaking with the natives, but only because they did not know their language.

The King hereupon sent a messenger in to the Queen to ask her to come to court and bring her daughter with her.

'Up we get, Isolde,' she said, 'we must go. Lord Tristan, you stay here. I will send for you immediately. When I do, take Brangane by the hand, and the pair of you follow us in!'

'With pleasure, ma'am.'

And so Queen Isolde, the glad Dawn, came leading by the hand her Sun, the wonder of Ireland, the resplendent maiden Isolde. The girl glided gently forward, keeping even pace with her Dawn, on the same path, with the same step, exquisitely formed in every part, tall, well-moulded, and slender, and shaped in her attire as if Love had formed her to be her own falcon, an ultimate unsurpassable perfection! She wore a robe and mantle of purple samite cut in the French fashion and accordingly, where the sides slope down to their curves, the robe was fringed and gathered into her body with a girdle of woven silk, which hung where girdles hang. Her robe fitted her intimately, it clung close to her body, it neither bulged nor sagged but sat smoothly everywhere all the way down, clinging between her knees as much as each of you pleases. Her mantle was set off by a lining of white ermine with the spots arranged diaper-fashion. For length it was just right, neither dragging nor lifting at the hem. At the front it was trimmed with fine sable cut to perfect measure, neither too broad nor too narrow, and mottled black and grey – black and grey were so blended there as to be indistinguishable. The sable beside the ermine curved all along its seam, where sable and ermine match so well! Where the clasps go, a tiny string of white pearls had been let in, into which the lovely girl had inserted her left thumb. She had brought her right hand farther down, you know, to where one closes the mantle, and held it decorously together with two of her fingers. From here it fell unhampered in a last fold revealing this and that – I mean the fur and its covering. One saw it inside and out, and – hidden away within – the image that Love had shaped so rarely in body and in spirit! These two things – lathe and needle – had never made a living image more perfect! Rapacious feathered glances flew thick as falling snow, ranging from side to side in search of prey. I know that Isolde robbed many a man of his very self! On her head she wore a circlet of gold, perfectly slender and ingeniously wrought. It was encrusted with gems, fabulous stones, emerald and jacinth, sapphire and chalcedony, which, despite their small size, were very dazzling and the best in all the land. These were so finely inlaid in their various places that no goldsmith's cunning ever set stones with greater artistry. Gold and gold, the circlet and Isolde, vied to outshine each other. There was no man so discerning who, had he not seen the stones already, would have said that there was a circlet there, so much did her hair resemble gold, and so utterly did it merge with it.

Thus Isolde went with Isolde, the daughter with her mother, happy and carefree. The swing of her steps was measured, they were neither short nor long, yet partook of the quality of either. Her figure was free and erect as a sparrow-hawk's, well-preened as a parakeet's. She sent her eyes roving like a falcon on its bough: they sought their quarry together, not too gently, nor yet too firmly; but softly they went hunting, and so smoothly and sweetly that there was scarce a pair of eyes to whom her two mirrors were not a marvel and delight. This joy-giving Sun shed its radiance everywhere, gladdening the hall and its people, as softly she paced beside her mother. Mother and daughter were pleasantly occupied with two different kinds of salutation – spoken greeting and silent bowing. The rôle of each was as fixed as it was clear. The one gave a greeting, the other inclined her head; the mother spoke, the daughter said nothing. The well-bred pair were engaged in this way, and such was their occupation.

When the two Isoldes, the Sun and her Dawn, had taken their seats beside the King, the Steward looked everywhere and asked in various places where the ladies' champion and attorney might be? – he had no information. He quickly took his kinsmen, who stood round him in a great throng, and went before the King to account to the tribunal.

'Now, Sire,' said the Steward, 'here I am to claim rights of judicial combat. Where is the good knight who hopes to turn me from my honour? I have kinsmen and vassals to call on, and my case is so strong that if I get my due in common law, my plea will be upheld. – As to force, I do not fear it, unless you alone employ it.'

'Steward,' said the Queen, 'if there is no avoiding this duel I do not know what to do, for I am not prepared for it. But I promise you, if you would let it rest on the understanding that Isolde should be exempt of this affair, I tell you, Steward, it would be as much to your advantage as hers.'

'Exempt?' asked the other. 'I can see you doing the same, madam! – you, too, would abandon a game already won! Despite what you say, I fancy I will quit this game with profit and with honour. It would have been senseless of me to go to so much trouble only to waive the matter now! Your Majesty, I mean to have your daughter; that is the long and the short of it. You are so sure that you know the dragon-slayer – produce him and have done with it!'

'I see there is nothing for it, Steward,' said the Queen. 'I must look to my own interests.' She beckoned to Paranis. 'Go and fetch the man,' she said. At this the knights and barons all looked at one another. There arose a great whispering, questioning, and gossiping as to who the champion might be, but none of them knew the answer.

Meanwhile, noble Brangane, the lovely Full Moon, came gliding in, leading Tristan, her companion, by the hand. The stately, well-bred girl went modestly at his side, in person and carriage beyond all measure charming, in spirit proud and free. Her companion, too, escorted her with dignity. He was marvellously blessed with every grace that goes to make a knight: everything that makes for knightly distinction was excellent in him. His figure and attire went in delightful harmony to make a picture of chivalrous manhood. He wore rare, fine clothes of ciclatoun of quite unusual splendour. They were not the sort of thing that is given away at court, the gold was not worked into the cloth in the amount that is usual there! You could scarce trace the silken ribbing – it was so swamped with gold and sunk so deep in gold, here, there and everywhere, that you could barely see the fabric! Over its outer surface lay a net of tiny pearls, its meshes a hand's breadth apart, through which the ciclatoun burned like glowing embers. It was copiously lined with silk dimity, more purple than a violet and quite as purple as the iris. This cloth of gold took fold and grain as smoothly as cloth of gold ought. It became the fine man most rarely and was altogether to his taste. On his head he wore an aureole of cunning workmanship – an excellent chaplet that burned like candlelight and from which topaz and sardonyx, chrysolite and ruby, shone out like stars! It was bright and full of lustre and made a lambent ring about his head and his hair. And so he entered, magnificent and gay. His bearing was fine and princely, his whole array was splendid, his person most distinguished in every particular. The throng began to make way for him as he came into the Palace.

And now the Cornishmen, too, had seen him. They ran, overjoyed, to where Tristan and Brangane were advancing hand in hand, and saluted him in welcome. Then taking the two companions by the hand, the maiden and the man, they conducted them in high state into the royal presence. The King and the two royal ladies gave him a mark of their quality by standing to receive him. Tristan bowed to all three. They then greeted Tristan's company with princely honours in a manner due to great lords.

At this the knights all came crowding in and welcomed the strangers, whose reason for coming none knew. As for the barons, they at once recognized their cousins and other relations who had been sent there from Cornwall as tribute. Many a man ran to his kinsman amid tears of joy. There was much rejoicing mingled with grief, which I shall not narrate in detail.

The King then took Tristan and his partner – that is, Tristan and Brangane – as they came before him, and seated them beside him with the former as the nearer. On his further side sat the good Queen and the Princess. Tristan's companions, the knights and the barons, had their seats below the dais on the pavement, but so that each could see the faces of the court and observe what was going on there.

But now the natives had begun to whisper and gossip a great deal on the subject of Tristan. I know for sure that in this hall many founts of praise began to well up and overflow concerning his every particular. They lauded and extolled him in many styles and manners. Said many: 'Wherever did God shape a figure more apt for the order of chivalry? Look how splendidly built he is for battle and all warfare! How lavishly designed are those clothes that he is wearing! You never saw such clothes here in Ireland, so truly fit for an emperor. His followers, too, are dressed with kingly splendour. And, indeed, whoever he is, so far as wealth and wishes go, he is free to do as he pleases!' There was much of such talk, and believe me, the Steward made a very sour face over it.

Now silence was called for throughout the hall, and the assembly complied. None spoke a word or a syllable.

'Steward,' said the King, 'speak! What do you claim to have done?'

'I slew the dragon, Sire,' he said.

The stranger rose at once. 'You did not, sir!'

'I did, sir, and will prove it in this place!'

'With what evidence?' asked Tristan.

'Do you see this head? I brought it away with me.'

'Your Majesty,' said Tristan, 'since he wishes to cite the head as evidence, have it examined inside. If the tongue is found there I will void my claim forthwith and withdraw my opposition!'

The head was accordingly opened, but nothing was found inside it. Tristan at once sent for the tongue. 'My lords,' he said, 'look and see if it is the dragon's.'

As a result they declared in his favour unanimously, with the sole exception of the Steward, who wished to deny it as before, but how, he did not rightly know. The wretch began to totter and sag at the knees, he could neither speak nor stay silent, he did not know how to comport himself.

'My lords one and all,' said Tristan, 'note this extraordinary sequence of events. When I had killed the dragon and after some slight exertion cut out the tongue from its dead jaws and carried it away, he afterwards came and killed the monster!'

'Little honour has been gained from these noisy boasts,' declared their lordships. 'Whatever anyone says, we are all of us convinced that, logically speaking, the man who arrived there first and took the tongue was the one who killed the serpent!' This found general assent.

Now that the rogue's case had collapsed and Tristan, the honest stranger, had obtained the verdict of the court, 'Your Majesty,' said the latter, 'remember your word – I am to dispose of your daughter.'

'I allow it, my lord, in the terms of your promise to me.'

'I object, Sire,' interposed the scoundrel. 'For God's sake do not speak in such terms! Whatever the explanation, there is some deception behind it; this has been arrived at by some trickery or other. But before I am robbed of my honour in defiance of justice, I must first lose it in a duel! Sire, I intend to essay the combat!'

'Steward,' said subtle Isolde, 'your wrangling is superfluous. With whom will you make appeal to arms? This gentleman will not fight – he has gained all he wants in Isolde. What a ninny he would be to fight for nothing at all!'

'But why, madam?' asked Tristan. 'I will fight him rather than that he should claim that we have won by force and chicanery. My lord and my lady, pronounce, and command him to arm at once! Let him make ready, and I will do the same.'

When the Steward saw that things were heading for a duel, he took his kinsmen and vassals and withdrew for a private discussion to seek their advice in the matter. But the affair struck them as so disgraceful that he received very little help from them.

'Steward,' they were all quick to say, 'your suit was evilly inspired and has come to a bad end. On what are you embarking? If you take the field with injustice on your side you may very well lose your life. What counsel can we offer you? There is no rescue or honour here. So that if you lose your life after utterly losing your honour, the damage merely increases. We are all of the opinion – and it is amply clear to us – that the man you would have against you is a stout fellow in a fight, and that, if you took him on, it would surely be the end of you. Since the promptings of the Devil have cheated you of your honour, at least hold fast to your life! Try and see if by some means this scandalous fraud can be settled.'

'How do you wish me to do it?' asked the impostor.

'Our advice is briefly this. Go in again and declare that your friends have told you to drop this claim, and that now you wish to abandon it.'

The Steward acted accordingly. He went in again and announced that his kinsmen and vassals had weaned him from his suit and he, too, wished to be rid of it.

'Steward,' said the Queen, 'I never thought I should live to see you abandon a game already won!'

There were jeers of this sort all over the Palace – they thrummed the wretched Steward as though he were a fiddle or rote, they bandied him round and round with their mockery like a ball, their taunts rose loud on the air. Thus this imposture took its end in public ignominy.

15

THE LOVE-POTION

WHEN this affair had been concluded the King announced to the knights and barons, the companions of the realm, throughout the Palace that the man before them was Tristan. He informed them, in the terms which he had heard, why Tristan had come to Ireland and how the latter had promised to give him guarantees in all the points which he, Gurmun, had stipulated, jointly with Mark's grandees.

The Irish court was glad to hear this news. The great lords declared that it was fitting and proper to make peace; for long-drawn enmity between them, as time went on, brought nothing but loss. The King now requested Tristan to ratify the agreement, as he had promised him, and Tristan duly did so. He and all his sovereign's vassals swore that Isolde should have Cornwall for her nuptial dower, and be mistress of all England. Hereupon Gurmun solemnly surrendered Isolde into the hands of Tristan her enemy. I say 'enemy' for this reason: she hated him now as before.

Tristan laid his hand upon Isolde: 'Sire,' he said, 'lord of Ireland, we ask you, my lady and I, for her sake and for mine, to deliver up to her any knights or pages that were surrendered to this land as tribute from Cornwall and England; for it is only right and just that they should be in my lady's charge, now that she is Queen of their country.'

'With pleasure,' said the King, 'it shall be done. It has our royal approval that they should all depart with you!' This gave pleasure to many.

Tristan then ordered a ship to be procured in addition to his own, to be reserved for Isolde and himself and any others he might choose. And when it had been supplied, he made ready for the voyage. Wherever any of the exiles were traced, up and down the land, at court or in the country, they were sent for at once.

While Tristan and his compatriots were making ready, Isolde, the prudent Queen, was brewing in a vial a love-drink so subtly devised and prepared, and endowed with such powers, that with whomever any man drank it he had to love her above all things, whether he wished it or no, and she love him alone. They would share one death and one life, one sorrow and one joy.

The wise lady took this philtre and said softly to Brangane: 'Brangane, dear niece, do not let it depress you, but you must go away with my daughter. Frame your thoughts to that, and listen to what I say. Take this flask with its draught, have it in your keeping, and guard it above all your possessions. See to it that absolutely no one gets to hear of it. Take care that nobody drinks any! When Isolde and Mark have been united in love, make it your strict concern to pour out this liquor as wine for them, and see that they drink it all between them. Beware lest anyone share with them – this stands to reason – and do not drink with them yourself. This brew is a love-philtre! Bear it well in mind! I most dearly and urgently commend Isolde to your care. The better part of my life is bound up with her. Remember that she and I are in your hands, by all your hopes of Paradise! Need I say more?'

'Dearest lady,' answered Brangane, 'if you both wish it, I shall gladly accompany her and watch over her honour and all her affairs, as well as ever I can.'

Tristan and all his men took their leave, in one place and another. They left Wexford with jubilation. And now, out of love for Isolde, the King and Queen and the whole court followed him down to the harbour. The girl he never dreamt would be his love, his abiding anguish of heart, radiant, exquisite Isolde, was the whole time weeping beside him. Her mother and father passed the brief hour with much lamenting. Many eyes began to redden and fill with tears. Isolde brought distress to many hearts, for to many she was a source of secret pain. They wept unceasingly for their eyes' delight, Isolde. There was universal weeping. Many hearts and many eyes wept there together, both openly and in secret.

And now that Isolde and Isolde, the Sun and her Dawn, and the fair Full Moon, Brangane, had to take their leave, the One from the Two, sorrow and grief were much in evidence. That faithful alliance was severed with many a pang. Isolde kissed the pair of them many, many times.

When the Cornishmen and the ladies' Irish attendants had embarked and said good-bye, Tristan was last to go on board. The dazzling young Queen, the Flower of Ireland, walked hand in hand with him, very sad and dejected. They bowed towards the shore and invoked God's blessing on the land and on its people. Then they put to sea, and, as they got under way, began to sing the anthem 'We sail in God's name' with high, clear voices, and they sang it once again as they sped onward on their course.

Now Tristan had arranged for a private cabin to be given to the ladies for their comfort during the voyage. The Queen occupied it with her ladies-in-waiting and no others were admitted, with the occasional exception of Tristan. He sometimes went in to console the Queen as she sat weeping. She wept and she lamented amid her tears that she was leaving her homeland, whose people she knew, and all her friends in this fashion, and was sailing away with strangers, she neither knew whither nor how. And so Tristan would console her as tenderly as he could. Always when he came and found her sorrowing he took her in his arms gently and quietly and in no other way than a liege might hand his lady. The loyal man hoped to comfort the girl in her distress. But whenever he put his arm round her, fair Isolde recalled her uncle's death.

'Enough, Captain,' she said. 'Keep your distance, take your arm away! What a tiresome man you are! Why do you keep on touching me?'

'But, lovely woman, am I offending you?'

'You are – because I hate you!'

'But why, dear lady?' he asked.

'You killed my uncle!'

'But that has been put by.'

'Nevertheless I detest you, since but for you I should not have a care in the world. You and you alone have saddled me with all this trouble, with your trickery and deceit. What spite has sent you here from Cornwall to my harm? You have won me by guile from those who brought me up, and are taking me I do not know where! I have no idea what fate I have been sold into, nor what is going to become of me!'

'No, lovely Isolde, you must take heart! You had much rather be a great Queen in a strange land than humble and obscure at home. Honour and ease abroad, and shame in your father's kingdom have a very different flavour!'

'Take my word for it, Captain Tristan,' answered the girl, 'whatever you say, I would prefer indifferent circumstances with ease of mind and affection, to worry and trouble allied with great wealth!'

'You are right there,' replied Tristan, 'yet where you can have wealth together with mental ease, these two blessings run better as a team than either runs alone. But tell me, suppose things had come to the point where you would have had no alternative but to marry the Steward, how would it have been then? I am sure you would have been glad of my help. So is this the way you thank me for coming to your aid and saving you from him?'

'You will have to wait a long time before I thank you, for, even if you saved me from him, you have since so bewildered me with trouble that I would rather have married the Steward than set out on this voyage with you. However worthless he is, he would mend his ways, if he were for any time with me. From this, Heaven knows, I would then have seen that he loved me.'

'I don't believe a word of it,' answered Tristan. 'It demands great effort for anybody to act worthily against his own nature – no one believes that the leopard can change his spots. Lovely woman, do not be downcast. I shall soon give you a king for your lord in whom you will find a good and happy life, wealth, noble excellence and honour for the rest of your days!'

Meanwhile the ships sped on their course. They both had a favourable wind and were making good headway. But the fair company, Isolde and her train, were unused to such hard going in wind and water. Quite soon they were in rare distress. Their Captain, Tristan, gave orders to put to shore and lie idle for a while. When they had made land and anchored in a haven, most of those on board went ashore for exercise. But Tristan went without delay to see his radiant lady and pass the time of day with her. And when he had sat down beside her and they were discussing various matters of mutual interest he called for something to drink.

Now, apart from the Queen, there was nobody in the cabin but some very young ladies-in-waiting. 'Look,' said one of them, 'here is some wine in this little bottle.' No, it held no wine, much as it resembled it. It was their lasting sorrow, their never-ending anguish, of which at last they died! But the child was not to know that. She rose and went at once to where the draught had been hidden in its vial. She handed it to Tristan, their Captain, and he handed it to Isolde. She drank after long reluctance, then returned it to Tristan, and he drank, and they both of them thought it was wine. At that moment in came Brangane, recognized the flask, and saw only too well what was afoot. She was so shocked and startled that it robbed her of her strength and she turned as pale as death. With a heart that had died within her she went and seized that cursed, fatal flask, bore if off and flung it into the wild and raging sea!

'Alas, poor me,' cried Brangane, 'alas that ever I was born! Wretch that I am, how I have ruined my honour and trust! May God show everlasting pity that I ever came on this journey and that death failed to snatch me, when I was sent on this ill-starred voyage with Isolde! Ah, Tristan and Isolde, this draught will be your death!'

Now when the maid and the man, Isolde and Tristan, had drunk the draught, in an instant that arch-disturber of tranquillity was there, Love, waylayer of all hearts, and she had stolen in! Before they were aware of it she had planted her victorious standard in their two hearts and bowed them beneath her yoke. They who were two and divided now became one and united. No longer were they at variance: Isolde's hatred was gone. Love, the reconciler, had purged their hearts of enmity, and so joined them in affection that each was to the other as limpid as a mirror. They shared a single heart. Her anguish was his pain: his pain her anguish. The two were one both in joy and in sorrow, yet they hid their feelings from each other. This was from doubt and shame. She was ashamed, as he was. She went in doubt of him, as he of her. However blindly the craving in their hearts was centred on one desire, their anxiety was how to begin. This masked their desire from each other.

When Tristan felt the stirrings of love he at once remembered loyalty and honour, and strove to turn away. 'No, leave it, Tristan,' he was continually thinking to himself, 'pull yourself together, do not take any notice of it.' But his heart was impelled towards her. He was striving against his own wishes, desiring against his desire. He was drawn now in one direction, now in another. Captive that he was, he tried all that he knew in the snare, over and over again, and long maintained his efforts.

The loyal man was afflicted by a double pain: when he looked at her face and sweet Love began to wound his heart and soul with her, he bethought himself of Honour, and it retrieved him. But this in turn was the sign for Love, his liege lady, whom his father had served before him, to assail him anew, and once more he had to submit. Honour and Loyalty harassed him powerfully, but Love harassed him more. Love tormented him to an extreme, she made him suffer more than did Honour and Loyalty combined. His heart smiled upon Isolde, but he turned his eyes away: yet his greatest grief was when he failed to see her. As is the way of captives, he fixed his mind on escape and how he might elude her, and returned many times to this thought: 'Turn one way, or another! Change this desire! Love and like elsewhere!' But the noose was always there. He took his heart and soul and searched them for some change: but there was nothing there but Love – and Isolde.

And so it fared with her. Finding this life unbearable, she, too, made ceaseless efforts. When she recognized the lime that bewitching Love had spread and saw that she was deep in it, she endeavoured to reach dry ground, she strove to be out and away. But the lime kept clinging to her and drew her back and down. The lovely woman fought back with might and main, but stuck fast at every step. She was succumbing against her will. She made desperate attempts on many sides, she twisted and turned with hands and feet and immersed them ever deeper in the blind sweetness of Love, and of the man. Her limed senses failed to discover any path, bridge, or track that would advance them half a step, half a foot, without Love being there too. Whatever Isolde thought, whatever came uppermost in her mind, there was nothing there, of one sort or another, but Love, and Tristan.

This was all below the surface, for her heart and her eyes were at variance – Modesty chased her eyes away, Love drew her heart towards him. That warring company, a Maid and a Man, Love and Modesty, brought her into great confusion; for the Maid wanted the Man, yet she turned her eyes away: Modesty wanted Love, but told no one of her wishes. But what was the good of that? A Maid and her Modesty are by common consent so fleeting a thing, so short-lived a blossoming, they do not long resist. Thus Isolde gave up her struggle and accepted her situation. Without further delay the vanquished girl resigned herself body and soul to Love and to the man.

Isolde glanced at him now and again and watched him covertly, her bright eyes and her heart were now in full accord. Secretly and lovingly her heart and eyes darted at the man rapaciously, while the man gave back her looks with tender passion. Since Love would not release him, he too began to give ground. Whenever there was a suitable occasion the man and the maid came together to feast each other's eyes. These lovers seemed to each other fairer than before – such is Love's law, such is the way with affection. It is so this year, it was so last year and it will remain so among all lovers as long as Love endures, that while their affection is growing and bringing forth blossom and increase of all lovable things, they please each other more than ever they did when it first began to burgeon. Love that bears increase makes lovers fairer than at first. This is the seed of Love, from which it never dies.

Love seems fairer than before and so Love's rule endures. Were Love to seem the same as before, Love's rule would soon wither away.

16

THE AVOWAL

THE ships put out to sea again and, except that Love had led astray two hearts on board, sailed gaily on their course. The two lovers were lost in their thoughts. They were burdened by the pleasing malady that works such miracles as changing honey to gall, turning sweetness sour, setting fire to moisture, converting balm to pain; that robs hearts of their natures and stands the world on its head. This tormented Tristan and Isolde. The selfsame woe afflicted them, and in the strangest way: neither could find rest or comfort except when they saw one another. But when they saw each other they were deeply troubled by this, since they could not have their way together for the shyness and modesty that robbed them of their joy. When from time to time they tried to observe each other through eyes which Love had limed, their flesh assumed the hue of their hearts and souls. Love the Dyer did not deem it enough that she was hidden in the recesses of two noble hearts: she meant to show her power in their faces. Indeed, they bore many marks of it, since their colour did not long stay the same. They blushed and blanched, blanched and blushed in swift succession as Love painted their cheeks for them.

With this they both grew aware (as is inevitable in such matters) that their thoughts for each other ran somewhat in the direction of Love, and they began at once to behave in affectionate accord and watch for time and opportunity for their whispered conversations. Love's huntsmen as they were, again and again, with question and answer, they laid their nets and their snares for one another, they set up their coverts and lurking-places. They had much to say to each other. The words with which Isolde began were very much those of a maid: she approached her friend and lover in a roundabout way, from afar. She reminded him of all that had happened: how he had come floating in a skiff to Dublin, wounded and alone; how her mother had taken charge of him and how she had duly healed him; how, in all detail, she had learned the whole art of writing, under his tuition, and Latin and stringed instruments. It was with much beating about the bush that she recalled his valiant exploit, and the dragon, too, and how she had twice recognized him – in the bog, and in his bath. Their talk was now mutual; she addressed him and he her.

'Alas,' said Isolde, 'when I had so good a chance and failed to kill you in your bath, God in Heaven, why did I do as I did? Had I known then what I know now, I swear you would have died!'

'Why, lovely Isolde?' he asked, 'why are you so distressed, what is it that you know?'

'All that I know distresses me, all that I see afflicts me. The sky and sea oppress me, my life has become a burden to me!'

She leant against him with her elbow – such was the beginning of their daring! The bright mirrors of her eyes filled with hidden tears. Her heart began to swell within her, her sweet lips to distend; her head drooped on her breast. As for her friend, he took her in his arms, neither too closely nor yet too distantly, but as was fitting in an acquaintance.

'Come now, sweet, lovely woman,' he whispered tenderly, 'tell me, what is vexing you, why do you complain so?'

'*Lameir* is what distresses me,' answered Love's falcon, Isolde, 'it is *lameir* that so oppresses me, *lameir* it is that pains me so.'

Hearing her say *lameir* so often he weighed and examined the meaning of the word most narrowly. He then recalled that *l'ameir* meant 'Love', *l'ameir* 'bitter', *la meir* the sea: it seemed to have a host of meanings. He disregarded the one, and asked about the two. Not a word did he say of Love, who was mistress of them both, their common hope and desire. All that he discussed was 'sea' and 'bitter'.

'Surely, fair Isolde, the sharp smack of sea is the cause of your distress? The tang of the sea is too strong for you? It is this you find so bitter?'

'No, my lord, no! What are you saying? Neither of them is troubling me, neither the sea nor its tang is too strong for me. It is *lameir* alone that pains me.'

When he got to the bottom of the word and discovered 'Love'

inside it, 'Faith, lovely woman,' he whispered, 'so it is with me, *lameir* and you are what distress me. My dearest lady, sweet Isolde, you and you alone and the passion you inspire have turned my wits and robbed me of my reason! I have gone astray so utterly that I shall never find my way again! All that I see irks and oppresses me, it all grows trite and meaningless. Nothing in the wide world is dear to my heart but you.'

Isolde answered 'So you, sir, are to me.'

When the two lovers perceived that they had one mind, one heart, and but a single will between them, this knowledge began to assuage their pain and yet bring it to the surface. Each looked at the other and spoke with ever greater daring, the man to the maid, the maid to the man. Their shy reserve was over. He kissed her and she kissed him, lovingly and tenderly. Here was a blissful beginning for Love's remedy: each poured and quaffed the sweetness that welled up from their hearts. Whenever they could find an occasion, this traffic passed between them, it stole to and fro so secretly that none discovered their mind but she who could not help knowing it, far-seeing Brangane. Quietly and covertly she kept glancing in their direction and, seeing how intimate they were, she thought to herself repeatedly: 'Alas, it is plain to me that these two are falling in love!' It did not take her long to see that they were in earnest, or to detect in their demeanour the pain within their hearts. She was harrowed by their suffering, for she saw them the whole time pining and languishing, sighing and sorrowing, musing and dreaming and changing colour. They were so lost in thought that they neglected all nourishment, till want and misery so reduced their bodies that Brangane was greatly alarmed and feared this hardship might prove the end of them. 'Now pluck up your courage,' she thought, 'and find out what is happening!'

One day the noble, discerning girl was sitting beside them in quiet and intimate conversation.

'There is nobody here but we three,' she said. 'Tell me, both of you, what is the matter with you? I see you fettered by your thoughts and sighing, moping, and grieving all the time.'

'Noble lady, if I dared tell you, I would,' answered Tristan.

'You may indeed, sir, readily. Go on! Tell me anything you like.'

'My dear, good lady,' he replied, 'I daren't say any more, unless you first assure us on your holy word of honour that you will be kind and gracious to us poor wretches – or else we are past all saving.'

Brangane gave them her word. She promised and assured them on her honour, calling Heaven to witness, that she would do exactly as they wished.

'My good and faithful lady,' said Tristan, 'first think of God and then of your hopes of Paradise: consider our sufferings and the fearful plight we are in. I do not know what has come over poor Isolde and me, but we have both of us gone mad in the briefest space of time with unimaginable torment – we are dying of love and can find neither time nor occasion for a meeting, because you are always in our way. And I tell you, if we die, it will be nobody's fault but yours. It is in your hands, whether we live or die. Need I say more? Brangane, dear young lady, have compassion on your mistress and me, and help us!'

'Madam,' asked Brangane, turning to Isolde, 'is your distress as great as he paints it?'

'Yes, dear cousin,' said Isolde.

'May God have pity on it that the Devil has mocked us in this fashion!' said Brangane. 'Now I clearly see that I have no choice but to act to my own sorrow and your shame for your own sakes. Rather than let you die I will allow you good opportunity for whatever you wish to embark on. From now on do not abstain on my account from what you will not forgo for your own good names. But if you can master yourselves and refrain from this, refrain! – That is my advice! Let this scandal remain a secret among the three of us. If you spread it any farther it will cost you your reputations. If any other than we three comes to hear of it you are lost, and I together with you. Dearest mistress, lovely Isolde, let me entrust to you now, into your own keeping, your life and your death: deal with them as you please. Henceforward have no fear as far as I am concerned: do whatever you like!'

That night, as the lovely woman lay brooding and pining for her darling, there came stealing into her cabin her lover and her physician – Tristan and Love. Love the physician led Tristan, her sick one, by the hand: and there, too, she found her other patient, Isolde. She quickly took both sufferers and gave him to her, her to him, to be each other's remedy. Who else could have severed them from the ill which they shared but Union, the knot that joined their senses? Love the Ensnarer knit their two hearts together by the toils of her sweetness with such consummate skill and such marvellous strength that in all their days the bond was never loosed.

A long discourse on Love wearies well-bred minds. But a short discourse on worthy love gratifies good minds.

However little I have suffered the sweet torment in my time, the gentle pain that wounds our hearts so agreeably, something tells me (and I am well inclined to believe it) that these two lovers were in a happy and contented mood at having got out of their way Love's enemy, cursed Surveillance, that veritable plague of Love! I have thought much about the pair of them, and do so now and ever shall. When I spread Longing and Affection as a scroll before my inward eye and inquire into their natures, my yearning grows, and my comrade, Desire, grows too, as if he would mount to the clouds! When I consider in detail the unending marvels that a man would find in love if he but knew where to seek them, and the joy there would be in love for those who would practise it sincerely, then, all at once, my heart grows larger than Setmunt* and I pity Love from my heart when I see that almost everybody today clings and holds fast to her, and yet none gives her her due. We all desire our amorous fancies and wish to keep company with Love. No, Love is not such as we make her for one another in the spurious way we do! We do not look facts in the face: we sow seed of deadly nightshade and wish it to bear lilies and roses! Believe me, this is impossible. We can only garner what has been put into the ground, and accept what the seed bears us. We must mow and reap as we have sown. We cultivate Love with guile and deceit and with minds as bitter as gall, and we then seek joy of body and soul in her! But, instead, she bears only pain and evil and poison-berries and weeds, just as her soil was sown. And when this yields bitter sorrow, festers in our hearts and there destroys us, we accuse Love of the crime and say she is to blame whose fault it never was. We all sow seeds of perfidy – then let us reap sorrow and shame. If the sorrow should chance to hurt us, let us think of that beforehand; let us sow better and better,

* Setmunt remains unexplained.

and we shall reap accordingly. We who have a mind for the world (whether this be good or bad), how we abuse the days which we squander in Love's name, finding nothing but the self-same crop that we sowed in her – failure and disaster. We do not find the good that each of us desires, and which we are all denied; I mean steadfast friendship in love, which never fails to comfort us and bears roses as well as thorns and solace as well as trouble. In such friendship joy always lurks among the woes; however often it is clouded, it will bring forth gladness in the end. Nowadays no one finds such steadfast affection, so ill do we prepare the soil.

They are right who say that 'Love is hounded to the ends of the earth'. All that we have is the bare word, only the name remains to us: and this we have so hackneyed, so abused, and so debased, that the poor, tired thing is ashamed of her own name and is disgusted at the word. She heartily loathes and despises herself. Shorn of all honour and dignity she sneaks begging from house to house, shamefully lugging a patchwork sack in which she keeps what she can grab or steal and, denying it to her own mouth, hawks it in the streets. For shame! It is we who are the cause of this traffic. We do such things to her and yet protest our innocence. Love, mistress of all hearts, the noble, the incomparable, is for sale in the open market. What shameful dues our dominion has extorted from her! We have set a false stone in our ring and now we deceive ourselves with it. What a wretched sort of deception, when a man so lies to his friends that he dupes himself. False lovers and love-cheats as we are, how vainly our days slip by, seeing that we so seldom bring our suffering to a joyful consummation! How we dissipate our lives without either profit or pleasure!

Yet we are heartened by something that does not really concern us; for when there is a good love-story, when we tell in poetry of those who lived once upon a time, many hundreds of years ago, our hearts are warmed within us and we are so full of this happy chance that there can be none who is loyal and true and free of guile towards his lover that would not wish to create such bliss in his own heart for himself, except that the selfsame thing from which it all takes rise, I mean heartfelt Fidelity, lies beneath our feet in misery all the time. In vain does she address us – we look the other way and without a thought tread the sweet thing underfoot. We have shamefully trampled upon her. Were we to seek her where she lies, we should at first not know where to look. Good and rewarding as fidelity between lovers would be, why have we no liking for it? One look, one tender glance from the eyes of one's beloved will surely quench a myriad pangs of body and of soul. One kiss from one's darling's lips that comes stealing from the depths of her heart – how it banishes love's cares!

I know that Tristan and Isolde, that eager pair, rid each other of a host of ills and sorrows when they reached the goal of their desire. The yearning that fetters thoughts was stilled. Whenever the occasion suited they had their fill of what lovers long for. When opportunity offered, they paid and exacted willing tribute from Love and from each other with faithful hearts. During that voyage they were in ecstasy. Now that their shyness was over they gloried and revelled in their intimacy, and this was wise and sensible. For lovers who hide their feelings, having once revealed them, who set a watch on their modesty and so turn strangers in love, are robbers of themselves. The more they veil themselves the more they despoil themselves and adulterate joy with sorrow. This pair of lovers did not play the prude: they were free and familiar with looks and speech.

And so they passed the voyage in a life of rapture, yet not altogether scatheless, for they were haunted by fear of the future. They dreaded beforehand what actually came to pass and what in days to come was to rob them of much pleasure and face them with many hazards – I mean that fair Isolde was to be given to one to whom she did not wish to be given. And another cause for sorrow tormented them – Isolde's lost virginity. They were deeply troubled about this and it made them very wretched. Yet such cares were easily borne, for they freely had their will together many, many times.

When they had sailed near enough to Cornwall to make out the land the whole company was delighted, all save Tristan and Isolde, to whom it brought dread and alarm. Had they had their way they would never have seen land. Fear for their reputations and standing began to rack their hearts. They could not think what to do to keep the King in ignorance that Isolde was a maid no longer. Yet however unresourceful youthful lovers are in their inexperience, a ruse was vouchsafed to the girl.

17

BRANGANE

When love takes to sporting with the young and inexperienced we are likely to find cunning and guile in them.

Let us not make a long story of it. Young though she was, Isolde devised the best ruse that she could at this juncture, namely that they should simply ask Brangane to lie at Mark's side during the first night in perfect silence and keep him company. He could be denied his due in no better way, since Brangane was beautiful and a virgin. Thus Love instructs honest minds to practise perfidy, though they ought not to know what goes to make a fraud of this sort.

This is what the lovers did. They begged and implored Brangane till they brought her to the point where she promised to do the deed. But she promised it most reluctantly. It was not just once that she turned red and then pale at this request under the stress of great emotion: after all, it was a strange one.

'Dearest mistress,' said Brangane, 'your mother, my lady the good Queen, entrusted you to me, and I ought to have shielded you from such calamity during this god-forsaken voyage. But instead, owing to my carelessness, sorrow and shame have come upon you, so that I have little cause for complaint if I have to endure the disgrace with you, and it would even be right and proper that I alone should suffer it, provided that you could escape it. Merciful Lord, how couldst Thou so forget me!'

'Tell me, my noble cousin,' Isolde asked Brangane, 'what do you mean, why are you so distressed? I am dying to know what is troubling you.'

'Madam, the other day I threw a flask overboard.'

'So you did: but what of that?'

'Alas,' replied Brangane, 'that flask and the draught it contained will be the death of you both!'

'But why, cousin?' asked Isolde. 'How can that be?'

'It is like this.' And Brangane told them the whole story from beginning to end.

'It is in God's hands!' said Tristan. 'Whether it be life or death, it has poisoned me most sweetly! I have no idea what the other will be like, but this death suits me well! If my adorable Isolde were to go on being the death of me in this fashion I would woo death everlasting!'

When all is said, if we pursue pleasure it cannot remain so without our having to suffer pain as well.

Whatever our contentment of love, we must never lose sight of honour. When we are unwilling to seek anything but the body's delight it means the ruin of honour. However much the life that Tristan led was to his liking, his sense of honour restrained him. His loyalty laid regular siege to him so that he kept it well in mind and brought Mark his wife. Honour and Loyalty pressed him hard: these two, who had lost the battle to Love when Tristan had decided in her favour, this vanquished pair now vanquished Love in turn.

Tristan at once dispatched messengers to land in two ship's boats and sent news to Mark of how things had gone with regard to the fair maid of Ireland. Mark promptly summoned whomever he could. Within that same hour a thousand messengers were hastening to assemble the knighthood. Natives and strangers alike were made welcome in great number. The worst and the best that Mark received in this pair with whom he passed his life he welcomed as warmly as a man should welcome that which he most esteems.

Mark at once had the baronage informed that they were to come to court within eighteen days in such style as was appropriate for his wedding. This was duly done. They came in magnificent array. Many an enchanting cavalcade of knights and ladies arrived there to see their eyes' delight – radiant Isolde! They gazed at her with indescribable fervour, and accorded her this unvarying tribute:

'Isot, Isot la blunde,
marveil de tu le munde!

Isolde is indeed a marvel throughout the world! – What they say of this heavenly girl is true: like the sun she brings joy to the world! No land on earth ever gained so enchanting a maiden!'

When she had been settled in wedlock and had received what was due to her (namely that Cornwall and England were made subject to her provided that, if she bore no issue, Tristan should inherit), and when homage had been done to her, that night, when she was to go to bed with Mark, she, Brangane, and Tristan had gone to great trouble in advance to choose their ground and plan of action wisely and have it all cut and dried. There were none but these four in Mark's chamber: the King himself and the three. And now Mark had laid him down. Brangane had donned the Queen's robes – they had exchanged clothes between them – and Tristan now led her towards him to suffer her ordeal. Her mistress Isolde put out the lights and Mark strained Brangane to him.

I do not know how Brangane took to this business at first. She endured it so quietly that it all passed off in silence. Whatever her companion did with her, whatever demands he made on her, she met them to his satisfaction with brass and with gold. I am convinced that it can rarely have happened before that such fine brass was passed as bed-money for a payment due in gold. Indeed I would wager my life on it that false coin of such nobility had never been struck since Adam's day, nor had so acceptable a counterfeit ever been laid beside a man.

While these two lay in bed disporting themselves, Isolde was in great fear and anguish. 'Lord God help and preserve me lest my cousin prove unfaithful to me!' Such was her constant thought. 'If she plays this bed-game over-long and too intently I fear she will take such a liking to it that she will lie there till daylight, and we shall all be the talk of the town!' But no, Brangane's thoughts and feelings were true and unsullied. When she had done duty for Isolde and her debt had been discharged, she quitted the bed. Isolde was ready waiting there, and went and sat by the bed as if she were the same person.

The King, for his part, at once asked for wine in obedience to tradition, since in those days it was invariably the custom that if a man had lain with a virgin and taken her maidenhead, someone would come with wine and give it them to drink together, the one like the other. This custom was observed. Mark's nephew, Tristan, at once brought lights and wine. The King drank, and so did the Queen. (Many assert that it was the same draught through which Tristan and Isolde were plunged into their love-passion. No, none of that philtre remained. Brangane had thrown it into the sea.) When they had honoured the tradition and drunk as custom required the young Queen Isolde, in great distress and with secret pain in her heart, laid herself down beside her lord the King who, clasping her close to him, then resumed his pleasures. To him one woman was as another: he soon found Isolde, too, to be of good deportment. There was nothing to choose between them – he found gold and brass in either. Moreover, they both paid him their dues, one way and another, so that he noticed nothing amiss.

Isolde was greatly loved and esteemed by her lord Mark, and prized and honoured by the people of the realm. Seeing her in possession of so many gifts and accomplishments, all who were capable of uttering praise sang her praise and glory.

Meanwhile Isolde and her lover passed the time in varied pleasures. They had their joy morning and night, for nobody had any suspicion. No man or woman thought there was anything amiss here, for Isolde was wholly in Tristan's keeping and she did as she thought fit.

And now Isolde surveyed her whole situation. Since none but Brangane knew the secret of her subterfuge, she need have little fear for her honour in future, once Brangane were gone. But now she lived in great fear and she dreaded keenly lest Brangane, perhaps loving Mark, might divulge her shameful deed to him and the whole story of what had taken place. In this the fearful Queen showed that people dread scandal and derision more than they fear the Lord.

Isolde summoned two squires, foreigners from England, and had them swear oath upon oath and give pledge upon pledge, and she further commanded them on their lives to perform whatever task she gave them and also keep it a secret. She then told them her wishes. 'Now attend to what I say, both of you,' said the would-be murderess. 'I am sending a girl along with you. Take charge of her, and all three of you ride quickly and secretly to a forest somewhere – no matter if it is a long way off or near to hand, provided that it suits your purpose, and nobody has his home there – and cut off her head! Take note of all she says and report it all to me. Bring me back her tongue and rest assured that, however I contrive it, I will knight you tomorrow with great magnificence and enfeoff you and make you gifts, as long as ever I live!'

This was duly confirmed. Isolde now addressed herself to Brangane. 'Brangane,' she said, 'pay attention. Do I look pale? I do not know what is the matter with me, my head aches so! You must go and fetch us some herbs. Unless we find some remedy for my ailment I shall die!'

'I am very sorry indeed to hear that you are unwell, ma'am,' said faithful Brangane. 'Now do not lose a moment, but have me shown to a place where I shall find something to help you.'

'Look, there are two squires in attendance here. Ride with them, they will show you the way.'

'I will with pleasure, my lady.' She mounted and rode off with them.

When they came to the forest where there were all the herbs, salads, and grasses they could desire, Brangane wished to dismount, but they led her deeper into the wilds. Having at length gained sufficient distance from the open country, they took the faithful, noble, well-bred girl, set her sadly and sorrowfully on the ground, and then each drew his sword. Brangane was so terrified that she sank to the ground and lay there as she had fallen for a long time, quivering in every limb, while her heart throbbed within her.

'Mercy, Lord!' she cried, looking up in great dread. 'In God's name, what are you going to do?'

'You must die!'

'Alas, tell me why?'

'What wrong have you done the Queen?' asked one of them. 'She commanded to have you killed. What must be, must be. Your mistress Isolde has ordained that you shall die!'

Brangane clasped her hands in supplication. 'No, sir!' she cried, all in tears. 'Of your charity and in God's name, defer the execution of this command and let me live so long that I may answer you! You can dispatch me soon enough when it is done. You must tell my lady, and know it for yourselves, that I never did a thing to displease her from which I might expect that any harm could befall her, unless it is a thing I will not credit. When we two sailed from Ireland we each had a garment that we had chosen and laid apart from the rest, and these we took abroad with us: two shifts as white as snow! When we got out to sea on our voyage to this country the sun grew so hot for the Queen during this time that she could scarcely bear anything on her body other than her pure white shift – and so she grew to like having it on. But while she was wearing her shift until she had worn it too often and had soiled all the whiteness of it, I kept mine in my coffer safely hidden away in pure white folds. And when my lady had come here and married her lord the King, and was about to go to bed with him, her shift was not as presentable as it should have been, or as she would have liked it to be. Unless she is annoyed that I lent her my own, but after first refusing, and to that extent offended her, I call God to witness that I have never at any time overstepped her wishes. Now do this for me, both of you, in God's name! Give her my greetings in such terms as a young lady owes to her mistress; and may the Lord of his goodness preserve her life and honourable estate! My death I do forgive her. I commend my soul to God, my body to your bidding!'

The two men looked at each other compassionately and took pity on the fervent tears of that blameless girl. They both bitterly regretted and reproached themselves that they had promised to carry out the murder. Since they had neither found nor could at all discover anything in her that called for murder or in any way merited death, they took counsel together and agreed that, come what might, they would let her live. The good fellows bound her high up in a tree lest the wolves should get her before their return, then cut out the tongue of one of their setters and rode away.

When they arrived, these two men told Isolde, the would-be murderess, that they had killed Brangane with great sorrow and regret, and declared that it was her tongue.

'Tell me,' asked Isolde, 'what did the girl say to you?'

They repeated her words from beginning to end just as they had been told, suppressing nothing at all.

'Very well,' said Isolde, 'didn't she say anything more to you?'

'No, ma'am.'

'Oh misery!' wailed Isolde, 'what do I have to hear! What have you done, you damned cut-throats? You will hang, the two of you!'

'God in Heaven!' they said. 'What does this mean? You amaze us, Lady Isolde. You know you begged and forced us most insistently to kill her, as we indeed have done!'

'What is this that you say about begging? I entrusted my maid to you so that you could escort her to a place where she was to fetch me something for my ailment. You will have to give her back to me, or it will cost you your lives! You cursed, blood-thirsty vipers, you will hang for it, the two of you, or be burned to death on the hurdle!'

'Good Heavens, ma'am!' retorted the others. 'Your thoughts are not honest and straightforward, you are very double-tongued! However, my lady, let us have no more violence! Rather than lose our lives we shall return her to you safe and sound.'

'Don't lie to me any more!' said Isolde, breaking into tears. 'Is Brangane dead or alive?'

'She is still alive, Isolde, you strange person.'

'Then bring her to me, in return for what I have promised you.'

'Lady Isolde, it shall be done!'

Isolde kept one of them with her and the other rode back without delay to where he had left Brangane and then brought her to her mistress. When she came into her presence Isolde took her in her arms and kissed her cheeks and mouth, not once but many times. She gave the two squires twenty marks of gold as a reward, on condition that they kept the matter secret.

Now that Queen Isolde had found Brangane loyal, constant, and altogether of upright character, and had smelted her in the crucible and refined her like gold, she and Brangane were so deeply devoted in mutual love and trustfulness that no difference was ever made between them in any of their affairs, so that their feelings for each other were of the happiest. Brangane was pleased with the court and the court was full of her praises. She was on terms of friendship with all, and harboured rancour towards none, either openly or in her heart. She was counsellor to the King and Queen. Nothing could happen in the Chamber without Brangane's being informed of it.

Brangane was assiduous in the service of Isolde: she served her in all her wishes with regard to her lover Tristan. They conducted this affair so discreetly that nobody grew suspicious. None paid attention to what they said, to how they comported themselves or to any concern of theirs. No one had any doubts about them. They were at their ease and as contented as a pair of lovers should be who can choose their meetings at their own time and convenience. The lover and his beloved were at all times hot in pursuit of love. Many times in the day did they ensnare each other's eyes with tender glances, in the crowd and in the presence of others, where glances are full of significance and mean whole conversations, and through which it is possible to communicate on all matters of mutual affection. They continued so night and day without danger of observation. Walking, sitting, and standing, they were open and unconstrained both in speech and in demeanour. At times they embroidered their public conversation, in which they were marvellously adept, with words that were meant to stick – one might often observe Love's handiwork in words caught up in their talk like gold in silk galloons. But nobody had any idea that their words or acts were inspired by any affection other than what came from the close kinship which all knew existed between Mark and Tristan, with which they trafficked dishonestly and won their sport by cheating. With this, Love beguiled the wits of very many people, none of whom could conceive of the true nature of their amity, which was indeed perfect between them. Their thoughts and wishes were in concord: it was 'yes' and 'yes' and 'no' and 'no' with them. As to 'yes' and 'no', 'no' and 'yes', believe me, there was none of it, there were no differences between them. Yea or nay, they were both of one mind. And so they passed their time delightfully together, now thus, now so. At times they were happy, at others out of humour, as is Love's custom with lovers; for in their hearts she brews pain besides pleasure, sorrow and distress as well as joy. And distress for Tristan and his lady Isolde was when they could not contrive a love-meeting.

Thus in one way and another these two were both mournful and happy. Nor did it fail to happen now and again that there was anger between them – anger without malice, I mean. And if anyone were to say that anger is out of place between such perfect lovers, I am absolutely certain that he was never really in love, for such is Love's way. With it she kindles lovers and sets fire to their emotions. For as anger pains them deeply, so affection reconciles them, with the result that love is renewed and amity greater than ever. But how their anger is roused, and how they are appeased without the help of others, you need no telling. Lovers who are very often able to have each other's company are apt to imagine that some other is more loved than they, and they will make a great quarrel out of a caprice, and for a tiff will make peace right royally. And there is good reason why they should do so. We must uphold them in this, since affection will grow rich, young, and fresh from it, and take fire in its attachment. On the other hand, it grows poor, old, cold, and frigid when it lacks its fire; when anger is spent, affection does not quickly grow green again. But when lovers fall out over a trifle it is loyalty, fresh and ever new, that will always be the peacemaker. This renews their loyalty, this refines their affection like gold.

Thus Tristan and Isolde passed their time in joy and sorrow. There was joy and sorrow between them in tireless succession. I mean joy without mortal sorrow, for as yet they were free of mortal pain and of such calamity as stares into one's heart. They said not a word of their affairs, they kept their secret very close, and long continued so. They were both in excellent spirits and free and gay at heart. Queen Isolde was on the best of terms with everyone, and everyone spoke about Tristan. His name was on every lip, and he was marvellously feared in the land.

18

GANDIN

TRISTAN was full of spirit. He spent much of his time at the wars and also at tournaments, he passed his leisure days in hawking and rode out stalking and hunting as time and occasion offered.

In those days a ship put into Mark's harbour in Cornwall. A knight rode ashore from on board, a noble baron of Ireland by the name of Gandin, courteous, handsome, rich in possessions, and so valiant in his person that all Ireland spoke of his exploits. He came riding up to Mark's court, elegantly dressed in all the fine trappings of knighthood and with the air of a grand seigneur, though unattended and carrying no shield or spear. But slung on his back he had a small rote, adorned with gold and precious stones, and strung to perfection.

When he had dismounted, he went into the Palace and greeted Mark and Isolde appropriately. At various times and in various ways he had been Isolde's knight and admirer, and it was for her sake that he had come to Cornwall from Ireland. She recognized him at once.

'God save you, Lord Gandin!' said the courteous Queen.

'Thank you, fair Isolde,' answered Gandin, 'in Gandin's eyes fair and fairer than gold!'

Isolde then told the King in a whisper who he was. Mark was much puzzled as to why he wore the rote and thought it absurd, and indeed they were all wondering and thinking about it intently.

Nevertheless, Mark was at great pains to honour Gandin, as much for his own good name as to meet Isolde's wishes; for she begged and entreated Mark to show him honour, as a fellow-countryman of hers. Mark was readily persuaded. He seated Gandin beside him without delay and asked him various questions concerning his country and its people, its ladies and manners at court. And when their meal was ready and the household were washing their hands and the water came to Gandin, they begged him repeatedly to lay aside his rote: but no one could get him to do so. The King and Queen graciously let it rest at that. But many thought it grossly discourteous, and it did not pass off without their laughing and scoffing among themselves. The Knight of the Rote, his Lordship of the Burden, nevertheless ignored it. He sat beside Mark at their meal and ate and drank as became him.

When the board had been removed, Gandin rose and took his seat among Mark's vassals. They gave him their companionship and entertained him with much gossip of the court. Noble King Mark courteously asked him in the presence of them all to have the kindness to let them hear him play, if he possessed any skill at the rote.

'Sire,' answered the stranger, 'I will not, unless first I know my reward!'

'What do you mean by that, sir? If you want anything of mine, it is all at your service. Let us hear what you can do, and I will give you whatever you please!'

'Agreed,' said the man from Ireland. And without more ado he played them a lay that gratified them all. The King asked him at once to play another. The deceiver laughed hugely to himself. 'My reward inspires me to play you whatever I am asked,' he answered, and he played it twice as well.

When this second lay was over, Gandin stepped before the King, rote in hand.

'Now, Sire,' he said, 'remember what you promised me!'

'I shall, most willingly. Tell me, what do you want?'

'Give me Isolde!' he answered.

'My friend, apart from her, whatever you command is here at your disposal. What you ask is quite impossible.'

'Take my word for it, Sire,' replied Gandin; 'there is nothing I want, great or small, save only Isolde!'

'I declare that shall not happen!' retorted the King.

'Then you do not mean to keep your word, Sire? If you are proved a liar you should not henceforth be king of any land. Have the law of kings read out to you – if you do not find what I have said there, I will abandon my suit at once. Alternatively, if you or some proxy maintain that you promised me nothing, I will pursue my claim against you and him as your court thinks fit to assign to me. I will risk my life in combat, unless I am given my due. Let whomsoever you please, or you yourself in person, ride into the battle-ground with me. I will attest at the appointed time that fair Isolde is mine!'

The King looked this way and that searching everywhere for someone who would dare to face Gandin. But no one was ready to hazard his life, nor was Mark willing to fight for Isolde in person, since Gandin was so strong, virile, and courageous. None of them made it his concern.

Now my lord Tristan had ridden out stalking in the forest. No sooner was he on his way back to court from the woods than he learned the hateful news that Isolde had been surrendered to Gandin. It was true, so she had been. Gandin had taken the lovely woman, who was passionately weeping with many signs of distress, from the court to the landing-place, where a magnificent pavilion had been set up for him. He and the Queen went inside to sit down and wait till the tide should come in and the ship get afloat; for it was lying on the sand.

When Tristan arrived back home and heard more and more of the affair of the rote, he mounted his horse without delay and, taking his harp, rode at great speed to the neighbourhood of the port, where he shrewdly turned aside towards a bush and tethered his horse to a branch. He also hung his sword there, and then hastened away with his harp and came to the pavilion, where, sure enough, he found poor unhappy Isolde all in tears sitting beside the baron, who held her in his arms. He was doing his best to comfort her, but this was of little use – till she saw that one man with his harp!

'God save you, good harper!' said Gandin in greeting.

'Thank you, noble knight,' replied Tristan. 'My lord,' he went on, 'I have hurried here at great speed. I was told you were from Ireland. Sir, I am from Ireland, too. Take me home again, as you are an honourable man!'

'You have my word on it, my friend,' replied the Irishman. 'Now sit down and play me something. If you console my lady so that she leaves her weeping, I will give you the finest clothes that we have in this pavilion.'

'Done, sir!' answered Tristan. 'Unless it is a case of her refusing to stop crying for any man's music, I fancy she will refrain from it.' He set about his business and at once struck up a lay of such surpassing sweetness that it stole into Isolde's heart and pervaded her whole consciousness to the point where she left her weeping and was lost in thoughts of her lover.

By the time the lay was ended the tide had reached the ship and the ship had come afloat. This was the sign for Gandin's men to call from on deck into the harbour: 'My lord, my lord, come aboard! If Sir Tristan arrives while you are still ashore we shall have trouble on our hands! He commands the whole land and people and is himself (so they say) so daring and mettlesome that he may easily do you some harm!'

This roused Gandin's ire. 'God hate me if I budge a moment sooner this day to go on board for that!' he said very indignantly. 'My friend, play me first the Lay of Dido. You play your harp so well that I am greatly obliged to you for it. Now play it well for my lady. In return I will take you away with us and give you the clothes that were promised you, here and now – the very best I have.'

'At your service, my lord,' answered Tristan. The minstrel struck up again, and drew such sweet sounds from the strings that Gandin hearkened to his playing most attentively. Nor did it escape Gandin that Isolde was engrossed in the harp.

When the lay was over, Gandin took the Queen with the intention of embarking. But the depth of water before the gangway was now so great that none could enter by it unless he had a horse which was very long in the leg.

'What shall we do now?' asked Gandin. 'How can my lady go on board?'

'Listen, sir,' said the minstrel. 'Since I am sure that you will take me with you, I mean to leave none of my Cornish belongings behind. I have a big horse near by and I fancy he is tall enough for me to take madam your friend in over the gang-board so nicely that the sea will not touch her!'

'Go quickly, dear minstrel, fetch your horse, and receive your gift of clothes at once!'

Tristan at once fetched the horse and as soon as he was back he slung his harp behind him. 'Now, my lord from Ireland,' he said, 'hand my lady up to me and I will take her on the pommel.'

'No, minstrel,' answered Gandin, 'you shall not touch her. I shall take her myself.'

'Nonsense, my lord!' said fair Isolde. 'This talk of not letting him touch me is quite pointless. Rest absolutely assured that I shall never go aboard unless the minstrel takes me!'

Gandin handed her up to him. 'Look after her, friend,' he said, 'and take her in so carefully that I shall always be beholden to you.'

When Tristan had got possession of Isolde he galloped his horse a short distance away, seeing which 'Hey, you fool, what are you up to?' Gandin cried indignantly.

'You are wrong,' retorted Tristan. 'You are the fool, Gandin! You are the one who has been fooled! Since what you tricked from Mark with your rote, I now take away with my harp! Deceiver that you are, you have now been duped in return. Tristan followed after you till now he has outwitted you! You bestow magnificent clothes, friend. I have the best that I saw in your tent!'

Tristan rode on his way. Gandin was beyond all measure sad and sorry for himself. His defeat and disgrace wounded him to the heart. He sailed back over the sea in sorrow and in shame. As to our two companions, Tristan and Isolde, they were heading for home. Whether they attained happiness anywhere on the way resting among the flowers, I shall leave unguessed: for my part I shall refrain from guesses and surmises.

Tristan brought Isolde back to his uncle Mark and took him severely to task. 'Sire,' he said, 'dear as the Queen is to you, Heaven knows, it is a great folly on your part to give her away so lightly for the sake of the harp or the rote. People may well scoff. Whoever saw a queen made common property for a performance on the rote? Don't let it happen again, and guard my lady better in future!'

19

MARJODOC

T R I S T A N'S renown flourished more than ever at court and in the country. People praised his skill and intelligence. He and the Queen were gay and happy again. They cheered each other's hearts whenever they could best contrive it.

In those days Tristan had a companion, a noble baron and vassal of the King and indeed his Steward-in-Chief, who went by the name of Marjodoc. He sought Tristan's friendship for the sake of the charming Queen, for whom he had a secret attachment, as many men have for many ladies, but to which these pay no attention. This pair, Tristan and the Steward, enjoyed each other's company and shared the same lodgings, and it was the Steward's way, since Tristan was a good talker, to lie down beside him of an evening so that he could readily converse with him.

One night it chanced that he had discoursed a good deal with Tristan on a variety of topics and had fallen asleep. Hereupon that lover Tristan stole silently along to his pasture, to the oft-repeated anguish both of himself and of the Queen. Though he deemed himself safe from exposure and master of the situation, Ill Fortune had set her snares, her baying pack, and t rouble ahead of him along that selfsame path which, now and again, in happy mood, he took to visit Isolde. That night the path was covered with snow. The moon, too, was very bright and clear. But Tristan gave no thought to spies and ambushes, but went boldly to the place of his secret assignation. When he had entered the chamber, Brangane took a chess-board and stood it in front of the light. Now I do not know how she overlooked it, but she failed to close the door, and went to sleep again.

While this was taking place the Steward saw in his dream as he slept a boar, fearsome and dreadful, that ran out from the forest. Up to the King's court he came, foaming at the mouth and whetting his tusks, and charging everything in his path. And now a great crowd of courtiers ran up. Many knights leapt hither and thither round the boar, yet none of them dared face him. Thus he plunged grunting through the Palace. Arriving at Mark's chamber he broke in through the doors, tossed the King's appointed bed in all directions, and fouled the royal linen with his foam. Mark's vassals all witnessed this, yet none made it his business to interfere.

When Marjodoc woke up, he brooded on the dream, since it pained him deeply. Then he called Tristan, meaning to tell him about his dream, but nobody answered. He then called again and again and reached out with his hand, but hearing no sound and finding no one in the bed, had a sudden suspicion of a clandestine affair. But of Tristan's intrigue with the Queen he had no notion at all. Yet, dear though Tristan was to him, he was piqued as a friend might be that Tristan had not told him his secret.

Marjodoc got up at once and dressed. He crept softly to the door, looked out and saw Tristan's footsteps. He then followed these tracks through a little orchard. The light of the moon, too, showed him the way over the snow-covered lawn, where Tristan had passed before him, as far as the chamber door. There in fear he halted, and was assailed by sudden displeasure at finding the door thus open. And so he pondered for a long time where Tristan might have gone, weighing good and bad. And now it occurred to him that Tristan had gone there for the sake of some young lady-in-waiting. But no sooner had the thought crossed his mind than he suspected he was there to meet the Queen. He wavered between these suspicions. Finally, plucking up his courage, he stole in very softly, but found neither candle nor moonlight – of the candle that burned there he saw nothing, for a chess-board stood before it. Thus he continued straight ahead, feeling along the walls with his hands, till he came to their bed and overheard the two of them and all that passed between them. This deeply offended him and wounded him to the heart, for all along he had had a warm regard for Isolde. But now this was all cut short by hatred and anger; now he felt hatred and anger, anger and hatred towards her. He was moved first by the one passion, then by the other. Faced with such a happening, he was unable to find a seemly course of action. Hatred and anger prompted him to be so unmannerly as to divulge their affair and make it known then and there. But his fear of Tristan – that he might do him some injury – restrained him.

And so he turned back and withdrew, and lay down again as a man much wronged. Soon Tristan, too, returned, and lay down on his bed very gently. He kept silent, as did the other, so that neither said a word, a thing that had not happened before and which was most unlike them. From this estrangement Tristan could tell that Marjodoc harboured some suspicion as to what was afoot, and so kept a closer watch on his speech and behaviour than hitherto. But it was too late: his secret was out, the thing that he wished to hide was now revealed.

Jealous Marjodoc took the King privately aside and told him that a rumour had sprung up at court concerning Tristan and Isolde which did the land little credit, and that he should take note of it and seek advice as to what to do about it, for it compromised his marriage and his honour. But he did not affirm to him that he knew the true state of affairs with such finality.

In his artlessness, Mark, the best and most loyal of men, was amazed and reluctant to agree that he should ever have the lodestar of his happiness in the person of Isolde under any suspicion of misconduct whatsoever. Nevertheless, he nursed it in his thoughts with pain and suffering and was always on the watch at all times of the day, in case he might unmask them through any factual proof. He took careful stock of all that the lovers said and did, yet failed to catch them at anything that amounted to firm evidence; for Tristan had acquainted Isolde with the Steward's suspicions and asked her to be on her guard. Nevertheless, Mark put it to the test most stringently, and was on the watch night and day.

20

PLOT AND COUNTERPLOT

ONE night as Mark lay beside the Queen and the conversation went to and fro between them, he set a cunning snare for her and succeeded in catching her in it.

'Now tell me, madam,' he said, 'what is your opinion, what do you advise? I mean shortly to go on a pilgrimage and may be away a long time. Under whose care and surveillance do you wish to be meanwhile?'

'Heavens!' answered the Queen. 'Why ever do you ask? In whose care should I and your land and people, too, be better off than in that of your nephew Tristan, who will look after us excellently? Your nephew, lord Tristan, is brave, prudent, and circumspect in every possible way.'

Mark grew very suspicious indeed at this answer; he did not like it at all. He set more and more watches and look-outs, and kept Isolde closer than ever. He at once told the Steward what he had discovered. 'Indeed, Sire,' answered the latter, 'that is just how it is. You can see for yourself from this that she is unable to disguise her passion for Tristan. It is very unwise of you to let him stay near her. As you cherish your wife and honour, do not suffer his presence any longer!' This angered Mark deeply. The suspicion and doubt which he was asked to entertain towards his nephew tormented him unceasingly, though he had failed to catch him in any misconduct at all.

Outwitted had she but known it, Isolde was jubilant. Laughing for joy and in great exultation she told Brangane of her consort's pilgrimage, and how she had been asked in whose care she wished to be. 'Madam,' interposed Brangane, 'tell me truthfully on your honour: whom did you ask for?' Isolde told her the truth, just as the thing had been schemed. 'How rash of you!' said Brangane. 'Oh why did you say so! It is clear to me that what was said on this subject was a trap, and I'll be bound it was the Steward who hatched the plot. They want to sound you with it. You must acquit yourself better in future. If he mentions it to you again, do as I tell you now. Say this, say that ...' and she told her mistress what answers she might make to counter such intrigues.

Mark, meanwhile, was burdened with a double sorrow. He was harassed by the doubt and suspicion which he had and could not fail to have. He deeply suspected his darling Isolde; he had doubts about Tristan, in whom he could find no sign either of deceit or of treachery. His friend Tristan, his joy Isolde – these two were his chief affliction. They pressed sorely on him, heart and soul. He suspected both her and him, and had doubts about them both. He bore with this double pain after the common fashion and desert, for when he wished to have his pleasure with Isolde, suspicion thwarted him, and then he wished to investigate and track down the truth of the matter. But since this was denied him, doubt racked him once more, and all was again as before.

What harms love more than doubt and suspicion? What constricts a lover's heart so much as doubt? In its grip he does not for one moment know where to go. From some offence that he sees or hears he could now swear that he had got to the bottom of it: but before you can lift a finger things are back to where they were, and he sees something else that arouses his doubts, as a result of which he gets lost again! Except that it is the way of the world, it is a very imprudent attitude and great folly to harbour suspicion in love: for none is at ease with a love of which he must needs be suspicious.

Yet it is far more remiss in a man to reduce doubt and surmise to certainty; since when he has gained his object and knows that his doubts are justified, the fact which he was at pains to track down becomes a grief surpassing all others. The two ills which troubled him before would now be welcome to him. If only he could have them back, he would now accept doubt and surmise, if only he need never know the truth. Thus it happens that evil brings about evil till something worse arrives: when this works greater ill, what once was bad seems good. However distressing suspicion is in love, its presence is not so irksome but that one would endure it far better than proven animosity. There is no help for it – love must breed doubt. Doubt *should* have part in love. Love must find her salvation with it. So long as Love has doubt there is some hope for her; but when she sees the truth, she is suddenly past all remedy.

Furthermore, Love has a way which has entangled her more than all else, namely, that when things are to her liking she refuses to remain steadfast and very easily lets go; and as soon as she sights suspicion she will not be parted from it. She is all impatient to join it and, stealthily pursuing it, goes to greater pains to discover her mortal sorrow than she will take for the joy that she can find and possess there.

Mark persevered in this same senseless habit. Day and night he bent his whole mind to ridding himself of doubt and suspicion, and was most eager to arrive through proof positive at his own mortal sorrow. Such was his set intention.

It happened again one night that Mark spread his toils before Isolde as he and Marjodoc had plotted it, in the hope of sounding her further by such subtleties. But things took the opposite turn: following Brangane's instructions, the Queen caught her royal master in the snare which he had laid for her and contrived for her downfall. Here Brangane was most efficacious. It stood them both in good stead that cunning had been met with cunning.

The King drew the Queen to his heart and kissed her eyes and mouth many times. 'Lovely woman,' he said, 'I hold nothing so dear as you, and my having to leave you soon is robbing me of my reason, may God in Heaven be witness!'

The well-tutored Queen parried cunning with cunning. Fetching a deep sigh, she addressed him: 'Alas, poor wretched me. I have been thinking the whole time that this hateful news was a joke, but now I see you really mean it!' And she gave vent to her distress with tears and laments, and fell to weeping so piteously that she forced the artless man to yield up all his doubt, and he could have sworn she did it from her heart. For (to take one's words from their own lips) the ladies have no greater harm or guile or duplicity in them of any description than that they can weep for no reason at all, as often as they please. Isolde wept copiously.

'Tell me, lovely woman,' asked Mark in his credulity, 'what is the matter, why do you cry?'

'I have good cause to cry,' answered Isolde. 'I have every reason to give way to my unhappiness. I am a woman in a strange land

and have but one life and the wits that I possess, and have so abandoned them to you and your love that I am unable to cherish anything in my thoughts but you alone. There is nothing so truly dear to me as you, and I know that you do not love me as much as you say and pretend. From the fact that you ever conceived the wish to go away and leave me in such strange surroundings, I can see that you heartily dislike me, so that I shall never feel happy again!'

'But why, lovely woman? You will have the land and the people at your command. They are yours as much as mine. Rule them, they are yours to dispose of. Whatever your bidding, it shall be done. While I am on my travels, my nephew, courtly Tristan, shall take care of you – he well knows how to do so. He is prudent and circumspect, he will make every effort to see that you are happy and to enhance your reputation. I trust him, as I have every reason to do. He has the same affection for you as for me; he will do it for the sake of both of us.'

'Lord Tristan?' asked fair Isolde. 'Indeed, I would rather be dead and buried than consent to be in his keeping! That sycophant is always toadying at my side with his flattery, and protesting how much he esteems me! But God can read his thoughts and knows with what sincerity he does so. And I know well enough myself, for he killed my uncle and fears my hatred. It is in dread of this that he is always fawning, beguiling, and flattering in his false way, imagining all the time that he will gain my friendship by it. But it is all to no purpose, his wheedling will not serve him. And God knows, were it not for you, for whose sake more than for my own honour I make a show of friendship towards him, I would never look at him with friendly eyes. And since I cannot avoid hearing and seeing him, it will have to happen without sincere affection on my part. I have, there is no denying it, occupied myself with him time and again with eyes devoid of warmth and with lies on my lips, merely to avoid censure. Women are said to hate their husband's friends. Thus I have beguiled the time for him with many a false look and with words lacking in affection, so that he would have sworn I did it from my heart. Sire, do not be deceived by it. Your nephew lord Tristan shall not have me in his keeping for so much as a day, if I can win your consent. You yourself must take charge of me on your travels, if you will. Wherever you wish to go, I wish to go there too, unless you alone should prevent me, or death should cheat me of it.'

Thus wily Isolde dissembled towards her consort till she had won him from his suspicion and anger with her tricks, and he would have sworn she meant it. Mark, the waverer, had found the right path again. His companion had rid him of his doubts. All that she said and did was now well done. The King at once told the Steward what she had answered in all detail, as precisely as he could, asserting that she was free of all deceit. This displeased the Steward and mortified his heart: nevertheless he instructed Mark farther as to how he could test Isolde once more.

At night, when Mark lay abed again conversing with the Queen, he once more spread his toils by means of questions, and decoyed her into them.

'Listen, ma'am,' he said. 'As I see it, we must bow to necessity. Show me how women guard the realm! My lady, I must go abroad and you must remain with my friends. My kinsmen and vassals and all who wish me well must afford you honour and resources when-ever you please to ask them. And if there are knights and ladies whose company irks you or whom you do not care to see about you, send them all away! You shall neither see nor hear anything that annoys you, whether it concerns people or property, if it goes against the grain. Nor shall I love anyone whom you regard with disfavour: this is the truth. Be merry and gay, and live as you think fit – you have my blessing on it! And since you cannot abide my nephew Tristan, I will shortly dismiss him from court on some convenient pretext. He must sail to Parmenie and see to his own affairs – both he and his country need it.'

'Thank you, my lord,' answered Isolde. 'You speak loyally and wisely. Since you now assure me that you are quick to take offence at whatever vexes me, it seems only right in return that I should defer to you to the utmost of my power in whatever suits your whim or finds favour in your eyes, and that I should help and advise, morning and night, in all that may serve your reputation. Now listen, Sire, to what you must do. I shall never wish or advise, now or at any time, that you should remove your nephew from court. For it would reflect on me if you did so. People would be quick to spread the rumour, here at court and in the country, that it was I who had put you up to it in order to settle an old score that rankles with me – namely, that he killed my uncle! There would be a good deal said on this topic that would be degrading for me and no great honour for you. I shall never consent to your humiliating your friend for love of me, or to your offending for my sake anyone to whom you owe favour. You should also consider this. If you go away, who is to guard your two territories? They will rest neither well nor peacefully in a woman's hands. Whoever is to maintain two kingdoms justly and honourably needs courage and intelligence, and, apart from my lord Tristan, there is not a baron in them who would do them any good if you permitted him to govern. Apart from Tristan, no one could take office whose commands would be respected. If the misfortune of war should come, for which we must be ready any day, it might easily happen that we should come off worst. Then, in their malice, they would twit and taunt you with Tristan. "Had Tristan been here" they would go on repeating "we should not have come to grief like this!" And then by common report they would all put the blame on me for having lost him your favour, to your injury and theirs. Sire, it would be better to refrain. Reconsider the matter. Weigh these two things: either let me accompany you, or place him in charge of your lands. Whatever my feelings for him are, I would rather he were on the scene than someone else should fail us and ruin us.'

The King realized in a flash that her whole heart was bent on Tristan's advancement, and immediately veered round to his former doubts and suspicions. As a result, he was more than ever immersed in angry resentment. Isolde for her part acquainted Brangane with their conversation in all detail and recounted one thing and the next without forgetting a word. Brangane was very sorry indeed that she had spoken as she had, and that the conversation had taken such a turn. She lectured her once more as to what she was to say.

At night, when the Queen went to bed with her lord, she took him in her arms and, kissing and embracing him and pressing him close to her soft smooth breasts, resumed her verbal stalking by means of question and answer.

'Sire,' she said, 'tell me as you love me: have you seriously ar-

ranged matters in accordance with what you told me about my lord
Tristan – that for my sake you mean to send him home? Could I be
sure of that I would thank you now and for the rest of my life. Sire,
I have great trust in you, as well I may and should, but at the same
time I fear that this may be some test. Yet if I knew for certain (as
you explained to me) that you meant to banish from my sight what-
ever was hateful to me, I would know from this that you loved me.
I would gladly have made this request long ago, but that I was re-
luctant; for I am well aware what I shall have to expect from Tristan
if I am to have long acquaintance of him. Now, Sire, make up your
mind to it – yet not because of ill-feeling on my part! If he is to
administer these kingdoms while you are on your travels and some
accident befalls you, as may easily happen on a journey, he will de-
prive me of my lands and title. Now you have learned in full the
harm that I can suffer at his hands. Think it over sympathetically,
as a friend should, and rid me of lord Tristan. You would be acting
wisely. Send him home again, or arrange for him to travel with you
and for Steward Marjodoc to care for me meanwhile. But if you felt
inclined to let me travel with you, I would leave our lands to be
governed and protected by whoever was willing, if only I might go
with you! But despite all this, dispose of your territories and of me
entirely as you please, that is my wish and intention. If only I can
be mindful to do what will please you, I shall not worry about the
realm and the people.'

She worked on her lord with her frauds till she forced him to re-
linquish his doubts for the second time, and once more to abandon
his suspicions concerning her thoughts and affections. He judged
the Queen in every way innocent of any misdemeanour; but the
Steward Marjodoc he judged in every way a liar, though Marjodoc
had informed him correctly and told him the truth about the Queen.

21

MELOT

WHEN the Steward saw that his plans were coming to nothing, he set to work another way. There was a dwarf at court, said to go by the name of Melot le petit of Aquitaine, who had some skill in reading the secrets of the stars, so it was alleged. But I will say nothing that concerns him beyond what I take from my source. Now I do not find anything about him in the authentic version of the tale other than that he was cunning, artful, and eloquent. He was one of the King's familiars and had admittance to the Queen's apartment. Marjodoc began to conspire with Melot that when Melot went in to join the ladies he should watch Tristan and the Queen; and he told the dwarf that, if he could serve him so far as to procure firm proof of love between them, Mark would reward and esteem him ever after.

And so Melot applied his lies and snares to this task, morning and night. He laid his traps in word and gesture at all hours of the day and had soon ascertained that they were lovers, for they behaved towards each other with such tenderness that Melot at once found the proofs of love in them and told King Mark without loss of time that it was assuredly a case of love. Thus they all three – Melot, Mark, and Marjodoc – pursued the matter, till by joint consent they settled on this ruse: that if my lord Tristan were forbidden the court, then the truth would be clearly revealed to them. This was at once given effect, exactly as it was planned.

The King requested his nephew for the sake of his own honour not to repair to the ladies' quarters or anywhere else where they foregathered, since the court was busy with a rumour (which was much to be guarded against) that could cause the Queen and himself much scandal and pain. Tristan at once complied with Mark's wishes. He avoided every place where ladies were among themselves. He never entered their apartments or the Palace. The house hold were much surprised at him and his aloofness. They said hard and unkind things about him. His ears were often full of undying malice. He and Isolde both spent an anxious time. Grief and despondency were very active between them. They suffered two kinds of sorrow. Sorrow at Mark's suspicion; sorrow that they had no opportunity for intimate conversation. From hour to hour their strength and spirits began to flag, and they lost colour. The man grew pale for the woman, the woman for the man; Tristan for Isolde, Isolde for Tristan. This gave them both great torment. It does not surprise me that their distress was mutual, and their suffering one and undivided; for there was but one heart and soul between them. Their pleasure and their pain, their life and their death were as if woven into one. Whatever troubled either, the other grew aware of it. Whatever gratified one, his partner sensed it immediately. For pleasure and for pain the two were at one. Their deep dejection was written so plain on their faces that there was little in their appearance to deny that they were lovers.

Mark at once discerned in the pair of them that their enforced estrangement made them suffer keenly and that they were longing to see each other, if only they knew how or where. He devised a stratagem to test them and without delay ordered his huntsmen to get ready with their hounds for the forest. He sent a message to inform them and had it announced at court that he would be out hunting for twenty days, and that those who were skilled in the chase, or who wished to pass the time out hunting, should make their preparations. He took leave of the Queen and told her to amuse herself at home as she pleased. He then privately charged the dwarf to spread his lies and stratagems round the lovers' secret doings, and assured him of his lasting gratitude. Mark himself rode off to the forest with much clamour. His hunting companion, Tristan, stayed at home and sent a message to his uncle that he was ill. The sick huntsman, too, yearned to go out to his hunting-ground! Both he and Isolde were engrossed in their sorrows, painfully searching in wildest flights of fancy how it could ever come about that they should see each other. But they could devise no means.

Meanwhile Brangane went to Tristan, realizing that he must be in agony, and they commiserated together.

'Ah, noble lady,' he said, 'tell me, what remedy is there for this desperate situation? What shall poor Isolde and I do to escape destruction? I have no idea how we can save out lives.'

'What advice can I give you?' asked the loyal woman. 'May God have pity on us that we were ever born! We have all three forfeited our happiness and honour. We shall never recover our freedom. Alas, Isolde! Alas, Tristan! that I ever set eyes on you, and that I should be the cause of your suffering! I can think of no plan or subterfuge by which I could help you. I can hit on nothing that would serve you. I know it as sure as I shall die that you will be in great danger if you are kept apart under such duress for long. Since there is nothing better to do, take my advice, nevertheless, for now and so long as you are separated from us. When you see that your chance has come, take a twig of olive, cut some slivers lengthwise, and just engrave them with a "T" on one side and an "I" on the other, so that only your initials appear, neither more nor less. Then go into the orchard. You know the brook which flows there from the spring towards the ladies' apartments? Throw a shaving into it and let it float past the door where wretched Isolde and I come out at all times of the day to weep over our misery. When we see the shaving we shall know at once that you are by the brook. Watch from the shadow of the olive-tree and keep a sharp look-out. Your love-lorn friend my lady and I will always come to meet you as occasion offers, and as you yourself desire. My lord, the short time I still have to live shall be spent together with you so that I may devote my life to you both and advise you how to act. If, at the cost of a thousand hours of mine, I had to buy but one in which I could live for your and Isolde's happiness, I would sell all the days of my life, rather than fail to lighten your sorrows!'

'Thank you, lovely woman,' replied Tristan. 'I do not doubt that you are loyal and honourable. Greater loyalty and honour were never implanted in one heart. If luck should come my way, I would use it to your happiness and advancement. Though my situation is wretched and my fortunes are toppling, if I knew how I might devote my hours and days to your happiness, believe me, I would gladly shorten my life to do so!' And then addressing her again through his tears: 'My good and faithful lady!' Whereupon he put his arms about her and drawing her very close, kissed her eyes and cheeks with many a pang, time and time again. 'Be kind and do as a loyal person should, pretty Brangane, and take care of me and dear Isolde, so full of sighs and cares! Bear us both well in mind.'

'I shall most willingly, sir. I will go now, by your leave. Do as I have told you and do not worry over much.'

'May God watch over your honour and handsome person!' Brangane wept as she bowed to him, and went sorrowfully away.

Doleful Tristan cut his slivers and threw them into the brook just as his counsellor Brangane had instructed him, so that he might mend his situation. Thus, as opportunity presented itself, he and his lady Isolde stole along the brook to the shadow of the tree no less than eight times in as many days without anyone being the wiser or their coming under observation.

But one night – I do not know how – it chanced that when Tristan was going this way, Melot (that cursed dwarf and tool of the Devil) most unluckily caught sight of him. He slunk after him all the way to where he observed him to go towards the tree and wait but a short time beside it when a lady joined him and he took her close into his arms. But who the lady was Melot could not say.

The next day a little before noon Melot sneaked out on his way again, his bosom well stuffed with dissembled regrets and vile deceit, and went to Tristan.

'Believe me, my lord, I have had an anxious time getting here; for you are so close beset with watchers and spies that, I assure you, I have made my way under cover here with the greatest difficulty, and only because I pity from my heart the good Queen, steadfast Isolde, who, I regret to say, is at this moment much troubled on your account. Finding no one else so apt for this purpose, she has asked me to come to you. She told me to give you her greetings, and did so from her heart, begging you most urgently to speak with her today at some place – I do not know where, but you do – where you met her last by night, and to keep careful watch for the time at which you are accustomed to come. I have no idea what she hopes to warn you of. And you must believe me that no worse thing has befallen me than her sorrow and your unhappiness have brought me! Now my lord Tristan, sir, I will go, by your leave. I will tell her whatever you please. I dare not stay any longer. If the court got to know that I had come here, I might have to pay for it heavily. You know, everybody says and believes that whatever has been done between you, all happened through me. I declare before God and the pair of you that it did not come about at my prompting!'

'Are you dreaming, my friend?' asked Tristan. 'What tittle-tattle are you foisting on me? What does the court believe? What have I and my lady done? Be off with you, and quickly, damn you! And rest assured of this: no matter what anyone says or believes, if I did not refrain for my own honour most of all, you would never get back to court to tell what you have been dreaming here!'

22

THE ASSIGNATION BY THE BROOK

MELOT left, and he at once rode to the forest and found Mark. He told the King that he had got to the bottom of the matter, and reported what had happened at the brook. 'If you will ride there with me tonight, Sire, you can see the truth for yourself. There is nothing on which I count with greater confidence than that they will meet there this very night, however they manage to do so. Then you can see for yourself how they behave.'

The King rode back with Melot to spy on his own chagrin. When they entered the orchard after dark and set about their business, the King and his dwarf failed to find any cover that would serve them for a lurking-place. Now beside the running brook there stood an olive-tree of some size, its foliage low, yet ample and spreading. Into this they climbed after some effort, sat, and said not a word.

When night was drawing on, Tristan stole out on his way again. Arriving in the orchard he took his 'messengers', placed them in the stream and sent them floating along. They always told love-lorn Isolde that her lover was at hand. Tristan at once crossed the brook to where the olive cast its shadow on the grass. There he took his stand, pondering his secret woes. And so it chanced that he noticed Mark's and Melot's shadows, for the moon was shining down through the tree very brightly. When he had made out these two forms distinctly, he was seized with great anxiety, for he realized in a flash that he was in a trap. 'Almighty God,' he thought, 'protect Isolde and me! If she fails to detect this trap from the shadow in time, she will come straight on towards me. And if that happens we shall be in a sad predicament! O Lord in thy mercy and goodness have us both in thy keeping! Stand guard over Isolde on this path! Guide her every step! Make the blameless woman somehow aware of this vile ambush which has been set for us, lest she say or do anything that could give rise to ugly thoughts. O my Lord, have pity on her and me! I commend our lives and honour this night to Thee!'

His lady the Queen and their friend, noble Brangane, went out unaccompanied to their garden of sorrows, where they always used to go to commiserate with each other when there was no danger in their doing so, to keep watch for Tristan's messengers. They walked up and down, sorrowing and lamenting, and sadly conversing of love. But Brangane soon noticed the message-bearing shavings in the current and beckoned to her mistress. Isolde retrieved and examined them. She read both 'Isolde' and 'Tristan'.

Quickly taking her cloak, Isolde wound it round her head and stole through the flowers and grass towards the tree by the brook. When she was near enough for them both to see each other, Tristan remained standing where he was, a thing that he had never done before – she had never approached him without his having come a long way to meet her. Thus Isolde was much puzzled to know what this could mean, and her heart sank within her. She drooped her head and walked towards him with apprehension – her going filled her with terror. As she softly drew near to the tree she caught sight of the shadows of three men, yet, to her knowledge, only one was there. From this, but also from Tristan's behaviour, she recognized at once that it was a trap. 'Oh what will come of this plot to have us murdered? What lies behind this ambush? I'll wager my master has a hand in it, wherever he may be lurking. I am sure we have been betrayed! Protect us, O Lord. Help us to leave this place without dishonour! Lord, watch over him and me!' But then she thought: 'Is Tristan aware of this calamity, or does he not know of it?' Then it struck her that, judging from his behaviour, he had discovered the trap.

She halted some way off and said: 'Lord Tristan, I am sorry you count with such assurance on my simplicity as to expect me to talk to you at this time of night. If you were to guard your reputation towards your uncle and me that would be more seemly and accord better with your allegiance and my honour than putting me to so late and secret a parley. Now tell me, what is it you want? I stand here in great fear because Brangane insisted on my coming and meeting you here in order to learn what was troubling you; after leaving you today she begged and urged me to do so. But it was very wrong of me to give way to her. She is sitting somewhere near by, and however safe I am here, I assure you, such is my dread of wicked people, I would rather lose a finger than that anyone should learn I had met you here. People have spread such tales about us; they would all take their oaths on it that we are embroiled in an illicit love-affair! The court is full of that suspicion. But God Himself knows how my feelings stand towards you. And I will go a little farther. May God be my witness when I say it – may I never be rid of my sins by any other test than the measure of my affection for you! For I declare before God that I never conceived a liking for any man but him who had my maidenhead, and that all others are barred from my heart, now and for ever. I swear to Heaven, lord Tristan, that it is very wrong of my lord Mark to suspect me so strongly on your account, fully acquainted as he is with the state of my feelings towards you. God knows, those who have got me talked about are very rash: they have no idea what my heart is really like. I have put on a friendly mien for you a hundred thousand times from affection for the man whom it is mine to love – not in with intent to deceive, Heaven knows full well! It seems right to me and very much to my credit, that I should show honour to any-one, knight or page, who is dear or near to Mark. Yet people twist it against me! But, for my part, I will never bear you any ill will as a result of all their lies. My lord, tell me what you have to tell me, for I wish to go – I cannot stay here any longer.'

'Good lady,' answered Tristan, 'I do not doubt that you would speak and act both virtuously and honourably if you had your way, but liars do not permit you, such as have brought suspicion upon you and me and lost us my lord's favour without cause, wholly innocent though we are, as God must recognize. Consider it, good lady, noble Queen, reflect how altogether guiltless I am with regard to you and Mark, and urge my lord of his courtesy to hide the animosity which he bears me without cause, and to put a good face on the matter for no more than this coming week. Till then let both of you behave towards me as though I enjoyed your favour. Mean-while I shall make my preparations to leave. We shall lose our good name, my lord the King, and you and I. For, if you behave as you do when I go away, our enemies will say: "There was most certainly something in it – see how my lord Tristan left court in the King's disfavour!"'

'Lord Tristan,' answered Isolde, 'I would sooner suffer death than ask my lord to do something for my sake that had anything to do with you. Surely you know that he has been ungracious towards me for a long time now on your account, so that, if he knew that I was alone with you at night at this very moment, I would be the subject of such a scandal that he would never again show me honour or kindness. Whether in fact he ever will, I truly do not know, and I am altogether puzzled as to how my lord Mark came by this suspicion, and who it was inspired it; while I for my part have never noticed (as women very quickly do, you know) that you have ever dissembled towards me, nor was I ever guilty of any falsity or laxness towards you. I cannot imagine of what treachery we are the victims, for your affairs and mine are in an ugly and lamentable state – may God Almighty remember them in time and mend and rectify them! Now, my lord, pardon me, I must go, as you must, too. God knows, I regret your vexation and troubles. I could claim that you have given me good cause to hate you, but I waive it now: rather am I sorry that you, through no fault, should now be in trouble because of me. I shall accordingly overlook your offence. And when the day comes for you to go away, may God preserve you, sir! May the Queen of Heaven watch over you! If I could be sure that the mission with which you have charged me would be furthered by any assistance that I could give, I would advise and act in any way I thought might help you. But I fear that Mark will misinterpret it. Yet whatever comes of it, and at whatever risk to me, I will give you your due for having acted loyally and honestly towards my lord and me. Whatever my success, I will further your suit as best I can!'

'Thank you, my lady,' answered Tristan. 'Let me know at once what response you meet with. But if I notice anything amiss and perhaps go away and never see you again, whatever comes of me then, may Heaven bless you, noble Queen! For God knows, neither land nor sea ever sustained so blameless a lady! Madam, I commend your body and soul, your life and honour, to God!'

And so they took leave of one another. The Queen went away sighing and sorrowing, pining and languishing, with secret pain both of body and of heart. Melancholy Tristan too went sorrowfully away amid a flood of tears. Sorrowful Mark sitting in the tree was moved to sadness by it, and was deeply distressed for having suspected his wife and nephew of infamy. He called down a thousand curses on those who had led him into it – in his heart and also aloud. He roundly accused Melot the dwarf of deceiving him and of slandering his wife. They descended from their tree and rode back to the hunt in a state of great dejection. But Mark and Melot were aggrieved for very different reasons: Melot because of the deception that he was alleged to have practised; Mark because of the suspicion which had induced him to put his wife and his nephew, and most of all himself, to such annoyance and get them so ill spoken of, both at court and in the country.

Next morning he lost no time in having it announced to the hunt that they should remain and carry on with their hunting: but he himself returned to court.

'Tell me, madam the Queen, how have you passed the time?'

'I have had needless sorrow to occupy me: to distract me the harp and the lyre.'

'Needless sorrow?' asked Mark. 'What was that, and why?'

Isolde's lips parted in a smile. 'Whatever the reason, it happened,' said she, 'and it will go on happening today and ever after. It is my nature like that of all other women to be sad and despondent without reason. We purify our hearts and brighten our eyes with it. We often conceive some great secret sorrow for a mere nothing, then suddenly abandon it.' And she went on trifling in this vein.

But Mark was passing it all through his mind and noting her words and meaning. 'Now, madam, tell me,' he said, 'do you or does anyone at court here know how Tristan is? When I rode away recently I was told he was in pain.'

'And you were told the truth, Sire,' was the Queen's answer. (She meant with regard to love – she was well aware that love was the cause of his suffering.)

'What do you know about it, and who told you?' continued the King.

'I only know what I suspect, and what Brangane told me of his illness a short time past. She saw him yesterday during the day and brought me a message from him asking me to bring you his complaint and beg you in God's name not to entertain thoughts so hurtful to his honour and to moderate your harshness towards him this coming week, so as to allow him time to prepare for his departure; and then to let him leave your court and go abroad with honour. This he asks of us both.' And she repeated his whole request in full, as he had made it beside the brook and as Mark himself had heard it, and the whole course of their conversation.

'May that man be eternally damned who led me into this, ma'am!' rejoined the King. 'I bitterly regret that I ever brought suspicion to bear on him, for only a short while ago I learned of his complete innocence and got to the bottom of it all! And, my dear Queen, if you have any affection for me, let this quarrel be yours to decide – whatever you do will be acceptable. Take the two of us, him and me, and compose the difference between us!'

'Sire, I do not wish to take such a labour upon myself, for were I to settle your quarrel today you would resume your suspicions tomorrow as before.'

'No, indeed, ma'am, never again. I will never again harbour thoughts that are injurious to his honour, nor shall I ever suspect you, my lady Queen, for any outward show of friendship!' This was duly vowed.

Thereupon Tristan was summoned, and suspicion was buried at once in amity and sincerity. Isolde was entrusted to Tristan's keeping with all due form, and he guarded and advised her in every way. She and her apartment were at his sole discretion. Tristan and his lady enjoyed a pleasant life again. The measure of their joy was full. Thus, following after their troubles, they now had a life of bliss again, however short-lived it was before fresh woes were on them.

23

THE ORDEAL

I SAY quite openly that no nettle has so sharp a sting as a sour neighbour, nor is there a peril so great as a false house-mate. This is what I call false: the man who shows his friend the face of a friend and is his enemy at heart. Such comradeship is terrible, for all the time he has honey in his mouth, but venom on his sting! Such venomous spite puffs up ill fortune for his friend in all that he sees or hears, and one cannot keep anything safe from him. On the other hand, when a man lays his snares for his enemy openly I do not account it falseness. As long as he remains an overt foe he does not do too much harm. But when he feigns friendship for a man, let his friend be on his guard!

This is what Melot and Marjodoc did. With deceit in their hearts they often sought Tristan's company, and, the one like the other, offered him their devoted friendship with cunning and dissembling. But Tristan had been amply warned, and he warned Isolde in turn. 'Now, queen of my heart,' he said, 'guard yourself and me in what you say and do. We are beset by great dangers. There are two poisonous snakes in the guise of doves who with their suave flattery never leave our sides – be on the alert for them, dear Queen! For when one's house-mates are faced like doves and tailed like the serpent-brood, one should cross oneself before the hailstorm and say a prayer against sudden death! Dearest lady, lovely Isolde, be much on your guard against Melot the Snake and Marjodoc the Cur!' Indeed, that is what they were – the one a snake, the other a cur, who were always laying their traps for the two lovers, whatever they did, wherever they went, like cur and snake. Morning and night they treacherously worked upon Mark with schemes and accusations till he began to waver in his love again and suspect the lovers once more and lay traps and make trial of their intimacy.

One day, on the advice of his false counsellors, Mark had himself bled, and Tristan and Isolde, too. They had no suspicion that any sort of trouble was being prepared for them and were entirely off their guard. Thus the King's intimate circle lay pleasurably at ease in their room.*

On the evening of the following day, when the household had dispersed and Mark had gone to bed, there was no one in the chamber but Mark, Isolde, Tristan, Melot, Brangane, and one young lady-in-waiting, as had been planned beforehand. Moreover, the light of the candles had been masked behind some tapestries to dim their brightness. When the bell for matins sounded, Mark silently dressed himself, absorbed in his thoughts as he was, and told Melot to get up and go to matins with him. When Mark had left his bed, Melot took some flour and sprinkled it on the floor so that if anyone should step to or away from the bed his coming or going could be traced. This done, they both went to church, where their observance had little concern with prayer.

Meanwhile, Brangane had at once seen the stratagem from the flour. She crept along to Tristan, warned him, and lay down again.

This trap was mortal pain for Tristan. His desire for the woman was at its height and his heart yearned in his body as to how he could get to her. He acted in keeping with the saying that passion should be without eyes, and love know no fear when it is in deadly earnest. 'Alas,' he thought, 'God in Heaven, what shall I do in face of this cursed trap? This gamble is for high stakes!' He stood up in his bed and looked all about him to see by what means he could get there. Now there was light enough for him to see the flour at once, but he judged the two positions too far apart for a leap; yet on the other hand he dared not walk there. He was nevertheless impelled to commit himself to the more promising alternative. He placed his feet together and ran hard at his mark. Love-blind Tristan made his gallant charge too far beyond his strength; he leapt on to the bed, yet lost his gamble, for his vein opened and this caused him much suffering and trouble in the outcome. His blood stained the bed and its linen, as is the way with blood, dyeing

---

* Strange to say, being bled had pleasant and companionable associations at this time.

it here, there, and everywhere. He lay there for the briefest space, till silks and gold brocades, bed and linen, were altogether soiled. He leapt back to his bed as he had come and lay in anxious thought till the bright day dawned.

Mark was soon back and gazing down at the floor. He examined his trap and found no trace. But when he went along and studied the bed, he saw blood everywhere. This caused him grave disquiet.

'How now, your Majesty,' asked Mark, 'what is the meaning of this? How did this blood get here?'

'My vein opened, and it bled from it. It has only just stopped bleeding!'

Then, as if in fun, he turned to examine Tristan. 'Up you get, lord Tristan!' he said, and threw back the coverlet and found blood here as there.

At this Mark fell silent and said not a word. He left Tristan lying there and turned away. His thoughts and all his mind grew heavy with it. He pondered and pondered, like a man for whom no pleasant day has dawned. Indeed, he had chased and all but caught up with his mortal sorrow, yet he had no other knowledge of their secret and the true state of affairs than he was able to see from the blood. But this evidence was slender. Thus he was now yoked again to the doubts and suspicions which he had utterly renounced. Having found the floor before the bed untrodden, he imagined that he was free of misdemeanour from his nephew. But again, finding the Queen and his bed all bloody, he was at once assailed by dark thoughts and ill humour, as always happens to waverers. Amid these doubts he did not know what to do. He believed one thing, he believed another. He did not know what he wanted or what he should believe. He had just found Love's guilty traces in his bed, though not before it, and was thus told the truth and denied it. With these two, truth and untruth, he was deceived. He suspected both alternatives, yet both eluded him. He neither wished the two of them guilty, nor wished them free of guilt. This was a cause of lively grief to that waverer.

Mark, lost man that he was, was now weighed down more than ever before by pondering on how he might find a way out and compose his doubts, how he might throw off his load of uncertainty and wean the court from the suspicions with which it was so busy concerning his wife and nephew. He summoned his great nobles, to whom he looked for loyalty, and acquainted them with his troubles. He told them how the rumour had sprung up at court, and that he was much afraid for his marriage and his honour, and he declared that in view of how the allegation against them had been made public and noised about the land, he felt no inclination to show favour to the Queen or to be on terms of intimacy with her till she had publicly vindicated her innocence and conjugal fidelity towards him, and that he was seeking their general advice as to how he could eliminate all doubt concerning her delinquency, one way or the other, in a manner consonant with his honour.

His kinsmen and vassals advised him forthwith to hold a council at London in England and make known his troubles to the clergy, to those shrewd prelates so learned in canon law.

The council was promptly called to meet in London after Whitsun week when May was drawing to a close. A great number of clergy and laymen arrived on the appointed day in answer to the royal summons. And now Mark and Isolde arrived, both weighed down with sorrow and fear – Isolde in great fear of losing her life and her honour, Mark in great sorrow that through his wife Isolde he might cripple his happiness and noble reputation.

When Mark had taken his seat at the council he complained to his great nobles of the vexation to which this slander was subjecting him and begged them earnestly for the sake of God and of their honour, if they had the skill, to devise some remedy whereby he could exact satisfaction and justice for this delict and settle the issue in one sense or another. Many aired their views on this topic, some well, others ill, one man this way, another that.

Then one of the great lords present at the council rose to his feet, a man well fitted by sagacity and age to offer good advice, the Bishop of the Thames, who was old and distinguished in appearance and as grey as he was wise.

'My lord King, hear me,' said the bishop, leaning over his crook. 'You have summoned us, the nobles of England, into your presence to hear our loyal advice, in dire need of it as you are. I am one of the great nobles, too, Sire. I have my place among them, and am of an age that I may well act on my own responsibility, and say what I have to say. Let each man speak for himself. Your majesty, I will tell you my mind, and if it meets with your approval and pleases you, be persuaded by me and follow my advice.

'My lady Isolde and lord Tristan are suspected of serious transgressions, yet judging by what I have heard, they have not been proved guilty by any sort of evidence. How can you allay this evil suspicion with evil? How can you sentence your nephew and your wife to forfeit their honour or their lives, seeing that they have not been caught in any misdemeanour and very likely never will be? Somebody makes this allegation against Tristan; but he does not attest it on Tristan, as by rights he ought to do. Or someone spreads rumours about Isolde; but that someone cannot prove them. Nevertheless, since the court so strongly suspects that they have misconducted themselves, you must deny the Queen community of bed and board till such time as she can prove her innocence before you and the realm, which knows of this report and busies itself with it daily. For alas, true or false, people's ears are eager for such rumours. Whatever is made common gossip when someone impugns a reputation, whether there be truth or falsehood behind it, it excites our baser feelings. However the matter stands here, whether it be true or not, reports and allegations have been gossiped about to such a point that you have taken offence and the court is scandalized.

'Now this is my advice, Sire: that since madam the Queen has had this fault imputed to her, you summon her here into the presence of us all, so that your indictment and her reply may be heard in such terms as shall please the court.'

'I will do so, my lord,' answered the King. 'What you have said by way of advice appears to me appropriate and acceptable.' Isolde was sent for, and she came into the Palace to the council. When she had taken her seat, the grey, wise Bishop of the Thames did as the King had bidden him.

He rose and said: 'Lady Isolde, noble Queen, take no offence at what I say – my lord the King has ordered me to be his spokesman and I must obey his command. Now may God be my witness that, if there is anything that will compromise your honour and rob you of your spotless reputation, I shall bring it to light most reluctantly. Would that I might be spared it! My good and gracious Queen, your lord and consort commands me to indict you in respect of a public allegation. Neither he nor I knows whether perhaps someone is paying back a grudge; but your name has been linked with his nephew Tristan's both at court and in the country. If God so will, you shall be innocent and free of this fault, madam. Yet the King views it with suspicion because the court declares it to be so. My lord himself has found nothing but good in you. It is from rumours fostered by the court that he brings suspicion to bear on you, not from any evidence; and he indicts you so that kinsmen and vassals can hear the case and discover whether, with our joint advice, he can perhaps root out this slander. Now I think it would be wise if you were to speak and account to him for this suspicion, in the presence of us all.'

Since it was for her to speak, Isolde, the sharp-witted Queen rose in person, and said: 'My lord Bishop, you Barons here, and the Court! You shall all know this for a fact: whenever I am called upon to answer for my lord's dishonour and for myself, I shall most assuredly answer, now and at all times. You lords, I am well aware that this gross misbehaviour has been imputed to me for the past year, at court and in the country. But it is well known to you all that there is none so blessed by heaven as to be able to live to everybody's liking all the time, and not have vices attributed to him. And so I am not surprised that I too am the victim of such talk. There was no chance that I should be passed over and not be accused of improper conduct, for I am far from home and can never ask here for my friends and relations. Unfortunately, there is scarcely a soul in this place who will feel disgraced with me – rich or poor, you are each one of you very ready to believe in my depravity! If I knew what to do or what remedy there were for it, so that I could persuade you all of my innocence in accordance with my lord's honour, I would gladly do so. Now what do you advise me to do? Whatever procedure you subject me to, I gladly accept it so that your suspicions may be set aside, yet more, by far, in order to vindicate my lord's honour and mine.'

'I am content to leave it there, your Highness,' answered the King. 'If I am to have satisfaction from you as you have proposed to us, give us your surety. Step forward at once and bind yourself to the ordeal of the red-hot iron, as we shall instruct you here.' The Queen complied. She promised to submit to their judgement in six weeks' time in Carleon in accordance with the terms laid down for her. Then the King, his peers, and indeed the whole council withdrew.

Isolde, however, remained alone with her fears and her sorrows – fears and sorrows that gave her little peace. She feared for her honour and she was harassed by the secret anxiety that she would have to whitewash her falseness. With these two cares she did not know what to do: she confided them to Christ, the Merciful, who is helpful when one is in trouble. With prayer and fasting she commended all her anguish most urgently to Him. Meanwhile she had propounded to her secret self a ruse which presumed very far upon her Maker's courtesy. She wrote and sent a letter to Tristan which told him to come to Carleon early on the appointed day when he could seize his chance, as she was about to land, and to watch out for her on the shore.

This was duly done. Tristan repaired there in pilgrim's garb. He had stained and blistered his face and disfigured his body and clothes. When Mark and Isolde arrived and made land there, the Queen saw him and recognized him at once. And when the ship put to shore she commanded that, if the pilgrim were hale and strong enough, they were to ask him in God's name to carry her across from the ship's gangway to the harbour; for at such a time, she said, she was averse to being carried by a knight. Accordingly, they all called out, 'Come here, good man, and carry my lady ashore!' He did as he was bidden, he took his lady the Queen in his arms and carried her back to land. Isolde lost no time in whispering to him that when he reached the shore he was to tumble headlong to the ground with her, whatever might become of him.

This Tristan duly did. When he came to the shore and stepped on to dry land the wayfarer dropped to the ground, falling as if by accident, so that his fall brought him to rest lying in the Queen's lap and arms. Without a moment's delay a crowd of attendants ran up with sticks and staves and were about to set upon him. 'No, no, stop!' said Isolde. 'The pilgrim has every excuse – he is feeble and infirm, and fell accidentally!' They now thanked her and warmly commended her, and praised her in their hearts for not punishing the poor man harshly. 'Would it be surprising if this pilgrim wanted to frolic with me?' asked Isolde with a smile. They set this down in her favour as a mark of her virtue and breeding, and many spoke highly in praise of her. Mark observed the whole incident and heard various things that were said. 'I do not know how it will end,' continued Isolde. 'You have all clearly seen that I cannot law-fully maintain that no man other than Mark found his way into my arms or had his couch in my lap.' With much banter about this bold rogue they set out towards Carleon.

There were many barons, priests, and knights and a great crowd of commoners there. The bishops and prelates who were saying mass and sanctifying the proceedings quickly dispatched their busi-ness. The iron was laid in the fire. The good Queen Isolde had given away her silver, her gold, her jewellery, and all the clothes and palfreys she had, to win God's favour, so that He might overlook her very real trespasses and restore her to her honour.

Meanwhile Isolde had arrived at the minster and had heard mass with deep devotion. The wise, good lady's worship was most pious: she wore a rough hair-shirt next her skin and above it a short woollen robe which failed to reach to her slender ankles by more than a hand's breadth. Her sleeves were folded back right to the elbow; her arms and feet were bare. Many eyes observed her, many hearts felt sorrow and pity for her. Her garment and her figure attracted much attention. And now the reliquary was brought, on which she was to swear. She was ordered forthwith to make known to God and the world how guilty she was of the sins that were al-leged against her. Isolde had surrendered her life and honour utterly to God's mercy. She stretched out her hand to take the oath upon the relics with fearful heart, as well she might, and rendered up heart and hand to the grace of God, for Him to keep and preserve.

Now there were a number present who were so very unmannerly as to wish to phrase the Queen's oath in a way that aimed at her downfall. That bitter-gall, Marjodoc the Steward, plotted her ruin in many devious ways, but there were no few who treated her cour-teously and gave things a favourable turn for her. Thus they wrangled from side to side as to what her oath should be. One man wished her ill, another well, as people do in such matters.

'My lord King,' said the Queen, 'my oath must be worded to your pleasure and satisfaction, whatever any of them says. There-fore see for yourself whether, in my acts and utterances, I frame my oath to your liking. These people give too much advice. Hear the oath which I mean to swear: "That no man in the world had carnal knowledge of me or lay in my arms or beside me but you, always excepting the poor pilgrim whom, with your own eyes, you saw lying in my arms." I can offer no purgation concerning him. So help me God and all the Saints that be, to a happy and auspicious outcome to this judgement! If I have not said enough, Sire, I will modify my oath one way or another as you instruct me.'

'I think this will suffice, ma'am, so far as I can see,' answered the King. 'Now take the iron in your hand and, within the terms that you have named to us, may God help you in your need!'

'Amen!' said fair Isolde. In the name of God she laid hold of the iron, carried it, and was not burned.

Thus it was made manifest and confirmed to all the world that Christ in His great virtue is pliant as a windblown sleeve. He falls into place and clings, whichever way you try Him, closely and smoothly, as He is bound to do. He is at the beck of every heart for honest deeds or fraud. Be it deadly earnest or a game, He is just as you would have Him. This was amply revealed in the facile Queen. She was saved by her guile and by the doctored oath that went flying up to God, with the result that she redeemed her honour and was again much beloved of her lord Mark, and was praised, lauded, and esteemed among the people. Whenever the King observed that her heart was set on anything, he sanctioned it at once. He accorded her honour and rich gifts. His heart and mind were centred only upon her, wholly and without guile.

His doubts and suspicions had been set aside once more.

24

PETITCREIU

WHEN Isolde's companion Tristan had carried her ashore at Carleon and done as she had asked him, he at once sailed from England to Duke Gilan in Swales. Gilan was young, wealthy, and single, as free as he was gay. Tristan was heartily welcome to him, since Gilan had heard a great deal in former days about his exploits and strange adventures. He was solicitous of Tristan's honour, and of his happiness and ease. Whatever offered a prospect of pleasing him Gilan sought most assiduously. Only melancholy Tristan was always fettered by his thoughts, moping and brooding on his fate.

One day, as Tristan sat beside Gilan, lost in doleful thoughts, he happened to sigh without knowing it. But Gilan noticed it and sent for his little dog Petitcreiu, his heart's delight and balm to his eyes, which had been sent to him from Avalon. His command was duly performed – a rich and noble purple, most rare and wonderful and suitably broad, was spread on the table before him with a tiny dog upon it. It was an enchantment, so I heard, and had been sent to the Duke by a goddess from the fairy land of Avalon as a token of love and affection. It had been so ingeniously conceived in respect of two of its qualities, namely its colour and magic powers, that there was never a tongue so eloquent or heart so discerning that they could describe its beauty and nature. Its colour had been compounded with such rare skill that none could really tell what it was. When you looked at its breast it was so many-coloured that you would not have said otherwise than that it was whiter than snow; but at the loins it was greener than clover; one flank was redder than scarlet, the other yellower than saffron; underneath, it resembled azure, but above there was a mixture so finely blended that no one hue stood out from all the others – for here was neither green, nor red, nor white, nor black, nor yellow, nor blue, and yet a touch of

all, I mean a regular purple. If you looked at this rare work from
Avalon against the grain of its coat, no one, however discerning,
could have told you its colour. It was as bewilderingly varied as if
there were no colour at all.

Round the dog's little neck went a chain of gold on which hung
a bell so sweet and clear that, as soon as it began to tremble, melan-
choly Tristan sat there rid of the sorrows of his attachment and un-
mindful of his suffering for Isolde. The tinkling of the bell was so
sweet that none could hear it without its banishing his cares and
putting an end to his pain. Tristan saw and listened to this marvel
of marvels, he studied and observed both the dog and its bell and
examined each in turn – the dog and its wonderful coat, the bell
and its sweet music. They both filled him with wonder. Yet, as he
looked, the marvel of the dog appeared to him more marvellous
than the dulcet sound of the bell that sang into his ears and took his
sadness away. He thought it a wonderful thing that his eyes, wide
open though they were, should be deceived by this medley of
colours and that he could identify none, however much he looked
at them. He gently stretched out his hands to stroke the dog, and as
he fondled it, it seemed to him as though he were fingering the very
finest silk, so soft and smooth was it everywhere. The dog neither
growled nor barked nor showed any sign of vice, whatever games
you played with it. It neither ate nor drank, so the tale declares.

When Petitcreiu had been carried out again, Tristan's sadness
was as fresh as ever. It returned with heightened intensity, so that he
gave his deepest thoughts to considering by what happy inspiration
or ingenious idea he might obtain the little dog for his lady the
Queen, in order that her longing might be eased. But he could not
conceive how this should ever come to pass, either by entreaty or
artifice, for he was well aware that Gilan would not part with it for
any precious thing that he had ever seen, except to save his life. Such
thoughts and anxieties weighed continually on his heart, yet he
never gave a sign.

As the authentic history of Tristan's exploits tells us, there was
at this time a giant who had settled near the land of Swales, a
haughty and arrogant man who had his dwelling on the bank of a
river, and who was called Urgan li vilus. Gilan and his land of
Swales were subject to this giant and, in return for his allowing his

people to live free of molestation, were obliged to pay him tribute.

During this time it was announced at court that the giant Urgan had arrived, and that he had gathered together what passed for his tribute – cattle, sheep, and pigs – and was having it driven off ahead of him. Hereupon Gilan told his friend Tristan how this tribute had first been imposed on them by force and villainy.

'Now tell me, my lord,' said Tristan, 'if I succeed in ridding you of this trouble, and quickly help you to be free of the tribute for the rest of your days, what will you give me in return?'

'Indeed, sir,' answered Gilan, 'I shall willingly give you anything I have!'

'If you will promise this, my lord,' continued Tristan, 'by whatever means I achieve it, I shall most certainly help you to be rid of Urgan for ever in a short space, or else die in the attempt!'

'Believe me, sir, I will give you whatever you fancy,' answered Gilan. 'You have only to say the word.' And he gave Tristan his hand on it.

Tristan's horse and armour were sent for, and he asked to be shown the way along which that brat of the devil would have to return with his plunder. They promptly directed him to Urgan's tracks leading into the wildest of forests, which abutted on the giant's territory in the region where the plundered cattle regularly crossed by a bridge. And now the giant and his booty were approaching. But Tristan was there before them and was barring the way of the stolen herds. Seeing the turmoil at the bridge, that damned giant Urgan immediately turned towards it with his huge long pole of steel, holding it poised in the air.

When Urgan saw the knight before the bridge so well armed, he addressed him scornfully:

'My friend on the horse, who are you? Why don't you let my cattle cross? That you have barred the way, I swear, will cost you your life, unless you surrender at once!'

'Friend, my name is Tristan,' answered the man on the horse. 'Believe me, I am not in the least bit afraid of you or your pole, so be off with you! And take my word for it that your plunder will not get any farther, so far as I can prevent it!'

'Oh yes, lord Tristan,' rejoined the giant, 'you plume yourself on having fought Morold of Ireland, with whom you arranged a combat under no provocation at all, and whom you killed from over-weening pride! But I am a different sort of person from the Irishman whose favour you gained with your strumming, and from whom you stole Isolde in the flower of her beauty, though he wished to fight a duel for her! * No, no, this riverside is my home and my name is Urgan li vilus! Quick, get out of the way!'

With these words Urgan began to measure off, using both hands, a mighty long swing and a throw straight at Tristan. He aimed its sweep and fall with the precise intention of making an end of him – but as Urgan was in the act of hurling the pole, Tristan swerved aside, yet not enough to escape having his mount cloven in two, forward of the croup. The grisly giant let out a roar.

'So God help you, lord Tristan!' he shouted with a grin. 'Don't be in a hurry to ride away! Do please wait for me, so that I can beg you on bended knee to permit me quietly and honourably to go on driving off my revenues!'

Tristan alighted on the grass, for his horse had been killed. Making for Urgan with his lance, he wounded him in one eye. With this blow the damned villain was hit fair and square. The grisly giant tore across to where his pole had fallen and, as he lowered his hand to lay hold of it, Tristan, having thrown down his spear, came up at top speed with his sword and struck him just where he wished to, for he cut off his hand as it sought for the pole so that it came to rest on the ground. He then gave the giant a second blow, on the thigh, and drew aside. The injured giant Urgan groped down with his left hand, snatched up the pole, and ran at his deadly enemy. He chased Tristan beneath the trees, with many a fearful twist and turn. In this way the gush of blood that issued from Urgan's wound grew so great that the fiendish man began to fear that his strength and spirit would shortly ebb away. He therefore let the knight and his plunder be, found his hand, picked it up, and at once returned home to his stronghold, while Tristan stayed in the forest with the booty. He was not a little afraid at Urgan's having escaped alive. He sat down on the grass pondering deeply and reflecting that, since he had no proof of his exploit apart from the stolen tribute, the terror and toil he had endured for it would not

---

* Urgan here refers to Gandin; see Episode 18.

advance him one jot, and he judged that Gilan would not honour his oath, in view of the terms they had agreed on. He immediately made after Urgan and ran at an even speed along the track where the latter had run in advance of him, and where the grass and soil were dyed red with his blood.

When he came to the castle Tristan searched for Urgan here, there, and everywhere, but found neither him nor any living person. For, as the story tells us, the wounded man had laid his lost hand on a table in the hall and run down the hill from the castle to grub for herbs with which to treat his wound and which he knew had the power to heal him. And indeed, Urgan had calculated that, once he had joined his hand to his arm in good time before it was quite dead, by a means that he was versed in, he would have emerged well from this peril with his hand, though minus an eye. But this was not to be. For Tristan came in at once, caught sight of the hand there, and finding it undefended, took it and immediately returned by the way that he had come.

Now Urgan came back and, to his sorrow and anger, perceived that he had forfeited his hand. Casting his simples to the ground he turned to pursue Tristan, who was now across the bridge and well aware that he was pelting after him. Tristan quickly took the giant's hand and hid it beneath a fallen tree-trunk. Now at last he was seriously alarmed at the monster, for it was plain that one of them must die, either he or the giant.

Tristan made for the bridge and met Urgan with his spear, thrusting at him with such force that it snapped; and as soon as he had made his thrust, cursed Urgan was upon him with his pole and he struck at him so avidly that, but for the blow overshooting its mark, Tristan would never have survived it, though he had been made of bronze. But Urgan's craving to get at him aided his escape, for the giant had come in too close and aimed the sweep of his blow too far to Tristan's rear. And now, before the gruesome man could withdraw his pole, Tristan feinted and pierced him in the eye – there was no denying he had pierced him in his other eye! Urgan now lashed out like the blinded man he was, and there was such a rain of blows that Tristan ran to cover out of range and left him to blunder about, striking with his left hand. Eventually it happened that Urgan stepped so near to the end of the bridge that Tristan ran up at speed and put his utmost strength into this exploit: he raced up to Urgan and, turning him with both hands from the bridge to where he must pitch headlong, thrust him down so that his monstrous bulk was shattered on the rock.

Elated with his victory, Tristan now took Urgan's hand and, making all speed, soon came upon Duke Gilan, who was riding from the opposite direction. Gilan deeply regretted in his heart that Tristan had ever taken it upon himself to join this battle, for it never occurred to him that he would emerge from it alive as in fact he had. Seeing Tristan running towards him, he joyfully addressed him. 'Welcome, noble Tristan!' cried Gilan. 'Tell me, dear man, how are you? Are you safe and well?' Tristan at once showed him the dead hand of the giant and told him of the good fortune which had blessed the whole enterprise, exactly as it had happened. Gilan was heartily glad of it. They then rode back to the bridge and found a man who had been dashed to pieces in accordance with Tristan's testimony, just as Gilan and his men had been told; and they accounted it a marvel. They thereupon turned back and happily drove the stolen beasts into their territory again. This gave rise to great rejoicing in Swales. They sang praise, honour, and glory to Tristan – never in that land was one man's valour held in higher esteem.

When Gilan and victorious Tristan had arrived back home and resumed their talk of their good fortune, Tristan, the wonderworker, addressed the Duke without delay.

'My lord Duke, let me remind you of the pledge and the terms that we agreed on, and what you promised me.'

'My lord, I willingly recall it. Tell me, what would you like? What do you desire?'

'Lord Gilan, I desire that you give me Petitcreiu!'

'But I have a better proposal,' answered Gilan.

'Well, then, tell me,' said Tristan.

'Leave me my little dog and take my handsome sister together with half my possessions!'

'No, my lord Gilan, I must remind you of your word; for I would not take all the kingdoms in the world in exchange, if I were given the choice. I killed Urgan li vilus with the sole object of winning Petitcreiu.'

'If your wishes run more on him than on what I have proposed to you, I will keep my promise and grant you what you want – I will use no trickery or cunning in this affair. Though I am very loth to do so, your wishes shall be met!' He thereupon ordered the little dog to be set before him and Tristan. 'Look, sir,' he said, 'I declare to you on oath by all my hopes of bliss that there is nothing I could have or that I ever cherished, apart from my life and honour, that I would not much rather give you than my dog Petitcreiu. Now take him and keep him, and may God give you joy of him! In him you deprive me of my eyes' rarest pleasure and much delight to my heart.'

When Tristan had gained possession of the little dog, he would truly have rated Rome and all the kingdoms, lands, and seas, as nothing in comparison. He had never felt so happy as then, except in Isolde's company. He took a Welsh minstrel into his confidence, an intelligent and well-versed man, and instructed him in a convenient stratagem by which he could give fair Isolde, the Queen, her happiness again. He shrewdly hid Petitcreiu in the Welshman's crwth. He wrote a letter to her in which he told her how and where he had acquired the dog for love of her. The minstrel set out on his journey in accordance with his instructions, and duly arrived at Mark's castle in Tintagel without mishap on the way. He got into conversation with Brangane and handed her the dog and letter, and she conveyed them to Isolde.

Isolde examined intently this marvel of marvels which she found in the dog and its bell, both one by one and together. She rewarded the minstrel there and then with ten marks of gold. She wrote and dispatched by him a letter in which she told Tristan with great urgency that her lord Mark was most favourably inclined towards him and would hold nothing that had happened against him, and that he must return without fail, since she had settled their differences.

Tristan did as he was bidden and returned home without delay. The King and his court and the land and its people all held him in high esteem, as before. He had never been shown greater honour at court, except inasmuch as Marjodoc honoured him on the outside of his heart, as did his yoke-mate Petit Melot. But, whatever the honour shown him by those who had been his enemies, there was little honour in it. State your opinions, all of you, on this point:

where you have only the semblance, is that honour or no? I myself say both yes and no. No and yes both have their share in it. 'No' for the man who renders honour: 'yes' for the one who receives it. These two are found between the pair of them – both 'yes' and 'no' are found there. What more is there to say? Here we have honour without honour.

Now, as to the little dog, Queen Isolde told her lord that her mother the wise Queen of Ireland had sent him to her with instructions to make him a delightful little kennel of gold and precious things, such as one might dream of. Inside, they spread a rich brocade for him to lie on. In this way Petitcreiu was under Isolde's observation day and night, in public and in private – such was her custom wherever she was or wherever she rode. He never came out of her sight, he was always led or carried where she could see him. Nor did she have this done for any relief it might give her. She had it done (so we are told) to renew her tender love-pangs out of affection for Tristan, who had been moved by love to send her Petitcreiu.

Isolde had no relief from Petitcreiu, she did not depend on him for solace. For as soon as the faithful Queen had received the dog and heard the bell which made her forget her sorrow, she had reflected that her friend Tristan bore a load of troubles for her sake, and she immediately thought to herself: 'O faithless woman, how can I be glad? Why am I happy for any time at all while Tristan, who has surrendered his life and joy to sorrow for my sake, is sad because of me? How can I rejoice without him, whose sorrow and joy I am? And however can I laugh when his heart can find no ease, unless my heart has a share in it? He has no life but me. Should I now be living without him, happily and pleasantly, while he is pining? May the good God forbid that I should ever rejoice away from him!' So saying, she broke off the bell, leaving the chain round the little dog's neck. From this the bell lost its whole virtue. It no longer sounded with its old music. They say that it never again quenched or made away with sorrow in any heart, however much one heard it. But this meant nothing to Isolde; she did not wish to be happy. This constant, faithful lover had surrendered her life and joy to the sadness of love and to Tristan.

25

BANISHMENT

ONCE more Tristan and Isolde had surmounted their cares and perils, once more they were happy at court, which again overflowed with their honours. Never had they enjoyed such esteem. They were as intimate again as ever with Mark their common lord. They also hid their feelings very thoroughly; for, when it was not propitious for them to seize their chance together, they deemed the will sufficient, which often consoles a pair of lovers. Hope and expectation of how to accomplish the desire on which the heart is set never fail to give it a blossoming vigour and a living ecstasy. Here is true attachment, such are the best instincts in matters of love and affection – that where one cannot have the deed in a way that is serviceable to Love, one should forgo it, and take the will for the deed. Wherever there is a sure will but no good opportunity, lovers should assuage their longing with that same sure will. Companions in love should never want what opportunity denies them, or they will want their sorrow. To desire when the means are lacking is a very impolitic game. When you have the means – that is the time for desiring. This game is rich in opportunities, it is not fraught with sorrow. When these partners Isolde and Tristan were unable to seize their opportunity, they let the occasion pass, content in their common will, which, never tiring, stole tenderly and lovingly from one to the other. A common desire and affection seemed sweet and good to them.

The lovers hid their love at all times from the court and from Mark, as much and as well as they were allowed to do by the blind passion that would not leave them. But the seed of suspicion in love is of a nature so accurst that it takes root wherever it is cast. It is so fertile, so fecund, and so sturdy, that even lacking moisture and all but dying, it can never die entirely.

Busy suspicion shot up luxuriantly and began once more to play about Tristan and Isolde. Here was excess of moisture, of their tender looks and signs in which Love's proofs were ever visible. How right he was who said that however one guards against it, the eye longs for the heart, the finger for the pain. The eyes, those lodestars of the heart, long to go raiding to where the heart is turned: the finger and the hand time and time again go towards the pain. So it was always with these lovers. However great their fears, they had not the power to refrain from nourishing suspicion with many a tender look, often and all too often. For alas, as I have just said, that friend of the heart, the eye, was ever turned towards the heart, the hand would go to the pain. Many a time did they enmesh their eyes and hearts with looks that passed between them, so intimately that they often failed to disengage them before Mark had found Love's balm in them, for he was always watching them. His eye was always on them. He secretly read the truth in her eyes many, many times, and indeed in nothing but her glance – it was so very lovely, so tender, and so wistful that it pierced him to the heart, and he conceived such anger, such envy and hatred from it that he forsook his doubt and suspicion; for now pain and anger had robbed him of measure and reason. It was death to his reason that his darling Isolde should love any man but himself, he valued nothing above Isolde, and in this he never wavered. For all his anger, his beloved wife was as dear and dearer to him than life. Yet however dear she was to him, this vexation and maddening pain brought him to such a frenzy that he was rid of his affection and wholly taken up by his anger – he was past all caring whether his suspicions were true or false.

In his blind agony Mark summoned them both to court in the Palace before the household. Addressing Isolde publicly in full sight and hearing of the court, he said: 'My lady Isolde of Ireland, it is well known to my land and people under what dire suspicion you have long stood with regard to my nephew Tristan. Now I have subjected you to tests and trials of many kinds to discover whether, for my sake, you would restrain yourself from this folly; but I see that you will not leave it. I am not such a fool as not to know or see from your behaviour in public and in private that your heart and eyes are for ever fixed on my nephew. You show him a kinder face than ever you show me, from which I conclude that he is

dearer to you than I am. Whatever watch I set on you or him, it is of
no avail. It is all to no purpose, whatever lengths I go to. I have put
a distance between you so often that I never cease to marvel that you
remain so one at heart all this long while. I have severed your tender
glances so many times, yet I fail to sunder your affections. In this I
have over-indulged you. But now I will tell you how it is to end. I
will bear with you no longer the shame and grief that you have
caused me, with all its suffering. From now on I will not endure
this dishonour! But neither shall I revenge myself on you for this
state of affairs to the extent that I am entitled, did I wish to be re-
venged. Nephew Tristan, and my lady Isolde, I love you too much
to put you to death or harm you in any way, loth as I am to confess
it. But since I can read it in the pair of you that, in defiance of my
will, you love and have loved each other more than me, then be with
one another as you please – do not hold back from any fear of me!
Since your love is so great, from this hour I shall not vex or molest
you in any of your concerns. Take each other by the hand and leave
my court and country. If I am to be wronged by you I wish neither
to see nor hear it. This fellowship between the three of us can hold
no longer; I will leave you two together, and I alone shall quit it,
however I succeed in freeing myself. Such fellowship is vile – I
mean to be rid of it! For a King to be partnered in love with open
eyes is beneath contempt! Go, the two of you, with God's protection.
Live and love as you please: this companionship in love is ended!'

It duly happened as Mark commanded. With moderate distress
and cool regret, Tristan and his lady Isolde bowed to their common
lord, the King, and then to the royal retainers. Then these steadfast
companions took each other by the hand and crossed the court.
They told their friend Brangane to keep well, and asked her to
remain and pass the time at court until she should hear how they
were faring – this they urgently commended to her. Of Isolde's store
of gold, Tristan took twenty marks for Isolde and himself for their
needs and sustenance. They also brought him his harp, his sword,
his hunting-bow, and his horn, which he had asked them to fetch
for his journey. In addition he had chosen one of his hounds, a
handsome, slender animal called Hiudan, and he took charge of it
himself. He commended his followers to God, telling them to return
home to his father Rual, all except for Curvenal, whom he retained

26

THE CAVE OF LOVERS

THE three of them together made steadily for the wilds, journeying over forest and heath for well on two days. Tristan had long known of a cavern in a savage mountainside, on which he had chanced when his way had led him there out hunting. The cavern had been hewn into the wild mountain in heathen times, before Corynaeus' day, when giants ruled there.* They used to hide inside it when, desiring to make love, they needed privacy. Wherever such a cavern was found it was barred by a door of bronze, and bore an inscription to Love – *la fossiure a la gent amant*, which is to say 'The Cave of Lovers'.

The name was well suited to the thing. The story tells us that this grotto was round, broad, high, and perpendicular, snow-white, smooth, and even, throughout its whole circumference. Above, its vault was finely keyed, and on the keystone there was a crown most beautifully adorned with goldsmiths' work and encrusted with precious stones. Below, the pavement was of smooth, rich, shining marble, as green as grass. At the centre there was a bed most perfectly cut from a slab of crystal, broad, high, well raised from the ground, and engraved along its sides with letters, announcing that the bed was dedicated to the Goddess of Love. In the upper part of the grotto some small windows had been hewn out to let in the light, and these shone in several places.

Where one went in and out there was a door of bronze. Outside, above the door, there stood three limes of many branches, but beyond them not a single one. Yet everywhere downhill there were innumerable trees which cast the shade of their leafy boughs upon the mountainside. Somewhat apart, there was a level glade through which there flowed a spring – a cool, fresh brook, clear as the sun.

* Cf. *Aeneid* IX, 571, and XII, 298; from here Geoffrey of Monmouth takes Corynaeus to make him the eponymous hero of Cornwall (I, XII).

Above that, too, there stood three limes, fair and very stately, sheltering the brook from sun and rain. The bright flowers and the green grass, with which the glade was illumined, vied with each other most delightfully, each striving to outshine the other. At their due times you could hear the sweet singing of the birds. Their music was so lovely – even lovelier here than elsewhere. Both eye and ear found their pasture and delight there: the eye its pasture, the ear its delight. There were shade and sunshine, air and breezes, both soft and gentle. Away from the mountain and its cave for fully a day's journey there were rocks unrelieved by open heath, and wilderness and wasteland. No paths or tracks had been laid towards it of which one might avail oneself. But the country was not so rough and fraught with hardship as to deter Tristan and his beloved from halting there and making their abode within that mountain-cave.

When they had taken up their quarters they sent Curvenal back to put it out at court and wherever else was necessary that, after many griefs and hardships, Tristan and fair Isolde had arrived back in Ireland in order to proclaim their innocence before the land and people. Further, he was to take up residence at court as Brangane should instruct him and earnestly assure the true-hearted girl, their common friend, of their love and friendship. He was also to find out what was rumoured of Mark's intentions – whether he might be plotting some villainy against their lives, and in that case inform them at once. And they begged him to keep Tristan and Isolde in his thoughts and to return once every twenty days with such intelligence as would enable them to counter such moves. He did as he was asked. Meanwhile Tristan and Isolde had taken up their abode together in this wild retreat.

Some people are smitten with curiosity and astonishment, and plague themselves with the question how these two companions, Tristan and Isolde, nourished themselves in this wasteland? I will tell them and assuage their curiosity. They looked at one another and nourished themselves with that! Their sustenance was the eye's increase. They fed in their grotto on nothing but love and desire. The two lovers who formed its court had small concern for their provender. Hidden away in their hearts they carried the best nutriment to be had anywhere in the world, which offered itself unasked ever fresh and new. I mean pure devotion, love made sweet as balm that consoles body and sense so tenderly, and sustains the heart and spirit – this was their best nourishment. Truly, they never considered any food but that from which the heart drew desire, the eyes delight, and which the body, too, found agreeable. With this they had enough. Love drove her ancient plough for them, keeping pace all the time, and gave them an abundant store of all those things that go to make heaven on earth.

Nor were they greatly troubled that they should be alone in the wilds without company. Tell me, whom did they need in there with them, and why should anyone join them? They made an even number: there were simply one and one. Had they included a third in the even pair which they made, there would have been an uneven number, and they would have been much encumbered and embarrassed by the odd one. Their company of two was so ample a crowd for this pair that good King Arthur never held a feast in any of his palaces that gave keener pleasure or delight. In no land could you have found enjoyment for which these two would have given a brass farthing to have with them in their grotto. Whatever one could imagine or conceive elsewhere in other countries to make a paradise, they had with them there. They would not have given a button for a better life, save only in respect of their honour. What more should they need? They had their court, they were amply supplied with all that goes to make for happiness. Their loyal servitors were the green lime, the sunshine and the shade, the brook and its banks, flowers, grass, blossoms, and leaves, so soothing to the eye. The service they received was the song of the birds, of the lovely, slender nightingale, the thrush and blackbird, and other birds of the forest. Siskin and calander-lark vied in eager rivalry to see who could give the best service. These followers served their ears and sense unendingly. Their high feast was Love, who gilded all their joys; she brought them King Arthur's Round Table as homage and all its company a thousand times a day! What better food could they have for body or soul? Man was there with Woman, Woman there with Man. What else should they be needing? They had what they were meant to have, they had reached the goal of their desire.

Now some people are so tactless as to declare (though I do not accept it myself) that other food is needed for this pastime. I am not so sure that it is. There is enough here in my opinion. But if anyone has discovered better nourishment in this world let him speak in the light of his experience. There was a time when I, too, led such a life, and I thought it quite sufficient.

Now I beg you to bear with me while I reveal to you on account of what hidden significance that cave was thus constructed in the rock.

It was, as I said, round, broad, high, and perpendicular, snow-white, smooth, and even, throughout its whole circumference. Its roundness inside betokens Love's Simplicity: Simplicity is most fitting for Love, which must have no corners, that is, Cunning or Treachery. Breadth signifies Love's Power, for her Power is without end. Height is Aspiration that mounts aloft to the clouds: nothing is too great for it so long as it means to climb, up and up, to where the molten Crown of the Virtues gathers the vault to the keystone. The Virtues are invariably encrusted with precious stones, inlaid in filigree of gold and so adorned with praise, that we who are of lower aspiration – whose spirits flag and flutter over the pavement and neither settle nor fly – we gaze up intently at the masterpiece above us, which derives from the Virtues and descends to us from the glory of those who float in the clouds above us and send their refulgence down to us! – we gaze at them and marvel! From this grow the feathers by which our spirit takes wing and, flying, brings forth praise and soars in pursuit of those Virtues.

The wall was white, smooth, and even: such is Integrity's nature. Her brilliant and uniform whiteness must never be mottled with colour, nor should Suspicion find any pit or ridge in her. In its greenness and firmness the marble floor is like Constancy; this meaning is the best for it in respect of colour and smoothness. Constancy should be of the same fresh green as grass, and smooth and gleaming as glass.

At the centre, the bed of crystalline Love was dedicated to her name most fittingly. The man who had cut the crystal for her couch and her observance had divined her nature unerringly: Love *should* be of crystal – transparent and translucent!

On the inside, across the door of bronze, there ran two bars. Inside, too, there was a latch most ingeniously let through the wall, where Tristan, indeed, had found it. This latch was governed by a lever, which passed from the outside to the inside and guided it this way and that. There was neither lock nor key to it, and I will tell you why. There was no lock for this reason – that any device which one applies to a door (I mean on the outside) for the purpose of opening and shutting it, betokens Treachery. For when anyone enters at Love's door who has not been admitted from within, it cannot be accounted Love, since it is either Deceit or Force. Love's gate is there to prevent it, the door of bronze bars the way, and none can get the better of it, unless it be by Love. Indeed, it is made of bronze so that no tool, whether of force or of violence, cunning or artifice, treachery or falsehood should ever have power to harm it. Within, two bars, two seals of love, were turned towards each other on either side, the one of cedar, the other of ivory. Now hear their interpretations. The bar of cedar stands for the Discretion and Understanding of Love; the other of ivory for her Purity and Modesty. With these two seals, with these chaste bars, Love's house is guarded, and Deceit and Force locked out. The secret lever which had been let into the latch from without was a spindle of tin, while the latch was of gold, as it should be. Neither the one nor the other, latch nor lever, could have been better applied in respect of their innate qualities: tin means Firm Intent for intimate dealings, but gold stands for Success. Tin and gold are appropriate here. Any man can guide his Intent to his pleasures, narrow, broaden, shorten, lengthen it, free it, or confine it, here or there, this way or that, with very little effort, as is the case with tin, and there is no great harm in that. But if a man can set his thoughts to love with a true will, this lever of humble tin will carry him on to golden suc-cess and the tender transports of love.*

Overhead, three little windows in all had been hewn through the solid rock into the cave, very secretly and neatly, through which the sun would shine. The first stood for Kindness, the second for Humility, the third for Breeding. Through these three, the sweet light, that blessed radiance, Honour, dearest of all luminaries, smiled in and lit up that cave of earthly bliss.

It also has its meaning that the grotto was so secluded in the midst of this wild solitude, in that one may well compare it with this – that Love and her concerns are not assigned to the streets nor yet to the open country. She is hidden away in the wilds, the country that

* Some erotic double entendres are lost in translation.

leads to her refuge makes hard and arduous going – mountains are strewn about the way in many a massive curve. The tracks up and down are so obstructed with rocks for us poor sufferers that, unless we keep well to the path, if we make one false step we shall never get back alive. But whoever is so blessed as to reach and enter that solitude will have used his efforts to most excellent purpose, for he will find his heart's delight there. Whatever the ear yearns to hear, whatever gratifies the eye, this wilderness is full of it. He would hate to be elsewhere.

I know this well, for I have been there. I, too, have tracked and followed after wildfowl and game, after hart and hind in the wilderness over many a woodland stream and yet passed my time and not seen the end of the chase. My toils were not crowned with success. I have found the lever and seen the latch in that cave and have, on occasion, even pressed on to the bed of crystal – I have danced there and back some few times. But never have I had my repose on it. However hard the floor of marble beside it, I have so battered the floor with my steps that, had it not been saved by its greenness, in which lies its chiefest virtue, and from which it constantly renews itself, you would have traced Love's authentic tracks on it. I have also fed my eyes on the gleaming wall abundantly and have fixed my gaze on the medallion, on the vault and on the keystone, and worn out my eyes looking up at its ornament, so bespangled with Excellence! The sun-giving windows have often sent their rays into my heart. I have known that cave since I was eleven, yet I never set foot in Cornwall.

Those true-hearted denizens, Tristan and his mistress, had arranged their leisure and exertions very pleasantly in the woods and glades of their wilderness. They were always at each other's side. In the mornings they would stroll to the meadow through the dew, where it had cooled the grass and the flowers. The cool field was their recreation. They talked as they walked to and fro, and they listened as they went to the sweet singing of the birds. Then they would turn aside to where the cool spring murmured, and would hearken to its music as it slid down on its path. Where it entered the glade they used to sit and rest and listen to its purling and watch the water flow, a joy they never tired of.

But when the bright sun began to climb and the heat to descend, they withdrew to their lime-tree in quest of its gentle breezes. This afforded them pleasure within and without their breasts – the tree rejoiced both their hearts and their eyes. With its leaves the fragrant lime refreshed both air and shade for them; from its shade the breezes were gentle, fragrant, cool. The bench beneath the lime was flowers and grass, the best-painted lawn that ever lime-tree had. Our constant lovers sat there together and told love-tales of those whom love had ruined in days gone by. They debated and discussed, they bewept and bewailed how Phyllis of Thrace and poor Canacea had suffered such misfortune in Love's name; how Biblis had died broken-hearted for her brother's love; how love-lorn Dido, Queen of Tyre and Sidon, had met so tragic a fate because of unhappy love. To such tales did they apply themselves from time to time.

When they tired of stories they slipped into their refuge and resumed their well-tried pleasure of sounding their harp, and singing sadly and sweetly. They busied their hands and their tongues in turn. They performed amorous lays and their accompaniments, varying their delight as it suited them: for if one took the harp it was for the other to sing the tune with wistful tenderness. And indeed the strains of both harp and tongue, merging their sound in each other, echoed in that cave so sweetly that it was dedicated to sweet Love for her retreat most fittingly as 'La fossiure a la gent amant'.

All that had been rumoured in tales of old on the subject of the grotto was borne out in this pair. Only now had the cave's true mistress given herself to her sport in earnest. Whatever frolics or pastimes had been pursued in this grotto before, they did not equal this; they were neither so sure nor so unsullied in spirit as when Tristan and Isolde disported themselves. These two beguiled Love's hour in a way no lovers surpassed – they did just as their hearts prompted them.

There were amusements enough for them to follow by day. They rode out into their wilderness hunting wildfowl and game with their crossbow now and then, when fancy took them, and sometimes they chased the red deer with Hiudan their hound, who as yet could not run without giving tongue. But it was not long before Tristan had trained him to run most perfectly through field and forest on the scent of hart and hind and of all varieties of game without giving

27

DISCOVERY

MEANWHILE, sorrowful King Mark had endured much grief as he mourned for his wife and his honour. With each succeeding day he became more of a burden to himself in body and in soul, and grew indifferent to eminence and wealth. It happened at this same time that he rode out hunting into this very forest, more because of his melancholy than in hopes of anything unusual.

When they came to the forest the huntsmen took their hounds and found a herd standing there. They cast off the hounds at them and these at once unharboured a strange hart from among them, maned like a horse, strong, big, and white, with under-sized horns scarce renewed, as though he had but recently shed them. They pursued him strongly and in great rivalry till well towards nightfall, when they lost the scent, so that the hart eluded them and fled to where he had come from, over towards the Cave. He fled there and saved his hide.

Now Mark was much annoyed, and the huntsmen were even more so that the affair of the hart had taken this turn for them, in view of his strange coat and mane. They were all in an ill humour because of it. They now gathered their hounds together and camped there for the night, since all were in need of rest.

Now throughout the day Tristan and Isolde had heard the clamour of the horns and hounds which had come into the forest, and they were haunted by the thought that it could be no other than Mark. This weighed upon their hearts. They were immediately siezed by the fear that their presence had been betrayed to him.

Early next morning before dawn the master-huntsman was up and doing and ordered his men to await daylight there and then follow him at speed. He took on his leash a track-hound well suited to his purpose, and put him on to the scent. The hound then led him over much rough country, over rock and stone, parched land

and grass-land, on and on, where the hart had ranged ahead of him as it fled during the night. He followed its tracks without fail till the country opened out and the sun was well up. He was then beside the spring in Tristan's glade.

That same morning very early Tristan and his companion had taken each other by the hand and stolen out through the dew and gone to the flowering meadow in their delightful valley. Calander-larks and nightingales began to blend their voices and salute their fellow denizens, Tristan and Isolde. They greeted them warmly – those wild woodbirds welcomed them most sweetly in their own parlance; the lovers were welcome there to many a sweet bird. They were all delightfully busy giving them their greeting. From their twigs they sang their joy-giving airs with many variations. There were innumerable sweet tongues singing their songs and refrains in tenor and descant, to the lovers' rapture. The cool spring received them, leaping to greet their eyes with its beauty, and sounding in their ears with even greater beauty, as it came whispering towards them to receive them with its murmur. How sweetly it whispered its welcome to those lovers! The lime-trees welcomed them, too, with fragrant breezes; they gladdened them outside and in, in their ears and in their senses. The trees in all their blossom, the lustrous meadow, the flowers, the green, green grass, and everything in bloom – all smiled its welcome! On either hand, the dew, too, gave them a tender greeting, cooling their feet and solacing their hearts.

But when Tristan and Isolde had had their fill, they slipped back into their rock and agreed together as to what they should do in their situation. For they were very much afraid – and events were to prove them right – that somehow someone might lose the hounds and come there, and so discover their secret. To meet this eventuality Tristan thought of a plan, which the two of them adopted. They returned to their couch and lay down again a good way apart from each other, just as two men might lie, not like a man and a woman. Body lay beside body in great estrangement. Moreover, Tristan had placed his naked sword between them: he lay on one side, she on the other. They lay apart, one and one: and thus they fell asleep.

The huntsman whom I mentioned just now as having arrived beside the spring, espied the tracks in the dew where Tristan and Isolde had walked in advance of him, and concluded that they could only be the trail of the hart. He dismounted and followed on foot the tracks which the lovers had left, right to the door of the cave. It was guarded by two bars, and he was unable to advance. Finding this way denied him, he tried a circuitous approach and, working his way all round it, chanced on a hidden window high up in the wall of the cave. Through this he peered in fear and trembling, and at once espied Love's retinue – one man and one woman in all! He wondered greatly to see them, for as to the woman he thought no creature so exquisite in all the world had ever been born of a mother. But he did not gaze for long; for, catching sight of the sword lying there so naked, he started back and leapt aside. It impressed him as very sinister – he thought it some strange enchantment ; and it made him feel afraid. He went back down the rock and rode to rejoin the hounds.

Now Mark, too, had advanced along this huntsman's tracks far ahead of the hunt and was hastening towards him.

'Oh my lord King,' said that wretched huntsman, 'I have some news to tell you! I have just found a rare marvel!'

'Tell me, what sort of marvel?'

'A lovers' cave!'

'Where and how did you find it?'

'Here in this very wasteland, Sire.'

'In this wild waste?'

'Yes.'

'Is there any living person in it?'

'Yes, Sire. There are a man and a goddess inside it. They are lying on a bed asleep, as if to see who could sleep deepest! The man is like any other man; but I have my doubts whether his bed-fellow, lying beside him, can be of human kind! She is lovelier than a fairy! It is not possible that anything more beautiful of flesh and blood should come to be on earth! And – I cannot guess for what reason – lying between them there is a fine, bright, naked sword!'

'Guide me to it,' said the King.

The master-huntsman led Mark back along his path into the wilds to where he had dismounted. The King alighted from his horse and followed in his tracks. Arriving at the place, the hunts-man paused, and Mark now advanced to the door. Leaving it on one side he passed round the face of the rock, and following the huntsman's instructions, made many a turn where it narrowed to its peak; and he, too, found a little window. He directed his gaze within, to his joy and to his sorrow – he, too, saw the pair lying high upon the crystal and still sleeping as before. He found them just as the huntsman had done, well away from each other, one on one side, the other on the other, with the naked sword between them.

As Mark recognized his wife and nephew, a cold shudder ran through his heart and all over his body at the pain of it, and yet for joy as well. Their lying so apart both pleased and pained him. Pleased him, I mean, because of the fond idea that they were innocent: pained him, I mean, because he had harboured suspicion. 'Merciful God,' he said to himself, 'what can be the meaning of this? If anything has passed between these two such as I have long suspected, why do they lie apart so? A woman should cleave to her man and lie close in his arms by his side. Why do these lovers lie thus?' And then he went on to himself: 'Is there anything behind it now? Is there guilt here, or is there not?' But, with this, Doubt was with him again. 'Guilt?' he asked. 'Most certainly, yes!' 'Guilt?' he asked. 'Most certainly, no!'

Mark bandied these alternatives to and fro till, pathless man, he was in two minds about their passion. Then Love, the Reconciler, stole to the scene, wondrously preened and painted. Over the white of her face she wore the paint of golden Denial, her most excellent cosmetic 'No!' The word gleamed and shone into the King's heart. The other that would have hurt him, the unpalatable word 'Yes!', Mark did not see at all. This was all done with, Doubt and Suspicion were no more. Love's gilding, golden Innocence, drew his eyes and sense with its magical enticement, drew them to where the Eastertide of all his joys was lying. He gazed and gazed at his heart's delight Isolde, who never before had seemed to him so very lovely as now. Heaven knows of what exertions the tale romances here that might have flushed her cheeks, whose radiance glowed up at the man with the sweet freshness of a rose in which red and white are mingled. Her mouth burned with fire like a red-hot ember. Yes, I recall what her exertions were. Isolde, as I said just now, had sauntered through the dew to the meadow that morning and this is what had given her her colour. And now a tiny sunbeam, too, had found its way inside and was shining on her cheek, on her chin, and on her lips. Two beauties were sporting there together, two radiances blending their light. The one sun and the other had set a high feast of joy there for the glory of Isolde. Her chin, her mouth, her colour, her skin were so exquisite, lovely, and enticing that Mark was captivated and filled with the desire to kiss her. Love threw on her flames, she set the man on fire with the charm of the woman's form. Her beauty lured his senses to her body, and to the passion she excited. His eyes were fixed upon her. His gaze dwelt with ardour on the beauty of her throat, her breast, her arms, and her hands where they shone out from her robe. She wore a chaplet of clover, but was without a headband – never had she seemed to her lord so bewitching and alluring!

Seeing the sun shine down on her face through the rock he feared it might harm her complexion, so, taking some grass, flowers, and leaves, he blocked the window. With a prayer to the good God to have her in his keeping, he made the sign of the cross over the lovely woman in farewell, and went away in tears. He rejoined his hounds, a man very sad at heart. He broke off the hunt and ordered the huntsmen to return with the pack at once. But this he did with the intention that no other should stray and glimpse the lovers there.

Scarce had the King left when Isolde and Tristan awoke. They began to look round them for the sunshine, but the sun was shining through two windows and no more. They looked at the third and were very much amazed to find that it gave no light. They rose together without delay, went outside their rock and at once found the leaves, flowers, and grass before the window. Moreover, in the gravel above and before the cave, leading towards and away from it, they detected the footprints of a man. This came as a great shock to them, and they were very much afraid. They thought that somehow Mark must have been there and observed them – such was the suspicion that presented itself; yet they had no proof that it was so. But their greatest trust and hope was that, whoever it was that had discovered them, he had found them lying as they were, so well apart from one another.

28

THE PARTING

The king at once summoned his councillors and kinsmen, at court and in the country, to ask them for their advice. He told them how he had found the lovers (as I have just narrated) and declared himself no longer willing to believe that Tristan and Isolde had misconducted themselves. His councillors realized immediately which way his wishes were tending, and that he had made his declaration with a mind to having Tristan and Isolde back. Like the wise men they were, they advised him according to his own desires and inclinations, namely, that since he knew of nothing contrary to his honour, he should recall his wife and his nephew and take no further notice of slanderous talk concerning them.

Curvenal was summoned, and since he was conversant with the lovers' affairs, was appointed ambassador to them. Through him the King informed them of his good will and favour, and asked them to return and harbour no malice towards him.

Curvenal repaired there and told them what Mark had in mind. This met with the lovers' approval, and they were glad of it in their hearts. But they were happy far more for the sake of God and their place in society than for any other reason. They returned by the way they had come to the splendour that had been theirs. But never again in all their days were they so close and familiar as they had been, nor did opportunity ever again so favour their amours. On the other hand Mark, his court, and his household were devoted to their honour. Yet Tristan and Isolde were never free and open again. Mark, the waverer, commanded them and urged them for God's sake and his own to keep within the bounds of propriety and to refrain from entangling their ardent looks so tenderly, and no longer to be so intimate or talk with such familiarity as they had been accustomed to do. This gave the lovers much pain.

Mark was happy once more. For his happiness he again had in

his wife Isolde all that his heart desired – not in honour, but materially. He possessed in his wife neither love nor affection, nor any of the splendid things which God ever brought to pass, except that in virtue of his name she was called 'Queen' and 'Lady' where he by right was King. He accepted it all and invariably treated her with affection as if he were very dear to her.

Here was a case of that foolish, insensate blindness of which a proverb says 'Love's blindness blinds outside and in'. It blinds a man's eyes and mind so that they do not wish to see what they see very well between them. So it had come to be with Mark. He knew it as sure as death and saw full well that his wife Isolde was utterly absorbed in her passion for Tristan, heart and soul, yet he did not wish to know it.

And who is to blame for the life so bare of honour that Mark led with Isolde? – for, believe me, it would be very wrong of anyone to accuse Isolde of deception! Neither she nor Tristan deceived him. He saw it with his own eyes, and knew well enough, without seeing it, that she bore him no affection, yet he cherished her in spite of it! But, you ask, why did he harbour tender feelings towards her? For the reason that many do today: lust and appetite suffer most obstinately what falls to their lot to suffer.

Ah, how many Marks and Isoldes you can see today, if one may broach the topic, who are as blind or blinder in their hearts and eyes! Far from there being none, there are very many who are so possessed by their blindness that they do not wish to know what stands before their eyes, and regard as a delusion the thing they see and know. Who is to blame for their blindness? If we look at it fairly we cannot take the ladies to task for it. When they let their husbands see with open eyes what they are about, they are innocent of any offence towards them. It cannot be said that one is deceived or outwitted by one's wife where the fault is manifest. – In such a case lust has obstructed a man's vision; appetite is the delusion that lies all the time in men's clear-seeing eyes. Whatever is said about blindness, no blindness blinds so utterly as lust and appetite. Although we avoid quoting it, it is a true word that says: 'In beauty there lurks danger'. Mark was blinded outside and in, in his eyes and in his senses, by the marvellous beauty of Isolde in her prime.

He could see nothing in her that he would account a fault, and all that he knew of her was the very best! But to make an end of this. He desired so much to be with her that he overlooked the wrong that he suffered at her hands.

How hard it is to ignore what lies locked and sealed in our hearts! How we long to do what keeps nagging at our thoughts! Our eyes cleave to their quarry. Hearts and eyes often go ranging along the path that has always brought them joy. And if anyone tries to spoil their sport, God knows, he will make them more enamoured of it. The more firmly you remove them, the more they like the game and the closer they will cling.

So it was with Tristan and Isolde. As soon as they were debarred from their pleasures by watchers and guardians and denied them by prohibitions, they began to suffer acutely. Desire now tormented them in earnest with its witchery, many times worse than before. Their need of one another was more painful and urgent than it had ever been. The ponderous load of cursed Surveillance weighed on their spirits like a mountain of lead. This devilish machination, Surveillance, enemy of Love, drove them to distraction, especially Isolde. She was in a desperate plight. Tristan's avoidance was death to her. The more her master forbade her any familiarity with him, the more deeply her thoughts were embedded in him.

This must be said of surveillance: those who practise it raise nothing but briars and thorns. This is the maddening fetter that galls reputation and robs many a woman of her honour who would otherwise gladly have kept it, had she received just treatment. But when in fact she is treated unjustly, her desire for honour begins to flag; so far as this is concerned, close-keeping spoils her character. Yet, when all is said, to whatever lengths you take it, surveillance is wasted on a woman in that no man has the power to guard a vicious one. A virtuous women does not need to be guarded; she will guard herself, as they say. But if a man neverthe-less sets a watch on her, believe me, she will hate him. Such a man is bent on his wife's ruin, body and soul, and, most likely, to such an extent that she will not mend her ways so far that some-thing of what her hedge of thorns has borne will not cling to her ever after. For once having struck root in such kindly soil, the bitter thorn-bush is harder to destroy there than in parched and other places. I am convinced that if one wrongs a willing heart so long that ill-treatment robs it of its fruitfulness it will yield worse ills than one that was always evil. This is true, for I have read it.

A wise man, therefore, that is, one who grants woman her esteem, should keep no watch over her privacy in defiance of her own good will other than by counsel and instruction, and by tenderness and kindness. Let him guard her with that, and may he know this for a fact: he will never keep better watch. For whether she be vicious or good, if a man wrongs a woman too often she may well conceive a whim that he would rather be without. Every worthy man, and whoever aspires to be one, should trust in his wife and himself, so that for love of him she may shun all wantonness.

However much he tries, a man will never extort love from a woman by wrong means – that is how to extinguish it. In matters of love, surveillance is an evil practice. It quickens baleful passions and leads to a woman's downfall. In my opinion it would be wise in a man to abstain from prohibitions. They give rise to much scandal among women. Women do many things, just because they are forbidden, from which they would refrain were it not forbidden. God knows, these same thistles and thorns are inborn in them! Women of this kind are children of mother Eve, who flouted the first prohibition. Our Lord God gave Eve the freedom to do as she pleased with fruits, flowers, and grasses, and with all that there was in Paradise – excepting one thing, which he forbade her on pain of death. Priests tell us that it was the fig-tree. She broke off its fruit and broke God's commandment, losing herself and God. But indeed it is my firm belief today that Eve would never have done so, had it never been forbidden her. In the first thing she ever did, she proved true to her nature and did what was forbidden! But as good judges will all agree, Eve might well have denied herself just that one fruit. When all is said and done, she had all the rest at her pleasure without exception, yet she wanted none but that one thing in which she devoured her honour! Thus they are all daughters of Eve who are formed in Eve's image after her. Oh for the man who could forbid all the Eves he might find today, who would abandon themselves and God because they were told not to do something!

And since women are heirs to it, and nature promotes it in them, all honour and praise to the woman who nevertheless succeeds in abstaining! For when a woman grows in virtue despite her inherited instincts and gladly keeps her honour, reputation, and person intact, she is only a woman in name, but in spirit she is a man! One should judge well of all her doings, and honour and esteem them. When a woman lays aside her woman's nature and assumes the heart of a man, it is as if the fir dripped with honey, the hemlock yielded balm, or what rooted as a nettle bore roses above ground! What can ever be so perfect in a woman as when, in alliance with honour at her side, she does battle with her body for the rights of both body and honour? She must so direct the combat that she does justice to them both and so attends to each that the other is not neglected. She is no worthy woman who forsakes her honour for her body, or her body for her honour, when circumstance so favours her that she may vindicate them both. Let her deny neither the one nor the other, let her sustain the two, through joy and through sorrow, however she sets about it. Heaven knows, a woman has to rise in merit at the cost of great effort. Let her commend her ways to seemly moderation, let her restrain her instincts and adorn herself and her conduct with it! Noble moderation will enhance her honour, person, and reputation.

Of all the things on which the sun ever shone, none is so truly blessed as a woman who has given herself and her life in trust to Moderation, and holds herself in right esteem. For so long as she esteems herself, by the innate fitness of things everyone else will esteem her. When a woman acts against herself and so directs her thoughts that she becomes her own enemy – who, in face of this, is going to love her? When a woman treats herself with contempt and gives proof of this in public, what honour or affection can one accord her? One quenches desire as soon as one feels the urge and yet wishes to bestow the exalted name on such meaningless behaviour! No, no, it is not Love, but her deadly enemy, the vile and shameful one, base Lechery! She brings no honour to the name of woman, as a true proverb says: 'She who thinks to love many, by many is unloved!' Let the woman who desires to be loved by all first love herself and then show us all her love-tracks. If they are Love's true traces, all will love in sympathy.

People should laud and extol a woman who, in order to please them, shows tender concern for her womanhood. They should crown her with garlands and fête her every day, and enhance their glory in her company. And on whomever she takes courage to bestow her love and person, that man was born most fortunate! He was altogether destined for present bliss, he has the living paradise implanted within his heart! He need have no fear that the thorns will vex him when he reaches for the flowers, or that the prickles will pierce him when he gathers the roses. There are no thorns or prickles there: thistly anger has no business there at all. Rose-like Conciliation has uprooted them all – prickles, thistles, and thorns! In such a paradise nothing buds on the twig or puts on green or grows but what the eye delights in – it all blossoms there by grace of a woman's virtue. There is no other fruit there but love and devotion, honour and worldly esteem. Ah me, in such a paradise, so fecund of joy and so vernal, the man on whom Fortune smiles might find his heart's desire and see his eyes' delight. In what would he be worse off than Tristan and Isolde? If only he would take my word for it, he would not need to exchange his life for Tristan's! For, truly, to whomever a virtuous woman resigns and surrenders her honour and her person, oh, with what deep love she will foster him, how tenderly she will cherish him! How she will clear all his paths of thorns and thistles and of all the vexations of love! How well she will free him from his sufferings, as no Isolde ever freed her Tristan better! And I firmly believe that, were one to seek as one ought, there would still be living Isoldes in whom one would find in plenty whatever one was able to seek.

Now let us return to Surveillance. As you have heard, the watch that was set on Tristan and Isolde was torment to those lovers, the royal command that they were to avoid each other so afflicted them that never before did they give such thought to their chances of a meeting, until, after all their pangs, they at last accomplished it. But they both reaped suffering from it, and mortal sorrow, too.

It was noon, and the sun was shining strongly, alas, upon their honour. Two kinds of sunshine, the sun and love, shone into the Queen's heart and soul. Her languor and the noonday heat vied with each other to distress her. She therefore intended by some means or other to elude this dissension between her mood and the hour – and was soon deep in trouble.

Isolde went to her orchard to study her opportunity. She went in search of shade for the chance that she meant to seize, shade that would assist her by offering her its shelter, and where it was cool and lonely. As soon as she had found it she ordered a bed to be made there with great magnificence – underquilts, linen, silks, and gold brocades – all that goes to make a royal couch was spread in abundance on that bed. And when it was made as well as possible, Fair Isolde lay down on it in her shift. She then told all her young ladies to withdraw, with the sole exception of Brangane. A message was sent to Tristan to tell him to come without fail and speak with Isolde immediately.

Now Tristan did just as Adam did; he took the fruit which his Eve offered him and with her ate his death! He came. And Brangane joined the ladies and sat down among them in fear and foreboding. She ordered the chamberlains to close all the doors and admit nobody, unless she herself allowed him in. The doors were shut, and when Brangane had sat down again she went over it all in her mind and deplored it that fear of watchers and spies should have failed to impress her lady.

Now while she was brooding thus, one of the chamberlains left by the door and was scarcely outside when the King came in past him and asked after the Queen in a manner that brooked no delay. 'I think she is sleeping, Sire!' the young ladies answered together. Lost in thought as she had been, Brangane was taken by surprise, and did not say a word. Her head drooped on her shoulder, her hands and heart dropped away from her. 'Tell me, where is the Queen sleeping?' asked the King. They motioned him towards the garden, Mark repaired there at once – and found his mortal pain there! He found his wife and his nephew tightly enlaced in each other's arms, her cheek against his cheek, her mouth on his mouth. All that the coverlet permitted him to see – all that emerged to view from the sheets at the upper end – their arms and hands, their shoulders and breasts – was so closely locked together that, had they been a piece cast in bronze or in gold, it could not have been joined more perfectly. Tristan and Isolde were sleeping very peacefully after some exertion or other.

Only now, when the King saw his woe so plainly, was his irrevocable affliction brought home to him. Once more he had found his way. His old overload of doubt and suspicion was gone – he no longer fancied, he *knew*. What he had always desired had now been given him in full. But truly, in my opinion, he would have been far better off with suspicion than with certainty. All his past efforts to rid himself of doubt had now ended in living death. He went away in silence. He drew his councillors and vassals aside. He made a beginning and said that he had been told for a fact that Tristan and the Queen were together, and that they were all to accompany him and take note of the pair, so that if they were found there as stated he should be given summary judgement against them in accordance with the law of the land.

Now Mark had scarce left the bedside and gone but a short way when Tristan awoke and saw him receding from the bed. 'Oh,' he said, 'what have you done Brangane, faithful woman! God in Heaven, Brangane, if you ask me, this sleeping will cost us our lives. Isolde, wake up, poor lady! Wake up, queen of my heart! I think we have been betrayed.'

'Betrayed!' exclaimed Isolde. 'How, sir?'

'My lord was just standing over us. He saw us, and I saw him. He is just going away and I know for a fact, as sure as I shall die, that he has gone to fetch help and witnesses – he means to have us killed! Dearest lady, lovely Isolde, we must part, and in such a way that, it seems, such chances of being happy together may never come our way again. Consider what perfect love we have cherished till now, and see that it endures. Keep me in your heart; for whatever happens to mine, you shall never leave it! Isolde must dwell in Tristan's heart for ever! See to it, dear mistress, that absence and distance do not harm me in your affections. Do not forget me, whatever befalls you! Fair Isolde, sweet friend, kiss me and give me leave to go!'

Isolde stepped back a pace and addressed him with a sigh. 'My lord, our hearts and souls have been engrossed with each other too long, too closely and too intimately, ever to know what forgetting could be between them. Whether you are near or far, there shall be no life in my heart nor any living thing, save Tristan, my life and being! It is a long time now, sir, since I surrendered my life to your keeping. See to it that no living woman ever comes between us to prevent us from remaining always fresh in our affection, in which we have been so perfect all this long time. Now accept this ring. Let it be a witness to our love and our devotion. If you should ever be moved to love any thing but me, let this remind you of how my heart now feels. Remember this farewell, and how deeply it affects us. Remember many an anxious time that I have gone through for your sake, and let none be nearer to your heart than your friend, Isolde! Do not forget me for anyone. We two have brought our joys and sorrows up to this hour in such companionship that we are bound to keep its memory till our dying day. My lord, there is no need for me to exhort you thus far. If Isolde was ever united with Tristan in one heart and bond, it will always remain fresh, it will endure for ever! But I will ask one thing: to whichever corners of the earth you go, take care of yourself, my life! For when I am orphaned of you, then I, your life, will have perished. I will guard myself, your life, with jealous care, not for my sake but yours, knowing that your life is one with mine. We are one life and flesh. Keep your thoughts on me, your very life, your Isolde. Let me see my life again, in you, as soon as ever possible; and may you see yours in me! The life we share is in your keeping. Now come here and kiss me. You and I, Tristan and Isolde, shall for ever remain one and undivided! Let this kiss be a seal upon it that I am yours, that you are mine, steadfast till death, but one Tristan and Isolde!'

When these words had been given their seal, Tristan went his way in great grief and anguish. His life, his other self, Isolde, remained there in deep sorrow. The two companions had never yet parted in such torment as here.

Meanwhile, having gathered a crowd of his councillors together, the King had returned. They arrived too late, however. They found Isolde alone, lying on her bed and lost in her thoughts as before. Seeing that the King had found nobody there but his Isolde, his councillors at once drew him aside and said: 'Sire, it is very wrong of you continually to drag your wife and honour to judgement on scandalous charges without reason. You hate your honour and your wife, but most of all yourself! How can you ever be happy so long as you thus injure your happiness in her, and make her the talk of the land? – for you have never discovered anything that goes against her honour. Why do you reproach the Queen? Why do you say that she is false, who never did a false act against you? My lord, by your honour, do not do so again! Have done with such infamy, for God's sake and your own!'

Thus they dissuaded him from his purpose, so that he fell in with their counsel and once more left his anger and went away, unavenged.

29

ISOLDE OF THE WHITE HANDS

TRISTAN went to his quarters. He took all his retainers and made for the harbour at a smart pace. He boarded the first ship he found and sailed for Normandy with his followers. But he did not stay there long, for he felt an urge to find a life that could in some way afford him relief from his sadness. Note a strange thing here: Tristan was in flight from toil and suffering, and yet he went in search of suffering and toil. He fled Mark and death, and yet sought mortal peril that was death to his heart – absence from Isolde. What was the use of his fleeing death on the one hand and following death on the other? What was the use of his eluding torment in Cornwall, when he bore it on his back, night and day? He saved his life for the sake of the woman, and his life was poisoned with that woman alone. No other living thing was death to his life and soul but his best life, Isolde. Thus he suffered the threat of two deaths. He thought that if this agony was ever to become supportable to a point where he could survive it, this would have to be through martial exploits.

Now there was a widespread rumour of a great war in Germany, and somebody told it to Tristan. He accordingly made for Champagne, and thence over here to Germany. He served the Crown and Sceptre so splendidly that the Holy Roman Empire never had under its banner a man who won such fame through deeds of arms. He reaped much success and good fortune in martial affairs and in hazardous enterprises which I shall not mention at length; for were I to give a detailed account of all the deeds ascribed to him in books, it would make an endless story. I shall cast the fables on this topic to the winds – since in dealing with the authentic version I have a load of work to carry as it is.

Isolde the Fair – Tristan's life and death, his living death – was in pain and torment. That her heart did not break on the day when she followed Tristan and his ship out to sea with her eyes was because he lived. That he lived helped her to survive. Without him she was powerless either to live or die. Both death and life had poisoned her: she could neither die nor live. The lustre of her bright eyes was often obscured. Time and again her tongue stayed mute in her mouth when she needed it – although they were both there, her mouth and tongue were neither dead nor alive. It was sorrow that made them forsake their rightful use so that she was aware of neither.

Seeing the sail flying, she said to herself in her heart: 'Ah me, ah me, my lord Tristan, now my heart cleaves fast to you, my eyes follow after you and you are fleeing fast away from me! Why do you hasten away from me like this? I know that when you flee Isolde, you are leaving your life behind you, since I am indeed your life. Without me you cannot live for one day longer than I can live without you. Our lives and very souls are so interwoven, so utterly enmeshed, the one with the other, that you are taking my life away with you and leaving yours with me. No two lives were ever so intermingled: we hold death and life for each other, since neither can really find life or death unless the other give it. And so poor Isolde is neither alive nor yet quite dead: both ways are denied me.

'Now my lord Tristan, sir, since you are for ever one life with me, you must teach me how to preserve my life, first for you and then for me. Now teach on! Why are you silent? We have dire need of wise counsel. But what am I saying, foolish Isolde? Tristan's tongue and my spirit are sailing away there together! Isolde's life, Isolde's soul have been entrusted to the mercy of the sails and the winds! Where shall I find myself now? Where shall I seek myself now, oh where? I am here and there, and yet I am neither there nor here. Whoever was so lost and bewildered? Whoever was so divided? – I see myself yonder on the sea, and yet I am here on dry land. I am sailing out there with Tristan, and sitting here at Mark's side!

'Meanwhile, life and death fight a mighty battle in me, by these two I am poisoned. I would gladly die, if I could – but he who keeps my life will not let me. But now I cannot live well, either for him or for myself, since I have to live without him. He is leaving me here and sailing away, and he knows full well that, without him, deep down in my heart I am dead. But, God knows, I say so without need – my sorrow is shared, I do not suffer it alone. His sorrow is as great as mine and, I imagine, even greater. Yes, his grief and pain are more than mine. His going away from me weighs on my heart, but it weighs heavier on his. If it grieves me that I miss him here beside me, it grieves him even more. If I mourn for him, he mourns for me. Yet he does not mourn with good cause like me. I may fairly claim that my pining and mourning for Tristan are justified, for my life depends on him, whereas his death depends on me; so that he mourns without cause.

'Tristan is most welcome to sail away and preserve his life and honour, since if he stayed with me for long he would have no chance of surviving; and so I must do without him. However much it hurts me, he shall not live in fear of his life for my sake! And so I must do without him. Whatever it costs me, I would much rather he were absent and unharmed than present and I in constant expectation that some harm might befall him at my side. For truly, whoever seeks his own advantage at his friend's expense bears him little affection. Whatever harm I reap from it, I desire to be Tristan's friend without any hurt befalling him. If only his affairs run a happy course I do not care if I am always wretched. I will delight in forcing myself, in all that I do, to forgo myself and him, so that he may live on for us two.'

When Tristan, as I was saying, had been in Germany for six months or more, he conceived a great longing to return to his homeland so that he could discover what rumours there were about his lady. He made up his mind and left Germany, and travelled back to Normandy by the way he had come and thence to Parmenie, to Rual's sons. He was hoping to find Rual himself and to tell him of his plight. But, alas, Rual had died, both he and his wife Floraete. Yet his sons, you must know, were heartily glad at Tristan's coming. The welcome they gave him was tender and true. They kissed his hands and his feet, his eyes, and his mouth, over and over again. 'Sir,' they said immediately, 'in you God has sent us back our mother and father. My good and faithful lord, settle down here again and take back all that was yours and ours. Let us prosper with you here like our father, who was your retainer, as we too shall always gladly be! Your friend our mother, and our father, too, are dead. But now, by bringing you back to us, God has most graciously provided for our need through you.'

Sad though he was already, Tristan drew fresh sadness from this news and gave way to wild laments. He asked to be shown his foster-parents' grave. He repaired there in sorrow and stood over it for a while weeping and lamenting and speaking words of mourn‑ing. 'May almighty God take note,' he said with fervour, 'that should it ever come to pass, as I have heard since childhood, that loyalty and honour may be buried in the earth, they both lie buried here! And if loyalty and honour keep company with God, as people say, then I have no doubt, and indeed there is no denying it, that Rual and Floraete are in the presence of God. Those two, whom God had made so splendid and noble on earth, are also crowned where God's children wear their crowns!'

Rual's good sons with spontaneous sincerity placed their resi‑dences, persons, and property at Tristan's disposal, together with their most willing devotion. They were at all times entirely at his service. Whatever he commanded was done in everything it was in their power to do. They went visiting with him to observe knights and ladies. They attended him to tournaments and to the hunt, both stalking and the chase, and to whatever pastime he followed.

Now there was a duchy lying between Brittany and England called Arundel, bounded by the sea. In it was a duke – fearless, courteous, and advanced in years, whose neighbours, so the history says, had ravaged and occupied his lands and jurisdiction. They had overwhelmed him by land and sea. He would most gladly have offered battle, but he lacked the means. By his wife he had a son and a daughter who were faultless in qualities of body and of mind. The son had been made a knight; he was entirely devoted to chivalry and had been earning much honour and renown by it for well on three years. His sister was beautiful and unmarried. She was called Isolde of the White Hands, her brother Kaedin li frains – the Noble and Free – her father the Duke Jovelin. Her mother the Duchess was named Karsie.

When Tristan was told in Parmenie that there was a feud in the land of Arundel, it occurred to him that he could again forget some part of his sorrows there. He left Parmenie at once for Arundel and made for a castle named Karke, where he found the lord of the land, and only there did he turn from the road.

Lord and retainers received Tristan as one is bound to receive a man of worth.* They knew him well by repute. For Tristan,

* Or: as one should receive a stout man when one is hard-pressed.

as the story says, was renowned for his manly prowess throughout the islands that lie towards the Ocean. For this reason they were glad of his coming. The Duke submitted to his advice and instruction and made him master both of his territory and of his honour.

Jovelin's courteous son Kaedin was deeply attached to Tristan. Kaedin studied everything which he knew would conduce to Tristan's credit, and all his thoughts were directed to it. Kaedin and Tristan vied continually to outdo each other in each other's service. This pair swore between them to be loyal companions, and kept their oath well to the end.

Tristan the stranger took Kaedin and went to the Duke and questioned him, asking him to tell him how his enemies had brought this feud upon him and from which quarter the worst damage by which he was being overwhelmed was inflicted.

When the nature of the feud had been explained to him, and he had been accurately informed of the enemy's dispositions and where they had approached with their war-train, Tristan and his friend Kaedin, with a company of knights of no great size, stationed themselves in a good castle which the Duke had in his keeping and which lay on the enemy's path. Their resources were not such that they could ever give battle in the open except inasmuch as they were able to harry the enemy's territories, from time to time, by stealth with fire and pillage. Tristan sent a secret message home to Parmenie to his beloved retainers. He informed Rual's sons that he was in need of knights as he had never been before, and that they were to give him convincing proof of their honour and worth by bringing him their aid. They brought him five hundred mounts in one company, splendidly caparisoned, and great stores of provisions.

When Tristan learned that help was coming from home he went in person to meet them, gave them escort through the night, and conducted them into the duchy without anyone being the wiser apart from those who were his friends and who had aided him in this undertaking. He left half of the men of Parmenie at Karke and commanded them to shut themselves in very strongly and ignore all who offered battle till they had made sure that he and Kaedin were engaged there, and that they were then to ride out and attack the enemy's vanguard and so make trial of their fortunes. This done, he took the remainder and continued his march. Under cover of night, he got them into the castle which had been entrusted to him and ordered these, too, to conceal their strength as strictly as those over in Karke.

By daybreak next morning Tristan had made a further division, this time of no less than a hundred knights. The rest he left in the town. He asked Kaedin to tell his men that, if he were pursued to its walls, the knights were to look out for him and come to his aid, both from there and from Karke. He then rode to the frontier, plundering and burning openly in the enemy's country wherever he knew the latter's fortresses and cities to be. Before night had yet fallen the rumour was flying through the country from place to place that noble Kaedin had ridden out on foray in broad daylight. This news angered the enemy's leaders Rugier of Doleise, Nautenis of Hante, and Rigolin of Nantes. During the night the latter summoned all the resources and strength they could muster.

The next day, round about noon, when their forces had been concentrated, the enemy at once made for Karke. They had upwards of four hundred knights in their number and were counting on camping there as they had done many a day before. But now Tristan and his friend Kaedin were following on their tracks. When the others imagined that they were safe and that nobody would dare to do battle with them at such a time, the men of Arundel flew at them from all sides – not one of them thought that he could close with the enemy soon enough!

When the enemy saw that battle was inevitable they at once turned to the attack, advancing all together. There and then, lance flew towards lance, charger against charger, man against man so fiercely that great mischief was done. They wrought havoc on either side, here Tristan and Kaedin, there Rugier and Rigolin. Whatever a man hankered for with sword or lance, he had it there, he found it. On one side they hailed each other with 'Chevalier Hante, Doleise, e Nantes!' On the other, 'Karke and Arundel!'

When those in the castle saw the fighting settle down before them, they galloped out at the gates into the enemy's ranks on the other flank and pressed them this way and that with bitter fighting. In a very short space they broke through them, first in one direction and then in the other. They rode slashing among them like wild boars among sheep. Tristan and his friend Kaedin now aimed their attack against the banners and coats-of-arms of their chief enemies. Rugier, Rigolin and Nautenis were taken prisoner and much loss was in- flicted on their retinue. Tristan of Parmenie and his compatriots rode striking, felling and capturing their enemies. When these real- ized that it was useless to resist, they all strove desperately to escape and save themselves as best they might, by flight or by some ruse. Flight, entreaties, or death ended that battle with a clear verdict for one side.

Now that the issue had been decided by a rout and the captives had been lodged and secured in suitable places, Tristan and Kaedin took all their own knights and available resources and turned the tables by invading hostile territory. Wherever they found any of the enemy or knew any of his possessions to be, property, towns, fortresses, these were forfeit where they lay. They sent their booty to Karke.

When they had utterly subdued their enemies' lands to their will, fully avenged their wrongs and had all the others' lands in their power, Tristan sent his own retainers back home again to Parmenie, after thanking them most gratefully for the honour and good fortune that he had won with their kind help. When his followers had left, far-sighted Tristan advised that the prisoners should be received into favour and should accept from their lord whichever of their fiefs he returned to them with his express pardon. This they duly signed and sealed, lest any further harm should arise for the land from their quarter as a result of these wrongs and this enmity; after which captains and men all went free.

After these events, great honour and praise were rendered to Tristan in Karke and in all Arundel. His courage and discernment were acclaimed at court and in the country, which were subject to his slightest command. Kaedin's sister Isolde, she of the white hands, the paragon of that region, was noble and intelligent, and had so advanced her reputation that she had made a conquest of the whole duchy, with the result that people spoke only of her fair fortune. When Tristan saw how lovely she was, it renewed his sufferings – his old sorrow was as fresh as ever. She reminded him strongly of the other Isolde, the resplendent one of Ireland. And because her name was Isolde, whenever he let his eyes go out to her he grew so sad and joyless at the name that you could read his heart's pain in his face. Yet he cherished this pain and held it in tender regard – it seemed sweet and good to him. He loved this suffering because he liked to see this Isolde; and he liked to see her because his pining for Fair Isolde assuaged him more than any pleasure. Isolde was his joy and his sorrow. Yes, Isolde, his distraction, both soothed and pained him! The more Isolde broke his heart in Isolde's name, the more gladly he saw Isolde!

'Heavens,' he would often say to himself, 'how far I have gone astray over this name! It plays true and false with my eyes and sense, and utterly bewilders them. It sets me in the strangest quandary – "Isolde" laughs and sports in my ears continually, yet I do not know where Isolde is. My eye, which regards Isolde, does not see Isolde! Isolde is far away and nevertheless beside me! I fear I have succumbed to Isolde for the second time. It is as if Cornwall had turned into Arundel, Tintagel into Karke, Isolde into Isolde. When anyone mentions this girl by the name of Isolde, I keep thinking I have found Isolde. But in this I am far from the truth. What a strange thing has happened to me: I have been longing to see Isolde for a great while, and now I have found her; but am not with Isolde however near I am to her! Isolde I look at every day, yet, alas, I do not see her. I have indeed found Isolde, but not the fair one, who gives me such gentle pain! It is Isolde that has put such thoughts into my heart and causes me to brood so, the maid of Arundel and not Isolde the Fair, whom, alas, I do not see. But I will always love and cherish whatever my eyes behold that bears the seal of her name, and bless the sweet sound which so often has delighted me!'

Tristan often occupied himself with such musings, when he glimpsed his gentle pain, Isolde of the White Hands. She renewed the fire of his passion with the glowing embers which nevertheless night and day lay damped within his heart. He no longer gave thought to war or tournaments. His whole heart and soul were bent on love and distraction. But he sought it in a strange fashion, since he bent his thoughts to entertaining fond hopes and affection for the maiden Isolde, and to forcing his feelings to love her, in the speculation that, through her, the load of his longing might dwindle. He regaled her constantly with tender looks and sent so many towards her that she grew to be very well aware that he had an affectionate regard for her. Before this, she too had had thoughts enough on his account; she had pondered much because of him. Ever since she had seen and heard people speak of him so highly everywhere, her heart had been turned towards him. And when, now and again, Tristan let his eyes go out to her to try their fortune, she let hers go out to the man no less tenderly, so that he began to consider by what means he could accomplish it that all his despondency should be quenched, and gave much thought to seeing her at all times of the day, whenever it could be arranged.

It was not long before Kaedin noticed how they looked at each other, so that he introduced Tristan into Isolde's company more often than before, in the hope that, if she took root in his heart, Tristan would take her and remain there, and he, Kaedin, would also have gained all his objectives. He accordingly urged his sister Isolde to entertain Tristan with conversation as he should instruct her, but to stop short of any deeds without his knowledge and without their father's advice.

Isolde did as Kaedin asked because it fell in with her wishes. She accorded Tristan twice as much favour as before. She now plied him with looks and conversation and with all those things which ensnare a man's thoughts and quicken love in his heart, from every side with every means, till she had set him on fire too; with the result that the name which had lately troubled him now fell gently on his ears and he heard and saw Isolde far more gladly than he wished. And so it was with Isolde. She was glad to see him and harboured friendly feelings towards him. She was in his thoughts, as he was in hers. They now swore companionship and affection and cultivated them on all occasions when they could do so with propriety.

One day, as Tristan was sitting at leisure, he was assailed by memories of his old sufferings, to which he had been born. He recalled in his heart the many and varied hardships which his other life Isolde, the fair-haired Queen, the key that ruled his love, had endured for his sake, she who had remained so steadfast through all her trials. He took it as a reproach to himself, and it pained him to the depths of his being, that he should have admitted into his heart any other woman than Queen Isolde with an eye to making love to her, and should ever have arrived at such thoughts. 'What am I doing, traitor that I am?' he asked himself in anguish. 'I know it as sure as death that my heart and my life, Isolde, towards whom I have acted like a man bereft of reason, neither loves nor has in her thoughts any thing on earth, nor can she treasure any thing but me; whereas I love a life that has nothing to do with her. I do not know what has come over me. Oh what have I, faithless Tristan, embarked on? I am enamoured of two Isoldes and hold them both dear, yet my other self, Isolde, loves but one Tristan. That one woman desires no other Tristan but me, while I hotly woo a second Isolde. Alas, insensate man, poor bewildered Tristan, have done with this blind madness, put this monstrous thought away from you!'

With this he got free of his desire. He laid aside the love and inclination that he had for the maiden Isolde. Nevertheless he gave her many signs of such tenderness that she imagined she had all possible proof of his love – but such was not the case. Things took their rightful path. Isolde had robbed Isolde of her Tristan through desire; but now, with desire, Tristan had returned to the love that he was born to. His heart and mind ran entirely on their old sorrow. Yet he did what courtesy required. Observing how the girl's languishings were beginning to run their course, he devoted his efforts to amusing her. He told her some beautiful stories, he sang to her, he wrote and he read and gave thought to whatever would entertain her. He kept her company, he whiled away the time for her, now by singing, now by playing. Tristan composed for every sort of strings many lays and much fine music that have been well loved ever since. It was at this time that he made the noble lay of 'Tristan', which will be treasured and esteemed in every land so long as the world remains.

And here is what happened, time and again. When the Court was sitting all together – he, Isolde and Kaedin, the Duke and the Duchess, the ladies and the barons – he would compose love-songs, rondels and courtly little airs, and always bring in this refrain:

> Isot ma drue, Isot mamie,
> en vus ma mort, en vus ma vie!*

And since he so loved to sing it, they were all taken up with the idea that he had their Isolde in mind and were very glad of it and none more than his friend Kaedin. Kaedin led him out and led him

* 'Isolde my mistress, Isolde my beloved, in you my life, in you my death!'

in and always sat him beside his sister, who for her part was very glad to see him. She received him into her keeping and gave him her attention. Her clear bright eyes and thoughts played full upon him then, and from time to time that fragile thing called maidenhood lost all track of modesty, for she often laid her hands in his quite openly, as if she did it to please Kaedin. But whatever Kaedin imagined, her own pleasure was bound up with it. The girl made herself so alluring to the man with her smiles and laughter, her talk, her prattle, her blandishments and coquetry, that she at last set him on fire for the second time and his affections once more began to waver because of his thoughts and desires.

Tristan was in two minds about whether he wanted Isolde or not. Indeed, her tender treatment disquieted him exceedingly. 'Do I desire her or don't I?' he was constantly asking himself. 'I think I do not, and then I think I do.' But Constancy was always at hand. 'No, lord Tristan, consider your pledge to Isolde, hold fast to faithful Isolde who never swerved an inch from you!' He was at once reclaimed from these thoughts and returned to his mourning for the love of Isolde, the queen of his heart, with the result that his looks and his manner were so changed that, wherever he was, he did nothing but pine, and whenever he joined Isolde and began to converse with her, he grew oblivious of himself and sat sighing endlessly beside her. The signs of his secret sorrow were so plain to see that the whole court declared that his melancholy and suffering were all because of Isolde. Indeed, they were right. The source of Tristan's pining and distress was no other than Isolde. Isolde was his misfortune, yet she was by no means the one whom they believed – she of the White Hands. It was Isolde the Fair, not the Maid of Arundel.

But they all imagined the contrary, and Isolde thought so, too, and was utterly misled by it. For at no time was Tristan consumed with longing for Isolde when the girl was not consumed with a greater longing for him. And so these two passed their time with suffering in which the other had no part. They were both filled with longing and grief, but their grief did not coincide. Their love and affection were unshared. Tristan and the girl Isolde did not keep step with one another in mutual affection. For his sole source of suffering Tristan desired another Isolde, but Isolde desired no other Tristan – she of the White Hands loved and had her thoughts on him alone, her heart and mind were centred upon him. His sorrow was her distress. And when she saw how the colour left his face, and that he then began to sigh most tenderly, she looked at him tenderly, too, and sighed with him in company. She bore his suffering with him most companionably, though it did not in the least concern her. His sufferings tormented her so much that they affected him more because of her than on his own account. He was filled with regret for the kindness and affection which she so faith, fully entertained for him. It filled him with pity that she had abandoned her thoughts so far to loving him for nothing at all, and had bestowed her heart on him with such vain hopes. Yet he did as courtesy required and devoted himself with all the charm of manner and conversation he could summon to freeing her from her op, pression, as he dearly would have done. But she was too far gone in it, and the greater the pains he went to the more he inflamed the girl, from hour to hour, till at last she reached the point where Love won the victory over her, so that she regaled him time out of number with looks and words and glances of such melting tenderness that for the third time he fell into the stress of indecision and the barque that was his heart once more came afloat to toss on the tide of dark thoughts. And little wonder, for, heaven knows, delight that lies laughing up at a man all the time blinds his eyes and thoughts and keeps tugging at his heart.

Here lovers can see from this story that one can bear a distant sorrow for an absent love with much greater ease than loving near at hand and missing love within one's reach. Truly, as I see it, a man can suffer want of dearest love in absence, desiring it from afar, better than wanting what is near and forgoing it; and he will be rid of his distant love more easily than he will refrain from love that is near. Tristan entangled himself in these toils. He desired love that was far away and endured great anguish for one whom he neither heard nor saw, whilst refraining from one that was near and often before his eyes. He never ceased to desire Isolde of Ireland, the radi, ant and fair, and he fled her of the white hands, the noble maiden of Karke. He suffered torment for the far and retreated from the near. In this way he was cheated of both: he desired yet did not desire Isolde and Isolde. He fled the one and sought the other. But the girl Isolde had bestowed her longing, her love, her whole integrity with complete singleness of will. She wanted the man who withdrew from her, pursued the man who fled from her. This was his fault – she was deceived! Tristan had so lied to her with the double action of eyes and tongue that she imagined she was quite sure of him and his affections. But of all the duplicity to which Tristan subjected her the crowning deed that compelled her to love him was that he liked to sing:

> *Isot ma drue, Isot mamie,*
> *en vus ma mort, en vus ma vie!*

This kept luring her heart towards him, this it was that engendered her affection. She made these words all her own and followed the fleeing man with the tenderest devotion until, at Love's fourth stride, she caught up with him as he fled and drew him back to her, with the result that he decided in her favour once again, and once again was musing and pondering and fearfully brooding night and day, about himself and the life that he was leading.

'Almighty God,' he thought, 'how utterly astray I am because of love! If this love that so distracts me, that robs me of life and reason and has brought me to this pass, is ever to be assuaged on earth, it must be through some other attachment! I have often read and am well aware that one love saps the strength of another. The flood and current of the Rhine are nowhere so great that one cannot by means of single channels draw off so much water that it slackens, and flows with only moderate force. Thus the mighty Rhine will shrink to a tiny rivulet. Again, there is no conflagration so great that if one gives one's mind to it one cannot distribute it into single fires until it burns but weakly. So it is with a lover – he can play a like gambit. He can draw off the flood of his passion through single channels and parcel out the fire in his heart at many points till at last it is so reduced that it does little harm. I may have a like success if I divide and apportion my love among more than one. If I direct my thoughts to more than one love I might easily become a carefree Tristan!

'I shall now put it to the test. If Fortune is to smile on me, it is time that I began. For the loyal love I have for my lady has no power to help me. I am consuming my life for her and can offer myself no consolation by which to go on living. I suffer this dejection and anguish with all too little hope. Ah, sweet mistress, dearest Isolde, the life we share suffers too great a separation! Things are not as they were when we two endured one good, one ill, one joy, one sorrow together. Alas, it is not so now! Now I am wretched, but you are happy. My thoughts are full of longing for your love, while yours, I imagine, long but little for me. The pleasure I forgo for your sake – ah, how it pains me! – you pursue as often as you please! You have your partner for it. Your master, Mark, and you are at home, you are inseparable companions; but I am abroad and alone. It seems to me that I shall have little solace of you, and yet I can never free my heart from you. Why have you robbed me of myself, seeing that you have so little desire for me and can so well do without me?

'Sweet Queen Isolde, with what numberless pangs does my life pass by with you, while I am not so pleasing in your eyes that you have sent me a messenger to inquire about the life I am leading. She send a messenger? What am I saying? Where should she send to me, and how could she inquire about my life? I have been at the mercy of such very uncertain winds now for a very long time – how could anyone find me? I cannot fathom how. If a man sought there I would be here, if he sought here I would be there. How or where shall one find me? Where am I to be found? Here, where I am – countries do not run away from one, and I am in those countries – so let Tristan be found there! Yes, if only someone began to look, he would seek until he found me. For whoever desires to trace a traveller has no fixed goal set before him, but must ply his endeavours for better or worse if he means to achieve anything. My lady, she on whom my whole life depends, ought in heaven's name to have explored all Cornwall and England most secretly long since. France and Normandy, my land of Parmenie or wherever her friend Tristan was rumoured to be, should have been searched long ago, had she cared anything for me! But she whom I love and cherish more than my body and soul cares but little for me. I avoid all other women for her sake, yet I must forgo her too. I cannot ask that of her which would give me joy and a happy life in the world. ...'*

* Gottfried's poem breaks off here.

Tristran

30

THE WEDDING

...TRISTRAN's feelings keep on changing, and he considers, this way and that, how to change his desire, since he cannot have what he wants. And then he says: 'Ysolt, dear mistress, our lives are very different: our love is so remote that it exists only to delude me. I lose joy and delight for you, while you have them night and day. I lead my life in great misery, but you lead yours in amorous sport. I do nothing but long for you, but you cannot help but have joy and delight and do all your pleasure. I suffer torment for your body, while the King has his pleasure of you. – He has his joy and delight – what was mine is now his.

'I yield my right to what I cannot have – for I know she is disporting herself, she has forgotten me in her pleasures. For the sake of Ysolt alone I scorn all others in my affections, but she does not wish to comfort me at all, and yet she knows the great anguish that I endure for love of her. For I am much wanted by another and am deeply afflicted because of it. Were I not so much desired by a new love I could better endure my longing for Ysolt, and I fear that unless she give heed to it, I may give up my longing for very weariness. Since I cannot have my true love, I shall have to take what I can (for it seems to me that I must). Thus does a man who cannot do otherwise. What is the use of waiting so long, for ever avoiding one's pleasure? Why maintain a love from which no good can come? I have suffered such pains and griefs for her love that I may surely withdraw from it. There is no profit for me in upholding it. She has forgotten me entirely, for her feelings have changed.

'Ah, God, good Father, Heavenly King, how is such a change possible? – How would she have changed, since affection still remains? How can she let love go? I cannot quit, for anything. I know that were she gone from our love, my heart would know it by hers. She did nothing, good or bad, that my heart was not quick to feel.

Through my heart I have clearly felt that her heart has held me fast, and strengthened me as well as it could. If I cannot have what I long for, I have no right on that account to seek a change and abandon her for a stranger: for we are too bound up with one another, and our bodies are too maltreated by love for me to languish for another, if I cannot have my true desire. And as to what Ysolt could do, she has the wish if only she had the means. Thus I must bear her no grudge, since she is well inclined; and if she does not do my will, I do not know how much that irks her. Ysolt, whatever your power to act, your intentions towards me are good.

'How, then, could she change? I cannot cheat in my love for her. I know that if she intended to change, my heart would sense it at once. But cheating or no cheating, I feel this severance keenly, and my heart clearly feels that she loves me little, if at all. For if she loved me more in her heart she would have found some way to comfort me. – She? In what? – In this anguish. – Where should she find me? – Here, where I am. – But she does not know where, nor in what land. – Does she not? Then, truly, supposing she sent someone to look for me! – For what purpose? – Because of my unhappiness. – She does not dare, from fear of her lord, even if the will were hers. – To what good, since she could not have the will? Let her love her lord, let her cleave to him.

'I do not ask her to remember me. I do not blame her if she forgets me – she ought not to languish for me. Her great beauty makes it unnecessary, nor does it suit her nature that she should languish for another when she has her will of the King. She should delight in him so much that she must forget her love for me, delight in her lord so far that she must forget her lover. And what does my love now mean to her, beside her delight in her lord? She must act as nature bids her, since she will not pursue her true desire. Let her hold to what she can have, for she must give up what she loves. Let her take what she can get, and suit it to her will. By disporting oneself, by much kissing, one can find agreement. It will soon be able to please her so well that she will not remember me at all. If she does not remember me, ah well, what does it matter? Whether she do well or ill, I do not care. To my way of thinking she can have pleasure in despite of love.

'How can she possibly have pleasure in despite of love or cherish her lord or consign to oblivion what she kept so long in memory? From where does a man get the will to hate what he has loved or bear anger and hatred towards one to whom he has given his heart? He must not hate what he has loved; but he may well withdraw from it, he may retire and depart when he sees no cause to love. He must not hate or love beyond the cause he sees. When a man sees noble behaviour followed by base, he should incline towards the noble, since he may not render evil for evil. The one thing must tolerate the other, so that they balance each other: a man must neither love too much, in view of what is base, nor yet hate over much in view of what is noble. One should love what is noble and fear what is base, and because there is nobility one should refrain from hating; but because there is baseness, too, one should refrain from doing service. Because Ysolt has loved me and given such signs of joy, I must not hate her for anything that may happen. But seeing that she forgets our love I ought not to remember her. I ought not to love her any more, nor yet ought I to hate her. But, if I can, I wish to withdraw as she has done, to try by my own experience how I can find pleasure in conduct contrary to love, as she does with her lord. How can I put this to the test, except by taking a wife? In doing what she does, Ysolt would not be justified, were she not lawfully married, for it is her rightful husband who thus divides our love. She has no right to withdraw from him; whatever her inclination, she has to do it. But I do not have to do it, except that I should like to try myself how she lives. I will marry the maiden in order to learn what life the Queen is leading, and whether marriage and union could make me forget her, as she has come to forget our love on account of her lord. I do not do this to her from hatred, but because I wish to leave her or to love her as she loves me: in order to learn how she loves the King.'

Tristran is in great anguish concerning this love on which it is possible for him to enter, and in great conflict and heart-searching. He can find no other justification for it except that he wants to try whether he can have pleasure in despite of love, and whether through the pleasure which he desires he can come to forget Ysolt; for he believes that she is forgetting him either because of her lord or her pleasure. He wishes to take a wife, so that Ysolt cannot blame him for seeking unlawful pleasure, which would not accord with his honour. He desires Ysolt of the White Hands for her beauty and the name 'Ysolt'. Tristran would never have desired her for the beauty that was in her had she not borne the name of Ysolt; nor for the name without the beauty. It is these two things which she has that cause him to embark on this enterprise, that is, to marry the maiden so as to know what the Queen's lot is, and how, in despite of love, he may have his pleasure with his wife. He means to test in his own person how Ysolt fares with the King, and thus he wishes to test what pleasure he will have with the other Ysolt. For his grief and his distress Tristran thus wants to seek revenge. For his suffering he seeks such vengeance that he will double his torment. He wishes to free himself from suffering, yet does nothing but embroil himself. He thought he would thus have his pleasure, since he could not have his true desire. Tristran has taken note of the Queen's name and beauty in the girl; but he would not have taken her for her name, or yet for her beauty, if it had not been for Ysolt. Were she not called 'Ysolt', Tristran would never have loved her. If she had not had Ysolt's beauty, Tristran could not have loved her. Both for the sake of the name and the beauty which Tristran has found in her, he falls into a wish and a desire to have the girl.

Hear this extraordinary thing, how strange people are, in that they can nowhere stay in one place. They are so changeable by nature that, although they cannot renounce their evil ways, they are able to change their good ones. They are so accustomed to evil that they account it right behaviour all the time, and are so much given to depravity that they do not know what nobility is and display such villainy that they are oblivious of courtesy. They are so intent on wickedness that they remain in it all their lives. They are unable to break with evil, so much is it a habit with them.

Some people are habituated to evil, others are curious of good. Their whole life is bent on change and on novelty, and they abandon the good in their power to follow their wicked will. Thirst for novelty makes them sacrifice the good in their power for wicked craving, and to give up the good which they can have in order to seek pleasure in evil. A man forsakes the better that is his to have the worse that is another's. He considers his own to be inferior, but another's that he covets to be better. If the good thing that he has were not his, he would not be averse to it; but in his

heart he cannot like what he perforce must own. If he could not have
had what he possesses, he would have longed to acquire it. He ex-
pects to find something better than what he has, and so he cannot
love his own. An itch for novelty deceives him when he does not
want what he must have and hankers for what he has not, or for-
sakes his own for worse. One ought, if one can, to exchange the
bad, abandoning the worse to gain the better, and act wisely and
give up folly; for it is not from fickleness that a man changes so as to
improve himself or escape from a bad situation. But many a man
suffers a change of heart and thinks to find in strange things what
he cannot find in familiar. So do men's thoughts vary; they wish to
try what they lack, and then they have to content themselves.[*]
Women do this, too: they abandon what they have for what they
fancy and try how they can arrive at their wish and their desire.
Truly, I do not know what to say on this topic; but men and
women equally are much too enamoured of novelty, for they change
too often their inclinations, their desires, and their wishes against
reason and possibility. One man seeks to advance himself in love,
yet only impairs himself; another thinks to cast love aside, yet he re-
doubles his pain; a third pursues vengeance, yet soon falls into
heavy sorrow; while a fourth imagines that he will free himself, yet
does nothing but embroil himself.

Tristran thought to forsake Ysolt and pluck love from his heart.
By wedding the other Ysolt, he hoped to escape from the first. And
were it not for the first Ysolt, he would not have loved the other so
much. But because he has loved Ysolt he is much moved to love –
Ysolt. And because he cannot have the first, his wish is for the
second; for if he could have the Queen, he would not love Ysolt,
the maiden. Therefore, it seems to me, I must assert that this
was neither love nor anger; for, if this had been true love, he would
not have loved the girl against the will of his beloved. Nor was
it true hatred, since it was from love of the Queen that Tristran
loved the maiden; and since he married her on account of his love,
it was not a case of hatred. For had he hated the Queen from his
heart, he would not have taken the girl for love of her; but had he
loved the Queen with true love, he would not have married the
other. Yet it so happened on this occasion that he was in such straits

* The text seems hopelessly corrupt at this point. I follow Wind.

of love that he wished to go counter to love in order to get free of it.

In trying to escape from his misery, Tristran fell into a greater. This happens to many people. When they have great torment of love, and anguish, great pain, and vexation, they do something to extricate themselves, free themselves, and avenge themselves, from which great trouble falls upon them. And often they do a thing deliberately that involves them in unhappiness. I have seen this happen to many. Unable to have their desire and that which they love most, they act within their means and do things out of desperation whereby they often double their affliction. And when they seek to get free they are unable to disentangle themselves. In such acts of vengeance I see both love and anger. This is neither love nor hatred, but anger mingled with love, and love mingled with anger. The man who by reason of some good that he cannot have does what he does not desire to do, does what he wants against his inmost desire, and this is just what Tristran is doing: he pursues what he wants despite his true desire. Since he suffers for love of one Ysolt he hopes to save himself through the other, and so much does he kiss and embrace her, and so earnestly asks her parents for her hand, that all are agreed on the marriage – he to take and they to bestow her.

The day is named, the term is set. Tristran arrives with his friends. The Duke is there, together with his men. All the preparations have been made. Tristran marries Ysolt of the White Hands. The chaplain says Mass and all that belongs to the service in accord with the rites of Holy Church. Then they go to feast at a banquet and afterwards to amuse themselves with quintains and jousts, javelins and reeds, wrestling and fencing, and various games of rivalry, such as go with a feast of this sort and such as the laity expect.

The day passes amid these pleasures, and the beds are ready for the night. They bring the maiden to bed, and Tristran has himself divested of the tunic that he is wearing. It sits very well on him and is tight round the wrists. But as they take off his robe they pull from his finger the ring which Ysolt had given him in the orchard on the last day he ever saw her.

Tristran looks and sees the ring and enters on a new train of thought. This puts him in such anguish that he does not know what to do. Now that he might easily do his will, his power to do so fails him. So searchingly does he think that he repents of what he has done. His action is now distasteful to him and he retracts in his heart through seeing the ring on his finger, and is much afflicted in his thoughts. He recalls the agreement which he made at their parting in the orchard when he had to go away, and he heaves a deep sigh from his heart.

'How can I do it?' he says to himself. 'This deed is repugnant to me. Nevertheless I must lie down as with my lawful wife. I am bound to lie with her, for I am unable to desert her. This is all because of my foolish heart that was so flighty and frivolous. When I asked the girl of her parents and relations – when I undertook this folly of breaking and betraying my plighted word – little did I think of my beloved Ysolt. I must lie down – how this grieves me! I have married her lawfully at the church door in the sight of the people. I can by no means repulse her, but must now commit an act of folly. I cannot hold aloof from this girl without great sin and misdemeanour. Nor can I unite with her, unless I mean to perjure myself, for I am so committed to the other Ysolt that it would be wrong for this Ysolt to have me. I owe so much to this Ysolt that I cannot keep faith with another and I must not break faith again, nor may I abandon this one! If I ever have my pleasure with any other, I shall be breaking my faith with Ysolt my beloved, and if I depart from this Ysolt, then I shall commit a sin, and evil, and wrong. For I may neither leave her nor take my pleasure of her by lying with her in her bed for my profit and delight. Indeed, I am so committed to the Queen that I must not lie with this girl, and am so committed to this girl that I cannot possibly retreat. I must neither betray Ysolt nor yet abandon my wife, I may neither separate from her nor may I lie with her. If I keep my promise to this girl, I shall break my vow to Ysolt; and if I keep faith with Ysolt, I shall break faith with my wife. But I must not break faith with her nor will I act against Ysolt. I do not know to which I should be false, since I must trick, betray, and deceive one, or, so it seems, play false to both together! For this girl has come so close to me that Ysolt is already betrayed. I have loved the Queen so much that the girl is betrayed, and I, too, am greatly betrayed. Unlucky was I to know either! Each suffers because of me, and I suffer for two Ysolts at once. Both are in love with me, and I am breaking faith with both of them. I have broken faith with the Queen and cannot keep it with this girl for whom I had to break it. Now, I can keep it towards one of them, and since I have already broken faith with the Queen, I must keep faith with the girl, for I cannot leave her. Nor must I betray Ysolt.

'Truly, I do not see what I can do. I suffer great anguish on all sides, since it is hard to keep faith with the Queen and worse to abandon my wife. Whether I enjoy the girl or not, I am bound to lie in her bed. I have now so avenged myself on Ysolt that I am the first to be beguiled; I wanted to avenge myself on Ysolt and am the first to be deceived. In going against her I have brought so much upon myself that I do not know what I should do. If I sleep with my wife, Queen Ysolt will be deeply offended; but if I refuse to sleep with her, it will be taken as a reproach to me, and I shall reap resentment and ill will from her. I should be hated and despised by her parents and all the others, and should sin in the eyes of God. I fear dishonour, I fear sin! What, then, when I am in bed, if I refrain at her side from what I most hate in my heart and am most reluctant to do? To lie there will do me no good. She will know by my condition that I long for another more. She is simple if she does not perceive that I love and desire another more, and that I would prefer to lie with one from whom I could have greater pleasure. When she is cheated of her joy with me I think she will love me very little. She will be justified in hating me, if I abstain from the natural act which should make us one in love.

'Abstinence breeds hatred. Just as love comes from doing, so hatred comes from refraining; love proceeds from the act, and hatred from a man's abstaining. If I refrain from the deed, I shall reap unhappiness and sorrow, and my prowess and noble qualities will turn to ignominy. What I have won by my valour I shall now lose through this love, and the affection she has borne me will now be denied me as a result of my refraining. All the fruits of my knightly service and nobility will be taken away from me by a dastardly act. Without the act of love, she has loved and desired me much in her thoughts; but now she will hate me for abstaining, because she does not have her desire. For this is what most joins a lover and his beloved in love. And for this reason I will not do the deed, since I intend to wean her from love. I am quite willing there should be hatred in her. I desire her hatred now more than love. I have surely brought it down on my own head, I have sinned against my beloved, who has loved me above all others.

'Whence did I get this wish, this longing, this desire, or the urge or power that I won her familiarity or ever married her, despite the love and faith which I owe my darling Ysolt? I intend to deceive her even more, inasmuch as I desire a closer intimacy with this girl. For by my words I seek a motive, a fetch, a colour, and a reason for breaking my faith with Ysolt – because I wish to sleep with the girl. In defiance of love I seek an excuse to take my pleasure with her. But I must not cheat as long as Ysolt, my beloved, lives, for the sake of my enjoyment. I act as a traitor and villain when I go in quest of love, despite her. I have already gone so far in it that I shall have cause to regret it all my life. And for the wrong that I have done, I intend that my dear one shall have justice, and I shall suffer penance for it according to my deserts. I shall now lie in this bed, but then abstain from my pleasure. I do not believe I can suffer torture that can give me pain more often, nor from which greater anguish could come to me, whether there be love or anger between us; for if I desire my pleasure of the girl it will hurt me much to refrain; whereas, if I do not lust for my pleasure, I shall find it hard to abide her bed. Whether I hate or love her, I shall have great pain to endure. But, since I am betraying Ysolt, I take such penance upon me, that, when she learns of my plight, she is bound to forgive me accordingly.'

Tristran lies down and Ysolt takes him in her arms. She kisses his mouth and his face. She strains him to her and sighs from her heart, and wants what he does not wish for. To give up his pleasure and to have it are both contrary to his will. Nature wants to take its course; but Reason stays true to Ysolt. The yearning which he has for the Queen takes away his lust for the girl. True desire dispels his lust, for nature is powerless in the matter. Love and reason constrain him and vanquish the lust of his body. The great affection which he has for Ysolt quells the urge of nature and conquers the loveless lust in his mind. His will to do the deed is strong; but love compels him to retreat. He feels that the maiden is charming, he knows that she is lovely, he longs for his pleasure and he hates his yearning for Ysolt; for did he not so yearn for the Queen he could now assent to his lust. But it is to his great yearning that he assents. He is in pain and torment, in great perplexity and anguish; he does not know how he may refrain, nor how to behave towards his wife, behind what pretext he ought to hide himself. Nevertheless, he is somewhat ashamed, and flees what he desires; he avoids his pleasures and flees from them, so as to have no more of his delight.

'Darling,' says Tristran, 'do not think badly of it, but there is something I wish to confess to you. I beg you earnestly to keep this hidden, so that none beside us may know it. I never spoke of it except now, and to you. Here on my right side I have a bodily infirmity that has long been with me. Tonight it has been giving me much pain. Because of my great exertions it has spread through my whole body. It keeps me in such agony and comes so near to my liver that I dare not exert myself, or give myself further to pleasure for fear of ill effects. I have never since made any effort without swooning three times over, and lying ill of it long afterwards. Do not let it vex you if I leave this for now – we shall have our fill another time, when you and I both wish it.'

'I am more sorry for your ailment than for any other ill in the world,' replied Ysolt. 'But I will and can well forgo the other thing I hear you speak of.'

31

CARIADO

QUEEN Ysolt sighs in her chamber for Tristran, whom she so much desires. She can think of nothing else in her heart save loving Tristran. She has no other wish or love, nor any other hope – all her desire is with him; yet she can learn no news of him. She does not know where or in what land he is, nor whether he is dead or alive, and her sorrow is the greater for it. She has heard no true report for a long while.

Ysolt has no idea that Tristran is in Brittany, but imagines that he is still in Spain, where he slew the giant, nephew to mighty Orgillos who came from Africa to seek out kings and princes from land to land. Orgillos was bold and valiant and did battle with all; he wounded and killed many men and took the beards from their chins. Orgillos made a cloak of beards, large, ample, and very long. He had heard about King Arthur, who had such renown throughout the world and such hardihood and valour that he had never been conquered in battle – that Arthur had fought with many men and overcome them all. When the giant heard this he sent to Arthur as to his friend to say that he had a new fur cloak, made of the beards of kings, barons, and princes of other realms whom he had conquered in battle and killed by violence in combat, but that it lacked a border and tassels; and that he had made of these beards such a garment as can be made from kings' beards – except that it needed a border. And since Arthur was the most exalted king, both in lands and honour, he requested him for his sake to have his beard cut off and sent to him for his glory; for he would do Arthur such high honour as to set his beard above the others. Just as Arthur was a high king and exalted above the others, so he would glorify his beard, if he would cut it off for him. He would set it uppermost on his cloak, and make a border and tassels of it. And if Arthur refused to send it, he would deal with him as was his custom; he would wager the cloak against the beard and fight with him, and the one who proved victorious should then without fail have both.

When Arthur heard this, he was grieved and angry in his heart. He informed the giant in reply that he would sooner fight than yield his beard out of fear, like a coward. And when the giant learned that the king had answered in these terms, he came to the very frontiers of his land to seek him out most forcibly in order to do battle with him. The two then came together and wagered the beard and the cloak, and then, in great anger, assailed each other. Hard was the battle, great the strife which they maintained all day. But on the morrow Arthur vanquished him, and took away his cloak and his head. In this way he conquered him with prowess and with valour.

It does not belong to this story, yet it is good that I should tell it you, for it was this giant's nephew who wanted the beard of the King and Emperor whom Tristran was serving while in Spain, before he repaired to Brittany. This giant came to ask for the beard; but the Emperor would not give it him, nor could he find any kinsman or friend in the country who was willing to defend his beard or do battle with the giant. The King was very downcast and complained in the hearing of his people. Tristran then undertook it for his sake and gave the giant a hard combat and a battle fraught with anguish that was full of pain for both of them. Tristran was badly wounded in it, and injured and hurt in his body. This saddened his friends; but the giant was slain there.

Since this wound, Ysolt had heard nothing of how Tristran had fared. For it is envy's way to speak evil and say nothing that is good; for envy conceals good deeds, but spreads news of evil works. For this reason does a wise man say to his son in ancient writings: 'It is better to be without company than to have an envious companion, and to lack a companion night and day, than have one in whom love is absent!' Such a one, hating his friend as he does, will conceal the good that he knows and tell the bad. If his companion does a good thing, he will not mention it; but he will hide the bad from no one. Thus it is better to want for a companion than to have one from whom comes nothing but evil. Tristran has fellows enough by whom he is hated and held in little affection. There are such around King Mark who neither love him nor keep faith with him. They conceal from Ysolt the good that they hear and broadcast the evil everywhere. They are vexed by the good which they hear because of the Queen, who desires it; and since they are full of envy they tell what she most hates.

One day she sat in her chamber and made a sad lay of love – how my lord Guirun became enamoured and was slain for love of the lady whom he cherished above all, and how thereupon, one day, in treachery the Count gave his wife Guirun's heart to eat, and what grief the lady felt when she learned of the death of her friend.*

The Queen sings sweetly and suits her voice to her instrument. Her hands are fair, her lay is good, her voice sweet, and her tone low. Then Cariado arrives on the scene, a mighty count of great inheritance, with fine castles and rich lands. He has come to court to sue for the Queen's love. Ysolt considers this great folly. He has wooed her many times before since Tristran left the country, and now he has come to stay at court. But never has he succeeded in achieving anything or doing in the Queen's eyes as much as would earn him a glove, either by gift or promise – he has accomplished nothing at all. Cariado has stayed at court for a long time and lingered there for this love of his.

Cariado was a very fine knight, courteous, proud, and haughty; but when it came to bearing arms he was not deserving of praise. He was handsome, and a good talker, gallant towards the ladies, and full of quips. And now he finds Ysolt singing a lay, and says with a smile: 'I am well aware that when one hears the wood-owl, madam, it is time to talk about a dead man, for its song forebodes death. And your singing, as I recall, means death of the owl! Someone has just lost his life.'

'You speak truly,' replied Ysolt. 'I quite agree that it does portend its death. A man who sings what dismays another is screech-owl and wood-owl enough! You may well fear your death, fearing my singing as you do, since you are owl enough because of the news that you bring. I believe you never brought news that gladdened anyone, nor did you ever come here without recounting bad news. With you, it is the same as once with an idle fellow who never rose from his hearth but to vex some man or other. You will never leave

* Guirun is no doubt the same person as Gurun in Episode 5, p. 89.

your lodgings unless you have heard some news that you can retail. But you will not stir abroad to do a thing that is worth recounting. No news will ever be heard of you from which your friends would reap honour, or those who hate you, sorrow. You love to tell the deeds of others: your own will never be remembered!'

'You are angry,' answered Cariado, 'but why, I do not know. He is a fool who is put out by anything you say. If I am a screech-owl and you are a wood-owl, ignoring the question of my dying, I bring you bad news on the subject of your lover Tristran. My lady Ysolt, you have lost him! He has taken a wife in another land. From now on you can get another lover, since he disdains your love and has taken a wife with great honour, the daughter of the Duke of Brittany.'

'You have always been a screech-owl to speak ill of lord Tristran,' was Ysolt's subtle answer. 'God grant I never prosper if I be not your owl of ill omen! You have told me bad news, and today I shall tell you no good. – I tell you truthfully that you love me in vain, you will never stand well with me. I shall never in my life like you or your love-making. I should have made a bad bargain had I accepted your love. I would much rather have lost Tristran's than gained your love. You have told me news from which I swear you will not benefit.'

Ysolt is now very angry, and Cariado is well aware of it. He has no wish to distress her by anything he says, or to berate or anger her. He quickly leaves the room, and Ysolt gives vent to great sorrow. She is distressed in her heart, and angered by this news. ...*

When Cariado had gone, Ysolt reproached her absent lover bitterly for his faithless pursuit of happiness elsewhere. But Tristran was very unhappy, although he hid his sorrow under a mask of gaiety and nonchalance.

* The connecting passages in italics between the fragments of Thomas are summarized from Joseph Bédier's reconstruction of Thomas's poem. See Appendix 1, p. 359.

32

THE HALL OF STATUES

One day Tristran overcame a giant in a forest just beyond the boundary of the Duke's domain and accepted the monster's homage. The following day Tristran commanded him and his minions, who were skilled carpenters and goldsmiths, to make a hall in a cavern and to fashion lifelike statues of Queen Ysolt and Brengvein. When these were finished, the image of Ysolt held in its right hand a sceptre with a bird perched on it that beat its wings like a live bird; in its left the image held a ring on which were inscribed the words which Ysolt had uttered at the parting. Beneath Ysolt's feet lay the image of the Dwarf who had denounced her to Mark in the orchard, while beside her reclined Peticru, modelled in pure gold; and as the dog shook its head, its tiny bell jingled softly. The statue of Brengvein held a vial, around which ran the legend: 'Queen Ysolt, take this drink that was made for King Mark in Ireland'.

Having achieved these things, Tristran returned to his castle, had his repast, and lay beside his spouse, for whom he had no desire, though people imagined that he lived with her as man and wife, a state of affairs which she suffered in silence. Nevertheless, when Tristran was away in the Hall of Statues, she wondered at his absence.

Whenever Tristran visits the image of Ysolt he kisses it and clasps it in his arms, as if it were alive....

... by means of the image Tristran recalls the delights of their great loves, their troubles and their griefs, their pains and their torments. When he is in a gay mood, he kisses it a great deal; but he vents his rage when he is angry, whether because of thoughts or dreams, whether because he believes lies in his heart to the effect that she is forgetting him or has some other lover; or that she cannot help loving another whom she has more to her pleasure. This thought bewilders him, and bewilderment drives out his courage. He begins to be afraid that the Queen may be transferring her affection to handsome Cariado. For Cariado is about her night and day, and serves and flatters her and often upbraids her because of him. He fears that, not having her desire, she will take what she can, that, unable to have Tristran, she will take another lover.

When Tristran imagines such maddening things he vents his hatred on the statue; he does not wish to look on her, nor to see or speak to her. Addressing Brengvein he says: 'My pretty one, I complain to you of my mistress Ysolt's change of heart and of the way she is betraying me!' He tells the statue whatever he thinks. Then he withdraws a little and looks at Ysolt's hand. She is about to give him the ring of gold. He sees the expression on her face as she looks on her lover at their parting, and recalls the covenant that he made at their farewell. At this he weeps, and implores her mercy for having imagined such folly, and knows that he has been deceived by the mad anger he has felt. He made this image so that he might tell it what is in his heart – his right thinking and mad aberration, his pain, his joy of love; for he did not know to whom to reveal his longing or desire.

Tristran behaves thus in his love – often he goes away, and often he returns. Often he shows her a fair face, often a foul, as I said before. It is Love that makes him do this and sends his heart astray. Did he not love Ysolt above all others, he would fear no rival. He is a prey to suspicion because he loves none but her. Were he in love with another, he would not be jealous because of this love; but he is jealous because he fears to lose her. But for the power of love, he would never fear to lose her. For a man does not care whether a thing that means nothing to him fares well or ill. How should he ever fear for a thing that was never in his thoughts at all?

Strange was the love among these four! They all had pain and grief of it, each lived in sorrow, and none had joy of it.

First, Mark dreads that Ysolt is unfaithful to him and that she loves another. He suffers this torment whether he will or no. And well may it torment him and give him anguish in his heart, for he neither loves nor desires anything save Ysolt, who draws away from him. He can have his pleasure of her body, but this gives him little satisfaction, since another possesses her heart. This maddens and enrages him. Never-ending is his grief that her love is inclined towards Tristran.

Next, after the King, Ysolt feels that she has what she does not wish to have. On the other hand, she cannot have what she longs for. The King has but one torment; but the Queen's thoughts are filled by double his pain. She longs for Tristran and finds herself powerless, and she has to keep with her lord. She can neither leave nor forsake him, nor can she seek her delight; for though she has the body she does not want the heart. That is one torment that she suffers. Another is that she desires Tristran, but her lord Mark forbids it her, so that they cannot talk together, and she can love none but him. She is convinced that there is no one under heaven whom Tristran desires so much. Tristran desires her, and she him, but she is unable to have him – there's the torment.

Lord Tristran has double pain and double grief because of his love. He is married to the other Ysolt, whom he cannot and will not love. He cannot rightly abandon her. Whatever his wishes, he is bound to hold to her, for she does not mean to release him. When he takes her in his arms he has little joy of it, except only because of the name which she bears – this at least comforts him a little. He is saddened by what he has, and is sadder still for what he lacks – his mistress, the lovely Queen, in whom are his death and his life. And thus the pain is doubled that Tristran suffers for Ysolt.

Because of this love at least, his wife Ysolt of the White Hands is full of sorrow. However it may be with the other Ysolt, this one suffers without carnal pleasure: she has no delight of her lord, nor does she love another. She desires this man, she has this man, and yet she has no pleasure of him. She is quite the opposite to Mark, since Mark can have his pleasure of Ysolt though he cannot change her heart ...* whereas she does not know where to seek delight, save in loving Tristran without pleasure. She longs to have enjoyment of him and has nothing from him but vexation. She would like further trial of his kisses and embraces, but he cannot allow it her, and she does not care to ask it.

I do not know what to say here as to which of the four was in greater torment, nor how to tell the truth about it, because I have not experienced it. I will put the case before you – let lovers pass their judgement as to who was best placed in love, or who, lacking it, had most sorrow.

* There is a line missing here in the original.

Lord Mark possesses Ysolt's body, he takes his pleasure whenever he likes; but it vexes his heart that she loves Tristran more than him, since he loves nothing but her.

Ysolt in her turn is at the King's disposal: with her body he does what he pleases. She often gives way to sorrow because of this vexation, for she has no love for the King. She has to suffer him because he is her lord, while on the other hand she wants nothing but her lover Tristran, who has taken a wife in a foreign land. She fears that he has run after a new love, and hopes nevertheless that he has desire for no one but her.

Tristran desires only Ysolt and he is well aware that her lord Mark has his whole will of her body, and yet, but for lust and longing, fails to have any pleasure. Tristran has a wife with whom he cannot lie, and whom he is unable to love in that way; but he does nothing that goes against his heart.

Tristran's wife Ysolt of the white fingers cannot covet anything in the world but Tristran, her handsome lord, whose body she has without love; she lacks what she most desires.

Now he who knows can say which was best placed in respect of love, or which had the greatest sorrow of it.

33

THE BOLD WATER

LOVELY Ysolt of the White Hands lies with her lord, a virgin. They sleep in one bed together. I know neither their joy nor their anguish. Never does he do to her as to a wife anything that can give her any pleasure. I cannot say what she knows of pleasure, or whether she loves or hates such a life. But I can aver that, had it irked her, she would never have hidden this from her friends as she has done.

Thus it chanced in this land that lord Tristran and lord Caerdin had to go with their neighbours to take part in some amusements at a festival. Tristran took Ysolt with him. Now Caerdin rides on her right, leading her on his left by her rein, and they go their way talking of entertainments. They are so intent on what they are saying that they let their horses roam freely. Caerdin's strays across, and Ysolt's rears up against it. She strikes her palfrey with her spurs. As it rears with flying hooves and she makes to strike a second time, she has to open her thighs. She presses back with her right leg to steady herself. Her palfrey dashes forward and, as its feet meet the ground, it slips into a hollow full of water. Its hoof is newly shod and it sinks right into the mud. As it squelches down into the hole, the water in the hollow leaps up, splashing against her thighs as she parts them in order to strike with her spur. Ysolt gets a shock from the cold water, she lets out a cry, but says nothing. But she laughs so deep down in her heart that, had it been a time of mourning, she could scarce have checked herself.

Caerdin sees Ysolt laughing in this fashion. He thinks she may have heard him say something that strikes her as absurd, or low or depraved; for he was a bashful knight, good, well bred, and gallant. He thus fears that he has committed some folly when he sees his sister laughing so. His shame makes him afraid. He therefore proceeds to question her.

'Ysolt, you were laughing deep down, but I have no idea why you did so. Unless I know the true reason I shall never trust you again. You may well deceive me now; but if I discover it later, rely on it, I shall never keep faith or affection with you as my sister!'

Ysolt hears what he says, she knows that if she refuses he will take it very ill. 'I was laughing at a thought of mine,' she answers, 'about something unusual that happened, and I laughed as I recalled it. The water which splashed up here came higher along my thighs than did ever the hand of a man or than Tristran ever sought me. Brother, now I have told you what ...'

Caerdin was shocked to learn of this slight to his family's honour. His manner towards Tristran changed, and Tristran was quick to perceive it and ask for an explanation. Caerdin reproached him with the affront that he had put on them all and demanded an explanation in return. Tristran then confessed that he loved a lady whose beauty and fine qualities were of quite another order than those of Ysolt of the White Hands, so that his passion for her left no room for any other attachment. Moreover, even her lady-in-waiting, whom she altogether outshone, outshone Caerdin's sister by as much. Caerdin requested proof of Tristran's claim and threatened that Tristran would pay dearly for it if he failed to provide it. Skilfully using Brengvein's beauty as a lure, Tristran then swore Caerdin into his confidence.

34

TRISTRAN'S RETURN

One day Tristran took Caerdin to the giant's cavern and into the Hall of Statues. Pointing out the image of Brengvein to Caerdin, who was overcome with fear and wonder, he himself went forward and embraced Ysolt's image. 'My love,' he whispered to it, 'the passion you inspire in me torments me night and day, and I have no other wish or desire than what you wish and desire.' Thinking the images were alive, Caerdin asked Tristran for Brengvein as partner, and Tristran gave her to him at once. Only when Caerdin tried to take the vial did he see his error. Piqued at this deception, Caerdin demanded to be shown the living originals and that he be given the girl in person. Tristran promised that he should have Brengvein, and he and Caerdin renewed their vows of friendship. They then returned to the castle.

Some days later the two friends equipped themselves as if for a pilgrimage, but they also took their arms, and left with only two kinsmen as attendants. ...

... and they go straight to England to see Ysolt and look for Brengvein; for Caerdin wishes to see her, and Tristran to see Ysolt.

What is the good of drawing out a tale or telling what does not belong to it? I shall tell the gist and the outcome.

Tristran and Caerdin together have ridden and travelled so far that they have arrived at a city where Mark is due to sleep that night. When Tristran hears that Mark is expected there, knowing the road, he goes towards him with Caerdin. They ride on and on, watching for the King's retinue; and when this has passed, they meet that of the Queen. They then dismount away from the road, and there their squires await them. They climb into an oak-tree beside the metalled road. They can look down on the retinue, but those in the retinue cannot see them. There come serving-lads and footmen, hunting-dogs and lyam-hounds, messengers, kennelmen, scullions, beaters, grooms, harbingers; sumpters, too, and hunters, chargers and palfreys, led by the right hand; and here there are birds of the chase, carried on the left. It is a great company on that road. Caerdin is greatly astonished at the size of the retinue, at the many wonders there, and that he does not see the Queen, or Brengvein, the fair maiden. But here are the laundresses and the outside chambermaids who see to things outside the Palace, such as making and lifting beds, sewing clothes, washing heads, and attending to other affairs.

At this, Caerdin said: 'Now I can see her!' 'No, on my word you cannot!' answered Tristran. 'So far, those are only the outside chambermaids who do the rough work.' Thereupon the chamberlain comes along, and after him comes the thick throng of knights and young gentlemen, well-bred, brave, and handsome. They sing beautiful tunes and pastourelles. After them come ladies, the daughters of princes and barons, and born in various countries. They sing delightful airs and songs. With them come their gallants, the well-bred and courageous. They are all talking of love-making, of true-loving, and of ...* Then says Caerdin: 'Now I see her! The one in front is the Queen! And which is the young girl, Brengvein? ...'

Caerdin was mistaken again; but when he had at last recognized Queen Ysolt he was amazed, and he admitted that she was the loveliest woman alive and that Brengvein was more beautiful than his sister. For some reason the cavalcade had halted there. Tristran gave Caerdin Ysolt's ring and told him to climb down, engage the Queen in conversation, and make sure that she saw the token. This Caerdin did, on pretence of having lost his way. He brought the ring to Ysolt's notice by fondling Peticru under her eyes. Ysolt divined at once that Caerdin was a messenger and that Tristran might be near. Fearing to arouse suspicion by further delay, Ysolt signed to the cavalcade to move on, but not before telling Caerdin indirectly that she would spend the night at the next castle. Tristran now knew that his message had been understood. He and Caerdin then rejoined their attendants.

The King, too, was to pass the night at that same castle, but, feigning an indisposition, Ysolt obtained permission to sleep in separate quarters near the forest, where Brengvein and a maid accompanied her. When all were asleep, Tristran and Caerdin went to the castle in disguise after leaving their horses with their pages. They found Ysolt's sleeping-quarters and, after showing their token, were admitted by Brengvein. Tristran and Ysolt ex-

* Several lines are torn in the manuscript.

changed tender signs of love after their long separation, while Caerdin paid ardent court to Brengvein, who did not discourage his advances. Wine and food were served, and then it was time for bed. Caerdin lay with Brengvein in his arms, but she took a magic pillow of silk and placed it under his head, at which he promptly fell asleep. When he awoke next morning Caerdin had no idea where he was. Seeing Brengvein already up, he guessed that he had been tricked. Ysolt began to mock him, and he was inwardly furious with Brengvein. After a merry day the comedy was repeated. But on the third evening, not wishing her new friend to be fooled any longer, Ysolt praised Caerdin to Brengvein so highly as a match in marriage that she overcame her scruples. Caerdin swore eternal gratitude to Tristran if only he would give him the girl. Brengvein then accepted Caerdin as her lover. Their enemies, however, got wind of this affair, but Tristran and Caerdin escaped unseen, though they failed to find their mounts.

35

BRENGVEIN'S REVENGE

Cariado and his friends were on the watch for the lovers and found their horses before them. Seeing them coming, Tristran's and Caerdin's pages fled. Cariado mistook them for their masters and challenged them to stop, else their mistresses would be disgraced; but the pages continued their flight. Cariado and his companions then returned to upbraid Ysolt and Brengvein, especially the latter, since he accused her openly of having slept with the most craven knight in the world who had fled like a hare before the hounds and refused to stand when challenged.

Hearing all these insults, Brengvein ...

... is grieved and very angry. She goes away from there in indignation, and comes to where she finds Ysolt, who sorrows in her heart for Tristran.

'Madam,' says Brengvein, 'I am as good as dead. It was a bad day for me when I met you – both you and your lover Tristran! For your sake I renounced my native land, and then, thanks to your wild desires, my lady, I lost my maidenhead. I did so, assuredly, because I loved you; and you promised me great honour, you and that perjurer Tristran – may God give him bad luck today and confound him all his life. It was through him that I was first put to shame. Remember where you sent me: you gave me over to be killed, it was not thanks to your generosity that I was not murdered by the serfs. Their hatred stood me in better stead, Ysolt, than your affection. How wretched and wrong I was to trust you after that or ever to have trusted you, since I learned from your own lips that you had plotted my death. Why did I not seek your death, seeing that you sought mine without cause? This wrong was wholly pardoned, but now it has been revived by the deception which you have practised on me regarding Caerdin. A curse upon your nobility, if that is how you reward my services. Was *that* the great honour you have given me for my love? Caerdin needed company to carry on his debauches! Ysolt, you made him do so to lead me into folly. You have had me dishonoured, madam, to indulge your malice. You have put me to shame, to the ruin of our affection. God, how I heard you praise him to make me fall in love with him! "There never was a man of his nobility, of his distinction, of his warlike spirit!" What a knight you made him appear! You rated him the best in the world, and he is now the most craven that ever bore shield or sword. May he be shamed and destroyed for having fled from Cariado! Since he took to flight before so worthless a man, there is no greater coward from here to Rome. Now tell me, Queen Ysolt, since when have you been a Richolt?* Where did you learn her trade of thus praising a worthless man and so betraying a luckless girl? Why have you had me shamed by the most cowardly man in this country? So many valiant men have come to woo me, and I have kept myself safe from them all. But now I have been given to a craven. This was at your enticement. I shall have my revenge on you, and on your lover Tristran! Ysolt, my friendship for you two is at an end! I shall seek your harm and mischief for the vile way in which I have been shamed!'

When Ysolt hears this outburst and ending of their friendship from the one she most trusts in the world and who best ought to guard her honour – such is Brengvein's joy and pleasure in saying such horrible things to her – she is deeply hurt in her heart that the girl is so very angry with her. Anger besets Ysolt's heart, a double anguish holds her heart in its grip: she does not know from whom to defend herself or whom to attack.

'Alas, poor me!' she says with a sigh. 'How pitiful that I live so long! For I have had nothing but ill in this foreign land. Tristran, a curse on you! It is through you that I am in such straits. It was you who brought me to this country, where I have been in torment all the time. It is through you that I am in conflict with my lord and with everyone in this land, either privately or publicly! But who cares? I have endured it well and could yet endure it, if only I had Brengvein's affection. Since she wants to thwart me and hates me so much, I do not know what to do. She used to sustain my happiness. Tristran, she now wants to disgrace me because of you. It was a bad day for me when I came to know your love, such anger and

* A type of female go-between.

animosity have I reaped from it. You have robbed me of all my kinsmen and of the esteem of all these strangers. And this all seems little to you unless you rob me in the end of all the comfort that I had, that of noble Brengvein. There was never a lady so loyal and worthy. But you and Caerdin between you have taken her away by cunning. You mean to take her home to wait upon Ysolt of the White Hands. Knowing her to be loyal, you wish to have her about Ysolt. You behave like a perjurer towards me when you rob me of the one who fosters me. Brengvein, remember my father, and what my mother asked you. If you desert me here, in a strange land, without a friend, whatever shall I do? How shall I live? For no one will give me comfort. Brengvein, if you intend to abandon me, you do not have to hate me to do so, nor seek an excuse against me for going to another land, since I am willing to give you good leave if it is to Caerdin you wish to go. I am convinced Tristran is making you do this, God confound him!'

Brengvein listens to what Ysolt says and cannot refrain from re-plying. 'You have a wicked heart to say such frantic things to me,' she says, 'things that have not entered my mind! There is no need to blame Tristran – it is you who must bear the shame of it, seeing that you do it as you can. If you did not wish me evil you would not have behaved like this so long. You are trying to make Tristran answerable for the wickedness that is so dear to you, although, if there were no Tristran, a worse man than he would have your love. I do not complain of his love, but I am very unhappy that you have made me your dupe so that you can gratify your malice. Dishonour take me, if ever I allow it! Be on your guard from now on, for I mean to have my revenge on you. Since you wish to have me mar-ried, why did you not give me to a gallant knight? Instead, by your trickery, you have given me to the greatest coward ever born.'

'Have pity, my friend,' answered Ysolt, 'I have never done you any wrong. This matter was never contrived through any wicked-ness or malice. Have no fear of any betrayal. I did it with good intent, so help me God! Caerdin is a good knight, a rich duke, and a trusty warrior. Do not imagine that he fled for fear of Cariado; people only say that out of envy, for he never ran away from him. If you hear people lying about him you must not hate him for that, nor Tristran, my lover, nor me. Brengvein, I assure you on my word

of honour, whatever comes of your affair, the whole court would
like us to be on bad terms – our enemies would rejoice in it. If you
hate me, who will wish me any honour henceforward? How
can I be honoured if I am abased by you? One cannot be
worse betrayed than by one's intimates and dependants. When a
familiar knows one's thoughts he can betray them if he hates one.
You who know all about me, Brengvein, you can disgrace me if
you like. But it would be a great reproach to you (since you are in
the position of a counsellor towards me) if in anger you revealed my
secret thoughts to the King. Moreover, I did it for your sake. There
must be no bad blood between us. Our dispute is of no account. I
did it not to humiliate you but for your great good and honour.
Forgive and forget your animosity. What good will it do you when
I am humiliated with the King? Most certainly my degradation will
not improve your position. Rather, if I am disgraced through you,
you will be loved and prized the less. There may be some who will
commend you only to bring blame upon you. By all well-bred
people you will be the more despised for it, and you will have for-
feited my affection and the favour of my lord. Whatever his attitude
towards me, do not imagine that he will not hate you for it. His love
for me is so great that none could put hatred there. None could em-
broil us so far that my lord could live apart from me. – He may dis-
like the things I have done, but he cannot hate me in any way. He
may hate all my follies, but he can never forgo his love for me. He
can detest my deeds in his heart, but, whether he wants to or not,
he must love me. Never has any good come from the King to any-
one who was ill-disposed towards me. Know that he bears ill will
towards those who tell him what he most dislikes. How do you serve
the King, if you speak ill of me to him? In what will you have
avenged him, when you have disparaged me? Why do you wish to
betray me? What do you mean to divulge to him? That Tristran
came to talk to me? And what harm has the King of that? What
good will you have done him when you have incited him against
me? I do not know what he can have lost by that.'

'Tristran's love and conversation were forbidden you – you con-
firmed it by oath, a year past,' answered Brengvein. 'You have
honoured the prohibition and your oath very badly. As soon as you
had it in your power, my poor Ysolt, you became a perjurer, you

broke your word and your oath. You are so inured to wickedness that you are unable to renounce it – you have to keep to your old ways. Had you not practised them since childhood you would not go on behaving so. If you did not delight in sinning, you would not have held to it so long. What a colt learns on being broken in abides with him a long time, whether he wish it or no: and what a woman learns in her youth, if she is not reproved for it, stays with her all her life, if she has the power to follow her inclinations. You learnt it when you were young, and your mind will always be set on it. Had you not learnt it in your youth, you would not have practised it so long. If the King had chastened you, you would not have indulged in this wickedness. But since he allows you to do it, you have followed it all this time. And he has allowed it you because he was never quite certain. But now I shall tell him the truth; then let him do as he pleases. You have pursued love so far that you have lost sight of your honour, and have so indulged in folly that you will never give it up in your life. As soon as the King grew aware of it, he ought by rights to have punished you. He has endured it for so long that he stands shamed before all his people. He ought to cut off your nose, or deal with you in some other fashion so that you should be held to scorn for ever. It then would be a great joy to your enemies. You ought to be thoroughly disgraced, for you are disgracing your lineage, your friends, and your lord. If you loved honour at all you would abandon your wickedness. I am well aware what you are relying on: on the easy-going nature of the King, who allows you to do as you please regarding him. Because he is incapable of hating you, you will not desist from dishonouring him – and he loves you so much that he suffers his dishonour. If he were not so enamoured of you, he would act differently and admonish you. I will not refrain from telling you, Ysolt, you do great wickedness and bring great shame on yourself, since the King loves you so very much and you treat him as a man whom you do not love at all. If you had any affection for him, you would not work his dishonour.'

When Ysolt heard herself so abused she angrily answered Brengvein: 'You judge me too harshly. A curse on your opinion! When you make me out to be so unfaithful you speak like an ill-bred woman. Surely if I am an oath-breaker, a perjurer or shamed to any extent, or if I have done amiss, you have given me good counsel. Without your consent there would have been no folly between Tristran and me. But, since you did consent to it, you taught me what I must do. The great deceptions and griefs, the fears and the sorrows, and the love that we maintained – whatever we did, it was all done through you. First you deceived me, next Tristran, and then the King; for the King would have known it long ago but for your duplicity. By the lies you told the King you sustained us in our mad passion. By wiles and deceptions you covered up our doings. You are more to blame than I, since it is your duty to guard me – and yet you bring disgrace on me. You now intend to expose me for the wrong which I did in your charge. But Hell's fire and flame consume me, should it come to telling the truth, if I hide a jot for my part! And if the King takes vengeance, may he take it first on you! You have deserved it at his hands. Nevertheless, I beseech you not to divulge the secret, but pardon me your anger!'

'I swear I shall not!' rejoined Brengvein. 'I shall go straight to the King and reveal it! We shall hear who is right or wrong! Then let things be as they may.' Bent on a spiteful deed, Brengvein leaves Ysolt forthwith, swearing she will tell the King.

In this anger and fury Brengvein goes to speak her pleasure to the King. 'Sire,' she says, 'listen. Believe what I am about to say is true.' She speaks to the King in secret, she has thought of a wonderful ruse. 'Hear me a little,' she says. 'I owe you fealty and allegiance, loyalty and firm affection, both as regards your person and your honour. Knowing as I do of your dishonour, it seems to me that I may not conceal it. And, had I known it earlier, I should certainly have reported it. I wish to tell you this much of Ysolt: she is growing worse than she was, her morals have declined. And if she is not watched better she will do some folly with her body. Till now she has not done so, but she is only awaiting her chance. Your suspicions in the past were fruitless; but I have suffered much distress and fear and dread, for she will not hold back for anything if only she can attain her desire. And so I am here to advise you to have her better watched. Have you ever heard this saying "Empty room makes wanton woman"? or "Opportunity makes a thief"? or "Wanton woman, empty house"? You have been long in error. I myself was in doubt and was on the watch for her night and day.

But I watched in vain, for we have been deceived regarding both error and doubt – she has tricked us all and changed the dice without throwing them. Let us trick her when she throws the dice, when she arrives at what she has in mind, so that she cannot have her way as long as she has this wish. For, if she should be restrained a little, I am convinced she will renounce it. Indeed, Mark, it is only right, dishonour is bound to overtake you if you consent to all her wishes and suffer her lover about her. I am well aware that I am acting foolishly ever to tell you a word of it, for you will bear me much ill will as a result. Now you know the truth of the matter, whatever face you put on it. I am well aware why you are dissembling: because you have not the courage to let her see what you know. King, I have told you enough, together with what you know already.'

The King listens to what Brengvein says and is much amazed that she should be able to speak of his doubt and dishonour and that he has permitted it, and that she knows he has, and that he is dissembling, whatever face he puts on it. Then he is in great perplexity and asks her to tell the truth; for he imagines that Tristran is in the royal chamber, as he used to be. He promises her faithfully that he will not divulge the matter.

Then Brengvein says very cunningly: 'Sire, in telling all that I am bound to tell I will not conceal the love-affair or the intrigue that she has devised. We have been deceived by the error into which we had fallen, namely, that she was in love with Tristran. She has a more powerful admirer, the Count Cariado! He is around her for your dishonour. He has wooed her so persistently that I think she means to surrender to him. He has flattered and served her so much that she wants to make him her lover. But of this I do assure you: he has advanced no further with her than he has with me. I do not say that if he had the opportunity he could not do all his pleasure; for he is handsome and full of wiles, he is with her morning and evening, waits on her, flatters her, and urges his suit. It would be no wonder if she commits a folly with so wealthy a gallant. I very much wonder, your majesty, why you allow him near her so much, and for what reason you favour him so highly. You are afraid only of Tristran, with whom, as I have well discerned, she is not at all in love. He, too, was deceived. When he came to England to seek your pardon and favour, as soon as Ysolt heard of it she had him ambushed with intent to murder him. She sent Cariado, who drove him out by force of arms. Admittedly we do not know how much Cariado achieved. This ambush was set for Tristran by Ysolt. Surely she would not have contrived such a disgrace for him, if she had ever loved him? If Tristran is dead, it is a great sin, for he is brave and well-bred. And then, my lord King, he is your nephew. You will not have another such friend for many a month.'

When the King hears this news his heart quakes within him, for he has no idea what to do about it. He is unwilling to prolong this conversation, since he sees no profit in it. 'Dear friend,' he says to Brengvein confidentially, 'this is your concern henceforward. I shall not interfere in any way, except that I shall remove Cariado as best I can, and you will be responsible for Ysolt. Do not let her take counsel with knight or baron, unless you are present at their meeting. I entrust her to your care. Let that be your responsibility from now on.'

Now Ysolt is in Brengvein's power and subject to her discretion. She neither says nor does anything in private unless Brengvein is present at the conversation. Tristran and Caerdin sadly and sorrowfully go their way. Ysolt remains in great sadness, and Brengvein, too, who passionately laments her lot. Mark, for his part, has great grief at heart; he is troubled at the thought of his error. Cariado, who suffers for the love of Ysolt, is in great anguish, and he fails to achieve anything in her direction that would induce her to grant him her love. Nor is he minded to make an accusation to the King. Tristran begins to think that it is base of him to flee, since he is in ignorance of how matters stand with the Queen, or of what noble Brengvein is doing. He commends Caerdin to God's keeping and returns the whole way, swearing he will never be happy till he has learnt how matters stand with them.

36

RECONCILIATION

✣

TRISTRAN was greatly overcome by love. He now rigs himself out in wretched clothes; in wretched clothes and vile dress, lest any man or woman should know or see that he is Tristran. He completely deceives them with a herb, by which he puffs up his face and makes it swell as if he were a leper. To conceal himself securely, he contorts his hands and feet, and altogether assumes the guise of a leper. He then takes a mazer-cup which the Queen had given him the first year that he loved her, puts a box-wood ball in it, and so makes himself a clapper. He goes to the royal court and approaches the doors, longing to see and know how things stand there. He begs persistently and keeps on sounding his clapper, but fails to hear news that could make him any happier.

One day the King was keeping a festival and went to the minster to hear the great service there. He has come out of the Palace and the Queen follows after. Tristran sees her and begs a gift of her, but Ysolt does not recognize him. He follows her, clacking, and loudly calls to her, appealing to her piteously by the love of God for alms in a most heart-rending way. The serjeants make great fun of him when they see the Queen advancing in this fashion. Some push him forward, others push him back, and they thrust him out of the pro-cession. One man threatens him, another strikes him. He follows after, begging someone in God's name to give him some alms, and not turning back for any threat. They all think him a great nuisance, they do not know in what dire need he is. He follows them right into the chapel, calling out aloud and clacking his bowl.

Ysolt is much annoyed at this, she looks at him as if she were angry. She wonders what can be the matter with this fellow who comes thus close to her – and then she sees the bowl which she re-cognizes. She perceives well enough that it is Tristran, from his noble body, form, and figure. Ysolt is deeply alarmed, the colour has mounted to her face, for she greatly fears the King. She draws a ring of gold from her finger, but she does not know how she can give it him. She is about to throw it into his bowl, but as she holds it in her hand Brengvein has noticed it. Brengvein looks at Tristran and knows him – she realizes his cunning and tells him he is a fool and a wretch to have at nobles in this way, and calls the serving-men knaves for allowing him among the healthy. To Ysolt she says she is a hypocrite. – 'Since when have you been so saintly as to have given thus generously to a leper or the poor? You want to give him your ring, but I promise you, madam, you shall not! Do not give so lavishly that you will regret it afterwards. If you were to give it him now, you would be sorry before the day is out.' She tells the serjeants whom she sees there that he is to be put out of the church; so they put him out at the portal and he dares not beg any more.

Now Tristran sees and is convinced that Brengvein hates him and Ysolt. He does not know what on earth he should do. He suffers great anguish at heart. Brengvein has had him thrown out very shamefully. He weeps most piteously, complains of his plight and his youth, in that he has ever given his thoughts to love; for he has endured such griefs for it, such pains and such fears, such anxieties, perils, hardships, and exile, that he cannot hold back his tears.

There was an old palace in the courtyard, tumble-down and dilapidated. Tristran hides below the stair and bewails his hardship and suffering, and his life so hard to bear. He is much enfeebled by fatigue and by so much fasting and waking. Tristran languishes below the stair, overcome by toil and travail. He longs for his death, he hates his life; he will never rise again unaided. Ysolt is deep in sad thoughts, she calls herself wretched and unhappy to see what she most loves go away in such a plight. Yet she does not know what to do. She often weeps and sighs and curses the day and hour that she lingers so long in this world.

They hear the service in the minster and then go to the Palace for their repast, and spend the whole day in gaiety and merriment. But Ysolt derives no pleasure from it.

Now it chanced that before nightfall the porter was very cold in his lodge where he was sitting. He told his wife to go and fetch firewood. The woman did not wish to go far. Below the stair she could find dry wood for burning, and old timber, and thither she goes without delay. Entering in the dark, she comes upon Tristran as he sleeps. She finds his shaggy wayfarer's cloak, lets out a cry, and almost goes out of her mind, taking him for a devil; for she did not know what it might be. There is great dread in her heart, and she comes and tells her husband. He now goes to the ruined hall, lights a candle, gropes and discovers Tristran lying there, who indeed is nearly dead. The man wonders what it can be, comes nearer with the candle, and then sees from its appearance that it is a human form. He finds him colder than ice, asks who he is and what he is doing there, and how he has come under the stair. Tristran soon told him all about himself, and his reason for coming to that house. Tristran put great trust in the porter, and the porter held him in affection. And whatever the toil and pain it costs, he takes him right inside his lodge. He makes him a soft bed to lie on and fetches him food and drink. He takes a message from him to Ysolt and Brengvein, as is his wont. But for nothing that he can say can Tristran mollify Brengvein. Ysolt calls Brengvein to her. 'My noble young lady,' she says, 'I beseech you, have mercy on Tristran! Go and speak to him, I beg you! Console him in his grief. He is dying of sorrow and anguish. You used to have such affection for him. Fair woman, do go and console him. He wants nothing but you. At least tell him the reason why, and since when, you have hated him.'

'You speak to no purpose,' answered Brengvein. 'He will never be consoled by me. I wish him death far more than life or health. Never again shall anyone reproach me with having helped you to commit a folly. I shall not cover up your crime. There was an ugly rumour about us that you had done all this through my help, and I used to cover up your deeds by means of subtle ruses. But this is just what happens to one who serves a traitor: sooner or later one loses one's labour. I have served you to the best of my power and must suffer ill will in return. If you had had any regard for generosity, you would have rendered me other service and have given me other reward for my pains than to dishonour me with such a lord!'

'Enough!' said Ysolt. 'You must not reproach me with what I told you in anger. I am indeed very sorry that I did so. I beg you to forgive me, and that you will go along to Tristran, for he will never be glad till he has had speech of you.'

So much does she wheedle her, so much implore her, so much promise her, so much beseech her mercy, that Brengvein goes to speak with Tristran and console him in the lodge where he is lying. She finds him ill and very weak, pale of face, feeble of body, gaunt of flesh, sallow of hue. Brengvein sees how he laments and how tenderly he sighs as he piteously implores her to tell him by God's love why she hates him, and to tell him truly. Tristran has soon assured her that what she was imputing to Caerdin was untrue, and that he would have Caerdin come to court to give Cariado the lie.

Brengvein believes him on his pledge; and thus they are reconciled and go up then to the Queen into a marble chamber. They are reconciled in great affection and then solace each other's grief. Tristran has his pleasure with Ysolt.

When a great part of the night has passed Tristran takes his leave as day is breaking and then departs for his country. He finds his ship awaiting him, crosses the sea with the first wind, and returns to Ysolt of Brittany, who is sad because of this business. Love is rooted deeply within her, there is great grief in her heart, much sorrow and unhappiness. The whole time he was away was a torment to her, seeing that he loves the other Ysolt so much. This is the reason why she suffers now.

37

TRISTRAN RETURNS AGAIN

TRISTRAN departs; but Ysolt remains behind, sorrowing for his love, because he is leaving in such unhappiness. She has no certain knowledge of how he fares. Because of the great ills which he has suffered and made known to her in private, because of the sorrow that he has endured for love of her, because of the anguish and the grief, she wishes to share in the penance. Having seen Tristran languishing, she wishes to share in his sorrow. Just as she has shared love with Tristran who has languished for her, so she desires to share the sorrow and the hardship. For his sake she busies herself with many things that ill accord with her beauty, and leads her life in great sadness. And she, truly in love with sad thoughts and heavy sighs, stills many yearnings (a more loyal lady was never seen); she dons a leather corselet over her bare flesh and wears it there night and day, except when she lies with her lord. Her familiars were none the wiser. She makes a vow and an oath that she will never remove it unless she learns how Tristran is faring. She suffers a very harsh penance for her love by many of the deeds she does; and many are the pains and toils which Ysolt endures for Tristran – discomfort, wretchedness, and sorrow.

And next Ysolt took a fiddler and by him informed Tristran of her whole manner of life, and then she begged him to tell her all that was in his heart by tokens through this same messenger.

When Tristran hears the news about the Queen whom he most loves, he grows melancholy and unhappy. He cannot be gay at heart till he has seen the corselet which Ysolt has donned and which will never leave her back until he comes to her country. He therefore speaks with Caerdin, so that at length they set out and make straight for England to win fortune and adventure. They have disguised themselves as penitents; their faces are stained, their clothes disguised, so that none may know their secret. They arrive at the court of the King, have private parley, and do much of their desire.

A great many people attend a court which the King is holding. After their repast they go to amuse themselves and begin various games of fencing and wrestling. Tristran proved master in all. Then they did a Welsh Leap and one they called the Waveleis; and then they made jousts and threw with reeds, javelins, and lances. Tristran was accounted best of all, and, after him, Caerdin beat the others by his skill. Tristran was recognized there; he was noticed by one of his friends. This man gave Tristran and Caerdin a pair of fine horses – there were none better in the land – for he was very much afraid that they might be captured before the day was out. They put themselves in great jeopardy, for they slew two barons on that field, one of whom was Handsome Cariado. Caerdin killed him in a joust for having said that he had fled, the last time he went away. Thus he fulfilled the pledge that was given when the lovers were reconciled with Brengvein. After this, Tristran and Caerdin took to flight to save their skins. The two companions went spurring for the sea with the Cornishmen in pursuit. But the latter lost them, nevertheless. The two of them, Tristran and Caerdin, found the path in the forest. They went through roundabout ways in the wasteland, and so saved themselves from their pursuers. And now they go straight to Brittany and are delighted with their vengeance.

38

THE POISONED SPEAR

My lords, this tale is told in many ways, so I shall keep to one version in my rhymes, saying as much as is needed and passing over the remainder. But the matter diverges at this point and I do not wish to keep too much to one account. Those who narrate and tell the tale of Tristran tell it differently – I have heard various people do so. I know well enough what each says and what they have put into writing; but to judge by what I have heard, they do not follow Breri, who knew all the deeds and stories of all the kings and all the counts that had lived in Britain. Moreover, many of us are unwilling to assent to what narrators say about the dwarf, whose wife Caerdin is supposed to have loved. The dwarf in turn is said by great guile to have dealt Tristran a poisoned wound, after maiming Caerdin; and because of this wound Tristran sent Guvernal to England to fetch Ysolt. Thomas declines to accept this and is ready to prove that it could not have been the case. Guvernal was a familiar figure in all that region, and it was known throughout the kingdom that he was a partner in their intrigue and messenger to Ysolt. The King hated him for it mightily and set his men on the watch for him. Thus how could Guvernal come to offer the King, the barons, and the serjeants his service at court, as if he were a foreign merchant, without being quickly recognized, so well known was he? I do not know how he could have avoided detection or fetched Ysolt away. Such narrators have strayed from the story and departed from the truth, and if they are unwilling to admit it, I have no mind to wrangle with them – let them hold to theirs and I to mine. The tale will bear me out.

Tristran and Caerdin returned to Brittany in good spirits and amused themselves happily with their friends and followers. They went often to the forest to hunt and to tournaments in neighbouring regions. They won praise and renown beyond all in that country for chivalry and honour, and when they were not on their travels they went to the woods to see the lovely statues. They delighted in these images on account of the ladies whom they loved so. During the day they pleasured their eyes for the torment which they suffered by night.

One day they were out hunting until it was time to return. Their companions had gone on ahead of them. There was none there but these two. They were traversing La Blanche Lande, keeping the sea to their right. They observe a knight approaching at the gallop on a piebald steed. He is armed very splendidly: he bears a shield of gold fretted with vair, and has the lance, pennant, and cognizance of the same tincture. He comes galloping down a path, covered and protected by his shield. He is tall and big and very robust; he is armed, and a fine knight. Tristran and Caerdin wait to meet him on the path together, very curious to know who he is. When he sees them he comes on towards them and then bows to them very courteously. Tristran returns his greeting and then asks him where he is going, what his business is, and why he is in such haste.

'Sir,' replied the knight, 'would you tell me the way to the castle of Tristran the Amorous?'

'What do you want with him?' asked Tristran. 'Who are you? What is your name? We will gladly take you to his house; but if you wish to speak with Tristran you need not go any farther, for Tristran is my name. Now tell me what you want.'

'This is pleasant news for me,' answered the other. 'I am called "Dwarf Tristran". I am of the Marches of Brittany and live hard by the Sea of Spain.* I had a castle there and a fair mistress, whom I love as much as life; but I have lost her through great misadventure. The night before last she was stolen from me. Estult l'Orgillus of Castel Fer has had her carried off by force. He holds her in his castle and does with her just as he pleases. I suffer such grief in my heart from it that I am almost dead of sorrow, misery, and anguish. I do not know what in the world I can do. I cannot find solace without her, for I have lost my happiness, my joy, and my delight, and I value my life now but little. Lord Tristran, I have heard say that whoever is bereft of what he most desires cares little for what remains. I have never been so unhappy, and this is why I

* The Bay of Biscay.

have come to you. You are feared and held in great dread and are altogether the best knight, the noblest, the most just and, of all who ever lived, he that has loved most! So I beg you to have pity, sir, I call upon your magnanimity and implore you to accompany me on this task and win me back my mistress. I will do homage and allegiance to you, if you will help me to accomplish this thing!'

'Indeed I will help you all I can, my friend,' answered Tristran. 'But now let us go home. We shall start out towards daybreak and execute our business.'

When he hears Tristran putting off the day, the other says in anger: 'On my faith, friend, you are not the man who possesses such renown! I know that if you were Tristran you would feel the sorrow I suffer; for Tristran has loved so deeply that he well knows the ill by which lovers are afflicted. If Tristran heard of my sorrow he would aid me in this love-affair. He would not subject such unhappiness and pain to delay. Whoever you are, fair friend, in my opinion you have never loved. If you knew what affection is, you would have pity on my grief. He that never knew love could not know sorrow either; and you, friend, who love no one, are unable to feel my sorrow. Were you able to feel my grief, you would be ready to accompany me. God be with you. I shall go in search of Tristran till I find him. I shall have no comfort unless through him. Never have I been so disconsolate. Ah, God, why cannot I die, having lost what I most desire? I would much sooner I were dead, for I shall never find any consolation, pleasure, or joy in my heart, since by such ravishment I have lost the one in the world whom I most love!'

Thus does Dwarf Tristran lament. He desires to take his leave and go. But the other Tristran takes pity on him and says: 'Noble sir, have done. You have shown very rightly that I must go with you since I am Tristran the Amorous, and I shall willingly go there. Allow me to send for my arms.'

He sends for his arms and equips himself, and then rides away with Dwarf Tristran. They go to lie in wait for Estult l'Orgillus of Castel Fer, to kill him. They have travelled until they have found his strong castle. They dismount at the skirts of a wood and there await events.

Estult l'Orgillus was very haughty, and he had six brothers who

were knights, bold, valiant, and excellent warriors; but in valour
he surpassed them all. Two of these were returning from a tourna-
ment, and the two Tristrans lay in wait for them by the wood. They
quickly shouted their challenge to them and then struck at them
fiercely. The two brothers were killed there. The cry was raised
through the countryside, and the lord heard the alarm. Those in the
castle mounted and attacked the two Tristrans with impetuous on-
slaught. The latter were excellent knights, and skilled at bearing
arms. They defended themselves against all as bold and valiant
knights. They did not cease from fighting till they had slain the four.
Tristran the Dwarf was struck down dead, the other Tristran was
wounded through the loins by a lance bated with venom. Stung to
anger, he took ample vengeance, for he killed the man who wounded
him. And now all seven brothers are slain, one Tristran is dead and
the other in evil case, in that he is severely wounded in his body.

Tristran has turned back with great difficulty because of the
anguish that grips him. By great effort he reaches home and has his
wounds dressed. He sends for doctors to aid him and many are sent
to him. But none can cure him of the poison, for they do not re-
cognize it, and so they are all misled. They cannot make any plaster
that will cast or draw it out. They bruise and pound roots enough,
they cull herbs and make medicines, but fail to do him any good.
Tristran only grows worse. The venom spreads all over his body
and makes it swell up, both inside and out. He grows black and
discoloured, he loses strength, his bones now show through the skin.
He now knows that he will lose his life unless he is succoured at
once, and he sees that none can cure him and therefore he must die.
No one knows any medicine for this malady: and yet, if Queen
Ysolt knew that he had this great ill and were at his side, she would
heal him completely. But he is unable to go to her or to suffer the
hardship of the sea. Moreover, he fears that country, since he has
many enemies there. And Ysolt cannot come to him either, so he
does not know how he may be healed. He suffers great sorrow at
heart; for his slow torment, his malady, and the stench of his wound
distress him. He laments his lot and is deeply afflicted, for the poison
cruelly torments him.

39

CAERDIN'S MISSION

TRISTRAN sends for Caerdin privately in the wish to reveal his sorrow to him; he had a loyal affection for Caerdin, and Caerdin loved him in return. He had the chamber in which he lay cleared of people, he would let none but themselves remain in the house while they took counsel together. But Ysolt of the White Hands wonders in her heart what it can be that he wishes to do, whether he means to forsake the world and turn monk or canon. She is greatly perturbed by this. She goes and stands beside the wall outside his chamber, opposite his bed, for she wants to listen to what they say. She gets a friend to stand guard for her for as long as she stays by the wall. With great effort Tristran has managed to lean on his elbow against the wall. Caerdin sits beside him and the two of them are weeping and lamenting piteously that their good fellowship, their love, and their friendship will be severed after so brief a space. In their hearts they have pity and sorrow, anguish, affliction, and pain. Each is sad for the other. They weep and make much lamentation, since now their affection, which has been so loyal and true, must be parted.

Tristran addresses Caerdin. 'Listen, fair friend,' he says, 'I am in a foreign country. Fair companion, I have no friend or relation but you. I have had no pleasure or happiness here apart from the comfort you have given me. I am convinced that, if I were in my own country, I could get help to cure me. But because I have no aid here I am dying, my fair, sweet friend. Without aid I must die; for apart from Queen Ysolt no human being can cure me. She can cure me if she wishes: she has the power and the remedy, and she has the wish, if only she knew of my wound. But, dear friend, I do not know what to do – by what stratagem she may know of it. For I am sure that she could help me with this illness and heal my wound with her skill, if she but knew of it. – But how can she come here? If I knew anyone who would go and take my message to her, she would give me some good help as soon as she learned of my great need. I trust her so well that I am quite sure that she would let nothing prevent her from helping me in my distress, so firm is the love she bears me. I certainly cannot help myself. For this reason, my friend, I appeal to you: out of friendship and generosity, undertake this service for me! Bear me this message for the sake of our companionship and by the pledge you gave with your hand when Ysolt bestowed Brengvein on you, and I will give you my own pledge here that, if you will undertake this journey for me, I will become your liege man and love you above all else!'

Caerdin sees Tristran weeping, he hears him lament and despair and it makes him very sad, so that he replies with tender affection. 'Dear companion,' he says, 'do not weep, and I will do all you wish. Believe me, my friend, to make you well I shall go very close to death and into mortal danger to win your comfort. By the loyalty which I owe you, it will not be my fault or for want of anything that I can do or for any distress or hardship if I fail to exert all my strength to carry out your wish. Tell me the message that you wish me to take to her, and I will go and make ready.'

'Thank you,' answered Tristran. 'Now listen to what I shall tell you. Take this ring with you – it is our secret token. And when you come to that country, go to court, pretend to be a merchant, and carry fine cloths of silk with you. Be sure that she sees this ring; for as soon as she has set eyes on it and recognized you, she will seek a subtle pretext for talking with you when she can. Greet her and wish her health from me, for without her there is none in me. I send her so many wishes for her well-being that none remains with me. My heart salutes her in hopes of healing, since, without her, health will not return to me. I sent her all my health.* I shall never have succour in my life, or health or healing, unless she bring them. If she does not bring me health or succour me with her own lips, then my health will remain with her and I shall die of my great pain. In fine, tell her I am dead, unless I have comfort of her! Make my distress plain to her, and the malady of which I am languishing, and tell her to come and succour me. Tell her to remember the pleasures

* In this passage there is a play on the two meanings of *saluz* = both 'health' and 'greetings'.

and delights that we had, day and night, in times now past, and the great sorrows, the sadness, the joys, and the sweetness of our love, so true and perfect, when she cured me of my wound long ago,* and the philtre we drank together on the sea, when it caused us to fall in love. Our death was hidden in that potion, and never shall we recover from it! It was given us in an evil hour, we drank our death with it. She must call to mind the sufferings I endured in loving her, as a result of which I have lost all my kinsmen, my uncle, the King, and his people, have been shamefully dismissed and exiled to other lands, and suffered such pain and hardship that I am scarcely alive and am of little worth.

'But none could ever sever our love and our desire. Never could pain, grief, and anguish divide it. For whenever they strove most to sunder it, they succeeded least. They put a distance between our bodies, but they could not take away our love! Let her recall the agreement she made with me at the parting in the garden, when I went away from her, and she gave me possession of this ring. She told me that whatever land I went to, I must never love anyone but her. Never since have I loved another. I cannot love your sister, nor shall I ever be able to love her, or any other, so long as I shall love the Queen. I love Queen Ysolt so much that your sister remains a maiden. Bid the Queen by her loyalty to come to me in this my need. Now let it be seen whether she ever loved me! Whatever she has done for me in the past will profit me little now, if she is unwilling to help me in my need or stand by me in the face of such sorrow. What store shall I set by her love if she fails me now in my distress? I do not know what good her affection is, if she abandons me now in my great need. All her succour has been of little avail, if she does not aid me against death. I cannot say what her love was worth if she will not help me to recover.

'Caerdin, I do not know what I should ask you more urgently than what I now request: act as best you can and greet Brengvein warmly for me. Describe my malady to her, saying that unless God attend to it I shall die. I cannot live for long in the pain and distress which I feel. Do your best, my friend, to accomplish this and to re-

---

* Thomas here reverts to the older version of the story according to which the younger Ysolt heals Tristran, not the elder, as he himself has narrated it. See Episode 10.

turn to me with speed, for unless you return with the utmost dispatch, rest assured you will never see me! Let it be done within forty days, and if you do as I have said, so that Ysolt comes with you, take care nobody except ourselves comes to know of it. Hide it from your sister so that she may have no suspicion of our love. You will pass the Queen off as a physician-woman who has come to heal my wound. Take my fine ship and carry two yards on board, one with a white sail, the other with a black. If you can prevail upon Ysolt to come and heal my wound, use a white sail when returning. But if you do not bring Ysolt, then use the black! I have nothing more to tell you, dear friend. May our Lord God guide you and bring you back safe and sound!'

And now Tristran sighs, and weeps, and laments, and Caerdin weeps likewise. He kisses Tristran and takes his leave. He goes away to prepare for his voyage. At the first wind he puts to sea. They haul up the anchors, they hoist the yard, and sail on their course before a gentle breeze; they cleave the waves and the billows and the great seas and the deep. Caerdin takes with him handsome youths, he carries silken wares worked in rare colours, and rich plate from Tours, wine of Poitou, and birds of the chase from Spain, so as to cover up his errand and afford him some means of coming to Ysolt – her for whom Tristran utters such sad complaints. He cleaves the sea with his ship and steers with all sail for England. He has been running for twenty days and nights before he makes the island, before he succeeds in reaching where he can hear anything of Ysolt.

Woman's anger is much to be feared, every man must be well on his guard against it. For where a woman has loved most, there she will soonest avenge herself. Just as their love comes lightly, so, lightly, comes their hatred, and their hatred, when it comes, lasts longer than their friendship. They know how to moderate their love, but not at all how to temper their hatred as long as they are angry. But I dare not voice my opinion, since it is no concern of mine.

Ysolt is standing beside the wall. She listens to what Tristran says and she hears it – she has well understood each word. She becomes aware of their love. It makes her very angry in her heart, that she has loved Tristran so much while his mind was set on another. But now it has been clearly revealed to her why she loses her joy of him. She well remembers what she has heard, but pretends that she knows nothing. But when at last she has the opportunity she will take fearful vengeance on the one she loves above all.

As soon as the doors are opened Ysolt enters the room and, concealing her anger from him, tends him and shows him a fair face as a lady should to her lover. She speaks to him very sweetly, and often kisses and embraces him, showing him great affection, but plotting evil in her rage, by what means she may be avenged. She keeps on asking and inquiring when Caerdin is due to return with the doctor who is to heal Tristran. It is not out of a good heart that she expresses sorrow for him. The wicked act she means to do, if she can, resides within her heart; for anger drives her to it.

Caerdin sails over the sea, and he does not cease to sail till he comes to the other land where he is going to look for the Queen. And this is the mouth of the Thames. He sails up-river with his merchandise and within the mouth, outside the entry to the port, has anchored his ship in a haven. Then, in his boat, he goes straight up to London beneath the bridge, and there displays his wares, unfolds and spreads his silks.

London is a very noble city; there is none better in Christendom or any of higher worth, of greater renown, or better furnished with well-to-do people. For they much love honour and munificence and bear themselves very gaily. London is the mainstay of England – there is no need to seek beyond it. At the foot of its wall there flows the Thames, by which merchandise comes from every land where Christian merchants go. Its men are very clever.

Lord Caerdin has arrived there with his cloths and hunting-birds, of which he has fine and excellent ones. He takes a great goshawk on his fist, a cloth of rare colour, and a beautifully wrought goblet, chased and inlaid. He presents it to King Mark and tells him courteously that he has come to his country with his wealth in order to gain and acquire more – may the King afford him protection in his territory lest he be brought to court or suffer harm or disgrace from chamberlains or sheriffs. The King grants him firm protection in the hearing of all in the Palace. Caerdin goes and speaks to the Queen, asking leave to show her his wares. He brings her in his hand a brooch wrought of fine gold (I think there can be no better in the world) and presents it to the Queen. 'It is very good gold,' he says, and indeed Ysolt had never seen better. He takes Tristran's ring from his finger and sets it beside the other, saying: 'Just look, your majesty, this gold is of a deeper colour than the gold of this ring! Nevertheless, I think the ring a fine one!'

When she sees the ring she at once recognizes Caerdin. Her heart quakes and she changes colour, she sighs from deep sorrow and dreads to hear some news. Calling Caerdin aside, she asks if he will sell the ring and what he will accept for it, or whether he has other wares? All this she does with subtle intent, since she means to trick her guardians. Caerdin is alone with Ysolt.

'My lady,' he says, 'listen to what I shall say, and bear it well in mind. Tristran sends you his love, service, and greetings, as a lover to his beloved lady, in whose hand lie his life and his death. He is your liege man and friend, and he has sent me to you in his need. He tells you by me that he will never have succour from death unless it be from you, nor health nor life, madam, unless you bring it him. He has been wounded to death by a spear whose steel was dipped in venom. We cannot find physicians who know how to treat his malady – so many have tried their hands that his whole body is in a sad condition. He languishes and lives in pain, in torment and an evil stench. He asks me to make it known to you that he will not live unless he has your help, and therefore appeals to you by me and urges you by that faith and loyalty which you, Ysolt, owe to him, to let nothing in the world prevent you from coming to him at once; for he was never in greater need, and thus you must not fail! Now remember the great loves and pains and griefs that you two have suffered together. He is losing his life and youth. For you he has been exiled and driven from this kingdom several times. He has lost King Mark because of it – consider the ills he has endured. You must bear in mind the agreement that was made between you at the parting in the orchard, where you kissed him on giving him this ring. You promised him your love. – Have pity on him, madam! Unless you help him now, I swear you will never cure him! He can never get well without you, so come you must, else he cannot live.

He loyally gives you this message and sends this ring in token. Keep it, he bestows it on you!'

When Ysolt hears this message there is anguish in her heart, and pain, and sorrow, and grief – never yet has she known greater. Now she ponders deeply, and sighs and longs for Tristran, her lover. But she does not know how to come to him. She goes to speak with Brengvein. She tells her the whole story of the poisoned wound, the pain he is in and the misery, and how he lies there languishing, how and through whom he has sent for her – else his wound will never be healed. She has described all his torment and then asks advice what to do. And as they talk there begins a sighing, complaining, and weeping, and pain, sorrow, sadness, and grief, for the pity which they have on his account. Nevertheless they have discussed the matter and finally decide to set out on their journey and go away with Caerdin to treat Tristran's illness and succour him in his need.

They make ready towards evening and take what they will re-quire. As soon as the others are all asleep, they leave very stealthily under cover of night by a lucky postern in the wall overlooking the Thames. The water has come up to it with the rising tide. The boat is all ready and the Queen has gone aboard it. They row, they sail with the ebb – quickly they fly before the wind. They make a mighty effort and keep on rowing till they are alongside the big ship. They hoist the yard and then they sail. They run before the waves as long as they have wind behind them. They coast along the foreign land past the port of Wissant, and then Boulogne, and Treport. The wind is strong and favourable and the ship that bears them is fleet. They sail past Normandy. They sail happily and joyfully, since they have the wind they want.

40

THE DEATH OF TRISTRAN
AND YSOLT

TRISTRAN lies on his bed languishing of his wound. He can find no succour in anything. Medicine cannot avail him; nothing that he does affords him any aid. He longs for the coming of Ysolt, desiring nothing else. Without her he can have no ease – it is because of her that he lives so long. There, in his bed, he pines and he waits for her. He has high hopes that she will come and heal his malady, and believes that he will not live without her. Each day he sends to the shore to see if the ship is returning, with no other wish in his heart. And many is the time that he commands his bed to be made beside the sea and has himself carried out to it, to await and see the ship – what way she is making, and with what sail? He has no desire for anything, except for the coming of Ysolt: his whole mind, will, and desire are set on it. Whatever the world holds he rates of no account unless the Queen is coming to him. Then he has himself carried back again from the fear which he anticipates, for he dreads that she may not come, may not keep her faith with him, and he would much rather hear it from another than see the ship come without her. He longs to look out for the ship, but does not wish to know it, should she fail to come. There is anguish in his heart, and he is full of desire to see her. He often laments to his wife but does not tell her what he longs for, apart from Caerdin, who does not come. Seeing him delay so long Tristran greatly fears that Caerdin has failed in his mission.

Now listen to a pitiful disaster and a most sad mishap which must touch the hearts of all lovers! You never heard tell of greater sorrow arising from such love and such desire. Just there where Tristran is waiting and the lady is eager to arrive and has drawn close enough to see the land – gay they are on board and they sail lightheartedly – a wind springs up from the south and strikes them full in the middle of the yard, checking the whole ship in its course. The crew run to luff and turn the sail, they turn about whether they wish to or not. The wind gains in force and raises the swell, the deep begins to stir; the weather grows foul and the air thick, the waves rise, the sea grows black, it rains and sleets as the storm increases. Bowlines and shrouds snap. They lower the yard and drift along with the wind and waves. They had put out their boat on the sea, since they were close to their own country, but by ill luck they forgot it and a wave has smashed it to pieces. This at least they have now lost, and the tempest has grown so in violence that the best of sailors could never have kept his feet. All on board weep and lament and give vent to great grief, so afraid are they.

'Alas, poor me,' cried Ysolt. 'God does not wish me to live until I see my lover Tristran. – He wants me to be drowned in the sea! Tristran, if only I had spoken with you, I would not mind if I had then died. Dear love, when you hear that I am dead I know you will never again be consoled. You will be so afflicted by my death, following your long-drawn sufferings, that you will never be well again. My coming does not rest with me. God willing, I would come and take charge of your wound. For I have no other sorrow than that you are without aid; this is my sorrow and my grief. And I am very sad at heart, my friend, that you will have no support against death, when I die. My own death matters nothing to me – if God wills it, so be it. But when at last you learn of it, my love, I know that you will die of it. Such is our love, I can feel no grief unless you are in it. You cannot die without me, nor can I perish without you. If I am to be shipwrecked at sea, then you, too, must drown. But you cannot drown on dry land, so you have come to sea to seek me! I see your death before my eyes and know that I am soon to die. Dear friend, I fail in my desire, since I hoped to die in your arms and to be buried in one coffin with you. But now we have failed to achieve it. Yet it may still happen so: for if I am to drown here, and you, as I think, must also drown, a fish could swallow us, and so, my love, by good fortune we should share one sepulture, since it might be caught by someone who would recognize our bodies and do them the high honour befitting our love. But what I am saying cannot be. – Yet if God wills it, it must be! – But what would you be seeking on the sea? I do not know what you could be doing here. Nevertheless I am here, and here shall I die. I shall drown here, Tristran, without you. Yet it is a sweet comfort to me, my darling, that you will not know of my death. From henceforward it will never be known and I do not know who should tell it. You will live long after me and await my coming. If it please God you may be healed – that is what I most desire. I long for your recovery more than that I should come ashore. So truly do I love you, dear friend, that I must fear after my death, if you recover, lest you forget me during your lifetime or console yourself with another woman, Tristran, when I am dead. My love, I am indeed much afraid of Ysolt of the White Hands, at least. I do not know whether I ought to fear her; but, if you were to die before me, I would not long survive you. I do not know at all what to do, but you I do desire above all things. God grant we come together so that I may heal you, love, or that we two may die of one anguish!'

As long as the storm endures Ysolt gives vent to her sorrow and grief. The storm and foul weather last on the sea for five days and more; then the wind drops and it is fair. They have hoisted the white sail and are making good speed, when Caerdin espies the coast of Brittany. At this they are gay and light-hearted, they raise the sail right up so that it can be seen what sail it is, the white or the black. Caerdin wished to show its colour from afar, since it was the last day of the term that lord Tristran had assigned when they had set out for England.

While they are happily sailing, there is a spell of warm weather and the wind drops so that they can make no headway. The sea is very smooth and still, the ship moves neither one way nor the other save so far as the swell draws it. They are also without their boat. And now they are in great distress. They see the land close ahead of them, but have no wind with which to reach it. And so up and down they go drifting, now back, now forward. They cannot make any progress and are very badly impeded. Ysolt is much afflicted by it. She sees the land she has longed for and yet she cannot reach it: she all but dies of her longing. Those in the ship long for land, but the wind is too light for them. Time and again, Ysolt laments her fate. Those on the shore long for the ship, but they have not seen it yet. Thus Tristran is wretched and sorrowful, he often laments and sighs for Ysolt, whom he so much desires. The tears flow from his eyes, he writhes about, he all but dies of longing.

While Tristran endures such affliction, his wife Ysolt comes and stands before him. Meditating great guile she says: 'Caerdin is coming, my love! I have seen his ship on the sea. I saw it making hardly any headway but nevertheless I could see it well enough to know that it is his. God grant it brings news that will comfort you at heart!'

Tristran starts up at this news. 'Do you know for sure that it is his ship, my darling?' he asks. 'Tell me now, what sort of sail is it?'

'I know it for a fact!' answered Ysolt. 'Let me tell you, the sail is all black! They have hoisted it and raised it up high because they have no wind!'

At this Tristran feels such pain that he has never had greater nor ever will, and he turns his face to the wall and says: 'God save Ysolt and me! Since you will not come to me I must die for your love. I can hold on to life no longer. I die for you, Ysolt, dear love! You have no pity for my sufferings, but you will have sorrow of my death. It is a great solace to me that you will have pity for my death.'

Three times did he say 'Dearest Ysolt'. At the fourth he rendered up his spirit.

Thereupon throughout the house the knights and companions weep. Their cries are loud, their lament is great. Knights and serjeants rise to their feet and bear him from his bed, then lay him upon a cloth of samite and cover him with a striped pall.

And now the wind has risen on the sea. It strikes the middle of the sailyard and brings the ship to land. Ysolt has quickly disembarked, she hears the great laments in the street and the bells from the minsters and chapels. She asks people what news? and why they toll the bells so? and the reason for their weeping? Then an old man answers: 'My lady, as God help me, we have greater sorrow than people ever had before. Gallant, noble Tristran, who was a source of strength to the whole realm, is dead! He was generous to the needy, a great succour to the wretched. He has died just now in his bed of a wound that his body received. Never did so great a misfortune befall this realm!'

As soon as Ysolt heard this news she was struck dumb with

grief. So afflicted is she that she goes up the street to the Palace in advance of the others, without her cloak. The Bretons have never seen a woman of her beauty; in the city they wonder whence she comes and who she may be. Ysolt goes to where she sees his body lying, and, turning towards the east, she prays for him piteously. 'Tristran, my love, now that I see you dead, it is against reason for me to live longer. You died for my love, and I, love, die of grief, for I could not come in time to heal you and your wound. My love, my love, nothing shall ever console me for your death, neither joy nor pleasure nor any delight. May this storm be accursed that so delayed me on the sea, my sweetheart, so that I could not come! Had I arrived in time, I would have given you back your life and spoken gently to you of the love there was between us. I should have be-wailed our fate, our joy, our rapture, and the great sorrow and pain that have been in our loving. I should have reminded you of this and kissed you and embraced you. If I had failed to cure you, then we could have died together. But since I could not come in time and did not hear what had happened and have come and found you dead, I shall console myself by drinking of the same cup. You have forfeited your life on my account, and I shall do as a true lover: I will die for you in return!'

She takes him in her arms and then, lying at full length, she kisses his face and lips and clasps him tightly to her. Then straining body to body, mouth to mouth, she at once renders up her spirit and of sorrow for her lover dies thus at his side.

Tristran died of his longing, Ysolt because she could not come in time. Tristran died for his love; fair Ysolt because of tender pity.

Here Thomas ends his book. Now he takes leave of all lovers, the sad and the amorous, the jealous and the desirous, the gay and the distraught, and all who will hear these lines. If I have not pleased all with my tale, I have told it to the best of my power and have nar-rated the whole truth, as I promised at the beginning. Here I have recounted the story in rhyme, and have done this to hold up an example, and to make this story more beautiful, so that it may please lovers, and that, here and there, they may find some things to take to heart. May they derive great comfort from it, in the face of fickleness and injury, in the face of hardship and grief, in the face of all the wiles of Love.

APPENDIX I

A Note on Thomas's Tristran

As with Gottfried, so with Thomas: nothing is known of him but what emerges from his story and from a passing reference by a fellow poet. Thomas several times refers to himself by his Christian name without further designation. But Gottfried von Strassburg names him 'Thomas of Britain' in his Prologue.* Gottfried uses 'Britain' for both Great and Little Britain (Brittany), so that it is not possible to demonstrate convincingly that he thought of Thomas as an Anglo-Norman, an Englishman, or a Breton. Nor does Thomas's French entirely decide the issue. In the opinion of Romance scholars, Thomas wrote in the literary French of the Angevin courts, but with traces of Anglo-Norman. This does not necessarily tell us anything about Thomas's origins, or even about where he was reared: but it agrees with what may be inferred from his story about his service as a court poet, namely, that the circle for which he wrote had strong associations with England, with London, and with the Angevins.

Near the beginning of his poem Thomas praises the natural wealth and the cultured people of England;† near the end (where Caerdin comes to England to fetch Ysolt to Brittany) he gives an interesting eulogy of London and its citizens;‡ and in the passage in which King Mark arms Tristan for his first battle it appears highly probable that Thomas conferred upon the hero the Angevin arms of a golden Lion on a red field.§

It would be good if we could know for sure whether Thomas was attached to the court of that literate and pleasure-loving pair, King Henry II and Eleanor of Aquitaine, and so perhaps accompanied them on their unending travels in England and France; or whether he resided in England in the suite of some great lord who courted the royal favour. In tone, the references to England and London show something of the pride of discovery, suggesting that Thomas is speaking more as a Frenchman to Frenchmen, which would accord well with the status of court poet to Henry and Eleanor. There can be no doubt that Thomas's free handling of amatory matters would have made his poem congenial to Queen Eleanor, who is known to have presided over literary 'Courts of Love', and scarcely less so to the future lover of Fair Rosamond and other ladies. But there is more.

* p. 43. † cf. p. 47; *Saga*, I.
‡ p. 346. § See Appendix 3.

The most astonishing of the innovations which Thomas introduced into the story is King Mark's voluntary separation from Ysolt.* None could hear this without being reminded that Eleanor had proved too much for her first husband, King Louis VII of France, whom she despised both as a king and as a lover, and that their union had been annulled by a Church council in 1152; whereupon Henry had snapped her up in marriage within the space of two months. While Eleanor was still Louis' queen, gossip was as busy on the subject of her virtue as it was concerning Ysolt's, and, later, the jaundiced Giraldus Cambrensis does not hesitate to repeat the rumour that Henry had been her lover before she was divorced. The grounds for the divorce were the usual ones for people of high station, namely relatedness within the forbidden degrees; but it would not be difficult to show political motives for Louis' plea of consanguinity, rather than of adultery and lese-majesty. However this may be, Louis can have had little idea of what Eleanor was contemplating, for her swift marriage to Count Henry of Anjou, as Henry II then was, transformed the power politics of western Europe and led to the Hundred Years' War.

If we turn a courtly blind eye to the fact that Henry was junior to Eleanor by some eight or ten years and that his standards of personal cleanliness left much to be desired, Thomas's conferment of the Angevin arms upon Tristran might, for that robust and thick-skinned age, be regarded as a flattering act of homage to Henry and Eleanor. If this was indeed the case, it would certainly require a date for *Tristran* anterior to the estrangement of the royal pair, that is, before about 1170, while such an allusion might still be affably received. In 1152, when she married Henry, Eleanor's beauty was as yet unravaged by the years; but by about 1165, the date often canvassed by scholars for the completion of Thomas's *Tristran*, she was a woman of well past forty. Since there are some grounds for thinking that, to begin with, Eleanor's and Henry's marriage had rather more to it than the considerations of prestige and dynastic advantage which made it so uniquely desirable, the nearer we place the date of Thomas's beginning to 1152, the more significant the assumption of royal patronage becomes.† And if we ask ourselves which of the two, Eleanor or Henry, is the more likely to have been Thomas's personal patron, the answer is undoubtedly Eleanor. The story of Tristran is associated with Eleanor's family several times. But a factor which directly

---

* pp. 258 ff.

† After coming to this conclusion I was gratified to find that Professor Rita Lejeune had already come to the same conclusion in *Cultura Neolatina* (1954).

invites us to think of her as the poet's patron and adviser is the deliberate way in which Thomas, with an open appeal to the audience, twice formulates the problem as to which was the better or worse off in love – Tristran, Ysolt the Fair, Mark, or Ysolt Whitehands? (See p. 316.) Eleanor was to show her skill with fine points of amorous doctrine just such as these, in judgements recorded by Andrew, the facile chaplain of her daughter, Marie de Champagne. If the eulogy of London was delivered in that city, about which there can be no certainty, then the dates would lie between December 1154 and the summer of 1156, or between September 1157 and the autumn of 1158, when Eleanor resided in London. However, the date must not be placed earlier than 1155, the year in which Wace finished his *Brut*, since Thomas quotes this poem unmistakably. In any case, before 1160 is a better date than after, as other considerations may also suggest.

Two closely linked innovations by Thomas point to Angevin connexions in the early part of Henry's reign. In the archetype of *Tristran*, the hero's father Rivalin is King of Lohnois, better known to English readers as Lyoness, probably the Pictish kingdom of Lothian, in agreement with Tristran's Pictish name. Thomas, on the other hand, expressly rejects both Rivalin's locality and his rank, and instead makes him a great noble well below a King in status, but elevated enough to have a marshal, with a domain by the name of 'Armenie' or 'Ermenie'.* 'Armenie' borders on Brittany, yet it is quite distinct from Normandy, which Thomas names. Now there are only two domains that suit such a description, Anjou and Maine, the ancestral lands of the Angevins. And until Henry became Duke of Normandy and King of England, their lords had always been counts, not kings.

'Armenie' had a port on the sea, but Anjou and Maine had none, except that ships, if unmolested, could sail up river to Angers past the Breton port of Nantes. But in 1156 Henry II gained possession of Nantes.† At this time Brittany was an independent power, like the Brittany of Thomas's romance; for no supreme overlord takes up the death of Duke

* The *Saga* and the Middle English *Sir Tristrem* agree on (H)*Ermenie*; bus Gottfried has *Parmenie* with an 'A', and other texts have *Armenie*, *Armonie*. Gottfried's form suggests that he added a 'P' to avoid confusion with *Armenie*, i.e. *Armenia* in Asia Minor, well known from the crusades. If Thomas's name for Rivalin's and Tristran's country is fancifully constructed from relevant elements, then *Arm-* will come from *Armorica* ('Brittany') and *-menie* perhaps from *-mania* in *Ceno-mania*, i.e. the country of Maine.

† If one can believe the *Saga*, Tristran helped his friend to conquer Nantes for Brittany.

Morgan with Tristran his slayer, or comes to the aid of Whitehands' father, the Duke of Brittany.* But this state of affairs in Brittany ceased when Henry incorporated the duchy into his empire by the joint suasion of war and the marriage of its heiress, Constance, to his son Geoffrey in 1166. Furthermore, in Thomas's version Tristran appears as a near-Breton, and the Angevins had Breton blood in their veins and even laid claim by ancient right to be the Seneschals of Brittany. And just as there was a separate fief in dispute between Tristran and Duke Morgan of Brittany in the story, so, in life, the petty domain of Ancenis had been in dispute between Anjou and Brittany. This would all suit a date for *Tristran* of 1160 or before.

There can, of course, be no question here of equating Anjou and Maine with 'Armenie', or of identifying Henry and Eleanor with Tristran and Ysolt. Henry's and Eleanor's marriage was in the first place most assuredly dynastic. After marrying one king, Eleanor must marry another (though a young and lusty one, if possible). And the Angevins had for long cast hungry glances in the direction of Poitou and Aquitaine. It was enough to show that Thomas sought and found the means of paying the Angevins a passing compliment on his own or less probably on a patron's account which could not fail to be appreciated, and that his political picture of the Breton Marches, sketchy though it is, agrees perfectly with a date of or prior to 1160. Nevertheless those who consider that Thomas's *Tristran* was written after Chrétien's *Cligés* are tied to a date post 1169.

It was said above that Thomas had the merit of presenting a courtly version of the old story.† This was a hazardous undertaking, since, whatever its faults, the older version had an elemental force, whereas courtly ideals were at best fashionable and social. Love-making itself was stylized in a courtly sense, so that 'courtly love' became an elaborate convention. But when all is said, in giving us his courtly version, in which love might have come without a love-drink, Thomas has not finally abated the elemental force of the story, as his impressive ending will show.

The measure of Thomas's success and of his influence is given by these facts. An outstanding poet like Gottfried based his own version of the tale on that of Thomas and kept closely to his narrative despite subtle changes. The Norwegian Brother Robert based his prose *Tristramssaga* of 1226 entirely on Thomas's poem, though he judged that his northern audience would miss the finer points and accordingly suppressed them. An Italian writer used Thomas's version in his *Tavola Ritonda* of the thirteenth century. And an English versifier, who had the distinction of

* Episodes 8 and 29. † p. 9.

being edited by Sir Walter Scott, retold it in short strophes of such exacting form that he had to omit everything for which he could find no rhyme. This version is known as *Sir Tristrem*. No manuscript or fragment of the archetypal text remains to us, nor is there any trace or even echo of the *Tristan* of the great Arthurian romancer Chrétien de Troyes (*c.* A.D. 1135–*c.* 1190); so that it is not illegitimate to infer that Thomas's version outmoded them, at least at the leading courts, for which it had been written.

Important though Thomas's *Tristran* was, it, too, suffered a sad fate. Although ten longer and shorter fragments of five different manuscripts are known,* making an effective total of 3144 lines, this represents at most one-sixth of the complete work. However, by close comparison of the German, Norse, Italian, and English adaptations, it is possible to reconstruct the narrative of the missing five-sixths, and indeed the great French scholar Joseph Bédier has done so but for minor points on which scholars are as yet not agreed. † Since the narrative data of Thomas's model, the archetype, too, can be reconstructed from the versions of Eilhart, Béroul, and Thomas himself, and from later prose romances, it is possible to watch Thomas at his work of recasting the story, in some detail. But this is not the place to do so. An examination of some of his more striking innovations must suffice.

Mention has been made above of Mark's voluntary separation from Ysolt. Thomas needs this separation so that he can show us the lovers at peace in their delightful grotto in the wilds. The archetype, too, shows us Tristran and Ysolt in the wilds, wilds so harsh and forbidding that the lovers need to be fortified against them by the love-potion; but its author brings his lovers into this situation in a very different way. Whereas in Thomas's version Mark wavers continually in unresolved suspicion, which the stratagem of the flour around Ysolt's bed can do nothing to dispel, till at last he can no longer endure it and sends the lovers away, the poet of the archetype has Tristran leave a tell-tale mark in the flour which Mark accepts as proof, so that he arrests the lovers and arraigns them for high treason, a situation from which they are freed by Tristran's cunning and prowess. After Mark has seen the lovers lying in apparent innocence with Tristran's sword between them and the time has come for them to return to court, the archetype motivates their withdrawal crudely as due to the abatement of the potion at the end of three or four years: but

* They have been edited by J. Bédier, *Le Roman de Tristan par Thomas* (Société des Anciens Textes), vol. I (1902).

† In the same volume as the fragments, on the basis of the arguments elaborated in vol. II (1905).

with Thomas it is due to concern for their worldly honour and for their station in society, a motive whose force modern readers must by no means underestimate.

The difference between the archetype and Thomas's version in the events narrated is everywhere overshadowed by differences in psychological motivation. The transformation of Mark's character from that of an affectionate and then violent and tyrannical monarch into a sensual waverer who can never make up his mind about his wife's guilt or innocence, has already been touched upon. Thomas the psychologist is at work again when, in the extant fragments, he deepens Brengvein's character by recalling all the indignities she has suffered and by making her turn at last when she thinks she has been deceived in her lover Caerdin.* A similar dynamic of the emotions is revealed in Thomas's interpretation of Ysolt of the White Hands' vengeance on Tristran as due to absolute frustration in love.† His deepened conception of Brengvein is entirely his own; his motivation of Whitehands' malice, however, is implicit in the archetype.

These examples may serve to show how Thomas rearranges traditional material and breathes a new spirit into it, which he is always at pains to do in things both great and small. He even gives us his own reflexions justifying his choice of Caerdin as Tristran's last messenger to Ysolt instead of the Guvernal of the archetype, and his rejection of Caerdin as the man who accompanied Tristran when he was wounded by a poisoned spear.‡ But in some instances Thomas goes quite beyond what the archetype has to offer him, perhaps beyond tradition altogether, and introduces episodes of his own creation.

Such are the episodes of Gandin,§ of the winning of Peticru,‖ and of the Hall of Statues.¶ In the Gandin episode, an Irish baron arrives at Mark's court with a rote on his back, and by holding Mark to his rash but royal word, wins Ysolt with his music, only to be tricked of his reward by Tristran's harping; whereupon, after dallying with Ysolt among the flowers, Tristran returns her to her husband with a stern warning. Mark had declined to fight for his queen, and the episode is clearly based on the frequent rapes of Guinivere, in which Arthur plays a similar rôle, reminding one of the light-hearted attitude of ancient Celtic poets towards the virtue of high-born ladies. This episode shows no great inventive capacity on Thomas's part. It was clearly introduced to tone down the double offence of adultery with lese-majesty; for – so we must read it – if

* p. 324.   † p. 345.   ‡ p. 338.
§ p. 214.   ‖ p. 249.   ¶ p. 315.

Mark refused to fight for his woman and it was left to another to fetch her back, that other – Tristran – might fairly assume his title to her favours.

The Peticru episode is light and graceful. At great risk to himself Tristran gains possession of a dog with a bell whose tinkling banishes all care. Although Tristran is full of sad thoughts for Ysolt, he sends her the dog to assuage her sorrows; but she, no less true to him, removes the bell and remains disconsolate.

The episode of the Hall of Statues shows very slight inventive gifts. All that can be called 'action' in it is where Tristran entices Caerdin into falling in love with Brengvein by means of her statue, so that Caerdin is now disposed to overlook Tristran's neglect of his sister and to go with him to Cornwall.

There is a neat and sophisticated touch in all three episodes, but they lack the primitive force, the starkness and symbolic profundity of the central episodes of the archetype. They come from the more superficial levels of a mind that was dominated above all by reason – a favourite word of Thomas – *raisun*.

Thomas was a great writer rather than a poet. He was undoubtedly one of the fathers of the European novel. Admittedly he was a vivid narrator in the direct manner when he wished, as the end of his story shows, even in translation; and how freshly he describes brother Caerdin's passionate and overbearing treatment of poor Whitehands when trying to wrest the secret of her marriage from her.* But Thomas was interested above all in his characters' minds and in the motives for their actions. It is rather unfortunate that the reader should meet him so soon in the middle of a complicated analysis of Tristran's feelings on becoming involved with the second Ysolt; yet this passage gives us the quintessence of Thomas.† It shows him quite as deeply interested in the disintegration of love as in its first tender growth, if not more so. With what gusto he rings the changes between Tristan and Ysolt and Mark in their seemingly eternal triangle; and how he pounces on the latent possibilities from all angles when, by addition of the second Ysolt, he has made it a quadrilateral! In the course of his analyses he even exposes the mechanism of wishful thinking. For as Tristran stands in interminable soliloquy beside the nuptial bed, Thomas makes him say: 'Whence did I get this wish, this longing, this desire, or the urge or the power that I won her familiarity or ever married her, despite the love and faith which I owe my darling Ysolt? I intend to deceive her even more, inasmuch as I desire a closer intimacy with this girl. For by my words I seek a motive, a fetch, a colour, and a reason for

* pp. 319 f.   † pp. 301 f.

breaking my faith with Ysolt – because I wish to sleep with the girl. In defiance of love I seek an excuse to take my pleasure with her.'

Thomas pursues his analyses *à outrance*, in more senses than one. He is inferior to Gottfried and Chrétien in his appreciation of artistic economy. It is psychological and moral truth that are of supreme importance to him. This, and his protestations of ignorance concerning feminine psychology (about which he displays so much knowledge), have led some to think that he must have been a priest, like Andrew the Chaplain, who wrote a Latin treatise on love for Marie de Champagne. But one need not go so far. The point is met if one concedes that Thomas had enjoyed a very thorough education in clerical logic and literature. He was a learned man who had made the human heart and mind his subject. In this chosen field he did not carry his learning too lightly.

Despite his use of fairy-tale motifs when he needed them, Thomas was nothing if not a rationalist. He wished everything to be made plain. One example will serve for many. I would refer the reader to the passage in which Thomas, with absurdly realistic mechanics, demonstrates precisely how the bold water leapt up between Ysolt's thighs, an event he was unwilling to leave to the imagination as tradition had been content to do.*

As an early writer who showed great academic understanding of human motives before the novel had been born of romance, Thomas has been (and so will always be) of incalculable influence. We may smile, now, at some of his psychological *tours de force*, but not often is it possible to speak so highly of a writer who was surpassed by a successor in the art of poetry so convincingly. There can be no doubt of Gottfried's respect for Thomas, and we may wonder if we can judge Thomas fairly with only one-sixth of his text before us. Aptly enough, Thomas is at his very best immediately after the surprisingly euphuistic passage in which Ysolt imagines herself and Tristran to have been drowned and then enshrined in one and the same fish, that is, when Ysolt lands in Brittany, finds Tristran dead, and yields up her spirit. This last scene is very moving, hushed, and muted. By it, I think, the reader should finally judge of Thomas's abilities.

*

Since Bédier's edition of the fragments,† there has appeared B. H. Wind, *Les Fragments du Tristan de Thomas* (1950), in which the editor attempts, with some measure of success, to vindicate the manuscripts against Bédier's emendations. The manuscripts teem with obscurities, so that I

---

* p. 319.   † See footnotes * and †, pp. 359.

have felt justified in making an eclectic use of Bédier's and Wind's texts, as common sense demanded.

The fragments have been translated into English at least twice before. Miss Dorothy Sayers rendered them into verse in 1929 under the title *Tristan in Brittany*. In 1923 Professor R. S. Loomis published a translation into an archaic form of English as part of *The Romance of Tristram and Ysolt*, the complementary and longer part being based on the *Tristrams-saga*. This was revised in 1931 and again in 1951. I did not consult the verse translation, except very occasionally, as a matter of principle; but I had Professor Loomis's rendering constantly before me. Although our versions sometimes offer divergent interpretations, I am happy to acknowledge my debt to him. It is always consoling to have a second opinion available when confronted with a difficult text. I frankly stole an heraldic passage from Professor Loomis because the language of heraldry is as precise as it is archaic and it was not possible to better it.

APPENDIX 2

The Scene in the Orchard

THE following scene, narrated by Gottfried in the episode of the Parting (pp. 280-2), has also survived in a fragment of Thomas's text of fifty-two lines. Comparison of the two passages will afford striking illustration of how Gottfried deals with his original.

... the Queen in his arms. They fully imagined they were safe. But, by a strange chance, the King suddenly appeared, led there by the dwarf. He was thinking he would catch them in the deed, but, thank God, they were decently composed when these two found them sleeping. The King sees them and says to the dwarf: 'Wait here for me a little. I shall go up to the Palace and fetch some of my barons. They shall see how we have found them. When the fact is proved I shall have them burnt!'

Then Tristran awakes. He sees the King, but gives no sign, for the King is making for the Palace. Tristran sits up. 'Alas!' says he, 'Ysolt, my love, wake up, do! We are being treacherously spied upon! The King has seen what we have been at and he is going to the Palace for his men. He will have us seized together, if he can, and condemned to be burned to ashes! I am going away, fair love! Your life is not in danger, for you cannot be convicted ...*

'... flee pleasure and seek exile, abandon joy, follow danger! This parting so afflicts me that I shall never be happy again! Sweet lady, I pray you, do not forget me – love me when I am far away as much as you have done while I was near. I dare wait no longer, my lady. Now kiss me at our leave-taking!'

Ysolt is slow to give her kiss. She hears what he says, and sees that he is weeping. Her eyes fill with tears and she sighs from her heart. 'My dear, fair lord,' she says tenderly, 'you must ever remember this day when you went away in such grief. This separation gives me such pain that never before have I known what it was to suffer. I shall never be happy again, dear love, since I have lost your consolation; I shall never know such tender pity as now when I must part from your love. Our bodies now must part, but our love will never be sundered. Take this ring, nevertheless. Guard it well, my love, for my sake! ...'

---

* Several lines have been cut away here by a bookbinder's knife.

Tristran's Angevin Escutcheon

THE possible implications of Tristran's coat-of-arms were first noticed by Professor R. S. Loomis.* The facts are these. In the twenty-fourth chapter of the *Tristramssaga*, Mark gives Tristran a war-horse draped with red trappers into which golden lions had been woven. The Middle English poem, which also derives from Thomas's version of the *Tristran*, describes in Strophe XCV how Morold thrust his spear through Tristran's Lion, while Tristran thrust his through Morold's Dragon. In the tiles from Chertsey Abbey, which take their matter from Thomas's version, as Professor Loomis has shown, Tristran appears twice in combat with Morold with a Lion rampant on his shield; when Tristran is wounded by Morold, the Lion faces to the rear; but when Tristran returns the blow, the Lion looks bravely forward! In the *Tavola Ritonda*, whose Tristran episodes are based on Thomas's version, the Italian author emphatically denies that Tristran's escutcheon was a golden Lion in a field of azure. This might have been in order to free him for an heraldic compliment to a local patron, though A. Colin Cole, Esq., Portcullis Pursuivant of Arms, whom I consulted, and wish to thank here for his help, is unable to suggest a suitable Italian house for the arms actually attributed to Tristran. Rather do these resemble the old Coat of Champagne.

So much for Professor Loomis's evidence. It should suffice to assure us that Thomas had indeed conferred the Lion on Tristran's shield and trappers, though it might leave us in some doubt as to the colour of the field.

With regard to the field this much can be said. Later heraldic material confirms the Anglo-Angevin escutcheon as having a red field, which agrees with the fact that as a source for what Thomas wrote, the *Tristramssaga* is greatly superior to the *Tavola Ritonda*. On the other hand, the portrait on Geoffrey of Anjou's tomb in Le Mans shows a shield with a Lion rampant in gold on a field of azure, which as a continental version of the Angevin arms might account for the field given by the *Tavola Ritonda*, although the available evidence is insufficient to maintain a regular contrast between azure for the continental and gules for the English branches.

* *Illustrations of Medieval Romance* (University of Illinois Studies in Language and Literature, II, 2), Urbana, 1916, pp. 50 ff., and in several articles of subsequent years in the *Modern Language Review*.

Geoffrey died in 1151. A shield with a Lion upon it had been hung round his neck by Henry I of England in 1127 on the occasion of his marriage to Henry's daughter, the ex-Empress Mathilda.

The question of whether the *Saga*'s attribution of Gules Lion Or to the charger's trappers could derive from Thomas's *Tristran* of *c.* 1160 can be answered in the affirmative: Henry II's brother William has a Lion rampant on both shield and trappers on his seal, dated 1156-63.

However, as early as 1902 Joseph Bédier had, on the sole evidence of Gottfried von Strassburg within the Thomas tradition, accepted the Boar as the device on Tristran's shield in agreement with Marjodoc's dream, in which Tristran figures as a boar. One may draw the parallel of Troilus dreaming that Criseyde lay in the arms of a boar, the device of his now successful rival Diomede, descendant of boar-slaying Meleager; for such symbolic relationships were well understood by medieval poets. Thus either Thomas led up to the interpretation of Marjodoc's dream of a boar by giving Tristran the Boar and not the Lion on his escutcheon, in which case all four Lions in the dependent sources above quoted must derive from a later English group of manuscripts; or Gottfried skilfully substituted a Boar for Thomas's Lion, a poetic refinement of which he was fully capable. Since, however, it is hard to imagine that both the Norwegian and the Italian versions derive from a late English edition of Thomas's *Tristran*, the balance of probability seems to be much in favour of the contention that Tristran's escutcheon was originally the Lion of Anjou, an attribution which is in agreement with other allusions in the poem to the Angevin house, referred to above.

It is not inappropriate to add here that the arms attributed in Thomas's *Tristran* to the hero's namesake Dwarf Tristran (p. 339) are quite possible in science, but that Mr Cole has been unable to identify them for the early period in question.

APPENDIX 4

Notes on the Poets referred to by Gottfried in the Literary Excursus

HEINRICH VON VELDEKE, more accurately Henric van Veldeken (*c.* 1140–50, d. before 1210), was a ministerialis or unfree knight bound to the service of an overlord, of Veldeke in Limburg, west of Maastricht. Heinrich had received a clerical education, and was the author of some attractive love-lyrics, of the versified legend of St Servatius, and of a celebrated adaptation of the French *Roman d'Eneas*. Heinrich was no poetic genius; but he was a highly competent writer and was well placed geographically to receive the new literary and cultural influences from France and to pass them on to German courts. Modern critics agree with Gottfried that Heinrich played a vital part in the evolution of classic canons of narrative. That his contribution owed much to his French models is recognized in Gottfried's phrase 'he grafted the first slip on the tree of German poetry'.

HARTMANN VON AUE (*c.* 1160–post 1210), was an Alemannic poet, probably of Eglisau in the Swiss Thurgau. Like Heinrich von Veldeke he was a ministerialis. Hartmann was the author of some love-lyrics, of two very accomplished short stories in verse, *Der arme Heinrich* and *Gregorius*, and of two Arthurian romances adapted from works by Chrétien de Troyes, the *Erec* and the *Iwein*. Hartmann brought the art of narrative to an appreciably higher level than Heinrich von Veldeke had done, and endowed it with humane values that it had not known before.

WOLFRAM VON ESCHENBACH (*c.* 1170–post 1220), to whom Gottfried does not give a name but who is easily recognized in Gottfried's irate caricature, was a Bavarian knight and ministerialis from a village near Ansbach, south-west of Nuremberg. In everything that matters in art and in much that matters in life, Wolfram was the exact opposite of Gottfried, with whom he shares the distinction of being one of the two greatest named narrative poets of an age abounding in literary genius. (The poet of the *Nibelungenlied*, a minstrel, was forbidden by custom to name himself.) Wolfram was a poet of astonishing originality and freshness. He wrote some love-lyrics, the narrative *Parzival* (in which he completed the unfinished *Perceval* or *Conte del Graal* of Chrétien, whom he followed in his own wayward fashion), *Willehalm* (unfinished), and the so-called *Titurel* (unfinished). Wolfram replies to Gottfried's parody not a bit less scathingly and effectively in *Parzival* and *Willehalm*. His main target is Gottfried's purely relative conception of truth and loyalty, Gottfried's weak spot indeed. One suspects that Gottfried chose not to name Wolfram because he would have condemned him to oblivion, if he could, rather than immortalize the intruder in the amber of his *Tristan*.

BLIGGER VON STEINACH (*fl.* 1210) came of a family of knights who were settled on the Neckar. Of extant poetry only a few unimportant lyrics are ascribed to his name. No word or even theme of the narrative poetry which Gottfried praises so highly has survived.

REINMAR VON HAGENAU (*fl.* 1185–*c.*1210), member of a family of imperial ministeriales in Alsace, was a leading *Minnesinger* or love-poet. He became the court poet of Vienna and served under three of the Babenbergers. He was also the tutor in the art of *Minnesang* of Walther von der Vogelweide. Much of Reinmar's restrained and plaintive poetry has survived, but not a single melody.

WALTHER VON DER VOGELWEIDE (*fl.* 1190–1230), an Austrian born, one feels, though proof is lacking. The greatest of the *Minnesinger*, all of whom he surpasses both in the range and in the humanity of his poetry. Walther was a poor knight of the class of the ministeriales. He learned his art in Vienna under Reinmar and then became his rival for favour. On the death of Duke Frederick of Austria in 1198 Walther had to leave his beloved Vienna and seek other patrons. The power of his political songs, which rank among the best ever written, gained him the patronage of three emperors in turn, the Ghibelline Philipp of Swabia, Otto IV, the Guelph, then Philipp's nephew Frederick II, 'Stupor Mundi'. A great deal of Walther's poetry survives. A few of his melodies have come down to us, though not one goes with a love-song.

Gottfried's Geography

GOTTFRIED'S knowledge of the whole region in which his story is situated is far from secure. The geography of the Arthurian romances and their associated stories in any case tended to be fantastic, and it is only kind to remember that, in Strassburg, Gottfried was many hundreds of miles away from England, Cornwall, and Brittany. Nevertheless, some of his notions are surprising in a man of his sharp perceptions.

The most disturbing thing is that Arundel, raised from an earldom or 'county' to a duchy with a chief city of 'Karke', lies across the Channel in France. This misplacement of Arundel is entirely due to Gottfried, though he was pushed into his error by carelessness on Thomas's part. For, early in his story, Thomas had introduced Morgan as a Breton duke, yet towards its end he introduced the father of Isolde of the White Hands as the Duke of Brittany. There was historically only one Duke of or in Brittany, and it was no doubt in order to avoid confusion that Gottfried made Whitehands' father the Duke of Arundel whilst leaving his duchy in roughly the same place. Thus one can ride on horseback from Gottfried's Parmenie (Thomas's Armenie or Ermenie), bordering on Brittany, to Arundel. But Gottfried says that Arundel is between 'Britain' and England, beside the sea. 'Britain' is ambiguous, since in Gottfried's text it stands mostly for Little Britain, that is Brittany, but sometimes also for Great Britain. Yet so far as Gottfried's Arundel is concerned, 'Britain' must stand for Brittany. It suits well that one of the Duke of Arundel's neighbours and vassals should be a lord of Nantes; but another neighbour is a lord of Hante, which in view of its proximity to 'Arundel' is under some suspicion of being Hampshire. It follows that Gottfried had only the haziest notion of the English Channel.

'Wales' seems to haunt 'Gales' and 'Swales', which both occur. Swales is contiguous with England, and Gales may be so. Whether Thomas said so or not, Gottfried believed that the name of Engelant (England) was derived from the name of Gales, which he peoples with Saxons. Having used up 'Gales' in this way, he may have felt compelled to adopt 'Swales' when he came to the Petitcreiu episode, which is located in and about 'Gales' in Thomas's version, that is, in Wales. There can be little doubt that Gottfried obtained 'Swales' directly or indirectly from a false division of the plural 'les Wales' (= Wales) as 'le Swales'.

Thomas, understandably, had much clearer conceptions of north-west European geography. On the way from London to Brittany, Queen Isolde passes Wissant, Boulogne, and Treport, as Thomas himself might often have done in the suite of Eleanor or Henry. The whole passage shows knowledge of and feeling for the sea and nautical matters.

APPENDIX 6

A Glossary of Geographical Names

ANFERGINAN: A mythical valley near Wexford in Ireland, haunted by a dragon.

ARUNDEL: A duchy situated 'between England and Brittany' by the sea. In fact, Gottfried places it on the French side of the Channel, and near to Brittany and Parmenie (*q.v.*, and see Appendix 5).

CANOEL: The seat or 'honour' from which Rivalin took his byname of Canel or Canelengres. The chief city of Parmenie.

CARLEON: Unlike the historic and Arthurian Carleon (Castra Legionis), situated by Gottfried not in Monmouthshire but in England. Tristan has to leave Carleon and England to get to Swales (*q.v.*, and see Appendix 5).

DOLEISE: Presumably misunderstood from the adjective Doleis = 'of Dol', a fortress on the Marches of Brittany.

GALES: Normally Wales, but according to Gottfried's notion the land of the Saxons before they drove the Britons from Great Britain, which was renamed 'England'. See Appendix 5.

GERMANY: 'Alemanje' in the original. The Holy Roman Empire of largely German speech.

HANTE: A domain, which, in view of its proximity to Arundel (*q.v.*), might be guessed to be Hampshire.

KARKE: The chief city of Gottfried's duchy of 'Arundel' (*q.v.*).

LOHNOIS: Better known to English readers as 'Lyoness'. The name of Rivalin's land in the archetypal version of Tristan which Thomas and Gottfried rejected in favour of 'Armenie' or 'Ermenie' and 'Parmenie' respectively.

LUT: Apparently a town in Brittany, which it is tempting but hazardous to equate with Lud. There was also Le Lude in Anjou.

PARMENIE: A domain in or near Brittany and also bordering on Normandy, ruled by Rivalin and eventually by Tristan in their own right (though it was associated with a separate fief which was held from a Breton Duke Morgan). Thomas had called it Armenie or Ermenie, but Gottfried modified it to Parmenie, no doubt to avoid confusion with Armenia (see p. 357).

SWALES: A land near England, distinct from Gales (*q.v.*, and see Appendix 5).

APPENDIX 7

A Glossary of the Characters' Names

Characters who appear only in the fragments of Thomas's Tristran have (T) after their names. Where Thomas's form of a name differs from Gottfried's, it is placed in round brackets. In my translation I have permitted myself the inconsistency of using the French forms Rivalin and Blancheflor for Gottfried's Riwalin and Blanscheflur.

BLANCHEFLOR: sister of King Mark; eloped with Rivalin, and was married to him; mother of Tristan; died on giving birth to him after hearing of Rivalin's death in battle.

BRANGANE (BRENGVEIN): companion and confidante of the younger Isolde, and related to her on her mother's side.

CANEL, CANELENGRES: bynames of Rivalin.

CARIADO (T): a great baron at Mark's court; disappointed admirer of Isolde the Fair, and enemy of her and Tristan.

CURVENAL (GUVERNAL): tutor and friend of Tristan since the latter's infancy.

ESTULT, li Orgillus (T): baron of Castel Fer; abductor of Dwarf Tristan's paramour; wounds Tristan with a poisoned lance and is slain by him in return.

FLORAETE: wife of Rual, and Tristan's foster-mother.

FOITENANT: see Rual li Foitenant.

GANDIN: an Irish baron, admirer and friend of the younger Isolde before she left Ireland.

GILAN: a duke of Swales (see Appendix 6).

GURMUN: King of Ireland; son of a king of Africa; husband of the elder Isolde, and father of the younger; has the byname of 'Gaiety'.

HIUDAN: Tristan's hunting-dog.

ISOLDE (YSOLT) the Elder: Queen of Ireland; wife of Gurmun, sister of Morold, and mother of Isolde the Fair; skilled in magic and medicine.

ISOLDE (YSOLT) the Fair and the Younger: daughter of Gurmun and the elder Isolde; niece of Morold; Princess of Ireland, then wife of King Mark and Queen of Cornwall and England; Tristan's fated lover.

ISOLDE (YSOLT) of the White Hands: daughter of Duke Jovelin and Duchess Karsie of Arundel; sister of Kaedin.

JOVELIN: Duke of Arundel (see Appendix 6); husband of Karsie, father of Isolde of the White Hands and Kaedin.

KAEDIN (CAERDIN): son of Duke Jovelin and Duchess Karsie of Arundel, brother of Isolde of the White Hands.

KARSIE: Duchess of Arundel; wife of Duke Jovelin and mother of Isolde of the White Hands and Kaedin.

MARJODOC: steward to Mark; at first an intimate friend of Tristan and admirer of Isolde the Fair, then, after discovering their intimacy, their bitter enemy.

MARK: King of Cornwall and England; brother of Blancheflor and maternal uncle of Tristan; married Isolde the Fair; tributary of Gurmun, until released by Tristan.

MELOT, petit, of Aquitaine: a dwarf who acts as spy for Mark and Marjodoc against Tristan and Isolde.

MORGAN: a Breton duke, not unambiguously the paramount Duke of Brittany. Thomas introduced a Breton duke Morgan, and a Hoel, Duke of Brittany. Gottfried tidies up the ambiguity by substituting Jovelin, Duke of Arundel (see Appendix 6), for Thomas's Duke of Brittany. Morgan was Rivalin's overlord for a separate fief; was engaged in a feud with Rivalin, whom he finally vanquished, and was killed by Tristan.

MOROLD: an Irish duke; brother of Queen Isolde of Ireland and brother-in-law of Gurmun, whose mainstay in war he was. As collector of Gurmun's Cornish tribute he was slain by Tristan.

NAUTENIS: a baron of 'Hante' (see Appendix 6), rebellious neighbour of Jovelin.

PARANIS: page to Queen Isolde of Ireland.

PETITCREIU: (PETICRU), a fairy lap-dog from Avalon, owned by Gilan and acquired from him by Tristan as a consolation for Isolde.

RIVALIN: lord of Parmenie (see Appendix 6); of undefined feudal status, though descended from a royal house and elevated enough to have a marshal; vassal for a separate fief to Morgan. Lover and then husband of Blancheflor; father of Tristan; slain in battle by Morgan or by one of his men.

RUAL, li Foitenant: marshal and burgrave to Rivalin; foster-father and guardian of Tristan; married to Floraete.

RUGIER: baron of 'Doleise' (see Appendix 6); rebellious neighbour of Jovelin.

TANTRIS: Tristan's cover-name when he is disguised as a merchant and minstrel, a name formed by the transposition of the syllables *tris* and *tan*. See Isolde's solution of the conundrum, p. 181.

TRISTAN (TRISTRAN): according to German law the illegitimate, but according to the Anglo-Norman law to which Thomas no doubt subscribed, the legitimate son of Rivalin and Blancheflor (see p. 24); maternal nephew of Mark; foster-son of Rual and Floraete. Although ultimately independent of any Breton overlordship whatsoever, Tristan seems to have been a Breton in a wider sense to both Thomas and Gottfried. Victor in battle over Morgan, Morold, the Irish dragon, Urgan, Jovelin's rebels, and (T) Estult. By killing Morgan, Tristan asserted his legitimacy in a *de facto* sense. On his adoption by Mark, Tristan became heir apparent to Cornwall and England, falling into second place in the line of succession when Mark married Isolde. (T) Also known as Tristran the Amorous in order to distinguish him from Dwarf Tristran.

TRISTRAN, Dwarf (T): a knight of the Marches of Brittany on the Biscay side; his paramour is abducted by Estult li Orgillus, and he claims the aid of Tristran as his namesake; killed in battle with Estult and Estult's six brothers.

URGAN, li vilus: a giant residing in or near 'Swales' (see Appendix 5); neighbour of Gilan.

MORE ABOUT PENGUINS, PELICANS, PEREGRINES AND PUFFINS

For further information about books available from Penguins please write to Dept EP, Penguin Books Ltd, Harmondsworth, Middlesex UB7 0DA

In the U.S.A.: For a complete list of books available from Penguins in the United States write to Dept DG, Penguin Books, 299 Murray Hill Parkway, East Rutherford, New Jersey 07073.

In Canada: For a complete list of books available from Penguins in Canada write to Penguin Books Canada Ltd, 2801 John Street, Markham, Ontario L3R 1B4.

In Australia: For a complete list of books available from Penguins in Australia write to the Marketing Department, Penguin Books Australia Ltd, P.O. Box 257, Ringwood, Victoria 3134.

In New Zealand: For a complete list of books available from Penguins in New Zealand write to the Marketing Department, Penguin Books (N.Z.) Ltd, Private Bag, Takapuna, Auckland 9.

In India: For a complete list of books available from Penguins in India write to Penguin Overseas Ltd, 706 Eros Apartments, 56 Nehru Place, New Delhi 110019.

THE QUEST OF THE HOLY GRAIL

TRANSLATED BY P. M. MATARASSO

The bright and colourful world of Arthurian Romance lends itself to medieval allegory in *The Quest of the Holy Grail*. The varied and often dangerous peregrinations and encounters of Arthur's knights in their search for the Holy Grail symbolize man's equally perilous search for the Grace of God. These chivalrous adventures sweeten the author's didactic pill, and the fusion of Christian symbolism and Celtic legend gives a mystical aura and tragic grandeur to the whole. The *Quest* is in fact a renunciation of the courtly ideals of the Romances sung by the early troubadours.

Wolfram von Eschenbach

PARZIVAL

TRANSLATED BY A. T. HATTO

In *Parzival*, one of the world's greatest narrative poems, Wolfram von Eschenbach (*fl. c.* 1195–1225) retells and ends the Arthurian *Story of the Grail*, left unfinished by its initiator Chrétien de Troyes.

Against alternating backgrounds of dazzling courtly ritual and the forbidding landscapes of the wilds is displayed Parzival's exemplary quest for the supreme goal of chivalry, the spiritual aspects of which are dramatized by juxtaposition of the more happy-go-lucky careers of Parzival's father and his amorous comrade-in-arms Gawan.

Beroul

THE ROMANCE OF TRISTAN

TRANSLATED BY ALAN S. FEDRICK

The tragic story of the illicit passion of Tristan and Yseut, which brought them only degradation, has lost none of its fascination since it was first composed about the middle of the twelfth century. Beroul's poem is perhaps the earliest version of the legend now extant, and the poet presents his narration in an abrupt, jerky style well suited to the violence and brutality of his matter. Of all the poets who have treated the *Tristan* legend, Beroul, about whom nothing at all is known, comes closest to preserving that elemental drive which is the very essence of the story and which has given it such tremendous vitality in the literature of western civilization.

THE NIBELUNGENLIED

TRANSLATED BY A. T. HATTO

Composed nearly eight hundred years ago by an unnamed poet, *The Nibelungenlied* is the principal literary expression of those heroic legends of which Richard Wagner made such free use in *The Ring*. This great German epic poem of murder and revenge recounts with peculiar strength and directness the progress of Siegfried's love for the peerless Kriemhild, the wedding of Gunther and Brunhild, the quarrel between the two queens, Hagen's treacherous murder of Siegfried, and Kriemhild's eventual revenge. A. T. Hatto's translation transforms an old text into a story as readable and exciting as Homer's *Iliad*

A CHOICE OF
PELICANS AND PEREGRINES

☐ **The Knight, the Lady and the Priest**
Georges Duby £5.95

The acclaimed study of the making of modern marriage in medieval France. 'He has traced this story – sometimes amusing, often horrifying, always startling – in a series of brilliant vignettes' – *Observer*

☐ **The Limits of Soviet Power** Jonathan Steele £3.50

The Kremlin's foreign policy – Brezhnev to Chernenko, is discussed in this informed, informative 'wholly invaluable and extraordinarily timely study' – *Guardian*

☐ **Understanding Organizations** Charles B. Handy £4.95

Third Edition. Designed as a practical source-book for managers, this Pelican looks at the concepts, key issues and current fashions in tackling organizational problems.

☐ **The Pelican Freud Library: Volume 12** £4.95

Containing the major essays: *Civilization, Society and Religion, Group Psychology* and *Civilization and Its Discontents*, plus other works.

☐ **Windows on the Mind** Erich Harth £4.95

Is there a physical explanation for the various phenomena that we call 'mind'? Professor Harth takes in age-old philosophers as well as the latest neuroscientific theories in his masterly study of memory, perception, free will, selfhood, sensation and other richly controversial fields.

☐ **The Pelican History of the World**
J. M. Roberts £5.95

'A stupendous achievement . . . This is the unrivalled World History for our day' – A. J. P. Taylor

A CHOICE OF PELICANS AND PEREGRINES

☐ *A Question of Economics* **Peter Donaldson** £4.95

Twenty key issues – from the City and big business to trades unions – clarified and discussed by Peter Donaldson, author of *10 × Economics* and one of our greatest popularizers of economics.

☐ *Inside the Inner City* **Paul Harrison** £4.50

A report on urban poverty and conflict by the author of *Inside the Third World*. 'A major piece of evidence' – *Sunday Times*. 'A classic: it tells us what it is really like to be poor, and why' – *Time Out*

☐ *What Philosophy Is* **Anthony O'Hear** £3.95

What are human beings? How should people act? How do our thoughts and words relate to reality? Contemporary attitudes to these age-old questions are discussed in this new study, an eloquent and brilliant introduction to philosophy today.

☐ *The Arabs* **Peter Mansfield** £4.95

New Edition. 'Should be studied by anyone who wants to know about the Arab world and how the Arabs have become what they are today' – *Sunday Times*

☐ *Religion and the Rise of Capitalism*
  R. H. Tawney £3.95

The classic study of religious thought of social and economic issues from the later middle ages to the early eighteenth century.

☐ *The Mathematical Experience*
  Philip J. Davis and Reuben Hersh £6.95

Not since *Gödel, Escher, Bach* has such an entertaining book been written on the relationship of mathematics to the arts and sciences. 'It deserves to be read by everyone ... an instant classic' – *New Scientist*

ENGLISH AND AMERICAN LITERATURE IN PENGUINS

☐ *Emma* **Jane Austen** £1.10

'I am going to take a heroine whom no one but myself will much like,' declared Jane Austen of Emma, her most spirited and controversial heroine in a comedy of self-deceit and self-discovery.

☐ *Tender is the Night* **F. Scott Fitzgerald** £2.95

Fitzgerald worked on seventeen different versions of this novel, and its obsessions – idealism, beauty, dissipation, alcohol and insanity – were those that consumed his own marriage and his life.

☐ *The Life of Johnson* **James Boswell** £2.25

Full of gusto, imagination, conversation and wit, Boswell's immortal portrait of Johnson is as near a novel as a true biography can be, and still regarded by many as the finest 'life' ever written. This shortened version is based on the 1799 edition.

☐ *A House and its Head* **Ivy Compton-Burnett** £3.95

In a novel 'as trim and tidy as a hand-grenade' (as Pamela Hansford Johnson put it), Ivy Compton-Burnett penetrates the facade of a conventional, upper-class Victorian family to uncover a chasm of violent emotions – jealousy, pain, frustration and sexual passion.

☐ *The Trumpet Major* **Thomas Hardy** £1.25

Although a vein of unhappy unrequited love runs through this novel, Hardy also draws on his warmest sense of humour to portray Wessex village life at the time of the Napoleonic wars.

☐ *The Complete Poems of Hugh MacDiarmid*

☐ Volume One £8.95
☐ Volume Two £8.95

The definitive edition of work by the greatest Scottish poet since Robert Burns, edited by his son Michael Grieve, and W. R. Aitken.

ENGLISH AND AMERICAN LITERATURE IN PENGUINS

☐ **Main Street** **Sinclair Lewis**   £3.95

The novel that added an immortal chapter to the literature of America's Mid-West, *Main Street* contains the comic essence of Main Streets everywhere.

☐ **The Compleat Angler** **Izaak Walton**   £2.50

A celebration of the countryside, and the superiority of those in 1653, as now, who love *quietnesse, vertue* and, above all, *Angling*. 'No fish, however coarse, could wish for a doughtier champion than Izaak Walton' – Lord Home

☐ **The Portrait of a Lady** **Henry James**   £2.50

'One of the two most brilliant novels in the language', according to F. R. Leavis, James's masterpiece tells the story of a young American heiress, prey to fortune-hunters but not without a will of her own.

☐ **Hangover Square** **Patrick Hamilton**   £3.50

Part love story, part thriller, and set in the publands of London's Earls Court, this novel caught the conversational tone of a whole generation in the uneasy months before the Second World War.

☐ **The Rainbow** **D. H. Lawrence**   £2.50

Written between *Sons and Lovers* and *Women in Love*, *The Rainbow* covers three generations of Brangwens, a yeoman family living on the borders of Nottinghamshire.

☐ **Vindication of the Rights of Woman**
  Mary Wollstonecraft   £2.95

Although Walpole once called her 'a hyena in petticoats', Mary Wollstonecraft's vision was such that modern feminists continue to go back and debate the arguments so powerfully set down here.

CLASSICS IN TRANSLATION IN PENGUINS

☐ **Remembrance of Things Past** Marcel Proust
☐ Volume One: **Swann's Way, Within a Budding Grove** £7.50
☐ Volume Two: **The Guermantes Way, Cities of the Plain** £7.50
☐ Volume Three: **The Captive, The Fugitive, Time Regained** £7.50

Terence Kilmartin's acclaimed revised version of C. K. Scott Moncrieff's original translation, published in paperback for the first time.

☐ **The Canterbury Tales** Geoffrey Chaucer £2.50

'Every age is a Canterbury Pilgrimage . . . nor can a child be born who is not one of these characters of Chaucer' – William Blake

☐ **Gargantua & Pantagruel** Rabelais £3.95

The fantastic adventures of two giants through which Rabelais (1495–1553) caricatured his life and times in a masterpiece of exuberance and glorious exaggeration.

☐ **The Brothers Karamazov** Fyodor Dostoevsky £3.95

A detective story on many levels, profoundly involving the question of the existence of God, Dostoevsky's great drama of parricide and fraternal jealousy triumphantly fulfilled his aim: 'to find the man in man . . . [to] depict all the depths of the human soul.'

☐ **Fables of Aesop** £1.95

This translation recovers all the old magic of fables in which, too often, the fox steps forward as the cynical hero and a lamb is an ass to lie down with a lion.

☐ **The Three Theban Plays** Sophocles £2.95

A new translation, by Robert Fagles, of *Antigone, Oedipus the King* and *Oedipus at Colonus*, plays all based on the legend of the royal house of Thebes.

CLASSICS IN TRANSLATION
IN PENGUINS

☐ **The Treasure of the City of Ladies**
Christine de Pisan £2.95

This practical survival handbook for women (whether royal courtiers or prostitutes) paints a vivid picture of their lives and preoccupations in France, *c.* 1405. First English translation.

☐ **Berlin Alexanderplatz** Alfred Döblin £4.95

The picaresque tale of an ex-murderer's progress through the underworld Berlin. 'One of the great experimental fictions . . . the German equivalent of *Ulysses* and Dos Passos' *U.S.A.*' – *Time Out*

☐ **Metamorphoses** Ovid £2.50

The whole of Western literature has found inspiration in Ovid's poem, a golden treasury of myths and legends that are linked by the theme of transformation.

☐ **Darkness at Noon** Arthur Koestler £1.95

'Koestler approaches the problem of ends and means, of love and truth and social organization, through the thoughts of an Old Bolshevik, Rubashov, as he awaits death in a G.P.U. prison' – *New Statesman*

☐ **War and Peace** Leo Tolstoy £4.95

'A complete picture of human life;' wrote one critic, 'a complete picture of the Russia of that day; a complete picture of everything in which people place their happiness and greatness, their grief and humiliation.'

☐ **The Divine Comedy: 1 Hell** Dante £2.25

A new translation by Mark Musa, in which the poet is conducted by the spirit of Virgil down through the twenty-four closely described circles of hell.

FOR THE BEST IN PAPERBACKS, LOOK FOR THE 🐧

PENGUIN POETRY LIBRARY

Arnold   Selected by Kenneth Allott
Blake   Selected by J. Bronowski
Burns   Selected by W. Beattie and H. W. Meikle
Byron   Selected by A. S. B. Glover
Coleridge   Selected by Kathleen Raine
Donne   Selected by John Hayward
Dryden   Selected by Douglas Grant
Hardy   Selected by David Wright
Herbert   Selected by W. H. Auden
Keats   Selected by J. E. Morpurgo
Lawrence   Selected by Keith Sagar
Milton   Selected by Laurence D. Lerner
Owen   Selected by Jon Silkin
Pope   Selected by Douglas Grant
Shelley   Selected by Isabel Quigley
Tennyson   Selected by W. E. Williams
Wordsworth   Selected by W. E. Williams